# GAD'S ARMY

*The unofficial war stories of Section M*

**Drew Bryenton**

Dedicated to the memory of
Vince Behr

'Not gone, but gone on ahead to seek out strange new adventures'
Travel easy, stay unique, make some worlds on your way

# Prelude – Holborn, West London Town, 1595

Will laid the quill down and gently blew a breath across the paper  He slowly closed the book, with the reverence a bishop might reserve for an ancient illuminated bible.

Then again, he'd always found it a good idea to handle things carefully, if they were prone to violently explode.

Holborn, in this year of our Lord, was still half cottages and fields, a straggly little addendum to London Town. Its only redeeming feature (to the mind of Will) was the Cockpit Theatre on Drury Lane. Even that street was an inauspicious place; Will's fellow Special Constable Angus McGillicutty, of Her Majesty's Chamber Praxis Occultis, had foiled the plot of some dastardly baker there back in '82. He'd heard stories about a monster made out of pastry, or some such. Blueberries had been involved[1].

That incident paled in comparison to what was afoot tonight. Tonight, in fact, fully merited the use of the term 'afoot' and probably an extra 'dastardly' as well. Tonight, Will could hear Them coming, and They were armed for war.

Hence the morris dancing outfit.

It's a little known fact that the traditional get-up of the English Morris Man is in fact a form of battle-dress as serious and deadly as the black pajamas favoured by certain Oriental assassins. Modern (and here we mean of course, *modern in 1595*) versions did away with several of the runes, wards, sprigs of unwholesome plants and the solid cast-iron codpiece. Will did not. His handkerchiefs were woven from spider silk by the light of a crescent moon, dipped in the tears of poets and embroidered with sigils of elder magic. His tiny bells were both a lure and a preventative against the razor-glass music of Those who were at war with humanity.

Then again, most contemporary morris men didn't carry a curiously

---

1 But of course, you know the Muffin Man...

shaped sword and a horrible squat blunderbuss either. But there'd be use for both of those tonight. Will picked up the sword, (more of a long, curved cleaver than a rapier blade), and its edge rasped across the table, leaving a faintly glowing blue line. He hefted his other weapon – the one Da Vinci's sketches called the 'Infernogunne' - and turned to face the door of the cottage.

In a fit of narrative predictability, stark white light burst out around its edges, and between the warped timbers. At the edge of his hearing and sanity, Will heard the sound of unhinged, merry laughter. That, and a voice like wild honey and decay.

"Come, mortal. Open up. You know how this must end. You are but lumpen clay, a puppet already thrown aside by your masters. Your virgin Queen and Doctor Dee both fear you cannot stop us."

Will's head felt like an egg in a red-hot vise as the voices closed in. Long, clawed fingers skittered across the cottage windows, leaving fern-frond trails of frost.

"And yet I must invite you in, it seems. Rules still bind you, deceivers. Rules which we mortal men have wrought."

The whole house creaked, as if squeezed in a giant's fist. Plaster dust rained down.

"You seek to bind us? To change us? We gave you just enough imagination to fear us, human! We will not be bound by **rules!**"

Will smirked. *But rules are all you are now, my unfortunate friends. Rituals and rhymes and snares which suited you so well, when we were a simple folk, and easy prey.*

"It's finished, you know!" he said, raising his voice as eerie music swelled, and the glass in the windows began to freeze solid. "The greatest working since Dante put the devils in their bloody circles back in 1320. When they perform it for the first time, it's butterfly wings and… and the *lids of biscuit boxes* for you. Forever!"

This time the pressure spike was like a fistful of daggers. That cloying, sweet voice became a howl, the likes of which the world would not hear again until the invention of the bandsaw.

**"Wretched creature! We will devour your soul!"**

William Shakespeare stood square to the door, bathed in the ever-shifting light which streamed in around it. He flipped a hidden switch on the side of the Infernogunne, setting a clockwork mechanism to spinning. Sparks crawled lazily inside its trumpet-shaped muzzle.

"Venture within, then, and speak such imprecations to my physiognomy!" he said, lapsing for a moment into the kind of language which the theatre-going public seemed to enjoy. It's hard for a blaze of eldritch light to look confused. But the one charring horrible images onto the cottage floorboards managed nonetheless.

"You *what*, mate?"

Will took a long, lingering look at the finished first folio of *A Midsummer Night's Dream*. Better than the one about those Italian kids, and less depressing than the one about the king, he thought. But the rest of the plays had just been the fletching and the shaft, the sinew and the bow. This one was the 'war-head', as it were. The tip of an arrow which would pierce all of Fae.

He looked back at the door. His morris bells jingled, setting up wyrd harmonics. The sword in his hand – actually the blade of a bookmaker's guillotine, forged for the use of one J. Gutenberg, glowed with thousands of tiny, tiny lines of script.

"Come here and say that to my face," he grated.

And the door exploded.

The first thing through it was tall and beautiful – so wild and free and pure that looking upon it with human eyes seemed a crime. The thought of killing it was as repulsive as that of strangling a majestic eagle while knee-deep in a cesspit. It was armed with copper claws, long as butcher knives, bound to its fingers with strands of maiden's hair. It was a lord of the Spring Court, ancient and cruel, suffused with magic and smiling like an explosion in a needle factory.

It was also phenomenally stupid.

Will demonstrated precisely why Leonardo Da Vinci had thought that the Infernogunne would 'end all warfare', because 'nobody who ever saw it used would want to see a person die like that, ever again'. The recoil slammed him backwards into the table with a kidney-bruising thump, and another shower of plaster dust came down.

But the Fae… well. Hot, electrified iron has a way of ruining anybody's mood, when fired at close to what would one day be called the speed of sound. The second two elves through the doorway met a cloud of splinters, bone shards and horrible wobbly chunks coming the other way, and promptly ceased to exist as well.

Will proved that Leo had been a tad optimistic. He slid the pump-action of the Infernogunne and reloaded, smiling. Blue blood dripped from every surface.

Behind him, glass smashed and tinkled. He heard the light footfall of more elves on the stairs. Another three hung back outside the doorway, their eyes glowing in the gloom.

"All right," said the Bard of Avon, spinning his sword in a limber figure-eight.

"Who's next?"

To all non-sworn officers of Section M
Condition three (gryphon) level clearance or lower!
(Including, though I am appalled to have to type this, Civilians and other lower life forms who may have come into contact with this document)
DO NOT READ ANY FURTHER
I understand that the piece of paper inside the cover of this dossier, which purports to be about Mr Shakespeare, is somewhat intriguing. But it never happened. Certainly not. Nothing exciting happened at all on that cold Autumn night in 1595, and I was certainly not there to write it down, because (and here I'd like you to imagine I'm raising an eyebrow meaningfully) I am NOT A WIZARD at all.

There's no such thing.

And if there was, there still wouldn't be.

But there isn't.

So STOP!

I can't help but note that YOU'RE STILL READING

Which means that you are either naughty, or stupid, or a combination of the two which I will, for the sake of convenience and less typing, call nupid. Stop now. There is nothing to gain from reading further. This is one of those boring, boring books about the retirement speeches of medieval tax assessors, or a long essay on the intestinal parasites of ducks. Unless those things are entertaining to you. Then, it's a big list of laundry receipts from the 1770s. A recipe for lichen soup. A brief history of the Nordic outhouse.

Blast it! I'm just not used to dealing with nupid individuals.

So…

Look, I didn't want to do this. But I'm going to have to ORDER you to STOP

By official decree of the sitting monarch of the realm, (blessings be on their particular bottom), I hereby abjure and command you forthwith to stop fondling this paper with your dirty, unsanctioned eyeballs! Aroint, and such!

There.

Right.

That didn't work, did it?

You're one of THOSE ones, aren't you?

Can't take the word of a perfectly sensible wiza… clerk or something.
Have to pry into matters of Wartime Security, with the capital W and
S, do you?

Well.

Let me tell you, matey. This chronicle is about Section M.
Not those prancing commandos or those silly marines!
Those who dare to read this document won't just get extra hair on
their chests, they'll get hair on their teeth! Hair on the inside of their
eyeballs! Possibly even the nigh- mythical hairy pancreas! They'll…

Not that it's interesting at all. Anything but.

It's so mind-curdlingly boring, in fact, that elderly geography
teachers read it to each other so they can fall asleep during long visits
to those incredibly dull old rickety libraries where blowflies knock
their heads against the windows all day amid piles of dust.

OK then.
If you have that much disdain for authority, burn it.
Go on.
Or are you a big soggy-bottomed coward?

BURN IT NOW

So - it's not looking too crispy in here.

Distinct lack of charcoal.

**Very well. Let me tell you straight.**

There have been some colossally bad ideas in history. Real disasters.

Back in the garden, there was a young lady who reckoned that a talking snake seemed relatively trustworthy, and thought – 'who doesn't like apple crumble?'

On the shores of a wine-dark sea, under the shadow of the walls of Troy, there was a fellow who yelled - "Hey sarge, they've buggered off, and left us a nice lawn ornament!"

In a little Austrian village, not so long ago, the postmaster invited his wife to come back to bed with a naughty smile on his face. And Mrs Hitler thought - 'what's the worst that can happen?'
A bit later, there was a kid called Eddie Weatherfield, who thought it would be a laugh to run away and join the Royal Air Force. Without him, large chunks of this document would not exist, and the world would consequently be a safer place.
Because that bit with Shakespeare before was right. He told me when we were both rascally drunk, you know. Reading something makes it just slightly more real. There's a reason why putting down letters in the right order is called 'spelling'.

So one last chance. STOP READING.
The last mistake on that list doesn't have to be you.

Ahhh, I thought as much.

Well, don't say you weren't told. You can't un-know things. Even if you do keep several fine distilleries in business trying.

One more try? Stop reading?

PLEASE?

Ahhhhh, to Hell with it. I suppose I'd best add, for any of those out there who ARE of condition three (gryphon) level clearance or above, that the following account is true and accurate, for a given value of quantum truth and probability-adjusted eleven-dimensional accuracy.

It takes place in the Year of Our Lord 19 hundred & 40, beginning during events which you young people are calling the 'Battle of Britain'. Though there have been at least sixteen of those throughout history, and this one didn't even have any talking skeletons in it. Well, maybe one or two.

Nevertheless.

It all begins with an aeroplane that's about to crash…

# Well bloody hell, don't stop now! [2]

---

2 Official addendum: The officer tasked with writing the official warning to this official official document has officially been relieved of his duties due to official stress. Officially, this didn't happen, but if you persist in believing that it did, please post any small change, lint, boiled sweets and miniature bottles of liquor to; The Distressed Wizards Charitable Trust (official), c/o the Suggestive Shrubbery, 92 Penharrowford Mews, Little Smuggling, just outside Doncaster.

# One - A Unnatural Accident

"This is what you get for being a liar," said a very unhelpful part of Eddie's brain, as he plunged toward the ground at what could only be called terminal velocity.

All the symptoms were there. The churning in his stomach, the sensation that his heart was trying to batter its way out past his tonsils, the white-knuckled, jangling terror... He supposed there was a good chance that his pants would be on fire any second now as well.

*It had all been going well up until the dragon.*

Well, no – that was a lie too. It had all been going slightly less fatally up until the dragon, although several hundred Germans had been trying their hardest to make the giant scaly red bastard unnecessary.

Adventure, eh?

It all seemed like a great idea until all the 'swaggering about in a cool uniform, heading down to the pub and impressing pretty English girls' turned into air-raid sirens in the small hours, shouting, cursing, trying to find your trousers and - to put a fine point on it - actual air combat.

*That* was the part he'd lied about.

That, and being able to control a slightly dragon-damaged Spitfire in a power dive toward a picturesque field near Dover. Eddie pulled back on the yoke until his eyeballs threatened to pop, but this only caused the giant, shuddering machine to spin like a sycamore seed. That oafish reptile had clipped the left wing, and none of the controls over there were responding.

*This was the kind of thing you thought they'd tell you about during basic training.*

The world went spinning upside down for a second, black sky and ragged clouds and cold, hard earth. Down there Eddie saw a farmhouse, pale and white in the moonlight. And out on the open heath, where the land rose up scrubby and barren past the fields, five little points of light.

Another loop. He wrestled the controls, got the plane steady, and homed in on those flickering little pinpricks.

Right between three massive mounds of earth. A flat patch, just big enough to bring the old kite down. Hard, admittedly, but far more softly than some of the landings which would be happening tonight. That dragon might have done him a favour...

It wasn't until he throttled back, and the great thundering pistons of the Merlin V-12 died, that he saw what the lights really were.

Five torches, arranged around a glowing circle. A star-shape inside. Some kind of magic?

Then there was no more time to think. Gravity came all scrabble-clawing at him, the ground made horribly real and hard as it whispered by, a few metres below and rising...

+++

There were times when Major Monkston was certain he was in the wrong line of business.

He'd be the first to admit that everyone had to do their part, what with there being a war on, and all – a fact he accepted in the same way that during a football match somebody has to cut up slices of orange for half time. It's just that *his* part – and here he was most certain indeed – probably wasn't standing about on a midnight heath with a witch and a skeleton, making unhallowed pacts on behalf of the British Crown.

On second thought, having the big red Government stamp on them probably *made* them hallowed. Major Monkston was, in fact, the Agent of Hallowing in this whole cold, uncomfortable process.

He stamped a bit of life back into his feet and smiled a thin smile at Mrs Tavistock and Ulfric Foesbane, fishing a very, very official-looking document from inside his greatcoat.

Say this for Major Charlie Monkston. He could look dapper in any situation. The fact that he insisted on wearing a black silk top hat, even now, was only part of it.

"There you go then, sir. With our appreciation. You're free to pass unbound through the veil, to tread the bridge of shadows and re-join your ancestors in the mead-hall of the gods."

Ulfric grinned – though he had very little choice. A grin was the one expression left to the Saxon chieftain after more than a thousand years buried under Tavistock Farm in a barrow.

"We haf fought ryte well against yon Visigoth foe," grated the old lich, in a voice like crumbling caskets. "Butte thenn agayne, showe mee a buggar who be readye to face a score of dragonnes, and I'll show you how to conquere the worlde!"

Ulfric was all preserved beard and yellow bone beneath a suit of armour and a helmet which the British Museum would wet themselves over, but Major Monkston got the idea that the old Saxon's ancestors had better square away a good supply of mead right now. Dead or not, he looked like the type who could quaff until the servants behind him needed snorkels.

"And what about the other thing, dearie?" asked Mrs Tavistock. As an official witch, she sported the obligatory pointy hat, secured with enough hatpins to moor a zeppelin. Other than that, she was simply a pudding-shaped elderly woman wearing a tweed suit jacket, woolen dress and immense gumboots. Until the power which leached up through the land and into her flashed in her eyes. "The apology, mind. It's only polite."

Major Monkston thought about all the things he could be doing on a cold English night, rather than standing outside a Saxon barrow-grave with a dead man and a witch. Even if she *had* brought a thermos of something which – had the spoon not stood up straight in it and started to bubble – could have been called tea.

Then he thought of all the things he could be doing in a few weeks time if he *wasn't* here, summoning the legendary Dragons of Albion for one last re-union tour. Things like speaking German, and having his fingernails pulled out by horrible little men in wire-framed glasses and black trenchcoats.

Up there, the very pride of the Royal Air Force was fighting an uneven battle against the biggest aerial invasion ever seen. They needed all the help they could get. What was a little supernatural diplomacy, compared to that?

"Very well," he said, nervously smoothing his pencil-thin mustache with one hand. "Ulfric Foesbane, son of Skaldi Hammerhand, Tamer of Dragons, Reaver-King of the Saxon Shore, I hereby apologise for the somewhat...errr... heavy-handed punishment handed down by the old Civic Power in your day. We have maximum sentences now, you know. Nice clean prisons. None of this supernatural mumbo-jumbo..."

A sharp elbow in the ribs from Mrs Tavistock shut him up. Then again, the cold blue light welling up in Ulfric's eyes would have done the same.

"Younge Arthur ande thatte olde bastarde were within their rytes.

Goode bloody enemies, those twoe! Propere fyre and the sworde fellowes, both of them! Anyhowe, whatt's a fewe centuries sleeping beneathe yon hille? I'm a bloody *legende* now. Me and the boyes. That's goode for more than a few jugges of mead, where we're going!"

The lich tucked the scroll in behind the rusted chestplate of his armour, and put two fingers to where his lips should have been. The whistle which followed was high and horrible enough to make dogs several miles away clatter to the floor, stiff as hairy planks of wood.

But the thing in the barrow behind Ulfric was no dog. It shouldered up to the massive trilithon door with a sound like a thousand leather handbags falling off the back of a truck. The smell of sulphur, dead sheep and old iron wafted out in a warm exhalation, making Mrs Tavistock pinch her nose.

"No bath in there then, is there? The poor thing would probably love a good rub down..."

Ulfric inclined his head. His helmet slipped forward on his polished skull.

"And you would like as notte appreciate the laste bitte of dragonne-scayle oil in Albion for your vile potions, thou dastardly midnight hagge." He chuckled. Mrs Tavistock blushed.

"Oooh, Major! What a gentleman! Nobody's called me a 'dastardly midnight hag' for *centuries*!"

Monkston was reminded, then, that Mrs Tavistock had been around these parts for nearly as long as Ulfric, and that she'd once been the siren-sorceress who lured sailing ships to their doom on the rocks of the Dover coast. A horrible image of her in a black and white striped Victorian bathing suit, with a ukulele, came unbidden to his mind.

"We'd best stand back, good lady. I think there's more dragon in this barrow than should be strictly possible..."

They didn't get to find out, though.

Because at that moment a plummeting mass of metal and wood came rushing down toward them, its engine still coughing and belching smoke. One of the Spitfire's wheels had unfolded, but the other was stuck, and it looked as though the stricken aeroplane was going to clip the barrow and shatter to pieces in the field beyond.

"You said we need every last one, didn't you?" asked Mrs Tavistock, as Ulfric's jaw dropped. Literally. He caught it before it hit the ground.

"By Wotan! You spaketh truthe! My lads are up there fighting these dragonne-engines, are they? Bloody *nice!*"

"Every last one, indeed," murmured Major Monkston, watching

that whirling, scything propeller come rushing toward him...

Mrs Tavistock sighed. Then the ground thumped beneath Monkston's feet, as if a vast stone heart had pumped once, miles below. Little crackles of green lightning bipped and fizzed across his skin, snapping from his fingernails and the ends of his mustache.

But the majority of the power came up through Mrs Tavistock's gumboots. The ground around her feet erupted with a small explosion of wildflowers. There was a scent like seaweed and spring sap, and a sudden blooming of warmth which turned the air to mist. But only for a second. The mist blew away as the old witch shrugged the power off her shoulders, rolled it forward, kneaded it in her hands, and unleashed it at the onrushing Spitfire.

A great clingy, springy, invisible spiderweb bound it up. Major Monkston, who, despite the top hat, had seen plenty of actual combat, was reminded of watching bullets fired into water. For a second Mrs Tavistock stood there with her hands outstretched, holding the entire aircraft up with sheer force of will. Then she grunted and set it down, gentle as you please.

"That was... *incredible!*" said the Major, though his threshold for 'incredible' was several levels above that of the common soldier.

"Not done yet..." puffed the witch. "Got to offset the kinetic energy..."

She licked her finger, closer her eyes, bent down and poked it into the ground. A pulse of something slippery and bright green shot away to the north, following a ley line. In the little village of Bishop's Corners, nine miles away, the steeple of the church exploded. She raised an eyebrow at Ulfric.

"How's that for some A-grade dastardly midnight haggotry?"

The lich-king actually bowed.

"Thatte be foul and arcane crone-level stuffe, Mrs Tavistock. Were I butte onne thousande yeares youngere..."

Major Monkston gave a gentle but utterly obtrusive butlery little cough, looking pointedly at the downed Spitfire.

"Hadn't we better take a look? I mean, dragons are all fine and good, Mister Foesbane, but an RAF pilot with all his arms and legs on is just as rare and useful right now..."

+++

They say your life flashes before your eyes when you are about to die - but somehow the flash must have known this wasn't the big one.

Eddie only got to see the bad bits in the indeterminable, black-and-purple chasm of time between his forehead smacking into the window and the Spitfire hitting the ground. This was, he thought, probably *exactly* what he got for being a liar. Not a hero's death, but a stupid bloody accident with an overstuffed flying alligator, a broken plane, and a lot of explaining to do.

None of which would be easy. Mentioning aerial collisions with dragons to a man like Fighter Group Commander Sir Horace Stackpole would be like mentioning Satan's nice new haircut to the Pope.

The whole story would go something like this, if he was stupid enough to tell the truth to the fearsome old Great War fighter ace with the two wooden legs.

"Well, you see... I was sort of bored living on a huge sheep station in New Zealand. My big brother Cyril had already come over here to volunteer in Spain against General Franco, and *he* could fly an aeroplane... we had an old Le Rhone Avro which he wanted to use to drop fertilizer. But the letters stopped coming, and I got worried, and Dad got angry, and I sort of stole his papers from the flying school, and got on a boat, and peeled a lot of potatoes, and came here to England and volunteered. And then..."

They'd been delighted that he could fly a plane. Which, in his defense, Eddie *could*, if only because he'd wheedled, begged, stolen and wrangled every turn he could get at the controls of that moth-eaten old Le Rhone. Training, then, was simple. Being yelled at a lot by Sir Horace Stackpole - who stumped around the airbase on two wooden legs, smoked a pipe the size of a chamber pot filled with foul-smelling brandy-cured tobacco, and possessed a mustache worthy of its own separate row of medals – was nothing compared to what his old man could belt out when it came to mustering and shearing time. There was plenty of time spent in lovely little country pubs. There were young men from America, Canada, Poland, France and more in the dashing uniform of the fighter pilots, and Eddie even grudgingly accepted the Aussies as comrades.

Then it was June of 1940. Then came the message from London which made Sir Horace look suddenly very sad and very, very old. Training was over. They were to report to the front lines. They'd given Eddie a beautiful new aeroplane which, he suspected, had recently been wiped clean of the last pilot's blood and other bits. They told him to get up there, at night, and shoot down just as many enemy planes as he could. When Eddie had asked the man on the refueling truck what he should do if he was shot down, all he'd got in reply was a twisted kind of smile.

"You religious, me lad?"

He'd shaken his head.

"Not much to do but curse, then, is there?"

He'd lied about his age. He'd lied about just how good he was behind the controls of an aeroplane. He'd even lied about why he was really here, in England, right now. But there was only a single truth up in the chilly darkness over the farms and villages of Kent, with the roar and shudder of that hammering great Merlin engine coursing through him. For a very, very small sliver of time he was actually happy, flying above the moonlit fields.

And then the first wave of Nazi fighters came.

It's a funny thing about war. In between the bits where you're actually being shot at, you can sort of forget that there's a whole nation full of people out there intent on blowing you to small crispy pieces. After weeks of very good ale, smiling young women, easy training flights and posing in front of a mirror in his new uniform, Eddie was not at all prepared for a sound like a sky full of hornets, and the impressive sight of rank after v-shaped rank of warplanes arrowing in toward them. He was even less prepared for what happened next, when more than a dozen of the swastika-blazoned machines peeled away and began raking him with machine-gun fire.

All of Sir Horace Stackpole's shouting and whacking the blackboard with a riding crop tried to squeeze into the front of his brain at once. In fact, his entire head seemed to have been frozen and cracked with a hammer. Different parts of his mind were yammering different strategies, ranging from complicated barrel-rolls and evasion techniques through to wetting his pants and crying.

Part of Eddie – a part which was probably welded on back in caveman times, right down in the dodgier neighbourhoods of the brainstem – took the middle path. He opened up the throttles, roared something incomprehensible but definitely rude, and let rip with all the guns they'd seen fit to give him.

The first German pilot was likely expecting some kind of clever maneuvers. Instead his entire craft was torn in half by the screaming-insane madman who had broken formation and come spiraling up toward him behind a storm of lead. Eddie brushed past a second Messerschmitt so close that he could see the pilot take his hands off the yoke, anticipating a fatal collision. Adrenaline plucked his spinal column like the devil on an upright bass. The plane reached the top of its arc, flipped, and looped back down, Eddie's vision blurring as he plunged back through the German formation, letting off another wild and unfocused burst of fire.

This time they were onto him. He swooped low, barnstorming a stand of moonlit poplar trees, and a glance over his shoulder was enough to confirm his fears. *Two of them.* They followed his curving, twisting ascent as if they were on invisible rails, and some half-remembered shouting from Sir Horace made him jink left and right, narrowly avoiding a chatter of machinegun rounds.

Pull back. Let the power of that great thunderous engine pull you clear. Up... and through the clouds, punching through wisps and veils into the open sky. A scatter of bullets followed, wide. They were still there. It was only a matter of time, then, before…

And this is where his mind stopped the film.

This is the part where sanity, if it was allowed free rein, would burn through the reel and nail up the doors of the cinema. Because...

There is a certain school of thought that says that dragons aren't real. And that if they are, they are creatures of magic and whimsy, borne aloft by tiny little wings too small for their big curly-wurly cursive bodies.

These people have never seen a Great Western European King Dragon stoop on its prey from high altitude, or smelled the stink of sulphur and sweat on leather as it collides, talons out.

But it's also worth noting that anything at all - even the most fantastical beast – can suddenly become *all too real* if it comes roaring past you at several hundred miles per hour, close enough so that you can see the flammable drool whipping back from its fangs, and the little skeletal viking on its back waving hello.

Of course, Eddie's brain only had time to scream DRAGON! once before the Messerschmitt on his tail ceased to exit. Spectacularly.

Several tons of red-and-copper aerial lizard met with a delicate concoction of German engineering and ripped it to shreds. A heartbeat later the beast turned its head on a long, serpentine neck, and a jet of superheated fire incinerated the second Nazi warplane. A red-hot engine block sailed up into the air, on an arc to land in the English Channel.

The dragon paused in the air as Eddie banked into a sharp turn, well aware that his jaw was hanging slack and his eyes were the size of barrage balloons. Those immense leathery wings clapped once, and the beast curved into a graceful ascent, that little armoured figure perched between its wings waving an axe in what seemed like a curiously festive manner.

*Yes! This was more like it! They hadn't told him about the dragons!* Of course, thought Eddie, they were probably Top Secret. Need-to-know-basis and all that. Nothing like some unexpected, quasi-mythical air support to boost morale in the flying corps. With a few of those beasts on his side, it might just be possible to survive this mission, then figure out how to never have to fly a plane again...

It was the tail which caught him. A dragon's tail really needs that tiny second brain which some dinosaurs were supposed to have grown, to make sure they knew what they were doing with all that scaly bulk. As it was, this dragon had as much control over its tail as a drunk human has over his little toe. It had no idea where it was, and it proceeded to slam it into the nearest hunk of unresisting metal – hard.

For the dragon, this was merely uncomfortable. But for Eddie, it was disastrous. It ended up, in fact, with all of this awful chain of events playing out behind his eyes while blue and yellow fireworks of pain exploded in close proximity.

He felt like a rag doll stuffed full of broken glass. He felt like the aftermath of a three-week pub crawl. He felt...

*Wait a second! That shape, rising up next to the cockpit window. That distinctively black and wide-brimmed pointy hat...*

*First dragons, and now witches?* thought Eddie.

And then, mercifully, he passed out once and for all.

+++

"He's out like a light, poor dear," said Mrs Tavistock, lifting Eddie down from the cockpit of the Spitfire. Despite appearing to be a plump old lady, the witch carried him with ease. This was nothing to do with supernatural powers - Eddie Weatherfield weighed only about sixty kilograms in his boots, and a lady farmer who can't carry a lamb under each arm through a blizzard soon gives up and moves to the city. Mrs Tavistock had seen blizzards which only Ulfric Foesbane would probably have believed in - ones with nasty personalities... and faces, and crowns of icicles. And she was yet to lose enough lambs, even after several hundred years, to make her prefer a flat in Notting Hill.

"Come on, come on. Let me take a peek," fussed Major Monkton. "He's hit his head, look. Did you have to stop the plane so suddenly?"

The witch shot him a glance with definite shades of frog transformation in it.

"I could have not bothered at all, and seen which of us survived," she said. But a second later her face crinkled up with worry. "Oh, he looks just like them young sailor boys, from all those years ago. I've gotten all soft-hearted in my later centuries, Major. Let's get him to the cottage. I can fix him up there."

Eddie really had taken a nasty knock. One of his eyes was swollen shut, and half of his face was the purple-black of a summer thunderstorm. A little trickle of blood ran from one nostril and dripped onto the moonlit grass.

"Ohhhh. Errrrmm..." coughed Ulfric, behind them. "I... ummm... looke, it's actually notte your faulte, goode lady..."

Mrs Tavistock turned, frog-making finger pointed like a revolver. Witches hate to be called 'good lady'. But she stopped when she saw what was in the old lich's skeletal fingers.

It was a copper-coloured dragon scale.

"Stucke inne the winge of yon engine, I'm afraide. Onne of the boyes ys gotte a bitte over-ethusiastic with the mead, methinks. Will... will our young warrior be all ryte?"

Major Monkston had seen his fair share of battlefield wounds.

"Nasty concussion. Hard to tell, with these things. He might be up and at the Germans again in an hour. He might be spark out for a week. And he might..."

He realized he'd gone too far when he saw the blue flash in Ulfric's eyes. Of course - the old Saxon warrior-king came from a time when a sprained ankle could be a death sentence. When gangrene made merry with the tiniest cut, and the term 'modern medicine' meant amputation with a slightly less rusty sword.

"Thys I cannot have upon my conscience," grumbled the ancient one. "He is onne of ours, yes? I shall notte go unto the feasting halle of mine ancestors as a betrayer..."

And with that he stumped off toward the barrow, where a huge scaly head came snaking out to meet him.

Major Monkston had no idea how all those dragons - twenty-four had come out from under the earth so far tonight - could fit inside three barrow-graves built over a trio of overturned longships. No doubt the boffins back at Section M would talk about quantum phenomena and pocket universe encapsulation, but Monkston preferred to think of it as just plain magic. Call it what you wanted, though - the last dragon could barely squeeze through the door. A big boy indeed. When it spread its wings and reared up against the moon for the first time in a thousand years, an atavistic shiver of dread and wonder ran all the way up the Major's spine.

"What exactly is he planning to do?" whispered Monskton. Mrs Tavistock shrugged.

"He's *helping*. Saves me boiling up a potion, and believe you me, the potion for fixing a knock to the head smells like a miner's underpants. He's doing us all a favour."

Ulfric reached up and patted his dragon on the snout, scratching its spikes and horns. One great back leg thumped the ground, as if the twenty-metre-long reptile was a gigantic labrador. Then came a whispered conversation in what must have been Very Old Saxon. The Dragon's eyes narrowed as it looked directly at Major Monkston. He pointed at himself, then Mrs Tavistock, then at the motionless body of Eddie Weatherfield. The beast nodded.

What happened next was very occult indeed, even by the standards of section M.

The dragon opened its mouth - a trap-jaw of ivory and sizzling phosphor-drool, a great blue tongue lolling out between those butcher-knife fangs - and Ulfric Foesbane reached inside. He spoke a few words which cut the air like chisels into stone - not words, in fact, but Runes, with a capital R. Runes of Power, to be precise.

And his hand came out holding a fragment of dragonflame.

Not a sticky ball of chemicals. Not a writhing globe of fire, all purple and green. Not a crystal made of reflections alone, facets sketched out with no mass behind them. No, *it was all three at once.* Ulfric carried it down to where Eddie lay in one hand, and it lit up his bearded, skeletal features with impossible angles and shadows.

"There we goe. As my olde dadde would saye, thee medicine doth tayste lyke shytte, butte it will putte hairs upon thy cheste, my sonne..."

And before either the Major or the Witch could stop him, he brought the blazing thing in his palm down hard, driving it into Eddie's forehead.

For an instant they waited for him to explode. For something eldritch to happen, perhaps - a spot of levitation, some head-spinning, some glowing eyes or a bit of speaking in tongues.

But there was nothing. Eddie sighed a little and rolled to his left, tucking his hands up under his head.

"He's gone from unconscious to just asleep," reported Mrs Tavistock, a little underwhelmed.

"I suppose that's a result," admitted Major Monkston. "Though I was expecting…"

Ulfric laughed, then - a sound like the wind through a graveyard.

"You gotte *dragonnes*, little man of Albion. And yon warrior will live. In facte, when he waketh uppe, he might putte a bit more fyre in your shield-wall."

The lich turned away, stomping back up the hill toward his waiting dragon.

"What do we do with him?" Shouted Monkston, as Ulfric swung up into the saddle and drew his sword.

"I might suggest some nyce soupe!" he bellowed, above the creak and groan of massive wings unfurling. "Butte in truth, alle this is your problem nowe. Young Arthur never spake anything aboutte healthe and safety! I'm off to batter some bloody foes, before all the goode ones are taken!"

There was a massive thunderclap of leather. There was a wind which flattened out the grass all around. There was a stench of hot metal and old offal, and Ulfric Foesbane was skybound, off to terrify the cream of the Third Reich's air forces.

"Well how do you like…" began the Major. He stopped when he saw the look in Mrs Tavistock's eyes.

"A powerful fate-weaving has been done here this night," she intoned, in a definitely witchy voice. "I see fire and darkness in this young lad's future. Fire, and darkness, and the salvation of England. That, and a humourous interlude where his leg gets stuck in a toilet bowl. Though I might be wrong about that one."

Major Monkston's dapper eyebrows rose.

"So what do we do?"

Mrs Tavistock smiled. It was not exactly sweet.

"You take his arms, and I'll take his legs, and let's get him back to the cottage. We'll all three of us catch our death if we stay out here much longer…"

High above, the battle raged on. Despite their small numbers, their raw, untrained recruits from all around the world, and the sheer might and momentum of the Luftwaffe, the Royal Air Force held the line.

Some German pilots swore they saw dragons over England that night, and for many nights to come. Those foolish enough to talk about this fact to their superior officers were shouted at in German, which is distinctly unpleasant. Those who pointed to claw marks and scorches on their aircraft were taken away and talked to in small, windowless rooms by horrible little men in wire framed spectacles and black trenchcoats. Most were swiftly convinced they had experienced hallucinations.

Others... well, their families were told, later, that they'd crashed into the sea.

And, in a bunker below Kew Gardens, a little dragon-shaped marker was removed from a big board in the shape of the British Isles. *They hadn't used that one up for the Spanish Armada, or for the French. They'd told Cromwell to go and stuff it up his puritan smock during the civil war. And the king, too, it must be admitted.*

But desperate times called for desperate measures. Such as melting down a few of the lesser magical swords Merlin had crafted to forge a line of Rolls-Royce aero engines with his name on them. And finally invoking the bargain he and his young *protege* had made with a Saxon sorcerer-king, back in the dark ages...

The General who clenched that little wooden dragon in his fist was old, and jaded, and quite weary of the world and its wars. He had been called the wickedest man alive, a servant of Lucifer, the Great Beast of Revelations. He'd also been called 'Big Al', 'Party Animal', and 'Mister Strangetrousers' - but despite his scandalous life, there was one thing he still cared about.

England must not fall. Adolf Hitler must not win. And above all, *he mustn't bring the magic back.* Because while we all know that absolute power corrupts absolutely - the old Fuhrer being a wonderful case in point - *magical power corrupts supernaturally.* And that's the kind of thing that can poke holes in the world.

Holes which General Crowley had seen through once or twice, thanks to absinthe, opiates, ritual sorcery and forbidden knowledge. Holes through which, he knew, *things looked back.*

They were looking now. And a world benighted by war had made them hungry...

# Two - The Labyrinth of Kew

Major Monkston's car roared on through the night, its slotted headlamps illuminating the winding back-roads of Kent. It zoomed past the great dark cathedral at Canterbury, then pressed resolutely on as dawn licked the rind of the horizon, toward the smouldering skies over London. That red glow was nothing to do with the sunrise. Monkston grimaced, his fingers tightening around the steering wheel, and he put his foot down.

Beside him on the passenger seat was a large metal drum - the kind which reels of flammable cinema film come in. It had been augmented with a padlock the size of a saucer, the key to which hung around the Major's neck. This was where his hat lived when he couldn't keep it on his head, for a variety of reasons. On the back seat, Eddie Weatherfield was curled up snoring, his efforts drowned out by the blatter and snarl of the car's mighty engine.

And mighty it was indeed. This was one of Section M's 'specials', a car designed by someone for whom the term 'engineering wizard' was more than just a colloquialism. The Merlin V-12 under the long and menacing hood really did contain a fragment of one of the old arch-sorcerer's magical swords. On the outside, it was a Talbot T150 grand tourer, with exquisite coachwork by Figoni, a Brooklands Racing Modified drivetrain and suspension, and the heavy-duty gearbox from an Albion double-decker bus. The entire chassis was engraved with runes, and the headlights were polarized with strange ritual bindings to see into realms far beyond the British A-road network.

That was why Major Monkston was able to race the dawn as he skirted the southern reaches of London town, blasting along the empty byroads at a confident two hundred miles per hour. Other traffic - and this consisted mainly of lumbering olive-drab army trucks - saw nothing at all as the Talbot streaked past, its wheels only kissing the tarmac for the sake of convention. Horses had nothing to do with it. The T150 put out 194 *broomstickpower.*

Eddie yawned and stretched as the Major slowed down to a

respectable one hundred and ten, navigating the early-morning streets of Croydon, into Mitcham, and past Wimbledon Common, where he silently saluted Section M's Private Rusk, perched in a tree with his binoculars, trying to catch sight of those things that kept knocking over the bins.

"Ahhh. Back with us, then? That was a nasty bump on the head you took, and no mistake."

Eddie nearly knocked himself out again on the low ceiling of the Talbot. He did the full 'where am I?' awakening, complete with rubbing his eyes, peering blearily through the little quarter-glass back windows of the car, and finally noticing all the blood on his uniform. He slumped back in the seat and sighed.

"I crashed, didn't I?"

"Rather spectacularly, in fact," confirmed the Major, nodding like a clockwork terrier. "But then again, you took a couple of German planes with you. All pretty good - *for someone who lied about just about everything to get in the cockpit of that Spitfire...*"

Eddie went a certain shade of greyish-green. The mists of sleep blasted away like cobwebs before a flamethrower.

"I... oh, my goodness, Sir, I can explain! You see, it's like..."

"Oh, no need, no need," smiled Monkston, who secretly liked to wind up the raw recruits. "You did better than some of our crusty old veterans up there. Good show! We were just surprised, what with all the little fibs, that you weren't a girl dressing up as a boy to join the services. Then again, it was pretty obvious..."

Eddie went from greenish-grey to red. He clasped the front of his trousers defensively. Monkston laughed.

"Lad, you've got an adam's apple so big it looks like your neck has a knee in it! Between that and the snoring we didn't really need a full medical. What I want to know is... do you remember *why* you crashed?"

They were coming in slowly now - well, slowly for the Talbot Special - towards Kew, approaching the great green park with its oriental pagoda peeking up through the foliage. Major Monkston flipped open a panel on the Talbot's walnut dash and tapped out a code on a set of brass keys. Ahead of them, the gates to the Royal Botanical Gardens creaked open.

It all came back to Eddie in a rush. He couldn't help the word from escaping his lips.

"*Dragons!*"

Monkston nodded.

"Indeed. Some of the last ones we could beg, borrow, steal, wheedle or cajole out of retirement. You saw them in action. But I'm sure you realize that such things cannot become common knowledge..."

Oh dear. Lots of disparate, grubby jigsaw pieces came together inside Eddie's aching skull, then, as they swept through the gates and crunched their way up the gravel drive toward a great glass building, all glittering peach and diamond in the dawn.

*He'd lied about nearly everything.* And then he'd seen something top, top secret. Now he was in a little car with a man whose uniform was covered in strange pips and bars, being hustled off to an unknown location for who knows what...

Well, he sort of *did* know what. Bang! *One little shot in the back of the head, and no more messy secrets being blabbed in the public bar by the snotty little liar from the Antipodes.*

The greyish-green came back with a vengeance. It brought with it the sensation of his innards being tied up with waxed string.

"Please sir - I didn't mean it! Don't kill me! I'll forget I ever saw them! I..."

Major Monkston sighed, as the Talbot eased through a pair of glass doors in the glass wall. Inside it was all tropical jungle plants, steaming hot and dripping. A large garden bed slid aside to reveal a metal platform, outlined in yellow paint.

"Oh, come on now, Son! The British Army doesn't just go around killing people!" He thought about this for a second. "Well... not like that. Only in what you might call a wholesale fashion, rather than bespoke. And only if you're in league with the dastardly Axis powers."

He raised an eyebrow, as the hatbox on the seat beside him rattled ominously. "*Are* you in fact in league with the dastardly Axis powers? That would make this all so much simpler. Whole other department..."

Eddie shook his head so hard he saw little blips of purple.

"Sorry, Sir. Totally committed to the Allied Cause, Sir. But... if I might ask... *where exactly are you taking me?*"

This question suddenly became a lot more pertinent as the Talbot came to a stop on the metal platform, and began sinking into the ground. A few seconds later a whole garden bed of tropical plants rolled shut above them, leaving the car in semi-darkness. Only the light from the dials and instruments lit up Major Monkston's face as he turned in his seat, his dapper mustache all but quivering.

"Well, that's the thing, see. We could have just given you a little drink of something which made you forget the dragons and all. We were even willing to send you back to your airbase, and forget all your little fibs and forgeries. After all, you *did* shoot down at least one German. That means you could have bagged a few more. But... something happened. So we're going to report back to the top brass, and see what we should do with you."

"Something happened? What kind of *something?*"

Eddie was just a bit frantic, now. Did he feel different? It was hard to tell, with his heart in his throat and his stomach somewhere in the vicinity of his boots. The little man with the pencil-thin mustache looked like a cheap woodcut of Lucifer in the orange light of the car's dashboard. He grinned.

"The kind of something people will talk about," said Major Monkston, flipping down the passenger's-side sun visor. It contained a little mirror, which he angled toward Eddie's face. "The kind of thing... well, you can see for yourself."

The platform reached the bottom of whatever stygian shaft the government had excavated under Kew Gardens. The lights came on all around them, flooding the interior of the Talbot T150 Special.

And Eddie saw. One of his eyes was bruised all around - a right shiner, but it was still the pale blue he remembered from his shaving mirror every morning.

The other, though.

Oh, cripes. Oh, yes indeed.

Eddie recognized the yellow-rimmed, gold-flecked red orb which bulged slightly from the left side of his face. He'd seen that slit pupil close-up, not so long ago. Hanging in the cold, moonlit skies above Kent, in fact.

*He now had the eye of a dragon.*

Eddie drew in a great deep breath to scream, but Major Monkston - who had been in this exact same situation, give or take a few supernatural variations, several times - clapped a hand over his mouth.

"Don't worry," he said. "We'll get you a nice pair of sunglasses. But first..."

+++

It turned out that 'but first' was actually slightly more worrying than having a great big evil lizard eye glaring back at him from one side of his face.

Eddie was hustled out of the Talbot and into a vast and echoing space, where little olive-drab carts scurried about on white rubber wheels, carrying a dizzying assortment of crates. Behind him, he heard a rattle of hinges, then a contented sigh as Major Monkston retrieved and donned his signature top hat.

"Now, you're going to be slightly surprised by the welcoming party, lad, but don't let it show. And for God's sake, no cattle jokes in front of Reggie, and no short jokes in front of... *dash it all,* I'm too late, aren't I?"

This was because Eddie was already looking up, and up, and *up* at a huge figure in military fatigues, visibly straining at the seams and buttons. You could hardly fit more muscle in with a crowbar. The reason he was drooling slightly and going 'Bu....bu....bu...', however, was probably something to do with this imposing presence's head.

"Spit it out, then," said the huge man-mountain, in a dolorous Welsh brogue. "They all have to. It's a laugh a minute down here in reception thanks to all the fresh, witty bull jokes. Load of old bull. Bully for you. Bull in a china shop. Take your pick..."

A face which was *definitely* not human leaned down until it was within an inch of Eddie's draconic eye. It possessed a glistening snout with a brass ring through it, big, soulful brown eyes, tufted black ears, and a pair of horns which looked fit to overturn a steam locomotive.

"You only get one." A mist, redolent of silage, blew Eddie's fringe back.

"*Minotaur.* You. You are, that is. One. If you hadn't noticed. With the..."

"Call me Reggie," said the immense bull-man, suddenly smiling. "Nice to meet someone with a classical education. Instead" (and here he frowned, as only a six- hundred-pound Minotaur can) "of those who care to speculate on how I got born..."

*That* hadn't occurred to Eddie. As a farm boy, he knew a whole telephone book full of coarse jokes about livestock - but right now his brain was out of the gutter and into the blender. He managed a lopsided smile, and extended one twitching hand.

"Magic, of course," said Major Monkston, deftly stepping between them, just as Eddie's hand was gripped in the Minotaur's huge fist and pumped enthusiastically. "Reggie here found a particularly interesting stone idol while on his holidays in Crete. Now he has a bit of an urge to guard labyrinths. Which is what we have here under Kew Gardens, in a big way."

"I like all the curly bits. And the distinct possibility of goring and stomping," confessed Reggie, with the same cheerful tone as a child discussing a prize finger-painting. "So far, no Nazis, but it's early in the war, eh?"

Eddie smiled in what he hoped was an encouraging way.

"And the short jokes?"

Something kicked him in the shin. It was only when he looked down that he realised it was, in fact, a tiny little headbutt.

"You'll forget all about them, if you know what's good for you!"

It was a garden gnome. Well - something like a garden gnome. It was short and round and possessed a pointy felt hat and a luxurious beard, but other than that... The beard was dyed lavender and curled. The hat was covered in tiny little white flowers.

"Miss Golightly is just a *smidge* sensitive about her height," said the Major. "But she is simply indispensable when it comes to our records. One incoming, Miss G - Born Conventional, Supernaturally Affected, Category 5, Attributes unknown, Nordic Mythos, Type C."

The tiny little lady gnome produced a clipboard the size of a postage stamp and ticked boxes.

"Weatherfield, E, Age seventeen, hair, dirty brown, eyes, one blue, one funny looking, 65 kilos, five foot eight with big boots on, slightly wonky teeth, and very bad at rugby."

She looked up, and batted a pair of immense mauve eyelashes.

"Reggie, the blindfold, if you would be so kind?"

"Sorry" whispered the Minotaur behind one immense hand, and he dropped a black hessian sack over Eddie's head with the other.

"Now, put him on the cart. Nice and gentle-like..."

Something picked him up. It felt as if it could have snapped him in half with but a fingertip's exertion.

"And off we go!"

Now they were moving. *Fast.* Strangely, for a person who never got airsick, Eddie found it remarkably easy to feel thoroughly nauseous when being whisked through an underground maze on a squeaky-wheeled electric cart with a sack over his head. The disorientation - combined with the musty odour left behind by the last denizen of the sack - combined to not only make him want to lose his breakfast, but also to remind him that he hadn't even had one yet.

".... really only got started when Dee and Shakespeare were in charge, during the Fae Wars. They had to expand when all that stuff happened with the lizard people, of course. And then Napoleon, with his bloody undead army! Whoops a daisy! Nearly all needed new trousers after that one!"

Eddie realized that Major Monkston had been happily wittering on all along, as if he was giving a guided tour. He tentatively raised a finger.

"Excuse me. But can I ask a very important question?"

A hand patted him on the shoulder as the little cart rounded a sharp corner, on what felt like two wheels.

"By all means, lad. Go ahead. Just nothing about any of the stuff I've just told you. Red tape. You know how it is."

Eddie had narrowed it down to two equally horrible possibilities.

"So. Am I mad, or am I dead?"

Major Monkston laughed. It seemed a little forced.

"The short but comforting answer - that is to say, the one I'd give you if I thought you were a stupid little berk - would be 'gosh no, you're chipper as a dandelion and *ever* so mentally stable'. But you're with Section M now. So you deserve the truth. The long, more disturbing answer which starts with 'we don't really know for certain about either.'"

"Starts with?" asked Eddie, as the Major plucked the bag from off of his head. They had pulled up to a stop outside a little half-round tin hut, of the kind soldiers everywhere were putting together right now, all over the world.

Monkston nodded.

"*Starts with.* Because, of course, we are *definitely* going to get to the bottom of both of those questions. Starting now, with a trip to the doctor's."

Inside, the hut was pale blue.

There was an old-fashioned record player playing old fashioned music, of the kind that makes you think of elderly people dozing in rocking chairs on a sunny Sunday afternoon. Someone had written, in huge white letters taking up an entire curved wall

They both took seats and waited. There were magazines, all of which were about people getting married, cakes, and small dogs. All of them were from 1927.

"Soooo..." said Eddie, after a long and awkward while. "About the hat..."

"What hat?" asked Monkston. Realization dawned. "oh, you mean this old thing? Well..."

"You're that Maskelyne[3] feller, aren't you? Magic, and top secret stuff with the army, and tricking the Germans and all. I suppose Reggie back there was wearing a very, very clever mask. And so-called Miss Golightly was a puppet of some kind. Though why you'd do all this stage makeup for my eye..."

Major Monkston sighed heavily, and tweaked the points of his dapper little mustache.

"No, no no! Why do they always... Listen. Maskelyne is in signals and camouflage. he's an *illusionist*. I'm a *magician*. There's a difference. And as for Miss Golightly being a puppet, I'll caution you to keep that thought to yourself, unless you'd like to find an oyster fork jammed into your shin at high velocity."

"So you've never done a kid's birthday party, then?"

Monkston looked a little deflated, then.

"There have been... *occasions*. Times were hard in the twenties. Me and the old man had to eat, God rest him. So yes, I've pulled the odd rabbit or two. But never with no *mirrors* or no *false bottoms*. Did you never wonder, lad, who all those stage illusionists were *copying*, with their black suits and white gloves and top hats? My great granddad, that's who. Barnabas Monkston, rightly called 'the Magnificent'. He taught..."

But at that moment a blue door opened in the blue wall, and a slightly nervous young doctor came shuffling into the room. He was - and this Eddie found slightly disappointing - the most normal person who had appeared all day.

"Sorry to keep you waiting, gentlemen. You would not *believe* the things you can catch from a ghoul..." He looked up over a pair of green-tinted half glasses with a pair of eyes like runny eggs. "But listen to me! All shop! You must be Eddie! And the Major, of course, we know. Any luck with that ointment for the..?"

Out of the corner of his eye, Eddie saw Monkston making frantic

---

3 Please do yourself a favour and look up J. Maskelyne. He's actually just as interesting as Monkston, and less classified. He once made an entire seaport disappear.

'don't go there' gestures with his hands. The Doctor lunged forward, enfolding Eddie's fingers in a grip just marginally less crushing than Reggie the minotaur's.

"Pleasure to meet you, of course. I'm Section M's resident quack, Doctor Jeckyll, and you, by process of elimination, must be my patient."

He wasn't about to let this slide.

"Wait! *Really?* I mean the witch, and the dragon, and even the little gnome lady I could... but... come on! *You're* the infamous, *totally fictional* Doctor Jeckyll?"

The medic smiled sheepishly, pushing his glasses up on his beaklike nose. They slid down immediately.

"Oh no. Nononono. Not him at all."

Eddie sighed contentedly. A bit of sanity, right now, was like a floating matchstick to a drowning man. But at least it was something.

"No, I'm his Grandson, to be precise. There's a lot of that kind of thing goes on, you know. Fictional! Ha! I wish! Do you know what you can get away with if you're *fictional?* I'd be bending the rules of causality like so many big arithmetical bananas! But no, don't worry about the stories. It's not as if I drink a magical potion and turn into a... hahaha... *raging monster*. How silly!"

Major Monkston got in on the laugh. Eddie tentatively joined the pair of them.

"Oh no," said Jeckyll. "I've got it quite under control now. Switch whenever I want to. It seems Granddad's potion was pretty darned heavy on the radioactive isotopes. Our opposite numbers in America have a fellow on their Manhattan Project with a similar ailment. Bruce somebody."

"Oh, really? The one with the temper? That's going to end badly, mark my words. I mean, I remember when we were on active duty, in Norway, and you threw that entire fishing boat..." Major Monkston and Doctor Jeckyll shared a certain look. Eddie stood between them, slack-jawed. The doctor squinted, tongue between his teeth, and poked the draconian side of his face with a pencil.

"I digress, though. What we're here for, young man, is to see just what's happened to you. And to that end, the good Major and I are going to ask you to participate in a few little tests."

The pair ushered him through the door, and into a vast and echoing space beyond. There was no doctor's office behind the little hut - just a concrete pier jutting out like an industrial tongue into a vaulted cave.

Bats chittered and jostled far above. Cold water licked the edge of the pier, bible-black and uninviting.

There was an iron desk and a single chair in the very centre of the pier. Several large wooden crates were stacked at its far end.

"Take a seat, my boy. Would you like a cup of... ahhh, sorry! Too late, I'm afraid!" Doctor Jeckyll looked at the huge, improbable brass pocketwatch on a chain which weighed down his starchy white coat. "Best press on. Lots of things to find out, and only so much time before those pesky Nazis come back, eh?"

Eddie sat down unsteadily. Major Monkston opened one of the desk drawers, and plopped a pile of paperwork down in front of him. He produced a slim silver pen from behind his ear with stage-illusionist aplomb.

"Right. First things first. Have you ever seen a ghost, spectre, wraith, or spirit?"

There was an awful lot of paperwork. At intervals Monkston would ask him to guess cards, or Jeckyll would lean in to tap him sharply with a small rubber hammer. The questions got weirder as the grating *tick-tock, tick-tock* of the Doctor's watch wormed into his brain. Did he know what a Fomorian looked like? Who was the Great God Dagon? Were there any zombies in his family? Did any of his relatives have extra nipples?

Time ground on, inexorable. Eddie's stomach made its presence known with a tectonic rumble. But still the paperwork came. Still the Doctor insisted on sticking thermometers in his ears and taping electrodes to his forehead. His draconic eye began to develop a twitch, which he was sure the pair of them wrote down.

There was no way of actually telling the hour, down here in the bowels of the earth. But it must have been about afternoon teatime by the time the pile of official documents was finished.

"Well," said Jeckyll, huddled together with the Major but still clearly audible. "He's not gotten any psychic powers. No indication of hyper-intelligence, no gravitonic anomalies, no tendency to shape-shift. There's only one thing for it..."

The Major sighed.

"I supposed it might come to this. Bad show and all that, but we are at war, after all."

Eddie was already thirsty, hungry, slightly dazed and very tired. Now he was also jangling with awful precognition. The Major and the Doctor turned to him, smiling like predatory fish from out of the dark and horrible bits of the ocean.

"Terribly sorry, young chap. The tests were a bit inconclusive. So... well, there's no easy way to say this, but..."

"I'm no good to you. I figured." Eddie slumped back in his chair, all the stuffing knocked out of him. "I suppose I'll at least get to wear an eyepatch, after you wipe my memory with your little drink, Major. That'll look dashing. And..."

"Oh, no. No, no. Sorry. I'm afraid you misunderstand. It's not that there's no easy way to say that you failed the test." He leaned forward, squeezed Eddie's shoulder, and looked him in the eyes. "You failed the test."

Behind them, the Doctor took out his pocketwatch. He opened it, and fiddled with the dial, setting what looked like far too many hands and giving it a tap on the edge of the desk.

"There's no easy way, he means, of saying *this!*"

The watch blazed orange. A star-shaped rune made of ember-coloured light flickered across it, and when the Doctor next opened his mouth, the voice which came out sounded like it had been dredged up from an abyss lit by lava.

"KHOL KALKO NA K'THAN DO..."

For a second he stopped, his voice slipping back into the normal register.

"It's Weatherfield, with a W, isn't it?"

Eddie nodded. That vast, sepulchral voice came back, along with a cold wind which smelled of cobwebs and dust.

"KHOL KALKO NA K'THAN DO - EDDIE WEATHERFIELD!"

Amber lightning streamed from the pocketwatch, crawling in sizzling arcs across the pier. It earthed itself against three of those huge wooden crates, blowing them to glowing splinters. And what was inside...

Opened its eyes.

The Doctor looked at Eddie brightly, taking a step back from the desk.

"Oh, silly me. There *is* an easy way of saying it. Although the Golems wouldn't have understood. Basically, I've just told them to crush, mangle and destroy you." He winked. "Good luck!"

Now the three hunched shapes in the wreckage of those crates were unfolding. Each one was twice the height of a man, with glowing orange eyes and rough, stony skin. Each one had fists like boulders, and the wide-shouldered, knuckling stance of a silverback gorilla.

*"Good luck!"* wailed Eddie. "Seriously? You utter, utter bas..."

But he was cut off by the bellow of the golems. They'd scented him. They were coming. Major Monkston smiled a knowing little smile, then doffed his top hat, reaching inside. What he pulled out was a shimmering, translucent paisley scarf, which grew bigger and bigger until it blocked off the entire end of the pier. With a snap of his fingers, the Major turned the entire thing solid. He and Jeckyll waved from behind their barrier as the Golems came thundering down on Eddie, like the most murderous rugby team in history.

Terror gripped him. Sheer nerve-twanging fear made him fast enough to duck under the desk as a fist like a rockery collapsed his chair down to a sad little hubcap. Another swipe of one rocky paw and the table went flying, clattering end over end, striking sparks off the concrete.

Eddie looked up at his assailant, and saw nothing human in that rough-carved face. Only two eyes like drill-holes in a lump of granite, weeping hot lava. A mouth, scrawled on by some ancient chisel in a sad but determined frown.

*So, this was how they got rid of the wrong 'uns, eh? Not even a bullet. Not even a nice funeral, he bet. That black water was likely full of bones, and all Dad and Mum would get would be a letter full of mealy-mouthed government lies...*

That was the spark that lit his anger.

Normally, Eddie Weatherfield's anger was like a garden incinerator. Stoked full of the scrap wood of his petty failures and frustrations. When it went off, that little spark tore through the fuel, and, outside the metaphor, some unfortunate schoolyard bully ended up fending off a flail of pipe-cleaner limbs, all the more terrifying for the fact that it was sure to fail. Being attacked by Eddie was, in fact, like being brutalized by a very agitated squirrel.

Only this time...

The little scrub-fire drum of his anger was sitting right under the tailpipe of one of Hitler's fancy new rockets. Eddie ducked under another swiping blow from the Golem, then screamed, his dragon eye suddenly blazing red. He leaped up and spun around the thing's nearly non-existent neck until he was on its shoulders, and he drew back a fist to batter its polished dome of a skull.

Now, this should have done nothing but splinter all his fingers like cheese straws. Instead, that first blow saw a shockwave of crimson light spiral up his arm, detonating from his knuckles. Cracks skittered out through the stone. He pulled his fist back to strike again...

But he'd forgotten the other two. A hand made of grinding sections of granite closed around his, and the second golem threw him, *hard*. He spun through the air, up into a realm of darkness, guano and stalactites. The world blurred, radial. Then he smacked into the roof of the cave, with a sound like a side of bacon being dropped on a marble floor. Pain drove its daggers in between every section of his spine.

And Eddie discovered that beyond the roaring, flaming rocket-exhaust of his rage, there was *more*. The warhead in that rocket, to stretch the metaphor to breaking point, was the one Bruce whatshisname and all those other Yankee scientists were working on. The one the world would find out about in five years, in a place called Trinity, New Mexico.

Flames boiled out from his red eye. They didn't touch him, but they burned nonetheless. Eddie had no idea what he was doing, but his body seemed to. It leaped from the cave ceiling, propelling him down as his hands opened up into flat-palmed blades. Tangerine fire flickered around them as he went into a spin, coming down hard, slashing with his left and right...

Eddie slid across the pier on one knee, his hands out at his sides. There was a shimmer above his skin, like the half-imagined outline of copper scales. Behind him, two of the golems tried to turn around. Both of them suddenly cracked across the middle, red-hot molten rock spilling out as they crumbled and fell.

Which left only one...

Eddie tried to get a handle on his rage. It burned white hot, a ball-bearing sizzling in the centre of his brain. *Perhaps these things were alive! Perhaps they had feelings. And families, and little rock-monster kids, and...*

But it was too late. He picked up the table with one hand, and advanced on the last remaining golem. It held up its huge fingers in a T for 'time out'. But the rage was inexorable. The table came down once, twice, thrice, with all the force of a steam hammer. The poor thing's stone head shattered on that third impact, spraying lava. It tottered a few steps, then keeled over backwards, plunging into the black water with a brief puff of steam.

Eddie gritted his teeth, turning on Jeckyll and Monkston. But just as he raised his fist, the rage dropped out of him. It was like slicing the bottom out of a paper cup. One second he was ready to tie the pair of smug, officious bastards up into a meat pretzel, the next he was sitting flat on his arse, feeling like the dregs in a spittoon. The table clattered to the ground, bent double.

"You..." he panted, clawing his hair out of his eyes. He was covered in sweat, his uniform shirt soaked through. "You... tried to kill me! What in the name of... was *that* all about?"

Major Monkston was very primly re-folding his barrier spell, collapsing it back down into the form of a blue paisley scarf.

"A calculated risk, based on the mythos, lad. There've been others with the same... *condition*, let's call it, throughout history."

"Talking about my grand-dad and that poor American fellow made it all click. You're a *berserker*, Eddie. Wyrmfire touched. Dragon-kin. There were at least two Vikings, a Saxon, a couple of medieval knights and a Barbary pirate who had the same gift. We just needed to know what switched it on."

Now Monkston was kneeling down next to him, offering a white silk handkerchief. It was pleasantly cool, as if it had come direct from a refrigerator.

"Never mind the technicalities, though! Dear boy, you were *sensational*! Section M needs people like you. People like *us*. The important thing is - how do you feel?"

A good question. Despite dripping like a wrung-out dishcloth, the adrenaline shock had left Eddie's brain all afire. He felt *alive*. As alive as he had, up above the clouds, at the controls of a roaring great V-12 fighter plane.

"To be honest, Sir, I feel like kicking you square in the plums. That was a dirty trick."

Monkston chuckled.

"You should have seen what they did to *me*, boy. Dirty tricks are what this section is all about. Though from now on, only against the enemy. Promise."

The Major and the doctor helped him up. They went back through the blue door, back into the waiting room, and all took seats around the sad little coffee table with its out-of-date magazines. The Doctor lit up a cigarette, and the Major soon fished a fine cigar from somewhere inside his immaculate coat.

"You must be hungry. We've got quite the commissary down here. I think, before we go any further, it would be wise to take a little break."

The mention of food made Eddie's head come up, his nostrils flaring.

"What exactly have you got?" he asked, as an unnatural hunger gripped him.

Monkston smiled. "Well, that depends. What do you want?"

Eddie licked his lips. It was a very alien, very inhuman motion. Gold flecks in his slitted red eye flickered.

"*Everything.*" he said. "With a side of chips."

# Three - The Glorious 27

Everything - chips included - was served up in a great steaming underground hall with mismatched antique tables and chairs and a crowd of bustling figures, all in uniform. Huge lights shone down from on high, illuminating a room the size of a football pitch and teeming with... well, Eddie supposed they were all people. Some were just more conventionally people-shaped than others.

Here walked the visibly strange, like the man all covered in bandages or the tall, thin woman who wore sunglasses and carried an open black parasol indoors. Others were simply odd-looking because they were in uniform at all - men who looked like college professors and circus performers, strongmen with arms like bags full of Christmas hams, ladies ranging from one or two pointy-hatted witches to what Eddie's mum would have called 'oldest professionals', and a few more who looked like Eddie's mum herself - that is to say, little and old and probably the kind to bake scones at the drop of a slightly frilly hat. Then there were things like Reggie the Minotaur. The bark-skinned, winged, scaly, two-headed, horned, cloven hoofed, multi-coloured, transparent, slimy and in one case *actually-on-fire* ones.

All of them were in the neat olive-green kit of the armed forces. Even the man in a turban with a thick Cockney accent who'd served Eddie his lunch, sitting-cross-legged in the air as he commanded a fleet of flying spatulas.

Oddly, it made him feel a bit better.

Even if things had gone very, very sideways, he was still in the starched, slightly itchy embrace of the Army (capital A); the Big Green Machine which ate paperwork and farted bugle calls and existed solely to remove Nazis from Europe wholesale. Compared to being in a foreign country, being given a state-of-the-art warplane, and being shot at by Germans, whatever was happening to him now seemed almost explicable. It was *Military*. Which meant there would be official forms, shouting, nonsense, the possibility of several cups of hot sweet tea, and, in the end, probably some Nazi-removal involved.

All Eddie had to do was obey orders, not get killed, and… for some reason keep his boots shiny. This, it seemed, was a keystone strategy when it came to kicking Hitler out of power.

Eddie sat, and ate. Copiously. The pile in front of him was comprised of the most fearsomely thick and heavy dishes ever devised by the British school system, yet he attacked it all with the force of a steam shovel. It said something about Section M's mess hall that nobody paid much attention. In between chewing and swallowing, he watched a silk top hat bob through the crowds.

Everybody knew Major Monkston. There were not that many actual salutes thrown his way, but there were a lot of significant nods, winks, nudges and clandestine little hand signals as he pushed through the commissary, saying his hellos. This grand circle route lasted until well after Eddie's plate was licked clean.

"They all think I'm going to tell them more than they need to know," he confided, as he hustled Eddie out through a side door and into a pale green corridor. They pressed themselves back to the wall as an electric cart came pinballing past with what seemed to be an orang-utan at the wheel. "But mum's the word, lad. The big plan is coming together nicely, and now…" here he cuffed Eddie playfully on the shoulder. "Squad 27 has it's other heavy-hitter! Won't the General be pleased?"

Eddie had no idea if the General would be pleased, but he nodded and smiled in any case. Hanging on to the fact that there *was* a General, and he was in the clutches of the Army, and that he was neither mad nor dead… well, it kept him putting one foot in front of the other. Until they reached his first assignment.

This turned out to be a good one, because he was ordered to get a good night's sleep.

Major Monkston showed him to a wood-paneled corridor lined with what looked like railway sleeper cabins, and were about the same size. One of them already had a little cardboard label affixed to the door, with the name 'Weatherfield' written in small, precise block capitals. Miss Golightly, he presumed.

"The alarm goes off at 0600 hours, soldier. For now, you're carrying the effective rank of Private in Section M, but in the field, to the norm-os, you'll be considered a Lieutenant. Don't try actually shouting at Sergeants, though, because Doctor J has better things to be fixing than broken noses. When the alarm rings, I'll expect you to be dressed and ready to go in ten minutes. Report to briefing room 12 for your new assignment. And Eddie… private Weatherfield?"

He stopped with one hand on the brass doorknob, looking into the tiny room. There was a new uniform laid out on the bed, including a pair of round-framed dark glasses.

"Sir?"

"Well done today. Most of 'em have what our American friends would call a 'bit of a freak-out'. They must build 'em tough in New South Wales."

"*New Zealand*, Sir. The long curly one east of Australia. And yes." He met the Major's twinkling gaze, remembering that he owed the dapper little bastard a kick in the plums for that golem nonsense. "Yes, they do."

He was out like a light before he'd even opened the little pamphlet on his pillow - cheerfully entitled *'So you think you're either mad or dead?'* - and deep in a dreamless sleep before he'd even gotten both boots off.

0600 Hours rolled around horribly fast, as it is wont to do in both civilian and military life. The jangling of the alarm clock made Eddie think, for a moment, that he was back home in the high country. Then he remembered *everything*. The information slammed into the front of his brain like a great iron filing cabinet falling from a considerable height, and he looked down at his one bare foot and his one booted one, frontal lobes gently fizzing.

*Ahhh well. Nothing for it. Let the Military take over for a while, and see where all this was leading. The power of routine should keep the screaming little voice in his skull quiet, at least until he'd had some breakfast…*

Eddie found a nice new uniform in the room's tiny closet. He found the mandatory boot polish and brush. He remembered to put on his new dark glasses before he went off out the door in search of somewhere with a sink, his brand new Section M toothbrush (marked - *type three, human, male, soft bristle*) clenched like a dagger before him.

The bathroom was empty. Eddie brushed his teeth and looked in the mirror, not knowing exactly what he hoped for. He let the glasses slip down his nose an inch, and saw that red-and-yellow eye staring back at him. He didn't quite know what to think about it.

I mean, we *all* believe we're destined for something different, right? How else do you convince a whole nation of people to pick up guns and go out into a wide world where other whole nations are shooting back? You have to be convinced that *you* - the one watching all this unfold, the *important* one - are destined to be missed. Destined to miss the dysentery and syphilis and punji stakes and big explosions and downright suspicious tuna sandwiches.

It's a story we tell ourselves. Now, Eddie Weatherfield had some proof that he was *right*...

He was also late. A quick check of a map on the wall outside the bathroom, and Eddie was off and running. Briefing room 12 was surprisingly far away. He stumbled, tripped, pelted and apologized his way through the mess hall, scooping up a half-eaten plate of porridge as he ran. He swung aboard a little electric cart and hitched a lift, leaping off and leaving an empty porridge bowl behind him. And he arrived outside the oak-paneled door of the briefing room just in time to see Major Monkston checking his watch.

"Twelve minutes thirteen seconds. Though I *do* notice you've polished your boots. Very military. A word to the wise, though, if any of them are in our general vicinity..." He leaned in, eyes twinkling. "Here in Section M we care a lot less about shiny footwear than we do about punctuality. Come on. The rest of them are already here."

He opened the door and ushered Eddie through, into what looked like a very small but well-appointed picture theatre. In the half-darkness, a row of mis-matched heads turned to look at him.

"Come on, come on!" muttered the shadowy figure at the front, a stooped and bent silhouette wearing what appeared to be a pointy hat and a dress. Another witch, Eddie supposed - and this one was *definitely* Scottish. "We havenae got all day, and the Krauts have just had another night of dragons out there. They need *answers*, and we're gonnae give them to 'em."

Monkston shoved Eddie down into a great green leather armchair. The figure beside him gave him a nudge, and offered a bag of what turned out to be salted cashews.

"This will be our first active assignment in enemy territory," continued that woolly Scots brogue. "So expectations are high. As you noo, we've just been assigned the last member of our squad, a young transfer from the RAF. He'll be taking the role of heavy-hitter opposite Lucky, so give him a nice welcome, aye?"

There was a polite round of applause. Eddie, as is traditional in these situations, was mildly embarrassed.

"That means Fyodor gets to scout, and hence the long gun. Percy and Mrs Hazelwood, you're front and centre. Patience and I will provide supernatural cover, *vis a vis* spells and suchlike. Monsieur Le Compte, you'll have the package, and of course serve as our medic in the field. Any questions?"

A pale hand with black fingernails went up.

"Fyodor?"

"Do I *haff* to scout? I mean, Mrs H would be just as good, and I'd really like to get into the thick of it..."

Unsurprisingly, the one called Fyodor had a Russian accent you could hammer a sickle around.

"Mrs Hazelwood might be able to see where the guards have been, and where they're *going tae be*, but *you* have the best eyesight in the here and now. And I don't want ye distracted, lad. We're there for work, not a picnic."

The figure next to Eddie leaned over. He caught a glimpse of ginger mutton-chop whiskers and a tiny little green hat perched atop a huge head.

"Sure an' the bloody vampire would *love* to bite off some German sausage, you know?" he chuckled. "And I don't mean for breakfast..."

"Corporal Lucky, do *you* have anything to share with the squad?" it was a question dripping with headmasterly sarcasm.

"Just offering the new lad some cashews, Sarge," grinned Lucky, who Eddie realized was wearing a tiny lincoln-green waistcoat, lime suspenders and little short pants made for a man many times smaller. The rest of him was all muscles and blue tattoos, knotted up like a whole week of bad laundry days.

"Then I hope ye've brought enoof for..."

"Oh aye, oh aye," said Lucky, just as determinedly Irish as the shadowy figure of the Sarge was Scots. "Anyone else?" A small paper bag was proffered. "Sure and it won't be like the business with the jellybeans last week, I assure you. That was a terrible, terrible prank to play on the lot of you, and I've learned me lesson well."

There were no takers. Eddie leaned in and whispered.

"Lucky? Do we *all* get nicknames, like in some kind of cheap war novel?"

The huge Irishman grinned even wider.

"Just me. What with being a leprechaun, my real name's a bit of a mouthful, you understand."

Eddie decided to let that one go, for now. Mainly because the figure at the front of the room had just made a flailing gesture to Major Monkston, who, after a series of muffled curses and pinched fingers, began to play a short black-and-white film. First came a very official looking coat of arms, featuring plenty of arcane symbols and a Union Jack on a shield supported by dragons. Then came a TOP SECRET warning, advising anyone not part of Section M to stop watching now, go to the nearest pub and drink a whole pint of the nastiest available gin, just to forget the fact that Section M *existed at all*. A long, long list of regulations and threats scrolled by. Eddie was certain that 'burning at the stake' and 'beheading' were in there amongst all the fine print.

Now came the good part. Eddie munched back a handful of Lucky's cashews, on the principle that you never know when the next snack is coming, during a war.

OPERATION POSTMASTER

Said the screen, in flickering monochrome. The Scots shadow produced a long pointer, and whacked the words for emphasis.

"Right, you horrible arcane lot. This is the village of Saint Mal-de-mer, on the coast of Brittany. Up until not so long ago, it was full o' nasty French fishing boats, cheap wine, dodgy seafood restaurants and the obligatory men on bicycles carrying large bags of onions."

A picture of a small, antique seaside town flickered across the screen. It looked like the kind of place which existed solely to produce novelty tea towels of itself.

"Now, of course, it's full of psychopathic Germans, including, we're told, a crack unit of Hitler's occult investigators, the Black Sun, led by this scallywag - Ubergruppenfuhrer-magischekriegseinheit Hans Schprinkler."

*A severe-faced middle aged man with half his head shaved bald, and tattooed with runes. A uniform heavy on the leather, silver skull buttons and big swastikas.* Was Eddie surprised to see that he wore a monocle engraved with a pentagram? Not in the slightest.

"Now, our old pal Herr Schprinkler will be *here* – " a map wobbled into focus – "at Le Chateau Mal-de-mer Chronique. Our job is tae deliver a wee present to the town, in the form of two dead bodies. Percy, you know the rules. No chewing!"

"*Frightfully* sorry about that last exercise, Sir," came a very, very upper-class voice indeed. "Won't happen again!"

The Scotsman pointed to the back, to Major Monkston.

"If ye'd be so kind as tae continue?"

"Body A, that is to say, the first stiff, is that of a boilerman from the merchant steamer *Lady Argyle*," said the Major. "He died last week after ingesting a very dodgy tuna sandwich. Tragic. However, he is the spit and bloody image of *this* man, Nazi secret agent and all around bad egg Heinrich Salzmann."

This picture was of an unassuming and tubby little man in a black sweater and massive cola-bottle spectacles.

"Herr Salzmann is currently helping us with our investigations as to why he was trying to break into the top-secret aircraft design department at Thackeray Hall. His double, here, is going to be horribly burned in an accident, but he's being equipped with all the right tattoos to make him look just like Salzmann. Even the very distasteful one of a famous cartoon duck playing the tuba. Now..." there was a prolonged fit of coughing from the stage, and the hunched figure produced and lit a corncob pipe.

"Yes. Body B, that is to say the second cadaver, is actually a poor lad who tried to clean his rifle while it was loaded, in basic training. He's getting a bit of a post-mortem promotion, though, to the rank of Captain. In the Intelligence Services, no less. For the benefit of Operation Postmaster, he's being renamed Philip Sidebottom. Our job is to get these actors in place, and make it look like the following..."

A map of Saint Mal-de-mer blurred into focus.

"We'll go in by boat, masquerading as French fishermen. You will all be issued bobble hats, striped sweaters and false mustaches for this purpose. Connor will summon a right pea-souping blinder of a fog as we reach the port, at which point Patience will put all their dogs to sleep with a handy cantrip. Under cover of fog, Fyodor will ascend the steeple of the parish church, *here* - and make sure nobody from the Chateau comes down the high road to assist. That is, until our two heavy hitters here, along with Percy and Hazelwood, bust into the tavern and really give the local garrison the old ten bells of shite.

At this point the Count will bring the bodies in, and Mr The Beige will conjure a suitable conflagration. Patience will tangle up the authorities so that they reach the old pub just in time to realize that a crack team of plucky Brit commandos have tried to stop poor old Salzmann from coming in from the cold. On his person will be plans for a radical new aircraft design, allegedly deployed by the RAF in the past few days. A type of plane armed with very, very powerful flamethrowers, and code-named the Wessex Dragon."

Eddie raised his hand, tentatively.

"So... we're going to use magic to convince the Germans that our side *isn't using magic?*"

"Exactly," puffed the figure on stage. "Eeeh, Monkston, ye've brought us a quick learner this time! Lad, who *else* can we trust to make sure the old Third Reich don't take magic seriously? Schprinkler and his scunners at the Black Sun want Uncle Adolf to give them money, and power, and *resources*. But thankfully, Der Fuhrer is more interested in tanks. Every time we use magic to stop the Nazis, we have to convince them that we didn't, and that it doesn't really exist. Otherwise the Black Sun will have their way, and we'll be in a magical arms race. We could end up back in the dark ages, nailing horseshoes over our doors and putting out cream for the bloody Fae."

The film clattered and whirred to an end. The lights came up. And Eddie saw the rest of the elite warriors who made up Squad 27.

"I'm not one for speeches, ye ken, so here we are. Eddie Weatherfield, the glorious 27th. Odds, sods and various bods of the 27th - Eddie Weatherfield, ex RAF, ex New Zealand, ex bloody Norm-o."

He may have gasped. It was possible that the bits of his brain responsible for believing in things were shut down for a second, hastily re-wired, and then shocked back into action.

Lucky was indeed a leprechaun. A seven foot tall, rail-thin leprechaun who resembled nothing less than a ginger Abraham Lincoln. What he'd taken to be a huge head was actually the most impressive set of mutton-chop whiskers in all Christendom, framing a face with a many-times-broken nose and eyebrows like orange caterpillars.

Mrs Hazelwood was a round little old lady wearing an army uniform and a floral headscarf. She carried a raffia basket almost bigger than she was, which contained, among other things, an immense crystal ball.

Percy was grey-green and gruesome, noseless, one-eyed and obviously long dead. His uniform was from the Great War, complete with a tin tommy helmet, and he smiled and waved with a hand that was mostly stitches.

Fyodor, on the other hand, was all style. There were little added touches to his army fatigues which made him stand out, even here. His long black hair was tied back with a red ribbon that managed to look anything but girly, and his grin showed more than a little bit of fang.

The man he'd heard called *'Monsieur Le Compte'* may have been dressed in olive green, but he also affected the huge powdered wig of a seventeenth century dandy. He actually sketched a little bow, causing unseen things to clink and rattle inside that mass of billowing white horsehair.

The one who caught Eddie's eye, though - and no surprises, considering - was Patience. Eddie might have lied about his age to join the air force, but this curvy, pale and dark-haired girl looked to be only a little bit older than he was. Even in a severe, no-nonsense military uniform there was the definite suggestion that she should in fact be wearing a black velvet dress and lots of skull-shaped jewelry. Her eyes were just slightly too large, just slightly too violet, and definitely just slightly too fixed on his for a moment, before she turned away, smiling enigmatically.

Which left the figure standing alone by the screen, puffing out a veritable cumulonimbus of tobacco smoke.

"New lad, Saint Germain, a word, if you'd be so kind? The rest of you, bugger off and stop staring. We'll meet for equipment check at 1800 hours."

Now, in the light, Eddie could see that it wasn't a witch at all. It was the *other* kind. Though he couldn't quite bring himself to lump this five-foot-tall, crook-backed little Scotsman in with the likes of Merlin. He was wearing a kilt and sporran, boots which looked to be hewn directly from stone, an army-issue cardigan rattling with medals, and a tartan pointy hat, bent backwards in the middle so that it looked like the fin of a rather drunken shark. The obligatory long grey beard came down to his belt, where the end of it was tucked in. It had, he noted, a woggle in it.

"Connor of Anstruther. Also known as Connor the Beige, ye ken? Last of a very, very long line of wizards, so I didnae get the same amount of height as the ones at the front of the queue."

The apparition held out a hand like a knob of preserved ginger, all lumps and leather. Eddie shook it.

"Eddie Weatherfield. I'm, ummm..."

"Oh, Monkey-boy there told me all about ye. The liar. *Lucky*, though. And now some daft old Saxon bag of bones has gone and put some dragonfire in your bonce. Typical!"

Anstruther went up on tip-toes and pulled Eddie's dark glasses down. He made a little huffing sound which could have signified anything from approval to bad gas.

"Just like old Bjarni Shield-Biter, eh? Whatever happened to that old sod?"

Major Monkston came down the stairs from the projection booth, with a look on his face like he'd just accidentally swallowed a lemon.

"That was in the *last* war, Connor. We dug him up on the Orkneys remember? Well preserved chap, for his age. Got blown to bits by Turkish artillery in Sinai."

"Bet they weren't expecting an undead viking, though!" cackled the Scotsman. "Still, a live one must be better. *Smells* better, anyhow." he turned back to Eddie. "You ready for this, lad? Fighting on the ground is different from fannying about in planes..."

The Major moved smoothly between them.

"I'm certain Private Weatherfield is quite capable. After all – " and here he gave Eddie a pointed look – "All you have to do is *follow orders* and make sure the bullets miss. Two simple tasks, correct?"

Eddie found himself nodding.

"Saint Germain," said Anstruther, addressing the massively wigged dandy. "Two bodies is a bit of a weight. You sure you've got this?"

The strange, powder-faced man rummaged with one hand inside his headpiece, his face lighting up with a smile.

"Never mind me, guv," he said, in a quite incongruously East-London accent. "Got a potion here that'll make em light as a feather. Two on a handcart and bish bash bosh. We'll 'ave 'em down the pub in no time, while old peepers here puts a few Nazi's horizontal-like."

The little wizard nodded.

"Right, then. Monkston, I'm sure you have lots to do, what with the Treaty being signed in a few days. That writer of yours must be right proud to be following in the footsteps of Willie Shakespeare."

Major Monkston looked slightly pained, as if someone had just trodden on his immaculate wing-tip brogues.

"Less said the better, old chap," he stage-whispered, following it up with a vaudeville smile. "And good luck tonight, all of you. I'm certain they won't know *what* to believe in once they see you in action. Or *don't*, of course. What with this being a top secret, covert kind of mission and all..."

Monkston and Anstruther shared the kind of dry little chuckle that teachers, regional managers and army officers often engage in after a not particularly funny joke.

"The two of you, fall out! Saint Germain, I'm sure you have lab work to be getting on with. And Weatherfield - I'd head down to the firing range and armoury if I were you. We've got some special kit for you that you might want to try out before horrible lads in coal-scuttle helmets start yelling 'Achtung!' at you from the shadows. As he said, it's a whole different world from..." (and here Monkston cleared his throat with malice aforethought) "*fannying about in planes.*"

Eddie and Saint Germain left the room as Anstruther produced a survey map from his sporran and unfolded it over the table. He and Monkston were already arguing by the time the door closed behind them.

"Good to have you on board," said the Count, extending a pale hand smothered in gold rings. Eddie noticed that he'd stitched a lace cuff to his army fatigues. "All the lads are keen to know, right? What's your party piece?"

Eddie shook, put more than a little off balance by the steely grip he found his fingers in.

"Party piece? Oh, you mean my... umm. *That.* The old supernatural thingy. I suppose we all..."

"Oh yes. Me, I'm immortal," said the Count. He delivered the information in the same tone someone else might announce they had hayfever. "But not like old Fyodor. He bloody hates it! An immortal Count who ain't a vampire! I dabble a bit in alchemy, too, which is a great help on the battlefield."

Eddie didn't have the heart to tell him that alchemy was pretty much rendered obsolete by a guy called Newton, some centuries before.

"So, what do you do?"

Eddie shook his head.

"I don't know what they're calling it. I've got a funny eye." He pulled his glasses down, to a low whistle from Saint Germain.

"No kidding! What, you get poked with some kind of magic stick? Some old three-stooges nonsense? Wait! I've got it! You looked right at a basilisk during an eclipse, right? Peed on a witch's vege garden? Close?"

"It was a big old dead viking with a dragon, actually. He might have saved my life. But it seems that when I get angry..."

"Oh, like Doctor J's old man! Right, right. Hence you're a heavy hitter, like our lad Lucky."

"Who's a *leprechaun.* A little magic man from the Emerald Isle who guards a pot of gold..."

"Well, more like a big lanky bastard from Dublin who guards a bottle of Jamesons, but you get the idea. When he hits something, it stays down. Up to and including small buildings."

"But... *Lucky*?"

Saint Germain patted him on the shoulder.

"He reckons Pádraig mac an Phríomhfheidhmeannaigh ar an

Gclaoch Airgid a Chodlaíonn Faoi na Cnoic Agus a Fhillfidh in am an Chontrála Mór Chun an Spéir a Roinnt le Toirneach is a bit of a mouthful, right? Look, don't worry. It's going to be weird for the first few weeks. Months, even. Me, I've had a couple of thousand years to get used to it, and it's even freaking *me* out a little. Now, the armoury's that way. If you want to catch one of those little carts, just whistle as high as you can. The gnomes aren't much good in the bass register."

Saint Germain set off down one arm of a T-junction, leaving Eddie stranded looking down the other. All the corridors in the Labyrinth of Kew looked quite the same, which was, perhaps, the nature of labyrinths.

"Count!" he shouted. "Saint Germain! What do you mean *two thousand years*?"

The big-wigged alchemist turned back with a rueful smile.

"When someone who claims to be the Messiah does a miracle right in front of you, son, don't be the guy in the crowd who yells 'I can see the loaves and fishes up the sleeves of his robe'. Simple advice, freely given. Wish someone had told me..."

And with that he reached a corner, swung on board a speeding gnomecart and was gone.

Eddie felt the madness tickling the edges of his mind. He was all alone under Kew Gardens, in a secret base full of wizards and monsters, and in a few hours, far from evading the front lines, *he'd be sailing into occupied France with a seven foot leprechaun, a posh zombie and someone who claimed to have heckled Jesus Christ as company...*

Right then. The Armoury.

There was nothing like some old fashioned Army-brand insanity (like learning the safety protocols around weapons of mass murder) to make the little details blur into the background. One foot in front of the other. Or, in fact...

Eddie put two fingers in the corners of his mouth and whistled, so high and loud that even his Dad's grizzled old drovers would have been proud. An electric cart squeaked to a stop in front of him.

*When in Rome*, or so they said.

It wasn't until they were halfway down the corridor that Eddie remembered. Rome was full of Axis soldiers too, these days...

# Four - Operation Postmaster

There were plenty of places where Eddie Weatherfield would rather have been than bobbing in the English Channel during the greatest armed conflict in history. Antarctic sulphur mines, horrible dank Turkish prisons and the crawlspace under the shearing sheds in high summer featured on this list.

Although any available tropical beach not staked out by Japanese machine-gunners would have been better. There might, he thought wistfully, have been those drinks served in hollowed-out pineapples, with lots of small umbrellas and hibiscus flowers in them.

Not here, though. Here, where duty and the sheer awful inertia of his life had wedged him in between a maniac in a three foot wig trying to play the violin, and a round little pensioner with a headscarf and a raffia basket. On a boat which, frankly, smelled of whole dead generations of very sick fish. On a sea aswarm, or so he was certain, with voracious, man-eating U-boats, big knobbly mines, and worse.

"Mermaids," said Fyodor, grinning his slick and pointy grin. "I bet they don't have mermaids down here. Sea hags, certainly. Deep Spawn, and serpents, naturally. But your average mermaid, she likes the - how you say - *tropical* waters."

"What about the one in Denmark?" asked Percy. He was trying, unsuccessfully, to remove a tangled mess of fish hooks and string from one of his hands.

"Da, this one I know. The story was written there, but she was definitely from further south. Even the poor bloody statue looks cold, yes?"

"*We've* got one. I've seen him. The American naval attache, from their Department of Arcane Intelligence. Colonel Spritzer, or whatever his name is."

Patience pulled off the combination of a striped cardigan, bobble hat and outrageous false mustache far, far better than she should have done. Eddie, of course, was gobsmacked.

"Ahhh, old Schwitzer. 'Wrath in a Bath' himself. You know he had that bloody tub of his put on tank treads so he could join the land assault, when it comes? He wants to be right there with his precious bloody MacArthur when they stomp back into Manila. Won't that be something?"

Her voice was very English, smooth as oiled steel, and ever so slightly intoxicating.

"Is different," replied Fyodor. "American Colonel is a Triton - an Atlantean. Whole different mythos. And *I* heard he got his famous bathtub on tracks made so he could smoke cigars. Cannot keep them lit underwater."

Connor of Anstruther grunted.

"Enough chit-chat, you lot. The Colonel and his bath are a long way behind us, even if we could use that Browning 50-cal he's got mounted on the thing. Now, we're nearly there. Everyone look extremely French, just in case they hit us with the spotlights. And then... showtime!"

Ahhh, yes, thought Eddie. *Showtime.* The whole production where he was expected to go hand-to-bayonet against the most lantern-jawed of Hitler's Aryan super-mensch. That was the bit he was having trouble with. Suppose, for example, that the thing… the red-misted, crazy thing… just failed to materialize? What was he meant to do? Apologize? He could just imagine.

*"Erm, sorry, Hans, Klaus, but this never usually happens to me. It must be stage fright..."*

He was almost certain that the crack SS troops wouldn't offer him condolences and say they just wanted to cuddle.

"Right-o then lads. Time for the fog, aye?"

Connor of Anstruther rolled up the sleeves of his ancient cardigan, which he still wore under this obligatory French stripey shirt. He had condescended to wear a kind of shapeless bobble hat, but something about the little Scotsman made the *suggestion* of a pointy wizard hat deflect the rain in a cone just over his head.

"I always love this part," whispered Mrs Hazelwood. "He's ever so keen to be impressive..."

Connor squinted up at the clouds. He removed his hideous pipe from within his sporran, and jabbed it heavenwards.

"Oh ancient spirits of the sea and sky, heed me eldritch call, if ye know what's good for ye! Brew and boil a binding mist, that we warriors should pass, and give yon sausage-munching scunners a right good kicking!"

Because he was a Wizard, and not a Witch like Patience or old Mrs

Tavistock in Dover, the power didn't come up from the sea or down from the clouds. It poured into Connor of Anstruther like a sleet of tiny motes, like a dandelion head exploding in reverse. Then he focused it like light through a lens, and folded it, and released it.

All around them the sea began to bubble. Thick tendrils of fog came roiling up, knotting and weaving together into an expanding cloud which raced out from their tiny fishing boat, leaving them adrift in a world of cotton wool and silence.

"Not how I would have done it, but..." began Patience, before a jab with the pipe-stem silenced her.

"That, I'll have ye know, was some A-grade wizarding. A fell incantation from mouldering tomes of yore, that was."

"Including the bit about giving them a damn good kicking?"

"Ye should have read it in the original medieval Gaelic, lass. Kicking was the bloody least of it. We Wizards may not be warlocks, be we ain't pixies either!" He tamped down a huge wad of something in the bowl of his pipe, and lit it with a flame struck from his naked index finger. "Haven't you got some dog-bothering to be getting on with?"

Patience raised one eyebrow with devastating effect, then fished a slim silver whistle out from what Eddie's mum would have called her *decolletage*, but what he simply thought of as 'that area he shouldn't be staring at'. She settled herself, closed her eyes, and drew in a breath…

The mist around the fishing boat turned to a glittering powder of ice. A paper-thin skin of frozen water formed and cracked in the time it took for the young sorceress to raise the whistle to her lips. Then she gave it a blast which would have made a football umpire proud, causing a great velvety sphere of silence to ripple out from the boat. The invisible dandelion-clock of anti-noise rushed ahead of them, muffling the waves, choking the sound of the boat's wheezing old motor, and Eddie could *feel* the seeking spell inside it, sniffing out canine minds, following doggy scent trails through the night air.

"That's odd," said Patience, dropping the whistle back into lavender-scented darkness. "There don't seem to be any. Never known the German Army to be without their ruddy huge dogs. All the good big, angry dogs are German. It's not as if they're only down to dachshunds, is it?"

"Good enough for me," grinned Percy. "The number of perfectly good legs I've gone through dealing with Rottweilers! I might as well have become a postman."

"Good enoof for me as well, lass. Even if my way was more…

dramatic," said Connor the Beige, packing another wad of foul-smelling tobacco into his pipe. "Now, ye all remember what to do? Germain, are ye ready with the cargo?"

The Compte popped up from the little hold of the boat, a bodybag over each shoulder.

"What I tell you, guv? Light as a feather! Me own special embalming fluid. I'll be right behind you. Look!"

Indeed, Eddie could now see the pale orange glow of lights on the horizon. Above the huddled radiance of the town, twin searchlights sliced the fog. Down the far end of the boat, gripping the wheel with his great callused hands, Lucky navigated them in with senses the Germans thankfully didn't have.

"Allright then. I'll take out the fellers on the pier, then. Lucky, Percy, Mrs Hazelwood and the new lad, get down the pub like it's happy hour and your neck's on fire. It shouldn't take much to start a punch-up with the local German lads. Some pointed remarks about sausages should do the trick."

Eddie was feeling more than a bit apprehensive now. Part of joining the air force had been the reassuringly big, solid aeroplane they put between you and the Fuhrer's finest. The frankly cobbled-together machine pistol they'd given him seemed futile compared to the old Spitfire's cannons, and as for the rest… he was sure he'd look a pillock carrying the round shield they'd dredged up for him out of some rust-eaten arms locker. That, and the short, chipped, dull-grey sword with the plain iron pommel. There were runes on it, but they looked like the kind that should read 'factory second'.

The keel scraped on good French continental sand. The bows sloped up and the motor coughed its last.

"Right-o, then, lads. Shall we go for a wee stroll?"

That was Lucky, already helping Mrs Hazelwood down into the ankle-deep water. He grinned at Eddie.

"Sure and the first time's always the worst. But don't worry. There'll be blood, and guts, and brains, and that horrible crackling noise you get when the gristle peels away, and eyeballs, and noses, and…"

"That's not a very reassuring outlook for us, is it?" asked Eddie, in a voice which cracked like a poorly made chamber pot. And threatened to leak exactly the same stuff.

"Oh, naw, naw," smiled the gangly giant leprechaun, reaching out to lift him bodily from the boat. Eddie might as well have been made of carpet fluff – the creature from the Emerald Isle picked him up effortlessly. "I was talking about the *Germans*, sure enough. Thought it might get the old berserker blood pumpin.'"

Eddie shrugged his shoulders, trying to settle the sword and shield on his back. It was impossible. They remained a huge lump of metal and leather grating on his spine. At least the machine pistol was from this century…

He gripped it tight as a searchlight sliced through the gloom, above them on the pier.

*"Achtung! Who goes there?"*

"Oooh! *Very* stereotypical. Very Nazi guardsmanly," said a second voice, with a slightly less thick accent. "You forgot the 'Heil Hitler', though."

"Look, Friedrich. *Someone* goes there. You can see the shadow. What was I supposed to shout?"

"Ahem," came a reply, suddenly downshifting in pitch and switching gears into pantomime French. "Eet ees just an honest fisherman, sil voo plait, avec some… aaaah… fresh fillets des haddock, or something."

That was definitely Patience, doing a scenery-chewing accent. The Germans seemed unimpressed.

"You were out *fishing?* In *this?* Here, Werner, give me that bloody searchlight a minute…"

"See? Bobble hat. Stripey vest. Outraaaaageous mustache. You, er, *garcons* wouldn't happen to have a d… *un chien* there, would you?"

"No, as it happens, we don't. But, if I may be so bold, *monsieur*, may I inquire why an honest French provincial fisherman like yourself is endowed with such a luscious, huge pair of…"

He never got to finish. Something loomed up behind the pair of soldiers in their little watchtower, like a spirit out of some horrible Scots nightmare.

"That really was an *atrocious* accent, dear. Some of us have a far better grasp of languages." Connor the Beige cheerfully puffed on his pipe, underlighting his wizened old face with red. For a second, he looked like a fresh-forged gargoyle destined for Hell's own toilet roll holder. He addressed one of the soldiers. "For example - *Kann deine Mutter jetzt nähen*[4], ye goose-stepping strudel-muncher?"

The man looked down at him, surprised. "Then *sag ihr, sie soll das nähen*[5], right pal?"Something sudden and awful happened, which resulted in two black-clad bodies toppling from the watchtower,

4 "Can your mother sew?" A popular street cry of merry old Glasgow
5 "Then tell her to stitch this"

gurgling. They bounced off the pier and disappeared into the dark water.

"*You lot. The pub. Pronto.* I bet the blood-sucker's already halfway up yon steeple. Patience, get out there and throw them some illusions!"

After that little display, Connor of Anstruther didn't have to tell them twice. The little band crept through the cobblestone streets of St Malde-mer, pressing their backs up against dripping brickwork, ducking low to crawl behind hedges and homing in on the sound of accordion music in the foggy gloom. Well, all apart from Mrs Hazelwood, who tottered along at a steady perambulation, her tiny little feet moving as if driven by clockwork under the hem of her great big housecoat. Her bag was clutched tight to her chest, and her face was plastered with a good-natured but more than slightly myopic grin.

"What happens if the Nazis see her?" hissed Eddie, as he pressed up nose-wrinklingly close to Percy behind a small shrubbery.

The zombie shrugged.

"She's an old lady, right? Even the French have old ladies. And even the Nazis have mums. I suppose it makes 'em hesitate. And then..."

"Quiet, you lot!" shushed Lucky, ducking back around a corner to glare at them. "The target's right around yonder. Let's check to see if the others are in position, and then we move! Mrs H?"

The smiling granny tottered over to them.

"You'll catch you death of cold huddling under shrubberies on a night like this," she confided, rummaging in her bag. One hand came out gripping that huge crystal ball, and she gave it a shake, as if it was one of those horrible little cheap souvenir globes full of fake snow.[6] "Hang on a mo, boys, I just have to tune it in..."

For a second the ball was filled with what looked like swirling coloured smoke. Then, for a fraction of an instant, a picture of a man in checkerboard suit, grinning like a lunatic in front of a row of automobiles the likes of which Eddie had never seen before.

"Cross-temporal interference," mumbled Mrs Hazelwood, giving the ball a whack. "There's background magic buggering up the transmission..."

With a silent pop the image wobbled into focus. There was Connor, standing on top of a gabled roof. He was looking through a pair of binoculars at something in the distance, inland. Another pop, and

---

6 Often these feature places and landmarks where it *never snows* – unless we accept that the Hong Feng Plastics Corporation of Xiamen, China, knows far more about the history of the great pyramids than we imagine

there was the Compte de Staint Germain, neatly arranging a pair of dead bodies so it looked like they'd both shot each other at once. There was a can of gasoline next to him, and a Citroen Traction Avant lying on one side. He was applying blood with a tiny paintbrush. Pop, again, and here was Fyodor, standing in the belfry of a church. Very appropriate bats hung upside down, waiting for him to do something important with the biggest gun Eddie had ever seen not mounted to a battleship. Being a militaria nerd, Eddie knew that this was in fact an old WW1 *tankgeschutz*, a recoilless rifle made to shoot through the engine blocks of tanks. It was equipped with sights involving a whole optometrist's shop full of sliding, brass-rimmed lenses.

"Everybody's home," said Mrs H, letting the ball float freely in front of her. "Charlie, come on out. We're going to have a visit with those bloody Germans again, you hear me?"

The fog in the ball cleared, and a face wobbled into focus. "What's that, dear? More Nazis? Where do they keep getting 'em from? I mean, only last week…"

Mrs Hazelwood gave the ball a flat-handed whack.

"Roger Hazelwood, you pay attention! We've got work to do!"

The face in the ball – which was that of a comb-overed, spectacle wearing, sad little man in a donkey jacket and a flat cap – looked contrite. "Yes, dear. Of course, dear. Just try to stay out of the way of the machine guns this time, would you?"

Mrs Hazelwood beamed. "Ready to kick some buttocks, lads! Which way is it again?"

Lucky gently grasped one shoulder and swiveled the old lady around as if she was on castors.

"Right around the corner. Sign of the Bell and Chicken. I count about thirty of the goose-stepping buggers, but well in their cups of ale, I reckon. Should be easy-peasy. We knock 'em down, set the place on fire, the Compte does the bodies and lights up yon Citroen, Patience befuddles the reinforcements while Fyodor pops anyone too keen, and the German brass get down here to discover *exactly what we want them to think*, while we take a wee boat ride back to Blighty."

Eddie popped his head out around the corner. There was indeed a tiny little French pub there, across the square with its obligatory fountain. Rosy light spilled out from its windows, and little groups of German soldiers were sitting around makeshift tables made from beer barrels, big steins in hand.

Now that it came to it, Eddie was almost certain he was going to die.

There wasn't so much as a flicker from his eye, and whatever was churning in his stomach was less like the flutter of butterflies and more like the mixing of cement. *Allright. Just shoot them, then. If you turn out* not *to be magic, they'll fire you. No more missions. No more silly fake 'stache and bobble hat. No more massive likelihood of weeing yourself.*

A traitorous little voice inside his head added more, though. *No more chance of finding your brother. No more Patience. No more being important...*

It's a hard thing, to realize that you're a bit of a coward.

It's even harder to realize it when you're just about to charge in and fight a large number of well-trained, confident and heavily armed soldiers.

Thankfully, that's what the big green machine they called the Army had invented sergeants for.

# Five – Nazi Psychos and the Holy Grail

Private Weatherfield swallowed what felt like a sandpaper golf-ball. Despite his strategy of waiting just another second or two, he didn't appear to be waking up from what was obviously a nightmare.

At times like this, they say, all it takes is a little push to turn a coward into a hero. Thankfully, Lucky's push was more along the lines of being flung bodily toward the Germans, arms and legs windmilling.

"*Achtung*, ye lily-livered Hitler-huggers!" shouted the huge gangly leprechaun, striding out of the mist behind him. "Which one of ye wants it first?"

Eddie managed to keep his balance, but only just. His finger tightened on the trigger of his machine pistol, and a three-foot tongue of muzzle flash lit up the night. Bullet holes stitched their way across the front of the pub, snapping the swinging sign from its chains. But that wasn't what got his attention.

No. *That* was the faces of the Nazi soldiers which now turned toward them. There was something more than a little wrong with them. For one thing, none of them were even mildly concerned about being attacked by an old lady, a zombie, a trigger-happy madman and a giant, mutton-chopped Irish maniac. This was because each of them was completely featureless – from coal-scuttle helmet to chin, every last one of them was as smooth and white as an eggshell.

Even Lucky came up short, turning his raised fist into an embarrassed little wave.

"Sorry, gents, I seem to have mistaken ye for a different bunch of horrible Nazi scumbags, so I'll just be… ooof!"

One of the faceless things moved so fast it was simply a monochrome blur. Lucky flew backwards, the hobnails on the bottoms of his boots scraping sparks from the cobbles. He winced, and cuffed a trickle of blood from the corner of his mouth.

"There's a fell enchantment going on here, lads," he whispered. "These are not your usual sturmtroopers, ye understand?"

Now all of them were standing. More poured out of the door of the pub, moving like clockwork puppets. Despite having nothing so prosaic as eyes, they all managed to stare at the four Section M commandos with utter menace.

Eddie smelled something in the air. For a second, he thought he might have wet his pants, but a moment's inspection proved that this hadn't happened just yet. The mist crackled. Little sparks bipped and whirred around his head. He tasted ammonia and old tin.

"Stinks like elf magic," said Mrs Hazelwood, disapprovingly. "What do you reckon, Sarge?"

Lucky's eyes narrowed.

"I reckon you and Roger should follow my lead. Percy, if they are what I think they are, no chewing and swallowing. And young feller. Eddie. Now's the time for the sword. That pop-gun will only make 'em angry."

Eddie gulped, and reluctantly grabbed the hilt of his sword. It was, as noted, a horrible workaday old thing, the kind which a Saxon warrior would have kept just for the nasty battles where having a big shiny blade marked you out as a poser. In the flux of magic, the runes down its fuller glowed green, picking out a name Eddie couldn't read.

"Do you think it's powerful? What kind of enchantment's on it?" he asked, ever hopeful.

Lucky squinted.

"The only one that matters. 'May my enemy get chopped into little bits, or at least get a nasty dose of tetanus', he said. "You have a good war-cry, lad?"

"Oh, bugger this," said Mrs Hazelwood brightly. *"Coo-eee! Nazis!* **Come and have a go if you think you're hard enough!"**

Lucky nodded.

"That'll do."

And it did. One instant the scene outside the Bell and Chicken was a silent horrorshow of faceless foes. The next a wave of the things was coming at them fast, heads craning forward as if to scent with non-existent noses, arms held back like featherless wings. There were at least thirty of them, and they pelted across the cobbles, knives blurring in their fingers like heat haze over a summer highway.

Eddie watched as one of them stabbed Percy, but the zombie seemed not to notice the knife at all. As the Nazi ghoul tried to pull it loose his grin tore open halfway around his head, and in a single bite he took the sturmtrooper's arm and shoulder clean off. Some of us, on the inside, are all love and kindness. Percy, on the inside, was all *teeth*.

Mrs Hazelwood gestured with her fingers, still gripping her immense woven purse, and the scrying glass containing her dead husband sliced through the air with the sound of an angry bandsaw. Several kilos of tempered crystal caved in skulls and cracked ribs as it pinballed left and right, lighting up bright purple with every strike. Lucky simply put up his dukes in what Eddie had always considered a comical parody of a vintage boxer… until he saw the leprechaun's horrible scarred-up fists punch clean through the torsos and bellies and heads of three ghouls.

Then it was too late to take notes, because they were on him. Eddie chopped wildly with his sword, blocking a knife thrust by luck rather than skill. A second came whispering in under his shield, but he leaned back, feeling the blade slice through his stripey French sweater. Another flailing swing, and he caught a ghoul with the flat of the sword, sending it reeling. For an instant the green fire from its blade slithered across the thing's face, revealing a complicated pentacle, the centre of which was a wide and staring eye.

Then the third ghoul stabbed him in the back.

There are said to be tribes from the arctic circle who have fifty words for snow. Eddie Weatherfield, over the last few days, had amassed several words for different kinds of pain, absolutely none of them printable here. The knife – one of those long, triangle-shaped, eagle-inscribed daggers so beloved of Team Hitler – scraped across his shoulderblade in a way which was far beyond thoroughly unpleasant. But he didn't bleed. He couldn't even scream.

Instead a jet of fire stabbed out from the wound, blue as a lizard's tongue and hotter than Satan's backside. The ghoul's knife evaporated in a spray of molten metal, taking its clammy white hand with it. And what came out of Eddie's mouth wasn't the feral shriek of the common-or-garden coward. It was a bellow that played the spinal cord like an electric guitar, reading from the sheet music of terror. The purple bits inside the brains of everybody present remembered hot primal jungles. They remembered being little scurrying things with fur, and the sound of huge lizards with yellow eyes and teeth like a butcher's cutlery drawer.

Eddie accelerated past Lucky and Mrs Hazelwood with his arms outstretched, gathering up a pair of Nazis in each. When he reached the doorway of the pub he didn't stop – he charged inside, slamming four eggshell foreheads against the massive granite pillars. There was a mess that all the toast and Marmite soldiers in the world couldn't clean up.

"That's the business, lad!" roared Lucky, kicking a ghoul so hard in the crotch that its legs literally fell off. "Give 'em hell!"

Somewhere above them a shot rang out. Then another. Percy pulled a Nazi arm out from between his teeth, and paused to dab his grisly lips with an embroidered handkerchief.

"We're due for company, boss!" he said, turning to block an onrushing ghoul. He absently twisted the thing's arm into a pretzel shape with his undead strength, then dispatched it with a punch that made its sternum kiss its spine.

"I think the laddie has us covered," chuckled Lucky.

And indeed, here was Eddie in the doorway of the tavern, armed with two bottles of suspiciously green and bubbling liquor. He upended both into his mouth, where magical pyrotechnics happened amid the gurgling and hissing. Then he swallowed. There was a noise like an industrial furnace with acid reflux.

"This one," he belched, his one mad eye blazing yellow. "Is for my bloody plane. I spe… spent… spenthours painting that lady onna front..."

He drew in a deep breath. He held up an American-army issue Zippo.

"Oh, you silly wee bas..." managed Lucky, before he hit the deck.

The Nazis weren't fast enough. And, let's be fair, it *was* one of the classics. Powered by two litres of the kind of absinthe which is sure to get you pages and pages of iconic gothic horror, as well. The click of the zippo was like the conductor tapping his baton before a symphony comes belting out.

And then…

Eddie exhaled a sheet of fire the colour of an autumn sunset, all orange and purple around the edges. It was a horizontal blast at head-height, roaring and crackling. Anything not hugging the cobbles was incinerated. The fountain in the middle of the square launched skyward on a plume of superheated steam. Nazi ghouls went up like plastic ornaments on a burning Christmas tree. Blank faces melted away from grinning skulls. Horrible pale hands curled up and blackened like spiders.

In the aftermath, amid the vile smell of burned hair and leather, the three surviving people in the square staggered to their feet. Percy's buttocks were still on fire – he patted them out with his handkerchief. Mrs Hazelwood's little pillbox hat had popped off and been reduced to ashes, and her massive blue-rinse perm had risen like a bad day for Medusa. Lucky was laughing as only a Leprechaun can.

"Remind me never to ask you for a light, pal," he managed, clapping Eddie on one shoulder with what would have been neck-breaking force at any other time.

"Wh… what's next, then?" croaked the erstwhile pyromaniac, letting two very empty bottles clatter to the ground beside him. "Don't feel so good, actually, Sarge. All the little green bubbles are going deedleydeedly deeeeee…."

"Dear oh dear. Absinthe without leave," said Percy. "DWI as well. Draconic While Intoxicated. But I won't tell if you don't." He waggled his eyebrows conspiratorially. One fell off.

"Right," said Lucky, hitching his thumbs in his tiny little waistcoat in a way which was supposed to mean business, but clearly meant he was stalling. "The way I see it, we've done our bit. More than our bit. Anyone know what those things were?"

"Changelings," said Mrs Hazelwood, in the kind of calm, reasonable voice old ladies use when you shouldn't argue with them. "Big ones, too."

"Thought they… hic… thought they wazza sort of babies, kindathing," slurred Eddie.

"Oh yes. The Fae love to swap out little faceless magical blanks for human babies. They can copy just about any features, you know. But these aren't those. These were changed *different*."

"Howd'ya mean?" asked Percy.

"Well, if one of the Fae change a little baby, they have a bit of a blank canvas. They've yet to grow into their features, you see. It's like drawing a face on a hard boiled egg. These, though… they've been changed the way a hard boiled egg gets changed when you drop it from the top of a stepladder. Nasty. Their brains are all curdled up."

Eddie could feel the fires inside him banking up now, but something still tweaked at his senses. And if nothing else, he *had* been to the movies a lot of times.

"So… something made these Nazis into… into whatever those were. They were *henchmen*. And that means…"

There was another cracking detonation from up in the mist, then something streaked through the air from inland, rattling the tiles on every roof as it passed. It was a bolt of green lightning, and it rung the church bell as it struck, making the steeple levitate, rotate ninety degrees and then crash back into place. Fyodor came down like a falling asteroid, his clothes on fire, his immense *tankgeschutz* bent into an iron banana. He actually carved a furrow in the cobbles as he cartwheeled to a standstill, cursing in Russian.

And Eddie heard a sardonic, slow round of applause from behind him.

"That means there's a *real* villain behind them. Of course. Because we *all* know that the story is so very, very important."

The voice was like razors dripping with treacle. It was as arch and as rotten as that of any proverbial apple-proffering serpent, and it jangled with aristocratic frequencies which politely suggested that it would be a good idea to kneel.

Eddie didn't, but only because the sheer arrogance of it put the bellows to his rage. What had been an orange firestorm became the tiny, ice-blue blade of a plasma torch as he turned.

"Oh dear," said Mrs Hazelwood. "It's only a bloody elf..."

It was. The creature that stood there in the tavern doorway wore a natty version of an SS officer's uniform, cut to accentuate its lithe, slim build. Elves are known as the fair folk, but it's only true for one meaning of the word[7]. Elves create a rapture, which, funnily enough, is a word associated with *raptors* – birds of prey. This one's eyes were hawkish amber, seething with hypnotic sparkles. It had the face of a thousand perfect movie stars, cheekbones which would have made Da Vinci weep, and hair like spun filaments of night. But there was a cruelty there which made the whole confection look like Arsenic Surprise.

"*Only a bloody elf?* Indeed, good lady. Except that *this* bloody elf happens to be Lord Herald of the Spring Court, emissary of the Rightful Queen."

"I've had enough of this bollocks," said Eddie, who had had enough of this bollocks. He drew back his sword and swung, charging his blow with enough anger to carve through a longship's keel.

*There was a flash of darkness, and...*

He woke up still airborne. The cobbles and the sky alternated in a great sickening loop. Then he hit the wall of a house and slithered

---

7 That whole load of cobblers about truth being beauty and beauty truth was dreamed up by the Fae's marketing department. There's nothing beautiful about truths like 'you have pancreatic cancer' or 'I'm sleeping with your best mate and so I'm leaving you, and taking the house and kids'. Similarly, many beautiful things – elves included – are nothing but the glamourous foil wrapper around a box of chocolate-dipped hand grenades.

down it, pain exploding in furry silent thunderheads.

"You should have warned him, Hoardkeeper," chuckled the elf. "We gave the humans rune magic. Using it against us is an affront to the Queen."

It was Lucky who replied.

"Me and mine have only got one thing for your bitch of a queen," he snarled. "But knowing her it'd likely freeze solid and drop off. Now, let's have your name, so we can make yer a nice accurate tombstone, eh?"

Even upside down behind a row of dustbins, Eddie could hear the stammer in the leprechaun's voice. Lucky was *worried.*

"Oh, I'm the one these stupid humans prayed to at midwinter. They've forgotten a lot, but when this war is over we'll help them remember. While they were afraid of the dark… *I was the one that the dark was afraid of!*"

Saint Germain slid into cover next to him, a huge silver revolver in one hand.

"Nice bloody speech, innit? These Fae snobs do go on. Now, let's see if anything's broken." Eddie just groaned. But he didn't miss what happened next.

There was a blast of coloured smoke. There was a rather flatulent shower of sparks. And a very small Scots wizard appeared in the middle of the square, his hands on his bony hips.

"Zeberith. Yes, yes. Nice speech. Where's yer bloody flower trumpet, eh? Up your arse?"

The elf coloured, a slash of pink on each pale cheek.

"*Shakespeare made that up!* I'm all man, you know! I ought to…"

"Oh, pack it in, you literal bloody fairy. It's time you heard *my* name, just so we can blast ye to pieces the old fashioned way, and no-one can go blubbering to the powers that be about rules and regulations." He flourished his hands. A staff which looked suspiciously like a horrible gnarled old shillelagh appeared with a pop. "You know they say the wisest of wizards are those who keep the balance, and understand that high magic is best left unused? That the world can be changed with nary but a quiet word in the right place, and all that?"

The elf Zeberith nodded, slowly, wondering just what was coming next. Being menaced by Connor of Anstruther was like being savaged by a hedgehog. His voice rasped like a hacksaw going through porcelain.

"Well… *I'm not one of them.*"

Roaring purple fire engulfed the staff. Hideous runes mamboed and slid all along its knotty old length.

"My name is Connor the Beige, ye servant of the banished Queen, and I am the keeper of the fire which *kicks arses like yours before breakfast, pal!* **You shall not pass!**"

"I… I don't *want* to pass," began Zeberith…

And then he exploded. In the aftermath, amid the patter of falling bits and tinkling silver buttons, Fyodor held up a finger from in this trench and croaked…

"A little help?"

"Nice!" said Connor, staring at the staff as it flickered out. "But that wasn't me. Was it you, Lucky?"

"Naw, boss. I just do the punching and general violence."

"Patience?"

The young witch materialized from out of the shadows, a spiderweb tangle of power evaporating from between her fingers.

"Not I, chief. I was ready to block anything he threw at you. Those Fae bastards love their archery. But no fireworks."

Eddie, who was now on his feet again, giggled. The fire and anger were being steadily bubbled away on a tide of absinthe.

"Sorry, Mr The Beige. I think that was me."

And indeed, the remains of the fountain from the middle of the square were definitely mixed up in the very sloppy, very crimson mess which was left of Zeberith, Lord Herald of the Fae.

"What goes up must come down, right?" said Saint Germain. "Come on then. Let's leg it!"

He didn't, though. Instead, he froze. The silence which followed gave birth to tens of thousands of individual goosebumps.

And *this* time the slow clap from behind them was more sarcastic than ever. If sarcasm was radioactive, it would have given all those present either super-powers or advanced lymphoma. Squad 27 turned as if on well-oiled castors.

"*Very good. Very good.* I was preeeeety sure that elf was going to betray me, but then again… when you're sure you'll be betrayed, you know *exactly* where you stand. Now his arrogant old Queen will have even more reason to hate you, Englanders'.

All this was delivered in a jovial German accent – the kind you would associate with a kindly old toymaker in lederhosen with rosy red cheeks. And a little shop in a cobbled street that looked like it was made of gingerbread. Unfortunately, it came out of a mouth filled entirely with gold teeth, framed by a face which was pale and haggard on one side and scarred like the surface of the moon on the other. The body under the face was wrapped in black leather. Are you at all surprised?

He chopped up his words with twitchy, random precision.

"So... now that you have fulfilled your pitiful farce, I can tell *Der Fuhrer* what I want him to hear, bless his drug-addled little brain. I've got the evidence that the Allies are covering up *vast magical operations* – the kind that are going to lose. Him. The war. Unless, of course, I get a very large amount of money for my research..."

Connor visibly bristled.

"You're a madman, Schprinkler. You know we use only a tiny bit of magic. A sorcerous arms race would tear this poor old world apart. Ye'd wake up each morning and have tae wonder which of your legs had turned to custard, and how many noses ye had!"

The German – who, it must be noted, was backed up by a host of very un-magical, very well armed SS guardsmen in full-face helmets – simply laughed. It sounded like someone sandpapering a duck.

"Yes, yes. *Of course.* But why present our noble leader with evidence of your real, clumsy, limited, frankly *amateurish* displays of magic? Evidence of a big cover up is the kind of thing that'll get the hamster. Wheels. In his head spinning. Nobody does conspiracy theories like Uncle Adolf!"

"And the elves?" asked Patience. "Tell me you're not actually trusting them with any part of this?"

Hans Schprinkler cocked his head on one side, peering through his pentacle-etched monocle.

"My dear, I would *never* trust one of those wily bastards. But they are *powerful*. Powerful enough to win this stupid, grubby little war of ours. What happens afterwards..." he grinned. "There will be ever so many lovely little twists and turns and betrayals! You, however, will not be there to enjoy them. I have what I came here for... so. How do you say? *'For you, Squad 27, ze var is over!'*" His raisiny little eyes twinkled with glee. "And incidentally, I have this, as well."

He held out one black-gloved hand, and made a gesture with his fingers. A guardsman gently placed the tip cup from the Bell and Chicken in it, then stood to attention.

"*Look! See!* This is what the elf needed for his plan. I just needed *you* for mine, but... how do you say in England? This is the. Cheeky. Bonus!"

Eddie looked. It seemed to be nothing but a fairly badly made pottery cup, the kind which slightly dim children make at arts and crafts fairs. Someone had written TIPS on it with nail varnish, more out of custom than actual hope.

Connor, however, drew in his breath as though he had been stabbed.

"*The Holy Grail?* I thought they buried it in Camelot?"

Schprinkler laughed again.

"In that silly place? What *they* had was a solid gold goblet covered in jewels. Do you think humble old Jesus drank his last abruzzio in an American brothel? This cup was stolen from a kosher smorgasbord in Jerusalem, and brought across the sea by the first Merovingians. The Black Sun only deduced its whereabouts with the help of the Fae, but it's really just an historic curiosity. Unless..." and here he grinned, like a cracked-open bank vault - "you have a plan. As evil. As their Queen does."

"And I don't suppose there's any chance, is there, that you'd like to tell us that plan in intricate detail, perhaps while laughing and rubbing your hands together in villainous glee?" asked Connor. He looked at his pocketwatch. "No?"

"No," said Schprinkler, his mouth set in a determined line. He gestured two ranks of SS troopers forward, and they raised their submachine guns. "I think not. I will let caution be the better part of villainy, and just kill you all now."

"Ach, weel," said Connor. "I suppose that was long enough..."

It's worth noting, at this point, that Major Monkston had been having a chilly night of it, sitting and smoking his pipe in the drivers seat of the Talbot Special out next to what would one day be called the A303 near Amesbury. Now a very specific little chunk of quartz crystal stuck to the dash with modeling clay began to glow red. Monkston sighed.

He got out of the car, shaking his head, popped open his top hat, set it determinedly atop his heavily lacquered hair-do, and fetched a pot of paint and a brush from the boot. Muttering under his breath, he walked through the long damp grass, dew-soaking his tuxedo trousers to the knees. He almost slipped over at the bottom of the ditch, but he kept his footing, the red paint in its little pail pitching wildly.

At last, he reached the stones. With a few precise brush strokes, Major Monkston laid out a set of very old runes indeed. Those pictoglyphs indicated, with elegant minimalism, that the British Government was quite willing to make a deal if certain ancient pacts were fulfilled, sharpish.[8]

Monkston stepped backward as the ground began to shake. There was a brief moment of paisley. There was a smell of burnt fox-fur and summer lightning.

And a serious tonnage of rock slipped down into the ground, disappearing beneath the turf with a sound like an old man losing his dentures.

POP

A passing policeman, riding his Lee-Enfield motorbike, was surprised *not* to see the massive shadows of a certain famous set of trilithons against the moon. Instead, there was nothing but an empty field, in which a man in a top hat was smoking a cigarette and looking very self-satisfied.

Meanwhile, in France…

Stonehenge doesn't look like much in real life. Well, allright - it *does* look like a huge ring of stones erected in the middle of a field by people without even the most rudimentary hydraulic excavator. But when it comes to weapons of war, a whacking great druidic calendar is one of the last things people would consider.

Unless, like Eddie Weatherfield, you had seen the steely eyes of a whole squad of SS Occult Division troopers narrow behind their black masks. And you'd been ready to see forty horrible squat little machine pistols tear you to pieces.

Only to have a wall of massive monoliths come erupting up out of the ground like the world's largest ever ornamental rockery, showering cobbles and lichen (and one very upset goose) in all directions. Bullets pinged and spanged off the wall just in the nick of time.

"Monkston, you little beauty!" shouted Saint Germain, hoisting Eddie to his feet. "Now, let's get out of here. Before all the crushing and bludgeoning starts."

Eddie couldn't get up fast enough. It was *certainly* time to leave. Lucky sprinted past, huge legs pumping, one hand holding onto his bowler hat. Mrs Hazelwood tottered by, her crystal ball once again clutched in that oversized raffia bag of hers.

"Come on!" said Patience, grabbing him by the arm as she jogged past. "Don't even *think* about going back for the Grail. I know what

---

8 It's notable that three of the stones at Stonehenge *were* in fact moved in the 1950s, and SOMETHING was put under them. In the 1920s the nearby Avebury stone circle was completely rebuilt by Alexander Kieller, the Marmalade magnate, in exchange for the Ultimate Recipe for Raspberry Jam – or so it's said.

happens next, and its the kind of thing that doesn't care what side you're on…"

Eddie looked back over his shoulder anyway, and was treated to a strange and pants-wettingly wondrous sight.

All of those great grinding megaliths were sliding up against each other, sizzling with green fire. Black soil stained the butt-ends of massive hunks of rock as they rose up, and up, flowing with a sound like continents flossing their teeth.

Stonehenge walked.

It reared up in a huge and hunched-over form, held together with a skin of magical force. A golem like the three he'd faced deep under Kew, but on a scale which dwarfed squad 27, the Nazis, Hans Schprinkler – even the town itself. A head made of a trilithon with bluestone eyebrows opened what passed for a mouth, and a bellow shook Eddie's teeth in their sockets. A plume of bilious flame lit up the night – prehistoric halitosis.

Then one of those immense stony arms came up, and a fist like the end of the dinosaurs came down on the Bell and Chicken. Rarely has anything, ever, been so utterly demolished.

"Leg it, you pillock!" roared Connor the Beige, riding side-saddle on his magic shillelagh as it skimmed through the air. "Yon thingy was built so long ago its little brain is all cracked quartz crystal! It'll last long enough to smash this town, but if it runs out of Nazis…"

Another tectonic howl split the night behind them. The crucifix from atop the village church went spinning by like a lopsided shuriken, to embed itself in the stone wall of a cottage near his head.

"Right!" said Eddie, all his soldierly instincts convincing him to, for once, obey his commanding officer. He ran as if Death himself was right on his heels.[9]

Back at the boat, there was a quick head count. Everyone piled in, while Fyodor – having ripped open a regulation Section M blood-bag and recovered a modicum of his former swankiness – pushed the vessel out to sea. Lucky kicked the motor once, twice, turned the key, and swung the wheel around, heading out into the mist as Patience wove it into an impenetrable dome behind them.

Eddie slumped in the bilges, not minding the crab's-armpit smell or the cold slop of what he hoped was mainly seawater. They'd survived.

---

9 Death, who famously attends to each job personally, was invisible to Eddie Weatherfield. He sauntered past in the opposite direction, naturally – toward where all the squashed Nazis were.

*He'd* survived. He gave his limbs and other bits a quick inventory, then smiled. Up above them, engines droned in the gloom – the unmistakable one-note dirge of big British bombers on a mission.

"The *other* clean-up crew," said Percy, slumping down next to him. "Major Monkston won't take any chances."

"Aye, that could hae gone better," admitted Connor the Beige. "But with any luck the old lawn ornament back there made raspberry jam outta yon scunner Schprinkler. In any case, those planes'll flatten whats left of St Mal-de-mer. Hitler won't believe shite wi'out any of us as prisoners."

"The holy grail, though," began St Germain. Connor cut him silent with a look.

"A historic curio, pal. I know you're one to be quite impressed with a certain carpenter from Nazareth, but..."

"But the elves want it." Patience looked more than a little worried. She covered it up by looking more than a little irate. "*elves*, Connor. Which means there's someone not happy about the Accords. I thought you said General Crowley had it all sewn up? This new fellow, the writer, had made it so every one of the Unmanifest races got what they wanted out of the deal?"

"Well, maybe ye cannae please everyone," grumbled Connor, packing a bowlful of nasty black tobacco into his pipe. "And especially not the old Queen. A more evil bitch has never worn high heels, lass. Not one of your sisterhood come close."

The mention of General Crowley made the whole crew go quiet for a second - except Eddie, who had never met him. It was a fair bet, though, that everyone aboard was thinking about the bollocking they were going to receive for failing so badly.

"Chin up, lads," said Percy, carefully hoisting his grey lips into a smile. "At least we're still alive. And this war just got a lot more interesting..."

Eddie groaned. 'Interesting', in his recent experience, was a good cypher for 'uncomfortable, weird, terrifying and painful'.

Meanwhile, far across the choppy Channel, in a strangely empty field, Major Charlie Monkston was having an argument with a policeman.

"Look, I'm only going to ask you one more time," said the red-faced constable. "*What have you done with the henge?*"

Monkston looked slightly hurt.

"Me? Nothing, I assure you. I could hardly have stuffed it up my jumper, could I?"

A big fat finger was waggled under his nose.

"Don't tell me it's classified, neither. Just coz there's a war on, you army types..."

"Whether or not it's classified..." purred Monkston...

"Yeeeessss..."

"Is *classified*. But it isn't. Because I didn't do anything to your precious henge."

"It's not bloody there!"

"An optical illusion." Monkston extracted a slim cigarette from a very elegant little case and lit it up.

The policeman stumped out into the field, letting his motorcycle drop. He waved an arm through the air where, he was certain, a massive, heavy, *very real* stone was supposed to be.

*"An optical illusion?* It's vanished! Gone! Disappeared!"

"The light can play funny tricks at this time of year, at this latitude," said the Major, cool as a frosty glass of iced tea.

The constable looked as if he would explode for a second or two. He spun around, leaving a heel-shaped divot in the turf. And he pulled his truncheon.

"Listen, pal, you're going to *bloody tell me* what you've done with a *very important* ancient relic, vital to the local tourist trade, and you're going to tell me *now*, or God help me, I'll..."

There was sound like two jellyfish wrestling in a rubber sock. There was a smell like stale bread and burning wires.

And a whole massive stone circle erupted, otherwise silently, just behind him. It rose like Atlantis in a bad movie, all stop-motion and strobe-flicker, each monolith in exactly the right place.

"Look," said Major Monkston, "it's *definitely* there. Perhaps you've had one too many, old chap?" He produced a penny coin from about his person and lobbed it over the policeman's shoulder. It stuck the rock with a satisfying little chime.

The poor officer turned around slowly, as if he was deathly afraid of what might actually be behind him. Several tons of featureless rock gave the distinct impression that it was grinning at him. Then it *winked*.

Major Monkston sighed. The poor constable was laid out cold in a dead faint. He reached in through the window of the Talbot, unhooked the radio, and tapped out a certain callsign.

"Yes, this is Top Hat. Send in a squad of Housekeepers." he paused for a second, listening. "Yes, at Stonehenge. Bring the long mops, some bleach, a stretcher, several buckets and a small bottle of whiskey. Don't delay."

The Major slipped into the driver's seat and placed his hat neatly in its armoured box. Behind him, the stones of the henge were gently steaming in the night. Quite a few of them were stained gruesomely red. A flattened Nazi helmet popped loose from one and clattered to the ground.

Thank goodness, thought Monkston, that the rural police force were not exactly picked for being perceptive…

# Six – The King of Nothing Much

They came back to the Labyrinth of Kew through the water-gate – sailing up the Thames in a Section M mini-sub which smelled suspiciously of rum. Now, at least (Eddie thought) he knew what the big cavernous pool behind Dr J's office was really for. Not that it was much consolation. A fug of despondency lay over the whole supernatural crew as they slunk back to their barracks in defeat. Even Major Monkston, standing on the concrete pier to welcome them, looked strained and haggard.

"Come on, now. You weren't to know about the elves. We'll have a debriefing meeting at oh-nine-hundred, but until then, I want you all to get a decent meal, wash up, and focus on the positive."

"What positive?" asked Lucky, his immense hands shoved deep in his waistcoat pockets. "The one where we failed our first mission, or the one where we saved a whole French town by turning it into a hole in the ground?"

Connor raised his staff, but the sparks fizzled out.

"Ahhh, lay off it, laddie. Ye cannae win 'em all, and there's boys out there who've lost worse than us. He's right about the elves, too. We couldnae ha' known."

His heart wasn't in the words, though. You could tell by the way his pointy hat deflated like a rather sad bagpipe, covering one eye.

At least the mess hall was still warm and steaming and full of the aromas of thick, hearty food – the kind you could lose your cutlery in. The whole squad bunched up at a long table, each with their own peculiar idea of a healthy breakfast. This meant porridge, porridge with extra haggis, a bowl of what was definitely not tomato soup, a fry-up with poached runny eggs, a raw t-bone the size of a toilet seat, one hard-boiled egg in a cup made of rune-etched rowan wood, some kind of American breakfast cereal with curiously shaped marshmallows in it, and for Eddie, a whole cauldron of leftover tikka masala with sausages floating on top.

There was nothing to be heard but chewing and slurping, and the odd 'pardon me' from the Compte. Until a seven-headed shadow fell upon the breakfast board.

"Well, well, well," sneered a voice so abrasive it could have been used to clean lavatories. "The losers return. How was your visit to France? I hear there's a *lovely* little village there called… oh, forget it."

Lucky carefully placed his spoon on the table with a deliberate little click. It was a sound not unlike that of the pin being pulled from a very big grenade.

"Ohhhh, shit. Squad 22." this was Percy, in a truly terrible stage whisper.

Eddie looked up into the grinningly smug face of a young wizard. He had the pointy hat, all right – and a pair of round-rimmed glasses, and spots, and the kind of fat little nose that reminds you of pug dogs weeing on the carpet.

"You're the new boy, then?" asked this apparition, in tones like lemon bleach. "God, what did you do to get lumped in with *this* shower of pillocks?"

"Yerr?" growled the thing next to him, which resembled a full-body wig. It was wearing just the collar of a russian uniform, complete with a hammer and sickle pin. "Vaat you do? Poop in the bed? Slap the commissar's auntie?"

"Hello… *Yevgeny*," grated Fyodor, just above the threshold of hearing.

"Hello… *Fyodor*." replied the hairy beast, in the same manner.

Eddie considered the young wizard for a moment. He looked over the rest of squad 22 – an old grandad carrying a cricket bat, a mummy in an ancient cavalry uniform, a haughty-looking young lady in a toga with her hair in a turban, what could only be called a Frankenstein (complete with neck bolts) and a Gnome much like Miss Golightly, although without the beard and sporting a pair of enormous machetes.

He figured he'd seen enough of all this in high school to know what to do next.

"You." he said to the wizard. "Down here. Come on. I've got something to tell you. You might find it quite amusing."

Wary, but still trying to remain smugly superior, the greasy little mage leaned in. Close enough for Eddie to grab him by one ear. Magic flared, but Patience made a gesture with her fingers, and a small cloud of orange sparks popped and faded into nothingness.

"Hello," said Eddie. "I'm the new guy. I've had a rough couple of days. But where I come from, I've had all sorts of problems with bastards like you." He gave the ear a twist. "Now, not so long ago, I got given some spiffy new powers by an undead viking, and I've had more than a few little idle thoughts about tracking down my old school bullies and giving them a look-see. But now here *you* are. And you're looking like a mighty fine stand-in. So, I suggest you fu..."

At this point, a massive, stitched-together hand closed around the top of Eddie's head like the jaws of a car crusher. At the same time, he saw Lucky stand up – and up, and up, his fingers clenching into fists.

"Allright," said Connor the Beige, finally looking up from his porridge with extra haggis. "Where's your C.O, young Snetterley? Haven't you got better things to be doing?"

"That's Archmage Snetterley of the Order of the Celestial Light to you, old man!" whined the wizard, pulling clear of Eddie's grip. A massive red fingermark throbbed on his earlobe. "I'll remind you that my father is the high ordinator of the..."

This time, the shadow which fell across the table was even bigger and darker. It was the kind of shadow which makes other shadows slink away to hide behind sundials and under rocks.

"And I'd remind YOU, Snetterley, that your dear old Dad is currently in Burma, fighting the Tcho-Tcho cannibals and the Japanese Imperial Coven of Sages. Which means the task of spanking your horrible bottom falls to the senior sergeant of this facility, vis-a-vis disipline, which is ME, Snetterley, and if you think your spotty posterior would **survive,** Snetterley, then you are about as right and correct as Adolf Hitler making plans to *re-decorate Buckingham sodding Palace!"*

Eddie had never been shouted at by a minotaur. He did not envy Archmage Snetterley of the order of the Celestial Light the experience. Reggie, it seemed, could literally blow any number of drill sergeants away sideways.

"Now – the lot of you! It looks like your commanding officer has been called away to work the security detail for our guest... who's *none of your damn business.* He's here to talk to squad 27 about the *vital intelligence* they recovered from their trip to France, see? But you..." and here the minotaur pulled out a large, reinforced clipboard. "*You* all have latrine duty." there was a chorus of groans from Snetterley and his cronies.

"But... but...."

"Now, don't bother hurrying along there," grinned Reggie, winking at Eddie with one huge brown bovine eye. "I just have to deliver this envelope to Mr Connor, here, and then... oooooh, I'm afraid I had a very, *very* big dinner. All that silage just ain't sitting right. I might just leave going anywhere near the latrines for an hour of so, if I were you lads..."

Seven looks of blank-eyed horror stared back at him. Reggie clapped his massive, leathery hands together.

"Chop chop, squad 22! Report to the janitorial stores for mops, bushes, disinfectant and… well, better stop by the armoury for some gas masks, eh?"

The unlucky squad 22 slunk away, shooting baleful glances back at all those around the table. Snetterley reserved a particularly toad-like glare for Eddie, who retaliated with a knowing little smile. It seemed that no matter where you went, and what kind of upside-down madness happened to the world around you, there would always be people like *that* to deal with…

"Don't be so sure they got the bad side of the deal," rumbled Reggie the Minotaur. "Because I wasn't kidding. The General really *does* want to see you all about what happened in France. They've sent a truck down to Wilmington to the gate there to bring in… *you know who.*" He tapped the side of his nose. The ring jingled.

Connor looked shocked. Patience doubly so.

"*Himself?*" she asked. "Well, it's a good thing they're using the gate at Wilmington. The one at Cerne Abbas always makes me uncomfortable."

The old wizard chuckled.

"They *do* say you can't keep a good man down…"

Patience actually blushed. It was adorable. Eddie felt a small, brittle sensation, like a tiny guitar string breaking in his chest.

"I just wish they had a pair of trousers big enough to… well, considering… and at least with the…"

"*What are they talking about?*" Eddie stage-whispered to Percy. The zombie waggled his eyebrows, both of which were now held on with drawing pins.

"The King's coming. Not *our* one - *their* one. On account of what we saw over in St Mal-de-mer. It's a diplomatic incident. And he has to come through one of the old gateways into Fae, see? They're using the Long Man of Wilmington."

Suspicions bubbled up through Eddie's mind.

"One of those chalk carvings? I bet he's called the long man because he's got a great big…"

"*Pair of staves,*" said Mrs Hazelwood, firmly. "Though it's actually the outline of a door. See, he's depicted as just a silhouette at that one. He sort of fills in his form once he's through into good, solid British reality. The one at Cerne Abbas, though, well, those neolithic people drew him with a whopping great huge..."

"*Club*," said Patience, getting control of herself. "A big knobbly club. And..." here she gave the assembled lads a look which dared them to contradict her - "he had absolutely nowhere to put it. Imagine three hours in a railway carriage having to stare at..."

"AHEM!"

Connor looked slightly more red than beige at the moment.

"Thanks tae what we saw over there, the big bastard is gonnae want to talk to us. You know what that means. Nae digressions. Nae funny little anecdotes tacked on. Nothing that could give Him *any cause* tae get involved in this bloody war. It's vital that He signs the accords next week, because where He goes, the Mountain King, the Hammerjarl and the whole bloody lot of them follow." He gave each of them a beady stare, of the kind usually found under baking-hot desert rocks. "Now, fall out, and be at the grand auditorium at three exactly. Full uniform. Even you, Percy. And bloody well find some superglue for those eyebrows, will ye?"

In ones and twos squad 27 carried away their washing-up and left the mess hall. Eddie had just handed over his cauldron – scraped clean – to what appeared to be a bearded lady with arms like duffel bags full of watermelons, when he felt a tap on his shoulder.

His heart expanded to fill his throat when he saw that it was Patience.

"Snurp. Glarph nrrrrrrrr," he said, in a doomed attempt at playing it cool. Up close, that combination of a severe military uniform, black braided hair and violet eyes made his collar feel like a vise grip. Eddie gurgled.

But there was something about the young witch which gas-axed through the hormonal fog. That was another thing about Patience. When she looked at you, she really looked *at* you – not just *toward* you, but at a point on the inside of your skull, like a scientist peering down a mile-high microscope at a paramecium.

"What you did back there. In France. It was very brave," she began, "But also *unbelievably* stupid." With a sense of creeping dread, Eddie realized that Patience felt sorry for him.[10] "Attacking an elf – especially one that powerful... well, it's sort of like taking on one of Hitler's fancy

---

10 Which, as we know, is the big boron control rod jammed into the nuclear reactor of prospective romance

new tanks with a cheesecake fork. You were lucky he thought you were funny."

Eddie remembered the sensation of being slapped with a rather large Alp. That was an elf's idea of *funny?*"

"I… I thought they were supposed to be little fairy things, with rainbows and flowers?" he found himself saying. Patience smiled, but it was the kind of smile you'd reserve for a slightly brain-damaged labrador.

"Shakespeare did that. Neutered the bastards during the Fae Wars. Did you ever wonder why we don't know exactly who he was? The Spring Queen used a level-twelve Working on him, tried to erase him from history. But it didn't stick. Before him, it was all horseshoes over the door and leaving out milk so they wouldn't steal your babies. After him, they were reduced to biscuit tins and storybooks. For a while…"

"So how did that one hit me so damn hard?"

"The war's got everything in flux. Energy levels are all over the place. And the Black Sun are prying into things they shouldn't. That's why these accords… Oh…"

Eddie followed her gaze. Connor the Beige was holding one finger to his lips in a clear 'shush!'.

"Look, I can't say much more. It's just that he can't scry like I can," she indicated Connor with a twitch of her head, 'and *you* – if you don't get a lot more cautious and smart, there's a good chance you could break reality."

That was a lot to be accused of. Eddie looked hurt.

"But that's where I keep all of my stuff! How? Isn't it… kind of permanent?"

"If you live, the Accords will go wrong. Someone will be left out. If you die, I can see swastika flags flying over London. It's very confused. If I had a piece of string, a brass key, a bowl of ink and a dead mouse I might be able to…"

"Miss Patience? Corporal? *I believe it's time to go!*"

That was Connor, looking at a very large pocketwatch he'd fished out of his sporran.

She patted Eddie on the cheek. It almost made up for what she'd just said.

Almost.

"Remember. Smart soldiers stay alive!"

Then she was gone, leaving behind only a lingering hint of lavender.

"Oooh," said the bearded lady, leaning up against the dinner counter.

She batted a pair of eyelashes like roller blinds. "That's a tricky one. Good luck, sonny."

Eddie tried to straighten himself out a bit, but succeeded only in looking slightly more foolish.

"I have no idea what you're talking about," he croaked. He didn't know exactly who he was trying to convince.

He gnomecarted. He took his boots off, and an automatic military part of his brain, screwed in there by hours of shouting, made his hands polish them to a mirror sheen. Then sleep hit him harder than Zeberith had, and he twitched and shuddered through a series of shallow but unpleasant dreams.

*A figure in the snow, carrying a huge axe and a formless sack. Elves inside a whole garden full of flowers, tiny faces contorted with cruel glee. Nazi flags flying from the burned-out buildings of London.*

Eddie awoke to a sense of nameless unease, and a pencil lifting up one of his eyelids.

"Oh, he's awake all right. *Yes*, it's the human eye," hissed a voice. "*No*, it's not gone funny!"

A tiny scrabble-slither of rage made Eddie's fingers snap the pencil in two before Fyodor could pull it back. The vampire grinned, which is *not* something you want to see after just waking up.

"Ahhhh, there he is! Come on, old chap, rise and be shiny as you Englishers say. We're off to see the General. Mustn't keep him waiting!"

Percy seemed to be part of his wake-up party too, and he pressed a huge tin mug of what Eddie hoped was coffee into his hand, making sure no rotting fingers stayed stuck through the handle.

"Thought you might have trouble shaking it off. Can't give the old boy another thing to grumble about!"

Eddie jack-knifed out of bed, still in full uniform, jammed his silly little air force hat onto his head, and concentrated on lacing up his boots. Things dipped and wobbled around him.

"You weren't watching me sleep, then, were you?" he asked, as he worked the knots. "That would be a bit... creepy."

"Force of habit," sighed Fyodor. "It's an undead thing. Now, if you were a young lady in a see-through nightgown..."

Percy snickered.

"Or, in fact, a middle aged lady in a terrycloth bathrobe, if the rumours are true."

Fyodor sniffed.

"Vampires are *romantic*. I can't help it if a bodice or two gets ripped here and there."

Eddie stood up, grabbed a shoulder each for leverage, and decided, on the whole, that he could remain upright without support. He knocked back about half of the mug of coffee in one go, finding it to be as harsh and gritty as the old primordial soup.

"Right! Shall we, lads? I hope this General Crowley of yours appreciates my sacrifice."

"You mean in France?"

"I mean that bloody drink I just had, Percy. If there was any more dirt in that mug I'd stick a flag in it and claim it for the Empire."

Eddie was grinning as he swung on board a gnomecart, thanks to something which had clicked into place in his mind in that blurry no-mans-land between sleeping and waking. His cheerful smile lasted long enough to get him all the way across the Labyrinth of Kew, and in through the doors of the great auditorium, held open by Miss Golightly.

It crumbled like mummy dust, however, when he saw what was happening inside.

Say this for General Crowley. Despite the terrible toll of waging a magical war against the Axis, he was still a striking figure. His huge, heavy head, bald as a bowling ball, shiny as polished oak, was thrust forward to leave him nose to nose with another... *thing* of equal stature. They had both obviously been shouting at each other – cords of muscle stood out on the general's neck like electrical cables, and he was red verging on purple. His adversary wore a green toga, a beard like a thicket, and a wreath of twigs, thorns and a small bird's nest twined around a massive pair of what could only be called antlers.

Both men's fists were on the tabletop; three-hundred-year-old solid mahogany creaked under the strain.

Off to one side, Connor the Beige waggled his eyebrows frantically. Squad 27 were all lined up in regulation un-comfy chairs along the wall, wearing the studiously uninterested look of subordinates who have just seen their boss utterly lose it.

Eddie, Percy and Fyodor slunk in, pressed to the walls. The tension in the room had the consistency of hot jelly.

"Now, if we can all just remain calm," soothed Major Monkston, placing a glass of water in front of General Crowley and his guest. "we might just be able to redirect some of that lovely animosity toward the Germans. Your Majesty? Was it *really* necessary to call the General a 'two bit carnival barker in two dollar underpants'?"

The immense leafy figure with the pointy ears gave a snort of frustration and collapsed back into his seat. It was a huge, high-backed club armchair, and it fielded him like a catcher's mitt collecting a sack of mud.

"Ahhh, of course, of course. Sorry, then. Allright? It's just… *Stonehenge?* You had to use that bloody stupid monument? Less brains than a zombie's diet plan, of course, but it's technically one of ours. Those stones, see? Our folk dug 'em up from Preseli Valley in Wales. Very magical place, that. Long associated with the elves.[11]"

Crowley sat down too, wincing a little.

"Fair enough, fair enough. And I'm sorry I called you a washed up old satyr with the morals of half a goat. Thing is, the henge is in *England.* And we're all doing our bit for the war effort."

"As I understood, *our* part was just to stay out of it. I *like* what your boy with the pens and paper is up to. I don't want to look like this forever, I'll tell you that for free. When me and mine get transformed into good-looking, immortal buggers with silver swords and a land over the western sea, I'll be happy to nail up three plaster ducks and call it a day. But…"

Major Monkston chimed in.

"But… none of us want your job either, Oberyn. Give your average human immortality and he'd just be asking what to do to fill the time in. We've all heard the legends, and *none of us* know what it means. That rubbish about Stonehenge is just Nostradamus all over again."

General Crowley took a long sip of water, looked mildly annoyed that it wasn't, in fact, something stronger, and sighed.

"He who commands the rock of elvish Preseli will be called King," he quoted. "Not one of Mother Shipton's best, was it?"

"Would-be monarchs have been looking for moody swords, iffy spadroons and suspicious yataghans around there since Merlin was a dustman," said Monskton. "Sorry, but the only use we could find for your load of old rockery was as a Nazi- smashing golem."

"And only then because of your ex-wife!"

King Oberyn - undisputed master of the Autumn Court of Fae and a God in his own right – wilted visibly at the mention of his ex. After all, mortal divorcees only take half the house and half the money. Titania, Queen of Spring, had taken half the year, give or take a solstice.

"Ooooh, I do know how to pick 'em, don't I? I hear your writer lad

---

11 This is an actual fact.

is setting me up with someone pale and fair and eldritch in the new Accords. Alright for ceremonial purposes, but I'm quite happy with the new wife." he sniffed. "Tania, of course, is still a bit jealous."

"A *bit?*" asked Crowley, with varnish-stripping levels of sarcasm. "She's been trying to kill you for the last three hundred years, hasn't she?"

"Off and on, off and on," agreed the King. "In between embarrassing denial, late- night telephone calls and horrible long rants about how we should get back together. The new wife thinks it's sweet."[12]

Major Monkston nodded decisively, like a salesman who had just handed somebody a very expensive fountain pen.

"And what..." he asked, mustache fairly quivering, "did she say to you the last time she called?"

"Some nonsense about getting the band back together. How this war among you humans would make a great backdrop for a reunion tour."

"The *band?*" asked Crowley. "You mean..."

"Thunderbeards," nodded King Oberyn. "My old mate Odin Allfather on lead guitar. Mithras on drums. Boozy old Dionysus belting out the vocals, I was on bass, and the rhythm guitarist was old what's-his-name. Helmet on all the time. Right into hunting... Ahhh, it's been too long."

The great horned God reached into the recesses of his toga – which smelled rather like the locker room of a neanderthal football team – and produced a huge fat wallet. From this he unfolded a photograph. Eddie craned his neck to see.

In the picture, mazed by time and coffee-cup rings and part of the photographer's thumb, was an image of a group of armoured, toga'd, immensely bearded celestial beings wielding musical instruments in the same way lesser mortals would swing around a double-headed war-hammer. They appeared to be standing atop an erupting volcano.

"Housewarming at old Vulkan's gaff, that was. 'Get Your Rocks Off Tour, Pompeii, about nineteen-hundred years back."

"What did you play?" asked Monkston. "Jazz? Some kind of folk music?"

Oberyn's eyes went dim. There seemed, from Eddie's perspective,

---

12 Oberyn's new wife was Eris, Goddess of Chaos, who loved intrigue, drama, soap operas, explosions and all kinds of carefully schemed and plotted capers in which she invariably won. She also baked a mean apple crumble, but it was advisable not to take the first slice.

to be lights and shadows spinning inside them, behind a veil of fire.

"Naw. It was something else. Something which has come before, and may yet come again. Alluring like gold. Brutal, like a lead cannonball in the face. Explosive, like that uranium stuff your lads are banging together..."

"Who told you about *that?*" yelped Monkston. Crowley shushed him.

"So – some kind of heavy, metal music, then. But how does that fit in with her plans with the Grail?"

Oberyn snapped out of his trance. Sometimes, especially when you are very, very old, the past isn't just another country. It's one your mind can get extradited to at the drop of a pina colada.

"Nothing, obviously. She's as mad a sack full of mallets. All I can think of is it's your Nazis who want to get through her, to me, to old Odin. But they're wasting their time. He's retired. Packed in the general Godding and Smiting centuries back."

Patience was on her feet before either Eddie or Connor the Beige could stop her.

"December 25th, she said, in a voice which carried like a dropped grenade pin in a very quiet bunker.

Three heads turned slowly to look at her. The combined stare of king Oberyn, General Crowley and a clearly agitated Major Charlie Monkston should have made the pretty young witch spontaneously combust. But you know what they say about evolution. Highly flammable witches had gone the way of the dodo, the self-biting viper and the now-infamous upright bass crab.[13]

"December. Twenty-five. All of them have the same holy day."
Crowley nodded.

"Very popular one," he rumbled. "Winter solstice and all."

"We actually… and this is funny," said Oberyn, in the classic preamble to an anecdote that isn't. "We only met because of a mix-up. We all took a year off at once, and ended up sitting about in a tavern at a crossroads, waiting to offer a poor traveler amazing musical skills in exchange for his mortal soul. Didn't work out, really. But we all had

---

13 This poor benighted creature is only known from the fossil record. A small group of fiddler crabs, isolated on some prehistoric island, became engaged in the kind of arms race which usually ends in radioactive tears. The end result was a tiny crustacean with one normal sized pincer, and one the size and shape of a hydraulic log splitter. The upright bass crab was unable to move, and spent most of its short and horrible life trying to lure seagulls in to be snipped in half.

our gear with us, and the new lad was doing most of the heavy lifting vis-a-vis god stuff that year, so we… oh dear."

There was a look on Oberyn's face. A look which spread from antlers to beard like a slowly advancing tide of cold porridge.

"The new lad."

Monkston snapped a pencil in half out of sheer nerve-twanging intensity.

"The bloody *grail!*"

Crowley slapped a meaty palm into his equally meaty face.

"Ohhhh, not him. Let's not get *him* involved. You *know* I think he's a pillock. And talk about a loose cannon! I hear he's fighting the Nazis out there already, you know. He's joined the French Resistance!"

"Typical showboating," said Monkston. "Then again, they gave him every reason. He *is* Jewish. Technically."

Next to Eddie, the Compte De Saint-Germain sat bolt upright and sniffed the air, like a rabbit about to get hit by a juggernaut full of gravel.

"*They're going to say it.* Ohhh, bugger, they're going to…"

"Who exactly are ye talking aboot?" asked Connor, cupping one ancient ear.

One witch, a Fae god, a highly strung magician and the so-called Logos of the Aeon answered him at once.

**"Jesus Christ!"**

Saint Germain sneezed so hard the back of his head hit the wall. He slumped down in his chair, unconscious.

"Well, there's no need to swear, said Mrs Hazelwood, disapprovingly.

"No, no, my dear Mrs H," said the General. "*Himself.* The halo'd Nazarene. Chippy the magic carpenter. Beardy-weirdy. Old Mr Jehovasson, as they call him in Sweden."

"And if there happened to be a Christ-shaped hole in the thaumic unconscious, say?" asked Major Monkston, who was quick on the uptake. "What would happen then?"

"Weeeeelllll," said Crowley, sucking his teeth in the fashion of a mechanic who is about to cripple your financial past, present and future. "We'd be looking at most of His armageddon-signifiers immanentizing. Four horsemen riding out. Seas turning to blood. The usual. And then there'd be a vacuum. Obie and his mates would sort of just… come back."

"But he's right here!" said Eddie, unable to contain himself any longer.

"Reality," said Patience, patiently, "Is rather like an old sofa. Turn the cushion over, and there's a nice bum-shaped indentation waiting, right where you left it. King Oberyn – excusing your presence, y'majesty – used to be a big, hairy, mean-spirited bastard who hunted humans for sport."

"We all did silly things when we were young, I'm sure," said the Fae King, looking a bit hurt.

"Yes, but *that's* when you were a focus of belief. Gnarly, *old* belief. Superstition, high octane blend. Uncut prayers. Get a taste of it again and -"

"And Tania might just get her wish. I don't want to go back. I *like* what your man's writing for me. elves with a beautiful language, and grace, and nobility, and a last great stand against evil. Going into the west..."

For a second the God's voice became wistful and fading, like the last breeze of summer. He seemed to shrink in on himself, until he was just an old man in a silly costume.

"She'll be two steps ahead of you, you know. And that young feller with the beard is flashy, but he's not one for cunning. I'll tell the others. We can go *away*. Far from the threshold. Go deep, and cold, so even if she wins..."

"Ermmmm..." came a reedy croak from floor level. A mass of white horsehair wobbled up to chair height, revealing the face of the Compte de Saint Germain.

Everyone turned to stare. The poor pseudo-French aristocrat looked like he'd battled hayfever and lost by knockout.

"I… have certain information about the umm…. gentleman DON'T SAY IT in question, right? If the Germans and your old missus want the grail, squire, then they'll want the other bits too, I'll bet. And J… jjjjjj… the *bloke from Bethlehem* DON'T SAY IT tucked away his three nails and the spear of Longinus in the old Byzantine capital."

"How do you know this?" asked Crowley, eyes wide with shock. Saint Germain squirmed. "Hitler would give his left… well, let's just say under normal circumstances..."

"Just the *facts*, Germain," said Monkston, in a steely, no-nonsense tone. The poor alchemist wrung his hands.

"Welll, it could be that, after I got given the old immortal eye, as it were, I sort of wanted to see the bugger get hung up by old Pontius. Could be that I figured he was gonna be a popular one, and I happened to pick up some souvenirs, like."

General Crowley cracked his huge knuckles, with a sound like walnuts collapsing under pressure in the depths of some benighted gas-giant.

"And it could be that, like, a while later I needed the money, and I happened to be in Constantinople, and I knew this bent orthodox priest, and I might have… sort of… pawned them for a moody donkey and a bag of falafel."

"Let me get this straight," said Major Monkston, into the tight, embarrassed silence which followed. "You know where the legendary Spear of Destiny is, because you *once sold it to a crooked preacher in Istanbul?*"

"If it's any consolation, that falafel was *well* on the turn," said the Compte.

Crowley turned to Monkston.

"Not much choice, is there?"

Monkston shook his head.

"Not really, Sir. Can't say I like it, but you know how it goes. Fate plays cards with the lives of men, but she's got a nasty bloody tell."

The General turned and grinned at squad 27. They were pinned up against the wall by that fervent, utterly believable smile, like roadkill about to happen in the headlights.

"Well then, lads. I hope you like hummus, big mustaches and buildings with onions on top. Because your King and Country need you in Turkey!"

"What about you?" asked Connor, pointing a pipe-stem at Major Monkston.

"Oh, I'd quite like you there too, old chap," he said, dapper as ever. "And it's not just one King, either. Remember, company?"

Oberyn totally misread all the very brittle, willing smiles in the room. He tried one on himself.

"Is this what you Mortals call a *suicide mission*? How very heroic!"

Eddie Weatherfield groaned inwardly. That was the problem with the army. It was great for wholesale Nazi smashing, but it contained *far* too many fiddly little bits which involved doing what you were told.

And they'd been told, alright.

Squad 27 was going to Istanbul.

# Meanwhile, elsewhere –

It was always the first day of Spring where the Queen lived.

There was a hint of ice in the air, but it was fading, and the flowers were clenched tight, waiting to bloom. She had held this eternal moment for thousands of years, ever since the old world of the Fae had met its doom – by her will, those blossoms would never feel the sun.

The Queen's world hung from the edge of reality in a way best described as exactly what it was – a blister. A pustule. A twisted-off little reality with a space-time curve so steep that you could, in some of the outlying, blurry parts of it, see the back of your own head.

But in here, it was perfect. There was a lovely forest. There were lovely meadows. Deer and bunnies and peacocks[14] walked around in a daze, like the living ornaments she'd made them into. Deep down, someone with the right kind of senses would have been able to feel their minds locked into buzzsaw loops of utter panic, but on the outside…

Titania knew that, despite all the nonsense spouted by well-meaning simpletons, it was what was on the outside that really counted. What was on the outside could be used like a gilded crowbar to rework the insides of the kind of people that thought insides counted.

Take the ladies who were here with her today.

Literal goddesses, each one – born of the strange magic humans didn't even know they possessed. The Fae didn't create Gods. They never used to have legends about people better than them, because they *were* the best. They didn't give parables and morals arms and legs and (she looked sideways at Eostre for a second) frankly ludicrously big bosoms without meaning to. It was all a bit messy.

Then again – they were *useful*.

Titania smiled.

---

14 But none of the dun-coloured, boring pea-hens. Titania's grasp of biology and her obsession with aesthetics did not match. Thankfully, new peacocks were easy to catch if, for example, one of the Spring Fae forgot its manners and tortured one to death just to see how it worked.

"So you see, ladies? Exactly as I promised. It's a damned shame what they tired to do to you, sidelining your holy days like that. I bet it played absolute havoc with your skin..."

Ishtar looked into the Queen's floating, silver-framed mirror, and smiled. It was the kind of smile that could raise a man from the dead, or at least one very specific part of his anatomy.

"I feel aeons younger!" she said, turning her face left and right. And there was another thing. Five thousand years old, and the poor little Goddess actually *believed* in what she saw in the magic mirror. When it came to what people wanted to believe, in her experience, they created their own blind spots. Ones big enough to park a zeppelin in.

Isis nudged her out of the way.

"Oooh yes! Those crow's feet have just disappeared! Tania, you are a *treasure!* It feels good to be back in the game!"

"Well, they *did* kind of keep the name. That made it easier. All that's happened, out there, is a psycho-theo-thaumatic chain reaction. Yesterday, Easter was all about the... well, the scruffy little prophet. Now, it's always been about eggs and bunnies and you-know-what."

Eostre, the big blonde, chuckled.

"Oh, they've *always* known what. It's just like you said. Their poor little minds lost sight of what's important."

Titania smiled. It was like a crack in the ice on the first day of spring. When you're far, far too far away from the shore.

"And when they forget, you forget. Aren't you glad I introduced you to my three-stage beauty routine?"

"Well, *you* never look a day over two thousand," said Ishtar, fiddling with her long black hair. "A bit of advice among us girls is always appreciated."

"What about the Nazarene, though? I do feel a bit sorry..."

Titania rounded on Isis, and for a second her face wasn't perfect. For a second, it was a mask of hatred so twisted it was hardly humanoid. But it was barely a flicker – like a single frame out of place in a flip book or a movie strip. She was all sparkle and honey as she patted the Goddess' cheek.

"Oh, how *kind*[15] of you to consider him! But doesn't he have enough, without giving you three wrinkles and spots and... well, the less said about that combination skin the better, dear. He'll do just fine with his lent and his pentecost and his... ahem... 'birthday'.

----

15 Titania said the word 'kind' in the way most people would say the word 'festering'

*For now.* She thought, smirking as only an elf queen can. *For now. Until I can get my lazy ex-husband back off the couch…*

"You just listen to aunt Titania, hmm? When it comes to beauty, I know best."

There was a second when Isis could have ruined it all. A spark of her old, haughty divinity snapped behind those dark blue eyes, remembering pyramids, and dynasties, and silent rituals in the choking hot dust of summer temples.

But doubt has inertia. There was no way these three – Eostre, Ishtar and Isis – had ever had a single wrinkle between them. Not really. Doubt built up like layers of silt, carefully laid down with a backhanded compliment here, a stab of fake sympathy there…

Say this about Titania, Queen of the Fae. She didn't become the most powerful female in a race of utterly beautiful sadists by being nice. She could lay on the fake 'sisterhood forever' schmaltz like a talk show host, while worming through self-esteem with the force of a power drill.

"Why, in a couple of days, you'll be down to having just the one chin again. And you, Eostre – that mole on your neck seems smaller already."

Eyes widened. Fingers smoothed and prodded. Just like the humans who made them, the Goddesses had *no idea they were doing it.*

"Now," said Titania, clapping her hands. This was the final masterstroke. "Who'd like some frosty mojitos?"

Servants appeared – male-model gorgeous, toga-clad and smiling. They carried glass jugs full of mixed drinks, trays of allegedly fat-free delicacies and, of course, little gift bags.

Each gift bag contained a pot of face cream, the likes of which could probably turn a decaying corpse into the spit and image of an artist's muse. It was made from things like moonbeams, and the tears of unicorns, and flowers which bloomed only by the light of rainbows. Well, *allegedly.* In fact, it was bog-standard cold cream from a large chain of chemists, cut with a certain powder. A few minutes work with the old pestle and mortar had been enough to reduce the tip cup from the Bell and Chicken to dust.

Titania and Oberyn weren't Gods. Not in the sense of the three featherbrained young ladies who were, even now, pouring out massive, sickly-sweet glasses of liquor and flirting outrageously with the help. But a part of them was. A part that got welded on when the humans saw what they could do, even after their world had been taken by the

Netherspawn, and they'd fled to this one.

It was *that* part which would kick-start old Oberyn's manhood. She'd get him back, and they'd take this world for their own. Then… then, even the Netherspawn would have cause to fear. They might not have the concept yet, but they'd learn.

The Queen of Spring smiled, this time to herself. Being private, it was an *honest* smile, and so it was a jagged nightmare of needle-sharp black teeth.

Already, the usurper was weakened. Perhaps, enough to make a call on the *other* member of the band. The one who got kicked out for creative differences…

# Meanwhile, elsewhere elsewhere...

The bombs hadn't hit *this* shop.

On either side, three-storey brick and tile buildings lay carved open, furniture and clothes and the little minutiae of people's lives strewn like confetti in the rain. At least the typical London weather had put the fires out. Someone in Berlin would be unhappy; then again, that was about par for the course, these days. Berlin was no longer a very happy place, unless you liked the kind of glazed, frantic fun which happens only when oceans of booze are needed to drown out the screams inside your head.

But back to the shop.

The big plate-glass window was tastefully inscribed with letters in black and gold.

EARL KINGSFORD,
TAXIDERMIST.

Peering through the glass, past a pair of tasseled velvet drapes, the persistent window-shopper would see a selection of very dead, very surprised-looking animals, frozen in poses of anger and nobility. Mr Kingsford was very good at what he did. Curiously, while customers often bought examples of his very skilled needlework, nobody ever seemed to deliver freshly dead hunting trophies around the back. On moonless nights, however, certain individuals[16] used the big metal doors with their hook-and-pulley system to bring in other stock. Stock wrapped in rugs, perhaps, or in suspiciously long brown paper parcels.

That's not to say that Mr Kingsford was a bad person. Just that he was not really a *person* at all, in the conventional sense. And there *was* a very eager clientele for empty spell books made from human skin, knives with handles made from human bone, hookah

---

16 These are the same 'certain individuals' who would be 'assisting the police with their inquiries' if they ever got caught...

pipes fashioned from skulls which could excite mystic visions, and even – remembering it was *other people* who bought these, not the Unmanifest races – whole preserved humans.

Tonight was not one of those nights. Tonight, as Mr Kingsford put down the telephone, there was a prickle of sweat on his pale brow. His eyes, which were a curious shade of yellow, widened as he licked his lips.

*Now that She mentioned it, he could feel it too.* A hollow in reality, like a missing tooth. Something to be probed at, because the pain there, electric and slick, was at least *different.*

*After so many years…*

The taxidermist moved slowly through his displays of mounted heads, half-finished skeletons glistening with wire, pelts hanging down like swatches of silk. He opened a dark, heavily carved cabinet, and his long-fingered hands brushed against a suit of armour, engraved all over with oak leaves and thorns. Its helmet throbbed to his touch, as if a living heart hid behind those void-black eyeholes.

A little later, and another door opened. A space full of dust and spiderwebs was revealed, and a figure all in metal stepped into the room. Here, there was nothing but junk – old picture frames, busted furniture, mouldering books. And a tarpaulin, which he pulled aside. Underneath lay something which seemed to writhe and flicker for a second, organic and transparent, before having *always been* a Brough Superior Alpine Grand Sport motorcycle, all in black.

There had been some modifications. The first one you'd notice, if you were unlucky enough to see this machine parked somewhere, was the immense side-slung scabbard, which held a sword that could only be called 'enormous', and a guitar which was blacker than the gap between stars.

The second, (and why it would be unlucky to even glimpse the oily, tweaked, fettled old Brough) was the fact that the headlight was gripped in the jaws of what appeared to be – by its profusion of butcher-knife teeth – a predatory stag's skull. Its antlers were the handlebars. Its eyes – and here we get to the bad part – were *still there,* red and raw, and they were filled with the kind of agonized madness which turns the mills of nightmare.

Earl Kingsford settled himself onto a seat upholstered in the fur of two species now extinct. The engine came to life with a roar which made people three streets away wee themselves in their sleep. The garage door slapped open, hinges shedding rust.

A second later, a single line of blue fire guttered and died on the cobbles, along with the sound of a thunderclap. Windows crazed and shattered up and down the street – but then again, there were only a few left which the bombs hadn't seen to.

One of those was the picture window of the taxidermist's shop. A frozen lightning-bolt of fissures had split the pane in half, feathering away to craze the name inscribed there.

To be fair, most of the letters hadn't been touched.

But those that were left spelled out far more truth than they used to.

Someone like Major Monkston, who was a student of the occult, and who didn't give a tinker's cuss for the idea of co-incidence, would have made a lot of the fact that they now read -

E RL KING

But then again, he wasn't there to ask…

# Seven – The Flight of the Black Buzzard

Eddie Weatherfield had imagined that the horrible part of Operation Longinus – which was the title that had shown up, in blurred and scratchy monochrome, when Major Monkston held his little briefing – would be dodging Nazi spies in Istanbul. His imagination was filled with rooftop chases, people shouting 'Halt, schweinhund!' and a certain amount of horizontal lead. Bazaars full of wicker baskets, angry men in robes, easily overturned fruit stands and irate camels had also been thrown in, thanks to far too many bad movies and a poor grasp of geography.

What he hadn't imagined was the *Black Buzzard*. Or the… well, he supposed he had to think of them as 'people' – who were working on her when squad 27 were gnomecarted into a vast and echoing underground hangar.

"We're under the pagoda right now," said Lucky, pointing at the ceiling. It was so high up there were small clouds skulking among the girders and trestles. "It makes for a grand control tower, and there's plenty of hidden guns in there too. Anti-air, right?"

"The vistas cut oot of yon gardens up above dinnae just form a great big magic sigil," explained Connor, as Eddie gaped at the huge iron bird which squatted on the runway before them. "They make it a lot easier tae land. Especially this thing, which I'm told..."

"Shhh!" scolded Patience. "I'm sorry, Sir, but you *know* how Darrin gets about his pet projects. He's also the only one of his kind we've got, so *please*. Don't insult the *Buzzard*."

Now Eddie could see the name written on the side of the odd aeroplane. It did indeed say '*Black Buzzard*', which was a fitting monicker for a vehicle which had – yes – birdlike talons gripping its landing gear, and wings outstretched with huge metal feathers flared. The real oddity – even by the standards of Section M – was the obligatory sexy lady painted next to the name. She was dressed in a brassiere made of two bombshells and a skirt so mini it was probably better defined as a belt. She also sported a luxurious curly grey beard.

Eddie tried very, very hard not to think of Miss Golightly.

"Ahhhh! Another test crew!" said the reason why, emerging from beneath the *Buzzard* in a great exhalation of black smoke. This figure was squat – three feet tall at most. It was also about three feet across. To be frank, it was a cube of muscle, covered in leather welder's gear and a pair of goggles. It had a beard in which whole new species of small woodland animal could probably be discovered. Some may have developed their own languages, folk songs and individual creation myths.

"No tests, old chap!" said Major Monkston, ducking under the wing with his usual dapper aplomb. "This is the real thing. An emergency airlift to Istanbul. There's nothing in the fleet faster than the *Black Buzzard*, or so I'm told!"

Connor made a sour face.

"Aye, and I heard the last two test pilots came back with their brains in their..."

Patience grabbed his lips between her fingers, making him splutter like a goose. But also shutting him up.

"I'm *certain*," purred Monkston, "That you've made *many vital improvements* in the months which followed."

"Weeks," volunteered the stocky, soot-blasted figure, popping his goggles off. "Well, *days*, really, if you count the work on the submari…." He trailed off, getting a good look at the skeptical faces of Squad 27. He smiled. "What I mean to say is, yes, of course! And good morning to you all! I'm Darrin Oakenbeard, and I'm pleased to be at your service."

Eddie snapped his fingers.

"Aha! I've got it. You're a dwarf, right?"

Major Monkston winced like a bulldog drinking lemon sherbet. Patience rolled her eyes.

"Well..." said Darrin. "Genetically. Genetically. But culturally – I'm afraid I'm an outcast. What they call *B'kraznah K'r'aakul*. I've been ritually undwarfed."

"But he's an amazing engineer and a great pilot and a bloody asset to our organization," filled in Major Monkston, ever the diplomat. "I agree with you, too. Gold's just some metal that comes out of the ground. No proper basis for a modern economic system."

There was a faraway look in Darrin's eyes for a moment, then he was all business again.

"Don't worry about it, mate," he said. "It were a long time ago, after all. And I'm happier here, where I can do some good. I hear when the accords go through, all the old *Kzrk'kaan* are gonna have to change their tune. Serves 'em right. And I'll already be ahead of the curve, building things like the good old *Buzzard* here!"

A clattering and banging came from within one of the cavernous engine inlets of the aircraft, and a figure popped out, holding a wrench bigger than its head.

"Number three thaumic cascade turbine's ready, boss!"

A second little person – even littler than Darrin, because it was slim, lithe and barely two feet tall – swung out of a hatch in the plane's belly.

"The alchemic digestor's ticking over nicely. No sign of resonance blowback this time. Remember the mess when…." A pair of huge green eyes took in Squad 27. "Ohhhhh. Right." It winked, very noticeably. "I mean to say that the little spinny thing, which has *never, ever* catastrophically come off at the wrong moment, is *definitely not* going to spray acid and sulphur everywhere due to low pressure at altitude again, boss!"

A third and final small, overalled figure emerged, yawning, from a toolbox.

"What did I miss?"

Darrin grinned.

"Ladies, this is our first batch of *actual passengers*. I trust everything's ready for takeoff?"

All three of the small people scrambled front and centre, standing to attention. Eddie noticed that all three were female, all had immense, pointed ears tufted with fox-fur, and tiny deer-like hooves instead of feet. They also possessed long, swishing opossum tails with furry red pom-poms at the tip. All three were tattooed, oily, scarred, clad in dirty overalls with sewn-on patches, and looked as hard as a bag full of hammers.

"Ilse, Lotte and Mica," said Darrin, "My assistants. And before you go guessing wrong, and get a number twelve crescent upside the head, they're gremlins." This was directed at Eddie, who offered the three tiny ladies a salute.

"Ohhh, he's a smart one. Officer material?"

"Hope not. I prefer a rebel."

"You prefer cutting pictures of Errol Flynn out of magazines, Lotte. Don't think I haven't seen you!"

"Well, a girl can dream. He's much cuter than any of the boys from our species."

"Shhh!" said Ilse, daintily knocking their heads together. "We're in slow time! They can hear you!"

The other two gremlins blushed. Ilse saluted Darrin.

"The *Buzzard* is ready to go. But… ummm… permission to remain on board for the maiden voyage? There are some tricky bits I don't think we should leave to the big 'uns."

"Mister Oakenbeard? Time *is* of the essence, I'm afraid…"

Major Monkston consulted his pocketwatch. Eddie was slightly disturbed to notice it was the one Doctor Jeckyll had been carrying not too long ago.

The undwarfed dwarf rubbed his thick fingers together.

"Very well, ladies. You have the controls. See to it that these people get to where they're going with all the right bits stuck on in the right way, won't you?"

Three heads bobbed up and down, under three different coloured oily bandannas.

"Gotcha, chief."

"Right, o."

"Fire 'em up, boss!"

Darrin watched them scramble on board with a gleam of pride in his eyes.

"It's the male ones what break everything, you know. The females *fix* things. These three are going to turn their society upside down after the war's over."

"How's that?" asked Eddie, stooping under the wing of the Black Buzzard to make way for Fyodor and Mrs Hazelwood.

"They're the first three gremlins who got the idea of fixing things that *haven't been built yet*. Half of this plane's their work. I just did the heavy lifting, as it were."

"Aboot that," put in Connor, unceremoniously handing Eddie a duffel bag which felt like it was full of anvils. "Are those broomsticks under yon wings, or have I finally gone completely mad?"

"I couldn't say for your mental health," ventured Darrin, "But yes. They're Demdike Mark Twelves. A whole ash tree for each handle, then about a half ton of willow twigs, woven on with spider-silk cordage. The runes will boost ten tons each, but they're just to get her in the air. Then the girls will fire up the dragon engine, and you'll feel some *real* speed!"

Eddie looked suspiciously at the immense, oversized brooms which had been clipped on under the *Buzzard*'s wings, where a sensible

Spitfire might sport auxiliary tanks or some useful bombs. Airman's pride made him ask the question.

"Just exactly how fast *is* she, Mister Oakenbeard?"

"Wellll..." the dwarf sucked the ends of his impressive mustache. "You know how they say a scandal can go around the world before the truth is out of bed in the morning?"

Eddie nodded.

"We're somewhere between a royal incest incident and the Pope being found drunk in a brothel." A huge, shovel-sized hand slapped him on the small of the back. "Don't worry. I think the girls like you. They'll make sure nothing happens like that time with the..."

"AHEM," said Major Monkston. "Private Weatherfield, the *bag*, if you would be so kind?"

That was how Eddie found himself hustled up the gangplank and into the hollow, echoing body of the great bird. Inside, muted jazz music burbled from hidden speakers. A row of seats with an unpleasant array of straps (and a further unpleasant array of stains) ran down the centre of the *Black Buzzard*, and a blur of tiny gremlin hands pushed him back into the cushions, webbing him up in beige leather and aluminium buckles.

This must be what they'd meant by 'slow time', he realized – because Lotte, Mica and Ilse moved about the cabin, and the *Buzzard*'s arcane, charm-hung cockpit, as a trio of tiny blurs. Orders were squeaked back and forth at bat-like frequencies. Metal rattled and chimed as bolts were tightened and levers rammed home. At last, the three small ladies slowed down, and Eddie realized (with a sudden shock of embarrassment) that they'd somehow changed their outfits during the last few minutes. Now all three were kitted out in female versions of the RAF's signature leather jacket and combat uniform.

"Welcome to Section M airways, flight 27," said Ilse.

"Direct service to Istanbul, and a boot in the arse for the Nazi war machine," said Lotte.

"I'll be your captain for this flight," continued Mica, tossing an adorably tiny flying scarf over her shoulder. "So, if you have any complaints vis-a-vis turbulence, acceleration, g-forces, or all that other tiresome human nonsense, you can address your remarks to the cabin crew."

The other two waved.

"Who also don't give a damn!" finished Ilse, clapping her hands cheerfully. "Questions?"

Lucky raised a huge, scarred-up paw.

"Who do ye pray at, if your species don't really have any gods worth talking to?"

Mica tipped her head to one side.

"That's theology. We only do engineering. So, if there's nothing else…"

They didn't give anyone else a chance to object. Three red-tailed motion blurs ricocheted into the cockpit, where stacks of cushions had been set up in the pilot's chair. A tug on a huge, toothed lever brought the whole pedal arrangement up on hidden arms.

"Ready for contact! Signal the pagoda for launch!"

"Aye aye! Lowering the ramp now!"

"Alchemic digestors are at capacity. Spinning up the turbines on one through six…"

Eddie squinted through the very thick, smoked glass window to his left. Out there, a huge section of the ceiling was grinding down, spinning orange lights spangling the scene in a surreal glow. Rain pattered across the skin of the *Black Buzzard*, sizzling in the aura of thaumic discharge which surrounded its four huge Demdike Mark Twelve solid-fuel broomsticks.

"Instigating the incantation," said Lotte, pulling an entire victrola record player down toward her on a kind of spring. She tapped the needle into the groove, and a voice began to chant in a reedy falsetto.

> *By tongue of newt and spider's eyes*
> *Let my broom ascend the skies*
> *To ride the moonlit clouds and soar*
>
> *O'er frosted peak and wind-swept moor*
> *By grim and gruesome rite satanic*
>
> *Make this, my broom, aerodynamic*
> *And charge with runes this mystic song*
> *To prove young Isaac Newton wrong…*

"I *do* love the classics," said Patience.

"*Young* Isaac Newton? Who wrote this stuff?"

"Come on, this one was top of the charts in the late 1600s, I'm sure…"

"Some of us weren't alive to buy the first copy!"

Then the sound of Squad 27's bickering was stretched out thin, compressed into a tiny hot core, and hammered flat. Something jammed both of Eddie's eyeballs into the back of his skull, as if trying to leave an impression of every single bloodshot vein in the living bone. It felt as if there was an elephant sitting on his chest. Scratch that – *two* elephants. Getting uncomfortably intimate.

Things rushed by outside the window. Then the whole world tilted upward at more than 45 degrees, and the amorous pachyderms were joined by a curious hippo. The whole structure of the *Black Buzzard* rattled and hummed like the inside of a tuning fork at an atomic level. Eddie's fingers, all unbidden, wrapped themselves around the arms of his chair in a death grip. His lips seemed to be retreating away from his gritted teeth as his cheeks made a bee-line for the back of his neck. Internal organs flipped and slithered like kids in a bouncy castle.

The world tilted again. Steel and aluminium howled like the unrepentant damned as the *Buzzard* stood on one wing-tip, slicing through the air so fast that its belly began to glow. But Mica held it. The great aircraft leveled out, and her sister gremlins leaped from their seats to grab a pair of overslung red handles each.

"Ready to release the brooms! On my mark!"

Then came an oily *clunk* like the world's largest shotgun being loaded, and the weight on Eddie's chest disappeared. Well, it halved. The elephants went off to have a quiet cigarette, anyway.

"One and four clear. The parachutes have deployed. Looks like they'll be coming down in Croydon."

Another *clunk*, and Lotte swung bodily from her pair of levers. Now the only sound was the hissing of the air around the slippery great bulk of the *Buzzard*.

"That's two and three clear. Ready on the turbines..."

This time, there was no massive punch in the throat. No incendiary roar. Instead, the *Black Buzzard* began to hum, the whole great machine resonating as its main engines began to burn pure sorcery.

It's often been said that knowledge is power. Pure, thaumic energy in this case. And like that other extremely intangible, utterly vital form of energy – light – knowledge is *fast*. We all know a vast mass of knowledge, such as a university or a museum, can turn actual discovery into a slow process, held back by the great sheet-anchors of tradition and self-assuredness. Knowledge compacted works like a black hole, and has an event horizon from which new and radical ideas often can't escape. But knowledge in its wild state crackles and arcs like lightning between thunderheads. A wild idea can sizzle through a whole population quicker than the thoughts of any of the people in it.

What you need, then, to turn a great mass of knowledge into the feral speed of inspiration, is something which converts mass to energy in a controlled reaction. Something like that Manhattan project the Yanks were working on...

Darrin Oakenbeard had done just that, with the help of his crew of female Gremlins. The *Black Buzzard* needed a kick to get it high enough to be out of the backwash of human thoughts, thick as a nine-day soup at ground level. Then hidden machines started dropping whole grimoires and tomes of occult knowledge into the alchemic digestors. Knowledge became power. Power became arcane fire. That fire turned huge silver turbines inscribed with potent runes.

And the *Buzzard* slit the air like a razor tearing through an infinitely long bolt of watered silk, sonic booms cupped within each other behind it like so many nesting dolls. Inside, however, it was as calm and smooth as a Sunday cruise. Mainly because *this* time, the little spinny thing didn't catastrophically come off at the wrong moment.

"Allright, allright!" shouted Major Monkston, as the English Channel blipped by underneath. "Eyes front, ladies and gents. We're about ten minutes out from Istanbul, so let's just recap the plan. Our aim is to infiltrate the Hagia Sophia and – ahem – *liberate* – the so called 'spear of destiny' before Herr Schprinkler and his men can work out where it is. Our operatives within the Black Sun report that he's narrowed it down to the old quarter of the city, but we have an ace up our sleeve. Mister Saint Germain here has *touched* the bloody thing, so we can find it with a bit of kit our research and development boys cooked up."

He took off his top hat, at fished around in it for a second. Despite being only elbow deep, the Major's arm disappeared up to the shoulder. When it came out, it was holding a kind of miniature scrying ball on a pistol grip, with a floating, spectral hand inside it.

"We've already attuned it to the Count, which means, unfortunately, we know exactly where that hand has been. But we also know that this gizmo will point the way directly to the resting place of the Lance of Longinus. So – we're going to drop in, using a variety of means. I'll levitate, Connor and Patience have their own flying accessories, Mrs Hazelwood will be ably assisted by Roger, and I'm certain Fyodor can transform into something appropriate. The rest of us will be using invisible parachutes which we've adapted from the latest cloaking technology."

"You mean special, stealthy countermeasures?" asked Eddie.

"No," said Monkston. "*Actual invisibility cloaks* sewn together to make parachutes. I understand they're also quite warm, so make sure to pack them back up when you land. Then we'll infiltrate the basilica, avoid the guards, nab the spear, and meet out front, where I will have appropriated some local transport from the Section M field office."

Down below them, the Alps flickered past like the world's iciest picket fence. Mica pulled the stick around and the *Black Buzzard* scudded down the Mediterranean, buzzing over Axis Italy so high and fast that anyone watching would have sworn they were a falling meteorite.

"No time to waste with tray tables and horrible little packets of rations pretending to be dinner, boys. Your combat gear is stowed under your seats. Kit up, and be ready for the drop in five minutes time."

Eddie poked around under his chair and found a black satchel containing a silenced pistol, his battered old shield and sword, and what appeared to be a signet ring with a radio control knob stuck on top.

"What's this?" he asked Lucky.

"Ahh. One of *those*. Oakenbeard and his lads in research came up with them a few months back. Put it on."

Eddie did so, gingerly, waiting for it to bite or glow red-hot. It did neither.

"Now, turn the dial, and look at your arm."

He gave the knob a tentative little twist. Everything he was wearing – coat, shirt, wristwatch, the lot – changed colour to a putrid shade of green. A wiggle the other way, and his clothes blurred through the spectrum to pink.

"Chameleon blood, apparently. They squirt it out their eyes when they get mad, see?[17] A bit of retro-sorcery, and you have that little piece of kit."

Eddie tried out lemon yellow, midnight blue and desert orange, before copying the giant leprechaun and turning the dial all the way down to black.

"Did he really say *ten minutes?*" he asked.

---

17 This is actually true. As a survival strategy, it's pretty unique, but then again, if *your* lunch started squirting blood from out of its eyeballs, you'd probably just opt for a salad too, right?

"Well, I hope so. I don't think there's a bathroom on this thing, if ye catch me drift..."

*Half an hour from London to Istanbul.* Never mind that the whole airframe of the *Buzzard* seemed to want to shake itself apart, and that gremlin-shaped blurs were zipping back and forth on the very edge of sight, tightening screws and applying what looked horribly like packing tape to sensitive bits of machinery. This thing was *fast.* It made his old spitfire seem like a steamroller! Something which was, perhaps, more dragon than human cracked a toothy grin at the back of his mind. Eddie suddenly wanted to stick his head out the window, like a dog in a speeding pickup truck. Never mind that at 3000 miles per hour, this may well have reduced him to a red-hot polished skeleton.

It was then that he noticed the piece of paper glued to the inside of his shield.

*"Checked and re-calibrated the kinetic bindings. NOTE! Impacts taken on the shield will now be stored for later re-distribution. Press the thunderbolt rune on the sword's hand-grip to release. Best of luck – Miss Golightly."*

"Ummmm..." he managed – before something hit the Black Buzzard like the croquet mallet of the Gods.

"Deceleration boosters fired!" shouted Lotte, bouncing up and down in her seat. "And this time we didn't explode!"

Connor the Beige (now all in black) rose creakily to his full height.

"As soon as yon doors open up, we jump," he grated, stowing his horrible pipe and gripping his staff in white-knuckled hands. "I'll try to offset the velocity with a wee slice o' magic, but it's gonnae feel a bit odd, ye ken..."

Sparks sizzled across every surface. Eddie felt his feet leave the floor as his head filled up with invisible bubbles.

Then a red light began to flash, and the aft of the *Black Buzzard* yawned open, revealing a huge expanse of ocean. It was night, and clouds tore past like scraps of paper in a hurricane.

"JUMP!" shouted the old wizard – and matched deeds to words, pelting past Eddie to throw himself into nothingness. Patience grabbed a broomstick from the overhead compartment and shrugged, following suit.

A dizzying memory of parachute training blurred through Eddie's head as he struggled to strap a heavy pack to his back. He hoped it actually *was* a parachute, and not the gremlins' lunch. Then it was too late, because Lucky had grabbed him by the waist, and was swinging him in an unstoppable arc, up and out into the slipstream…

For a second, everything was silent. Titanic forces tried to rip Eddie in half, as the sonic booms trailing behind the *Buzzard* lined up to pummel him senseless. Then Connor's spell went off, and it felt as if he had plunged through a mile-wide sheet of taut bubblegum. Far below them, an unfortunate goose became the focus for several hundred pounds of displaced velocity. It exploded, and sailed on through the air completely cooked. Due to narrative causality, it did so wearing those little paper fiddly bits on its drumsticks, and with a nice sage and onion stuffing spilling out behind it like a comet tail.

Eddie saw the city of Istanbul unfold below him, a glittering shawl of lights spread across the meeting of the Black Sea and the Med, the East and the West. Clouds came whipping past him as he sighted out the rest of Squad 27 – Connor leading the way on his flying staff, Patience keeping in close on what appeared to be a thoroughly modern broomstick, Mrs Hazelwood looking like the spore for a very weird mushroom indeed as she floated down, holding the handle of her wicker basket over her head…

The lights were closer now. Eddie's heart battered against his ribcage as he remembered, for no apparent reason, all the stories and legends and snippets of history about grand old Constantinople. Rather than an exotic myth, it looked like a very large, flat and solid surface right now.

And there was their target. The gently curling peninsula called the Golden Horn, where in ages past a few nomadic tribesmen had said - 'Blimey, you couldn't half defend that bit of land with a few lads with spears'. And later, a few lads with even bigger spears had said 'You're not getting your boat through here without paying us a toll...'

"Ready to release parachutes on my mark," came the voice of Major Monkston in his ear. Eddie looked up and around, and saw the magician outlined against the clouds. He was drifting down through the air, apparently unperturbed, both hands gripping the brim of his hat. "try to land on the roof, and do miss those towers. They seem awfully pointy now we're actually on the ground, as it were."

Eddie pulled the ripcord and felt the great mass of fabric in his pack slither out, catching the air with a jolt. He swung for a moment, weightless, looking down as individual buildings and parks, lawns and fountains became visible among the blur of light below. One of those buildings was huge and domed, ringed about with minarets like spikes of pale stone. Missing those *would* be quite important…

So he pulled on the strings which tilted his 'chute, swooping in closer now, seeing the streets laid out in a dusty grid, the little lights of tram cars and lorries bumbling along, the little gardens planted on the roofs of buildings – those, and the immense dome he was aiming for, right between his boots. Something made Eddie look up, just before impact, and he yelped at the sight of clouds and stars – his parachute was, indeed, completely invisible.

Then it was time to tuck and roll. Only – well, all the bail-out exercises had ended up in a nice grassy field. Eddie hit the dome of the Hagia Sophia like a bug hitting a windshield, and went sliding down the curved surface in a tangle of cloth and spider-silk strings. He caught up against the parapet on a narrow ledge, trussed up like a caterpillar who wasn't quite sure about all this butterfly business.

For a second, he thought he must have hit his head. Rainbow light flickered on the ledge next to him, and then, with a feeble 'phut' of sparks, a cauldron appeared. Lucky stepped out of it, adjusting his black combat gear and his tiny little green bowler hat.

"No time for napping, soldier," grinned the leprechaun, unclasping a huge and horrible knife from about his person. He knelt, and with a few deft strokes cut Eddie free. "Here. Wrap a bit o' that parachute around ye shoulders. Invisibility might not be a bad thing, right?"

He pulled the square of cloth around him, feeling a tingle of magic. And yes – Eddie could see the lights of downtown Istanbul right through himself. Then came another voice in his ear.

*"A little favour, perhaps, comrade Weatherfield? I can't seem to do this right way up. Could you hold out your arm?"*

Eddie looked left and right, and caught sight of what had to be the largest and most well-groomed bat he'd ever seen. If bats had competitions like dog shows, it would have been wearing a silly big blue rosette. It was, of course, Fyodor.

Eddie held out his arm, and the huge flying rodent came swinging to a stop, using him as a kind of human tree branch. Then it winked, and something indescribably horrible happened in between bat and human on the evolutionary spectrum. Something like radio static, and like mincemeat, and like a badly knitted cardigan re-knitting itself at the speed of light...

Fyodor rolled to his feet in a neat little gymnastic motion, now wearing a very stylish all-black combination of an opera tux and a commando's uniform. It had satin ammo belts. It had swallow tails, and grenade pouches.

"Many thanks. If I rematerialize out of the air I *always* fall on my head. And you know, with this haircut..."

Lucky rolled his eyes.

"All right then, lad. It's not a bloody fashion show! We're to break into the dome through yonder skylight, rappel down to the Empress' Loge – that's a little fancy balcony – and meet up with the others. Monkston's called in to the local field office, and he's preparing our getaway. The good news is, Turkey's not in this war of ours, and there's nothing in the German arsenal as fast as what we came here on..."

Eddie was looking past him, though. Up into the air over the Straits of Marmara, where something was pulling and twisting the clouds into a kind of horizontal tornado. His draconic eye narrowed as it focused far beyond what a human telescope could achieve.

"Not... and I want you to be *very* clear on this one, Lucky... not even *a man with antlers riding a huge black motorcycle?* Followed by what appear to be undead elves on even more motorcycles? Carrying Nazi sturmtroopers as passengers?"

Lucky could see the twisting, curdling sky. He could see the flickers of green and purple lightning. In fact, as a creature from one of the lost worlds – an immigrant to reality just like the elves - the presence of whatever was up there had every ginger hair on his body sanding to attention and crackling with power. He couldn't see it – but he *felt* it.

"Big antlers, are they? All hung up with chains and bits of bone and little wee shiny stones?"

Eddie nodded, ashen-faced. The rider had reached into a holster beside the machine's saddle, both hands off the handlebars. In clear violation of all health and safety protocols, he began banging out a complex, screaming riff on a jet-black guitar. Frost evaporated from the strings as little wisps of blue fire.

Primal parts of Eddie Weatherfield wanted to run away, possibly urinating at the same time. Other bits, though, knew bone-deep that this was *absolutely the coolest thing he'd ever witnessed.*

"That, then, would be the Erl King. And following him, the Wild Hunt. I'd say that puts our mission on the clock, lads. So let's hustle!"

Fyodor had produced – and Eddie did not care to speculate about *where from,* seeing as he'd been a bat only seconds ago – an immense sniper rifle with a scope the size of a thermos flask.

"I think I can hit him from here, Sarge," he whispered, licking his lips. "Come on, give the order..."

"No," said Lucky. "That's a *hunter's* weapon. It'll miss him. He's kind of the God of those sort of things. Arrows go through 'im, bullets twist away… we have to get to the spear. That thing is just the opposite. Stabbing the life out of a man nailed to a tree? That's the kind of thing the Erl King hates. And *fears.*"

Eddie risked another glance over his shoulder, as the three of them jimmied open a skylight and played out long lengths of black rope. The inside of the museum seemed dusty and hot compared to the night air. But he'd be glad to have walls between himself and what was coming…

Out over the bay, the Wild hunt had come down right to the deck, the wheels of their phantasmal motorbikes churning up a roostertail of spray. Only a couple of miles out, now. Outriders, all dead-skin grins and silver armour, hoisted pennants like medieval knights, depicting a red-eyed, antlered skull.

Ahead of them, the thing which was once Earl Kingsford, Taxidermist, smiled behind his full-face helmet. This was the real stuff. The *good* stuff! Bless the Queen for loosening the shackles of faith! They'd remember one of the rites of Spring straight away, of course, those poor human masses huddled in their cities. They'd remember the eggs and the bunnies as their little Nazarene carpenter faded away. But he'd be happy to teach them the rest again. What were fluffy little bunnies, after all, but prey? Spring was the time of the *predator*, and the old rites would come again, the dances in wolfskins, the ritual blood…

He had to say he liked the motorcycles, too. Flying over France, he'd felt the minds of certain men catch fire as they saw his Hunt go roaring across the sky. Two of them were volunteers, who'd gone to fight Franco, and continued on into the French Resistance. Lads who knew about riding fast with no lights along country roads. Boys from California, as it happened, who had thought war would be an adventure.

"Holy shit! Frank, do you see that? In the sky! A whole… bunch. A horde. I dunno. A *gang* of motorbikers! Flyin'!"

"Ahh, whatavya been drinkin', Harry? I…

There was a very uncomfortable pause.

Well, I'll be damned! Look at that! Do ya reckon they're *angels?*"

This time, Harry was well justified in taking a deep pull on the little flask he kept for such crises of faith.

"If they are, Frank, I don't think they're Heaven's. Must be the other kind."

The Erl King grinned. Already, his human teeth were becoming sharp and pointed.

Little sparks of faith. Soon they'd join together. And once again, the whole world would be lit by nothing but fire...[18]

---

18 The legend goes that the Erl King was once entirely human, but that he'd wandered into Tirfeynn by mistake, and been twisted into something horrible and over-compensating by the background magic of the place. He leads the Wild Hunt for one reason alone – out of all the Fae, he's the only one who can touch iron or steel This means that the honour of leading the Hunt is his, as the position is won by a duel to the death, and the Erl king's sword goes through copper like a fat policeman through a discount tray of donuts. Of course, his Huntsmen can't ride REAL motorbikes, as they are made of the forbidden metals. A closer look at what they're riding will put most people off their dinner, because it involves horses, vague ideas about motorcycle design, origami, copper and extra bones. The GLAMOUR of motorbikes covers this bleeding mess up, for the most part.

# Eight – Allies of Inconvenience

There are a lot of terms which can describe the huge, vaulted inside of the Hagia Sophia. Some talk of faith and incense, and some of arches and architecture and antiquity. Some describe a lingering smell of mustard, or a vague sense of being watched by things more dust and whispers than actual specters.

There are lots of terms.

One of them is, of course, 'bloody enormous'. Another – if you were to ask Eddie Weatherfield – was 'full of Nazis'.

Mrs Hazelwood had tied one to a pillar with an immense, tangled skein of knitting before Fyodor, Eddie and Lucky even arrived at the ornate balcony called the Empress' Loge. Apparently unperturbed, she was sitting on her wicker basket and enjoying a slice of cake on a tiny china plate.

"Caught 'im creeping about all stealthy-like', she said, showering crumbs. "I think they've done for the Turkish guards. Found one of them too, out like a light. Snoring, the poor dear. Lemon tart?"

Percy ducked back behind a pillar, pulling something thin and glistening from his neck. He sucked it experimentally.

"Cyanide. No…perhaps riacin."

Mrs Hazelwood bristled.

"Nothing but lemon juice and icing sugar, you cheeky bugger," she said, pointing with her cake fork. The zombie smiled, teeth appearing like a row of smashed-up headsdtones.

"*Poison darts*, my dear Mrs H. I think they have blowguns. And it's actually… a nasty mix of frog poison and mushroom juice. Tastes like boiled cabbage." He leaned back, and fired off a couple of shots with his silenced pistol into the dark. There was a muffled yelp, and then silence.

"Nice shot!" said Lucky. "Right in the forehead!"

"Well, he shouldn't be firing poison darts at strangers. How was he to know it wouldn't kill me? That's just bad manners!"

A red ember flared in the darkness, and a pair of guns, a sword and a very sharp- looking knitting needle twitched toward it. But it was only a burning dog-end dangling from the Compte De St Germain's lips. He surfaced from the gloom behind it with a stricken look on his face.

"Wotcher, all. This place gives me the willies, so it does, and me all immortal. *He's* here. I know it. The interfering bastard..."

"Who's here?" asked Eddie.

"J...j... *the baby from Bethlehem*, all right? I can sense him. It's *eerie*, is what it is. A premonition of uncertain life!"

"Don't you mean certain death?"

The Compte's look was withering.

"I know what I mean, pal. Death would be a *picnic* compared to some of the things I've had to live through. The black plague, for example, was no box of butterscotch. And *you* try being burned as a warlock seven times! Just because you don't die doesn't mean it doesn't hurt – plus, you spend a fortune on new clothes..."

Percy tried to calm him down.

"Of course you'd feel the presence of J... I mean, the beardy fella – here. This was once the biggest cathedral in Christendom!"

St Germain took a long, bitter drag on his roll-up and scowled.

"It's more than that. Or at least, I hope it isn't. But let's just get this over and done with, right? Where's Monkston with that bloody tracking scryer?"

"About that..." drawled a very dapper voice from the great black throne at the centre of the Loge. "We have a bit of a problem, chaps."

Major Monkston vaulted down from the high seat, combat-ready in a black opera cape, tuxedo and, of course, his obligatory top hat. Slung across his hip was a great silenced Thompson 'trench broom' submachinegun, and in his other hand…

Monkston threw the tracking scryer to the ground, and popped its glass globe under one immaculate patent-leather oxford. Something red, glowing and slippery flickered up and out, only to be caught between the Major's fingers. It disappeared with a pop of sparks and a horrid little squeal.

"*That* was a Black Sun tracing spell. Hidden inside *our* tracing spell, so it couldn't be detected. That means Schprinkler's boys know exactly where we are. We've led them to the spear of destiny."

"Crikey!" said Percy. "But that means..."

"Aye," said Lucky, cracking his knuckles. "We've got a mole in Section M HQ. There'll be bloody work to do when we get home."

"*If* we get home!"

"Och, don't be hysterical, Weatherfield. There's only so many Nazis in the Istanbul field office. What - ten, maybe twenty..."

"Mhhhhpty mmmmph," said the trussed-up German assassin, through Mrs Hazelwood's formless knitting.

"What was that?"

"Mhhhhmpty. Mmmphhh!"

Fyodor pulled the gag from his mouth. And at that moment, the lights came on.

Not the gentle glow of candles which usually filled the great house of worship. No – a pair of spotlights on wheeled trailers. They were accompanied by the sound of many, many weapons being loaded and cocked. That, and a familiar, smug voice.

"What he means to say is *sixty-eight*, my dear. Allied. Friends. Thanks to your silly little tracking spell, we have not only been able to follow you, but as you see, we have also… how do you say? Made the right. Old. Bastard of your day, yes?"

"We're not afraid of you, Schprinkler!" shouted Lucky, now ducked down tight behind the marble railing.

"I'd like a second opinion on that one," muttered Eddie.

"Whyever not?" chuckled the leader of the Black Sun. "You are caught between the hammer and the anvil, hmmm? My jolly pal the Erl King and his chums are behind you. I am in front of you. And here you are, eight. Silly. Little misfits, with nowhere to hide. Flies in my spiderweb in this game of cat und… *spider*, I suppose."

"*The Erl King?*" asked Major Monkston, his composure slipping for a single sickening moment. "Is he right?"

Eddie thought about the onrushing horde of spectral motorcyclists he'd seen coming out of the sky.

"Wellllll….." he began.

"Aye, sure and it's him all right," confirmed Lucky. "We were going to tell ye, but well, you know how it is..."

"Now!" shouted Schprinkler, displaying the enthusiasm Nazis always have for a good, loud megaphone. "Tell me the whereabouts of the spear, and you. May. Live."

Up on the balcony, several eyes of different colours met.

"We don't *know* where it is," hissed Percy.

"And even if we did – you know, honour, dignity, that sort of thing," said Monkston.

"Not to mention, he was a bit light on the details." put in Eddie.

"If we buy some time by telling him it's in the privies, or something..." suggested Fyodor.

"See, he didn't say how *long* we'd live for. Or *where*. I mean, he could mean we may live… in a horrible damp German dungeon somewhere. Or we may live… for another three and a half minutes."

Eddie was right into this new tangent of treachery. Lucky nodded.

"So your real problem is with the sort of dot, dot, dot thingy. The ellipsis."

"It's implied. *Heavily*. I frankly don't think he's the kind of evil Nazi magician we can trust."

Major Monkston sighed the kind of heavy sigh which is normally associated with plumbers looking deep into clogged-up lavatories.

"I suppose, King and Country and all that, we should just kill them."

Lucky waggled his impressive eyebrows.

"You reckon the old Isambard for starters? I'll follow up with the classic Dublin Dazzler?"

"What about Patience and Connor?" asked Saint Germain.

"Well… I hope old Schprinkler doesn't know they're on the roof. He called us *eight* misfits – not six. Between the two of them, they might be able to slow down the Erl King."

"For how long?" asked Eddie.

"How long do you reckon an ice lolly would last, in a toaster, in summer, in Hell?"

"Even the stick?"

"Even the box it came in. But don't worry – Connor the Beige is not one for famous last stands. And Patience is old enough to look after him."

This was neither the time nor the place, but Eddie just had to know.

"Erm… just exactly how old *is* Miss Patience?"

The magician stopped halfway in the act of taking off his top hat and shot him a pitying glance.

"A gentleman doesn't ask, you know, Weatherfield. But I'm accurately informed she was born in the Great Fire of London. Wren had to build a church over the spot she was… ahh, but not now. For *now*…" he rummaged elbow deep in the hat again, making goosebumps flow like cold custard across Eddie's skin. "There it is!"

Lesser mages must conjure with great tomes bound in human skin, slicked over with arcane lightning. Some prefer tablets carved in living stone with fiery runes, or scrolls dug up from inside mouldering desert tombs. Major Charlie Monkston, however, had learned a lot from his old granddad. He could confidently take on a small army of Nazis armed only with the 1938 Great Western Railway almanac. It was a slim volume, containing table after table of locomotive movements and departure times.

"Stall them for a minute, would you?" he asked, as he ran one white-gloved finger down the pages.

Saint Germain stood up.

"Fine. Fine. But you don't have forever, Sir, even if I apparently do."

The Count twisted the dial on his wrist, and made a complex series of passes with both hands, fingers blurring. Suddenly he was dressed in garish red and gold, a seventeenth-century costume of velvet and satin. He leaped up to the rail and whistled, one of those piercing, two-fingers-in-the-mouth jobs which can peel wallpaper and put a skin on a pitcher full of cream.

"*Hear ye, hear ye!* Welcome to the all singing, all dancing Squad 27 Punch and Judy show! For all you Nazi chaps who don't know him, old Mister punch is a lovely depiction of the typical London gent – to wit, a violent, drunken, cackling sod who assaults policemen and murders his own wife and child. Tonight, we present the tragical comedy of ol' Puncinello, with you bastards playing the role of everyone he whacks!"

There was even a spotlight. Saint Germain stood there like a gaudy gargoyle, gesturing wildly as his audience aimed a whole oily armoury of black steel up at him.

"Gentlemen? Kill. The. Wanker," ordered Hans Schprinkler. Sixty-three soldiers squeezed their triggers.

And this was the nature of M. Le Compte's immortality.

*All of them missed.*

A storm of lead chewed into the marble around him – at least, from those guns which didn't mysteriously jam, or explode, or have their magazines fall clattering to the floor in a most embarrassing fashion. Up on the balcony, Saint Germain took a long drag on his roll-up.

"Pillocks," he muttered. "You ready, boss?"

And Monkston was.

He came up wielding his hat between both hands, its unknown depths gaping like a tunnel to Hades. It seemed to grow bigger *while still staying the same size*, all while Monskton chanted a mysterious spell involving the names of stations along the old Great Western line.

It won't surprise many of you to learn that Isambard Kingdom Brunel was a wizard. Or that the rails he had laid down all those years ago reinforced a powerful telluric ley line, boosting its signal strength.

*"Displace the driver and fireman, calculate for the rotation of the Earth..."* muttered Monkston...

Somewhere between Chippenham and Bath a locomotive roared through the night, its lights blacked out and the orange glow from its firebox shielded by special wartime plating. Behind it came a train of boxcars hauling materials for the war effort – in this case, roll upon roll of barbed wire, can upon can of baked beans and a single crate of fine scotch whiskey.[19] Ahead loomed the black escarpment and the ancient arch of the Box Tunnel.

"'Ere,' said the fireman, peering through a slit in the armour plating. "Did the old tunnel used to have them glowing runes all round it, Tommy?"

"Enochian or Armaic?"

"Just take a butcher's, you pikelet!"

Tommy's mouth gaped open as something silvery and tenebrous flickered in the mouth of the tunnel. For a second he saw ornate columns, and spotlights, and black-clad Nazi soldiers...

Then there came a pop like a small, embarrassed thunderclap. There was a smell of sawdust, engine oil and old blood. And the driver of the 9:15 Special Freight found himself sitting at the table of a small country pub in rural Scotland. Across from him sat his fireman, staring in bemusement at a large plate of haggis and chips. A half-smoked roll-up dropped from his open mouth and into a pint of best bitter.

The driver's eyes swiveled like those of a ventriloquist's dummy.

Somebody had to say it.

"If we're here, Albert..."

"Yuuuuurrrsss?"

"Well... if we're here... *where's the sodding train?*"

Where it was would have taken a lot of explaining at that point. The space it twisted and howled through was outside of this and any world – a place where things with too many tentacles and feelers and teeth fumbled for the light and solidity of it, so hungry there was room for nothing else in their hacksaw-scrabble minds...

Where it *emerged*, though, was directly from the hole in Charlie Monkston's hat. Out into the great vault of the Hagia Sophia, its

---

19 For the trainspotters, this was in fact one of the Stanier class 8F locomotives, of which British Rail inventoried exactly six hundred and sixty six. Because we all know who's really running the railroads, and He is not a subtle entity when it comes to magic numbers.

whistle piercing the night, its blackout lamps casting a fan of light ahead of it.

This was where it all began to go wrong for Hans Schprinkler.

Several tons of red-hot, blazing locomotive came smashing down out of nowhere, utterly obliterating a score of his soldiers. Flames belched from its twisted smokestack as it tore itself apart on impact. Iron wheels bounced and rolled and wrecked… all while a chain of boxcars smashed themselves to splinters against the marble pillars of the nave.

It was an impressive sight for Eddie Weatherfield, who whooped as the great metal beast slid across the floor in a shower of sparks.

*"Up and at the bastards!"* roared Lucky, leaping over the balcony as if the drop below just wasn't there. Percy looked over the railing, shrugged, and then grinned.

"Come on!"

Private Weatherfield pelted after the zombie and down the stairs, knuckles white around the grip of his sword. He ran into Percy's back as he skidded to a stop inside a recessed doorway.

"Gosh, this is pretty exciting, isn't it?" asked the long-dead Percival. "And not a second too soon. I'm feeling a bit peckish, you know."

Eddie peered out into the main vault of the great museum, where chaos reigned. As he watched, Lucky let loose a dazzling blast of reflected rainbows. Where they struck they burned like concentrated acid, raising a chorus of screams. Nazi skeletons turned bright yellow, shocking pink and sky blue as they dissolved, howling.

"You actually *eat* the enemy?"

"Well, I know it's silly. I'll only be hungry again in half an hour. But you know, old chap. Fortunes of war and all that… plus, they often taste of sauerkraut. Yum yum!"

Now Eddie could see that Mrs Hazelwood was amid the fray as well, her possessed crystal ball sizzling with magical discharge. Without Connor or Patience to counter him, Hans Schprinkler was able to hurl bolt after bolt of raw magic at his enemies, and it was only the mad medium's dead husband who could stop them. Saint Germain fought with a curious, sidling efficiency, shuffling amid his foes as if he was ballroom dancing to an invisible orchestra. Around him Nazis fell on their own bayonets, pistols blew up in their hands… and once or twice the wig-wearing old scoundrel had to reach out and offer a desultory stab with his thin, jewel-encrusted rapier.

"Tally ho!" shouted Percy, unlacing the stitches at the corners of his mouth. His head hinged open, revealing a glistening red maw which would feature in Eddie's nightmares ever after. Any thoughts of just hanging back were dashed, as a group of Black Sun sturmtroopers pointed and shouted, leveling their guns.

It was at precisely that moment that Eddie realized *he had no idea how to turn his powers on.* There was no obvious magic word. Both other times he'd been terrified, but this time he was beyond all the gibbering and twitching. Adrift in a calm place, while his brain refused to believe he was watching, for example, a seven-foot leprechaun punch the head off a gas-masked Nazi's shoulders.

Perhaps a good battle cry?

"Aaaaaarrrrggggghhh!" roared Eddie Weatherfield, as terrifying as an enraged sheep. There was definitely something lacking there. Ahead of him, Percy had reached his first target (perhaps a small entree), and had bitten off his arm and half of his shoulder with it.

Eddie clenched his buttocks, clenched his fists around the grip of his shield and sword, screwed his eyes shut, and tried the battle cry again.

"Aaaaaaaaaaaaaaaaaarrrrrrrggggggggghhh!"

This time there was a little flicker of magic. It was about as powerful as the pop of static you might get from a cat on a plush carpet. But Hans Schprinkler noticed.

"STOP! HALT! EVERYONE!"

His voice was backed up with a great thaumic slap, like an invisible mattress *whumphing* down over the whole battle. *Everyone* stopped. On both sides. Here and there, little knots of sturmtroopers paused in loading and aiming a collection of guns. Saint Germain stood still, his fencing sword jammed through a dying man's throat. Mrs Hazelwood was a little head-scarf-wearing statue, hands held high as her crystal ball thrummed with power. Percy was frozen in mid-bite, his intended snack caught just in the act of screaming. Eddie wondered where he'd produced the knife, fork and napkin from. Even Lucky and Monkston stopped, turning to look where the leader of the Black Sun pointed.

Right at Eddie.

"Who brought *this* guy, hmm? Come on. Own up. You know, this is a *war*, right? A proper one, for. The. Grown-ups!" Now he turned his pentacle-etched monocle and horrible scars on Eddie, a prim little smile on his face.

"So, what exactly were you trying to do, boy? Are you… *keine scheisse*… what is the Englander word… *constipated?*"

If red-hot, searing embarrassment could be harnessed to a generator, Eddie Weatherfield would have been able to power a medium-sized city at that moment. He looked down at his feet and scuffed his combat boots in the dust.

"'s a war cry. Trying to turn into a monster."

Schprinkler cupped one leather-gloved hand around his ear.

"Louder, please. I can't hear you."

*"I'm trying to turn into a berserker, right? It's just..."*

Schprinkler nodded, sadly.

"It's just that good old Charlie Monkston, the clever-clogs fecking Englander magician man, *didn't bother to tell you how.* Yet another terrible thing to weigh on his conscience, if he even has one left." He shook his head. "No, you and your General Crowley think we Nazis are sooooo evil, but *you* are the. Ones. Sending. Children to die. *It's not even as if he has enough power in him to bother draining!"*

Monkston took a step forward, his hand out, his mouth open as if he was about to say something...

But Hans Schprinkler was too fast.

And in that instant, he shot Eddie Weatherfield in the head.

+++

Up on the roof of the great museum, Patience heard the shot. It plucked at some invisible thread deep within her soul – a part of her which was once known as Mother Greycap, the Seeress of Oxted. Because of the echo of that ancient, seventeenth-century crone, Patience could sometimes see fragments of the future.

Right now, that future featured swastika flags flying from the cracked and blackened tower of Big Ben.

She gritted her teeth, and pushed the vision aside. She blinked back tears. And she reached out to grab Connor the Beige by the scruff of his cardigan.

*"We should be down there! It's all coming to a tangle, and I can't see past it!"*

Connor scowled, as only a Scots wizard can. His eyebrows locked into a titanic death-grip over the top of his nose.

"Lass, I need ye to bloody *concentrate!* If we cannae raise yon shades and specters, we're all gonnae be wearing tyre-tread tattoos in aboot ten seconds!

For indeed, the Wild hunt was upon them. A ghostly light flickered around the onrushing horde of motorcycles as they came up off the waters of the straits, engines thundering. In the lead, a figure in ornate green armour, huge antlers jutting from his brows like twin explosions of bone.

"Stand aside, mortal fools!' bellowed the Erl King, his voice carrying like a foghorn in a library for the deaf. "Or become my prey!"

"Och, pack it in, ye old livestock-botherer," said Connor, rolling up the sleeves of his cardy. "Patience? Have ye got any names for me?"

The Revenge of English Witchcraft furrowed her very pretty brow and concentrated, hard. Deep below the museum – deep, in fact, below the cathedral it had once been, when emperors still wore garden clippings on their heads and the toga was the height of fashion – were the tombs of Byzantium's sages. Each one of them was a wizard the equal of any alive today. Though, sadly, the majority had been reduced by time and worms and general bad maintenance to a few bones, and a gaggle of somewhat confused ghosts.

"Ummm… Connor. *They say they don't want to come out.*"

Now the Erl King was half a mile out and closing. He drew a sword which seemed to writhe uncomfortably against the darkness, as if the metal itself was allergic to reality. It made the sound, as it cleared the scabbard, of a fingertip across oiled glass.

"What do ye *mean* they don't want tae come out?" asked Connor, his eyes bulging like boiled eggs. "We're helping them save their bloody last resting place, aren't we? We're the sodding *good guys* in this situation, unless I'm verra' much mistaken!"

Once again, Patience sent a great spike of power spearing down through the roots of the Hagia Sophia. What came back was a red-hot, itchy feeling of acute embarrassment.

"They… they say they don't actually want to meet Him. If it's all right by us, they'll just let him do his thing and they'll stay in the crypt until he's gone…"

"Who? The bloody Erl King?"

Patience was almost at the end of her namesake. This time, the power she sent sizzling through the stones was more than a little interrogative. The ghosts of a hundred dead sages howled, a sound like Hell's own hillbilly jug-band.

"Not him. **Him**. With a capital… oh, *shit!*"

Patience and Connor turned at the same time, just as a golden light flared atop the dome. It was pretty fair to say it was almost completely out of place, but then again, who knows what arrangements exist between the higher powers? What that light revealed, in a glissando of crazed harp and trumpet fanfares, was a figure all in white. And army camouflage. With crossed bullet belts, and sandals floating a foot above the marble slabs before he got to grips with the whole gravity thing, and slid down to the parapet, hair streaming out in an invisible breeze. This strange and bearded apparition carried an entire drum-magazine-fed Bren gun in each hand, with apparently no effort.

"Jesus Christ!" exclaimed Connor the Beige. "I see they taught ye all about turning up in the nick of time, then?"

Somewhere far below, the Compte De Saint Germain threw up just a little bit in the back of his mouth.

"Please," said the newcomer, winking over the top of his aviator sunglasses at Patience. "There's no need for formality. Call me J.C."

A wave of hovering motorcycles came up to meet them, then – the whole Wild hunt, the ghostly images of horses flickering like a very bad special effect around the outlines of a gang of elves in fur and silver mail, brandishing obsidian and copper blades. The Erl King recoiled in horror as he dragged his sword to a halt, pointing accusingly at a face recognizable to anyone who had ever seen a nativity play.

"No! That's… **impossible!** We have *weakened* you! We have taken away your apoth… apitho… aposto…" he clicked his fingers, head tilted on one side. "Help me out here, will you?"

"Australopithacus?" ventured Connor, puzzled.

"Apologies?" tried a thin-faced elven hunter, his helmet an entire bear's skull.

"Apoplexy?" guessed another, fiddling with a great hook-bladed copper sickle.

Patience smiled. It was a sharp, horrible little smile.

"I think the word you are looking for is *apotheosis*. Which means…"

Jesus of Nazareth gently nudged her out of the way, leveling both of his guns at the green-armoured leader of the hunt.

"It means I magicked up these bad boys with my holy powers. So the bullets in them might still be nothing but the *ghosts* of full-metal-jacket hollow-point slugs engraved with the names of my mates the Saints, then marinaded in that cheeky communion beaujolais which pumps through my veins. *Or they might be horribly real.* The question you have to ask yourself is… *are you feeling lucky?*"

Connor hefted his staff, sending magic sizzling down its length.

"Before ye answer, remember, *we're* the ones with the leprechaun."

Patience moved her hands in a complex pattern, causing great green-glowing pentacles to spring shimmering from her palms.

"And for the record, 'apotheosis' means elevation to divinity. For you slower elves in the back."

The Erl King's faceless helmet scrunched up in rage, with a sound like a hubcap being crushed in a vise.

"There's still only three of you! Hunters – **take them!**'"

It would be nice to say that there were no words for the noise which followed. But there were. A kind of buzzsaw shriek came from the horde of the Wild Hunt, a titanic thunder of motorcycle engines, the war cries of a hundred demented elves… and then the silence which bloomed from Patience's fingertips, an anti-sonic shockwave behind a wave-front of green. This was the old witchcraft of England, and despite the testimony of many silly little children's storybooks, the wildwood had no love for the elves, who capered through nature like a combine harvester through a kindergarten.

Patience Goodhallow's magic moved through them the same way, impaling and throttling with the scent of new sap, old blood and summer flowers.

Through it hammered the blasts of Connor's gnarled old wizarding staff, like a shotgun loaded with needles of ice. While the jade-green coils and thorns of Patience's magic tied them up, those icy detonations shredded them to scraps of fur and velvet and copper mail, with the blue blood of the elves misting the air between. Wrecked motorcycles fell from the sky in a fortean confusion.

But it was not enough. Not when the Erl King himself broke away and circled back, picking up speed, his sword held aloft like a crack in the sky. A roundhouse swing of the blade sent out a wave-front of black flame, withering up the sorcery of both witch and wizard alike.

"Your human magics are weak!" screeched the demented, antlered figure as it came flying at them, exhaust pipes trailing oily smoke. "Behold the true fire of *Tirfeynn*!"

Patience stole a look at Connor.

"Is he *mad*? The lost realm of the elves? Even bloody Titania's not *that* unhinged..."

Connor nodded.

"Does that look like a rational demigod to ye, lass? And ken the sword. Those who took Tirfeynn have their hooks in him, too!"

*Horrible pointy death rushed on, needle teeth glistening...*

But at the last moment – very much in his particular idiom – there was Jesus Christ.

"Bless you, my children, for I am with you," he drawled. "And now - let He who is without sin blast the first elf!"

Muzzle flash erupted in a pair of slow motion reflections across his mirrored sunglasses. The receivers of his twin bren guns jackhammered back and forth, stitching glowing lines of fire across the sky. And where those sacred bullets hit, whole engine blocks were punched through. Fuel tanks erupted into twisted metal fireballs. elves were plucked from their saddles and thrown tumbling into the night, only to detonate like damp little fireworks above the Straits of Marmara.

The hail of sanctified lead pummeled the Erl King, who heeled his Brough Superior around on its back wheel, carving a blazing skidmark in the air. His sword, held high, really *was* a gap through into a darkened otherworld, where far too many horrible bloodshot eyes were pressed up against it, hungry and intent.

"Curse you, Nazarene! *You will fall!*"

"Not before you, though," replied Jesus, throwing his guns aside, spent. His hand slipped inside his robes and came out holding a very real, very large hand grenade[20]. He pulled the pin with his teeth. "Catch!"

The Erl King, for all his madness, was still a stalker. A *predator*. And like a cat entranced by a ball of yarn, there was no way the master huntsman could stop his hand from lashing out, and his armoured fingers plucking the grenade from the air. It was as natural to him as breathing.

Unfortunately, in this case, it was as smart as breathing concentrated mustard gas.

In one instant all those hungry, gelid eyes were gone from the blade of his sword, sucked away with a series of oily pops. He looked at the bomb in his fist with a mask of green copper, and his antlers seemed to droop.

"Oh, bugge..."

The explosion threw Connor, Patience and Jesus backwards, sliding across the rooftop and halfway around the dome. A spinning chrome badge reading 'Brough motorcycle company' whickered past Connor's ear and embedded itself an inch deep in the marble.

Amid the echoing, ringing aftermath, Patience struggled to her feet. She offered her hand to Christ, who she hauled up and out of the

---

20 Not that one. But he did count to exactly three.

way as (according to the narrative laws which govern such events) a flaming wire-spoke wheel rolled past where he had been lying.

"Do you think that'll do it?"

Jesus shrugged.

"Not for long, I suspect. That guy and his little crew were juiced up on some wild magic. Some of *mine*, if I'm not mistaken. That means they're less like regular people, and I'm..."

"Less of a supernatural personification of the principle of death and rebirth, than an actual Jewish carpenter with a fancy pair of sunglasses?" finished Connor.

"Pretty much nailed it. Only so much magic to go round."

Patience nodded.

"Which is why we need that spear. Listen? Can you hear what's going on down there in the museum?"

"You mean *my* spear?" asked Jesus. "Only, see, I kind of wanted to take care of that myself..."

Patience bristled, her eyes literally flashing.

"*Yours?* Where the heck were you when the bloody Nazis stole your precious grail, then? We were arse-deep in changelings, while you were probably hanging out in the Vatican, enjoying a nice communion cabernet!"

The erstwhile King of Kings winced.

"In a very real way, miss, this version of me has only existed since Schprinkler and his goons started taking away my powers. One minute you're the nebulous collective spirit of a billion people's belief, then poof! You wake up outside a kebab shop in what turns out to be modern Bethlehem, stark naked, with horrible scars on your hands and feet and a burning desire to punch Caesar in the nose. It's not easy!"

There might have been a very interesting metaphysical argument just then.

There might even have been a full-blown slap fight between Jesus Christ and an actual, factual witch, of a type not seen since the 12th century.

But at that moment, a curse rang out in the silence below them, followed by a scream.

Not a scream of pain, mind you. And not one that stopped.

This was a scream of pure inhumanity, like a slab of white-hot metal being pulled in half by titanic pincers. Clear across the dome from them, a section of ornate marble glowed red for a second, then blasted outwards in a spray of molten rock.

"Team up?" asked Jesus, his grin more than a little shaky.

"Team up," agreed Connor and Patience at once.

*While behind them, a figure emerged slowly from the waters of Istanbul harbour, dripping, trailing seaweed and garbage and slime.*

It came ashore clear across the bay from the Hagia Sophia, squelching up an incline of mud, then a slipway where boats were hauled out of the water for repairs.

One of its antlers was comically bent upside down. Its armour was scorched black and dented like tin foil. But a terrible red light burned in the eye-slits of its helm, and across its back it carried a frosty, steaming greatsword.

This apparition staggered between the warehouses until it reached a road, and stepped out just as a local came blattering along the cobbles on an antiquated 1919 Indian Scout. The rider took one look at the huge, mud-dripping figure blocking the roadway and slid to a halt, his eyes wide behind a pair of aviator goggles. Some kind of horrible imperative, bounced back and forth through the years and resonating in a strange part of his brain, made him gulp as he looked at those red eyes in a metal face, those segmented metal fingers curled up to point a finger at him.

"I need your clothes, your boots, and your motorcycle," said the Erl King, drawing his sword…

+++

The thing with your life flashing before your eyes…

The thing is…

Well, you really have to have *both eyes.*

Eddie Weatherfield's head snapped backwards as his eyeball made the acquaintance of a sizable chunk of honest German lead, spiraling in at just under the speed of sound. There was a horrible little gristly pop. There was a sensation of many, many shards springing apart, hovering in a glittering cloud, then fusing back together again.

And, true to form, a sped-up filmstrip of all the weird, strange, arcane, occult, macabre and downright silly things which had happened to Eddie in the past couple of days stuttered across half of his mental movie screen. The other half, though -

Well, the other half was *on fire.*

From the outside, it looked something like this.

Eddie tried to clap a hand to his ruined eye socket. That was the first surprise for Hans Schprinkler, who was;

a) no stranger to shooting people in the face

b) himself a victim of spectacular ocular trauma and

c) kind of expecting the bullet to come out the other side, in a splattering style soon to be made famous by Jackson Pollock.

Instead, that hand was forced aside by a lance of fire. It was a hundred feet long if it was an inch, white at the core and feathering away to blue. Eddie gurgled and spun about, sending the beam scything through a trio on SS soldiers. They didn't so much catch on fire as *disintegrate*, chopped neatly across at chest height before they exploded into red-hot dust. Burning bones clattered down.

"Wuuuuuurgh," attempted Eddie, as the fire narrowed even further, becoming a filament of purple light, hot as Hell's condiment selection. Several of the great hanging lamps which studded the vault of the Hagia Sophia were sliced from their moorings, exploding against the ground.

And *here* came the change.

Private Weatherfield was not what anyone would call a large man. So when his right arm suddenly bulged with muscle, it looked as if a particularly clumsy butcher was using him to make a string of sausages. His left arm followed suit, as a glow like banked-up embers outlined his whole frame. The flames from his eye guttered out, and he was pulled to his feet, back arched, bones stretching and bending with a sound like a fat lady's corset in a class-five hurricane.

"Fascinating!" whispered Schprinkler and Major Monkston at the same time.

Eddie landed on his knees, his body now grotesquely bulked out, with muscles in all the wrong places. His sword looked like a mere pocketknife, clenched in fingers like saveloys. He lifted his head and a great glowing eye revolved back around from the white, revealing a yellow iris and a slit black pupil. Hellfire danced merrily within.

"Mister Schprinkler?" he purred, his voice like the rasp of an oiled bonesaw. "I know how it works, now. The pain, and the fear...*they call the dragons*. They let me see the place where the dragons went, when the Netherspawn came calling. And Mr Schprinkler? The battle cry I was going for..." he fumbled around in his too-wide mouth for a second, fishing something from between his too-sharp teeth. It clattered to the floor, small and pitiful. A flattened bullet.

"It went something like *this*..."

The roar was heard across the sleeping city of Istanbul. Children cried. Dogs howled. Cats shat themselves, then immediately pretended that it hadn't happened. Even the Erl King, throwing his leg over the saddle of a rather battered old 1919 Indian Scout, shuddered in his armour. It shivered the foundations of the Hagia Sophia, and set all those hanging lamps on their long, long chains to jangling.

Lucky took his fingers out of his ears as the echoes subsided.

"Aye, that's more like it, boy. Though you were a bit flat in the top end..."

Eddie turned a look on him which was part wild-eyed grin and part terrible, terrible hunger.

"I reckon you should get along with the others and grab that spear about now, Sarge. I have a feeling that *berserk...* urrrgh... means what it does for a... *arrrgh...* reason...."

Hans Schprinkler wasn't having it.

"Oh, you may have found your voice. But we have ways. Of. Making you... not talk? Did that come out right?" He turned to his soldiers, who seemed suddenly far less keen on fulfilling the glorious destiny of the fatherland. "All right." He shrugged. "See if you can kill him."

There was a general shuffling of feet and scratching of coal-scuttle helmets.

Schprinkler reached into his coat, and - with the most menacing sound of steel on steel ever committed to paper - drew forth a sword of ancient design, carved with runes. One of which was a glowing red swastika.

"Or do I have to do *everything* around here myself! For the love of all things evil, Hans, Jurgen, Rudolf? We are the *bad guys*, remember!"

Forty-odd remaining guns were leveled at Eddie as he watched the squad fall back. He hefted his shield, waiting for the storm of lead. And somewhere in the background, he heard one of the sturmtroopers mutter a question.

"Wait? What? *Are* we *the bad guys*? Seriously?"

But before the first bullet could fly, there came a piercing whistle from the gallery above.

"*Not so fast, ye Nazi scunner.* We'll be taking the spear, and we'll be leaving ever so polite-like. You, however, can go back an' tell yon Fuhrer that ye've lost again."

It was Connor the Beige, along with Patience... and another fellow, who seemed to be wearing a bathrobe and combat trousers. The Compte De Saint Germain pointed, groaned, turned green, and threw up noisily behind a pillar.

"We will. See. About...' began Schprinkler, but Connor's face – never the most pleasant of physiognomies – was contorted into a gargoyle scowl.

"*Incantus ferrus magneticum!*" he snarled, gesturing with his shillelagh. At once, all of the guns flew from the Nazi soldiers' hands, along with several buttons and – in one painful and unlucky case – a couple of dental fillings. Hans Schprinkler held onto his sword with both hands, grimacing with effort. Red lightning crawled and raved from the runic swastika on its blade. Connor held the ball of slowly spinning metal for an instant, perspiration beading his brow, then he shrugged and threw it out through the nearest stained-glass window, scattering it all into the night amid a storm of colours.

Schprinkler staggered, holding his sword aloft.

"A valiant effort, wizard. But it's all you had in you, yes? And I still have one. More. Card to play..."

Before anyone could stop him, the leader of the Black Sun reached into his greatcoat and produced a small black box. He threw it to the floor, where it sat, steaming gently. As Squad 27 watched, horrified, it began to play a rather soppy little tune.

"Nice," said Patience, "But you can't really *dance* to it. Mrs Hazelwood, would you be so kind as to try the column in the far north corner. The one with the picture of an eye on it." she looked scornfully at the remaining Nazis, many of whom were having to hold up their pants with both hands. "By the way, boys. *Rubus Plicatus Incapacitatus!*"

Blackberry vines – thick as hosepipes, spiked like razorwire – erupted from nowhere, binding up hands and feet, and in some cases (with quite a bit of squealing) other parts as well. The only one who escaped was Schprinkler himself, who simply swiped left and right with his blade, withering the vines as they sprouted from the smooth marble floor.

"That's right, witch!

This is the sword *Unaussprechlichelangeweileklingdunkelheit* – forged for an opera by Wagner which was supposed to last for seventeen weeks! It can suck the magic out of *anything* and render it down into pure. Tedious. Mathematics!"

"Coo-ee!" called Mrs Hazelwood. "This pillar's all cold and slimy. They ought to call a plumber. But you're right, dear. There's a hole."

Schprinkler inclined his head, grinning like a cat who has just invented the canary sandwich.

"Thank you *so* much for retrieving my spear for me, ladies," he said, sketching a little bow. "And tell the zombie not to bother. This sword will slice his bullet in half faster than he can say 'personal hygeine'. As for your pet monster…"

They all heard it, just as the pillar rumbled open, revealing a hollow, frozen space inside. A single tap from her floating crystal ball and Mrs Hazelwood broke the sheath of ice which had formed around the Spear of Destiny, the product of theological resonance condensing inside a powerful thaumic field.

But it wasn't the grind of stone on stone which made every last person in the great museum pause.

It was a footstep.

The kind of footstep normally only associated with giants. Or with big huge lizards which should have the decency to remain extinct. At Hans Schprinkler's feet, the music box tinkled and plinged, while he chuckled. Another footstep rocked the building, closer this time.

"Now, young Herr Weatherfield," smiled the Nazi sorcerer, as something immense and dark loomed up behind the tiny windows inset in the dome. "What is the delightful English saying? Ahhh, yes. ***Say hello to my little friend!***"

# Nine – The Obligatory Horror of Nazi Super-Science

Erdem Serkat had a legitimate reason to be skulking around the docks of Istanbul at midnight. He had, in fact, carefully memorized one he prepared earlier, just in case the police took an interest in what the ragged, furtive-looking little fellow with the long coat and comically small fez was up to.

It was quite convincing. It involved a lost dog, a ruined dinner, an irate mother-in-law, and a bucket of crabs.

What he was *actually* doing was helping to promote neighbourhood security awareness. By way of the old tradition of trying every doorknob in a row of warehouses to see if any of them were unlocked.

He had expected, perhaps, to have to answer some sharp questions about the crowbar slipped down inside his trouser leg, or the as-yet empty hemp sacks which he hoped might yet be filled as the night went by. He had also brought his second-best shoes, as it might be possible he'd have to run.

What Erdem Serkat had not expected, of course, was for the pier behind him to suddenly make a horrible, splintering, cracking noise, and lever up and over into the street like a great salt-crusted tongue. He certainly hadn't been prepared for the reason *why*, either – an enormous black submarine, red lights picking out its conning tower and superstructure. If the little puddle which dripped from the leg of his pants was any indication, what happened next was a bit of a stumper as well.

As the hapless thief watched, searchlights fore and aft slammed on, bathing the decks of the U-boat in a hard, clinical glow. Pneumatic couplings chuffed and hissed as they blew away, hoses writhing against the glare. Serkat tried very hard to become one with the brick wall he was pressed up against, as a cylinder the size of a building rose up from the belly of the submarine, ratcheting upright on what seemed to be a single great trunk of metal. Then two more erupted from the sides of the cylinder, popping out from hidden trap doors. They were tipped with three-fingered claws, and they came down on either side of the sub, one into the turbid black water, one smashing clear through a warehouse roof.

The cylinder rose. What appeared to be a tank turret grew from its upper surface, with a series of oily clunks and whines. And now more trapdoors rattled open, revealing a pair of mechanical arms. One ended in a gigantic bunch of 88mm cannons, the other in a cleaver the size of a trolley bus.

This behemoth, all black iron and stinking diesel smoke, dragged itself ashore, its three segmented legs moving with a jerky kind of stop-motion gait. Flares of orange fire chuffed from a pair of smokestacks protruding from what, had Erdem Serkat been a vulgar man, he would have identified as its arse.

A test-swing of that giant serrated cleaver lopped the chimneypot off of the warehouse. The clutch of cannons spun on clattering cog-wheels, shells snicking into place.

And then the machine screamed.

It was not a sound which Erdem Serkat ever wanted to hear again. In fact, as soon as he found another pair of trousers, the poor miscreant bought a fast donkey and headed east, where he changed his name and settled in far-off Samarkand, making and selling a range of herbal soaps.

The scream was part fury and part agony. It was part bloody and organic, part cold and mechanical. The worst part, though – the part which made Serkat eat his comically tiny hat – was that it was *right here*. A sound from nightmares, amplified through a crown of dripping wet bullhorns.

The little thief was the only one who heard it. In fact, it should have been hard to miss the great war-engine as it stomped its way through the city, preceded by a shimmering exhalation of sorcery.

But people *did* miss it. Something made them slam their shutters and look away, or roll over in their sleep, cursing and mumbling. A glamour unfolded from the great clanking, striding tripedal thing as it headed purposefully for the Hagia Sophia, periodically giving vent to a sound like a moose being torn in half.

No – people didn't *want* see it. Their brains turned to cottage cheese at the mere insinuation of such a thing. It was a vast, bible-black cutout in their memories, seconds after it shouldered its way past the next row of buildings. But the Erl King saw it. And what he saw inside it made him clench his armoured fingers tight around the handlebars of his newly stolen motorcycle.

His helm bloomed with fern-fronds of frost as the mind behind it – already so far beyond the horizon of sanity that it should have remembered to bring a towel – recoiled with horror.

Because there's a certain gravitas to being a crazed villain. It's almost expected, when you're the huntsman for an immortal fey maniac in a million-dollar evening gown. But then there's the oily, clockwork type of mind which considers the whole sanity spectrum to be a meaningless sideshow. *The kind which would carve up and flay a live elf, and weld it into a machine made of cold iron, still breathing.*

The Erl King tried not to remember the hooks and the blood and the raw nerve-endings he soared into the sky. He tried to blot out the harmonics of gibbering madness which radiated from the war-engine like stink from a week-dead skunk. That, and the tiny voice which scrabbled inside his head, whispering 'kill me kill me kill me kill me kill me kill me...'

*The Queen would hear of this! These treacherous Nazi humans were* **monsters***, worse than those which had swallowed up Tirfeynn!*

After all, *those* monsters had had an excuse.

And in the meantime – well, perhaps this blasphemous thing would be enough to crush that horrid little human demigod. Perhaps that meant he could leave now, without it looking like running away.

This was an unspeakably welcome thought for Earl Kingsford, Taxidermist. He'd filled a lot of creatures which didn't know when to make a hasty exit with foam rubber and old newspapers.

The Erl King laid down a track of tyre-tread fire in blue and purple, slamming the clouds shut behind him as he went.

But the massive war-machine lumbered on, weeping and howling as the elf inside it followed the sound of a very precisely tuned music box.

And an order to *kill*.

+++


Eddie Weatherfield was ready when a great black-iron blade came bulldozering through the wall. More ready than he'd been for any maths test, or funeral, or air raid drill, or date, or even for his own tenth birthday party.

In fact, it really didn't matter what Hans Schprinkler had summoned. He'd never felt so *angry* before. Not even when his tenth birthday party had proven to consist only of his grandparents, an incontinent sheep, and a lopsided cake that read 'sorry about your bunions'.

A pure, crystalline state of fury lifted him up, focusing his mind down to a flame which could slice through steel.

*Shoot me in the head, will you? That's worse than nasty. That's downright* **impolite!**

So as the entire eastern end of the Hagia Sophia was ripped away, and a great tripedal monstrosity swung at him with a cleaver the size of a banqueting table, Eddie leaped forward to face it.

Up, and he stepped off one of the hanging lamps, setting its long chain to jangling. Then his body was spinning in midair, shield flashing out, runes all scarred and glowing around its rim.

Metal struck metal in a detonation of gold and blue sparks. The impact should have driven the poor little human into the marble floor up to his neck, magic or no magic – but it spectacularly failed to do so. Instead, that immense cleaver-blade was stopped dead in its blurring arc, and Eddie felt an immense force vibrate deep in the metal of his shield. He pushed himself off the blade, spun backwards, and lashed out with his sword, scoring a deep gash in the black iron barrel of the thing's body.

He landed lightly, bringing up his guard, and the machine-beast *howled*, the bullhorns clustered around its tank-turret head spitting rage.

Inside that gash, coolant and hydraulic fluids bubbled. Electricity sparked from severed wires.

"Sorry to break it to you, Hans," grinned Eddie. "But your little toy here isn't quite what it's cracked up to be."

A three-clawed foot stomped down, lightning fast, trying to flatten him. Eddie put the shield up over his head and fended it away, making the war-machine totter and collapse against the ruined wall of the museum. It righted itself, bringing its clutch of cannons to bear and rattling off a series of shots. Each one rung Eddie's shield like a bell, ricochets punching holes in the dome, the walls, and in one case the war-engine itself.

Hans Schprinkler was still laughing, though. He was perched atop one of the hanging lamps, swinging back and forth like a sailor in a hurricane. It was definitely the kind of laugh which doctors who stock coats that zip up at the back would be familiar with.

"You. Cannot. Defeat me, Weatherfield! I am the *bad guy!* Have you any idea the *power* you can unlock, if you admit to yourself that you're truly rotten? Hundreds of years of stories. Thousands! And all you have to do is never actually fight the hero. Never tie the bastard up and deliver the big *sprechen*, you know?"

Another swipe with that immense cleaver, and Eddie rolled under it, coming up to strike at the arm which wielded it. Hydraulic pipes writhed like licorice serpents. He split them in a shower of hot fluid.

"It looks like I'm doing all right, pal," grunted Eddie, leaping back out of the way of another stomping claw. Behind him, he heard the roar of a motor. One of the artfully inlaid, massively carved wooden doors came sailing past, then slid across the marble floor. He jumped over it as it was chopped to matchwood.

"But you are no *hero*, Private Weatherfield. A fool. A liar. An imbecile who was in the wrong place at the wrong time. All you did was crash a very. Expensive. Aeroplane, hmm? Now, look at what your *dumbkopfery* has bought you!"

The great iron war machine screamed with pain as Hans Schprinkler held out his hand, red lighting pouring from his fingers. For an instant, Eddie could see the shape of something almost human trapped inside, with tubes and needles stuffed into its eyes and ears and... well, it seemed that they'd just kept making holes until they ran out of tubes and needles. Its back arched in pain.

And then – the metal began to *heal*.

Pipes knit back together. Ragged gashes in its armour melted and flowed. The bullhorns around its head let loose a sound that could have been laughter, and it squared up again, pistons arms chuffing and clanking.

"Amazing species, the elves," commented Schprinkler. "Their ability to survive is truly unsurpassed. And their fear of iron generates such a wonderful amount of magical vitae. Tangible hatred. A resource I have so. Many. Uses for..."

Eddie came up at him snarling, his sword a blur. It met the blade of the terrible *Unaussprechlichelangeweileklingdunkelheit* in a detonation of flame, and Eddie felt the power of that cursed relic gnawing at him, sucking the magic from his bones.

Parry, thrust, swing, stab, hack... each time Schprinkler blocked him – one handed, damn it! And smiling! - a little of his strength and rage bled away. The *Unaussprechlichelangeweileklingdunkelheit* filled his mind with the oppressive tedium of blowflies blattering aimlessly against midsummer attic windows. Of rainy Sunday afternoons in the parlours of spinster aunts. Of the last hideous stretches of mathematics exams…

But Eddie Weatherfield was armed with the least magical sword in the universe. If Connor's staff, or Patience's wand, Mrs Hazelwood's crystal ball (or any number of big enchanted pieces of cutlery) had slammed into that silvery, swastika-blazoned blade, they would have acted like a drinking straw in a coconut, turning wizards and witches into mere dead civilians. Dried out, mummified ones.

Eddie's sword was just the opposite. It was a big lump of sharp steel made to kill people with. It was as determinedly unromantic as a shopping trolley or a boot scraper. And it had a trick up its metaphorical sleeve.

"You are no hero, Weatherfield! You're a bit-part character at best! I mean, *come on! Jesus Christ himself* is over there! And the fearsome bloody Connor the Beige! Charles Monkston, hero of Dunkirk! You're a footnote. An obituary. A never-been, has been, **won't be!**"

These last insults were accompanied by a series of scything blows from the *Unaussprechlichelangeweileklingdunkelheit*, leaving after-images in the air. Eddie caught all three on his blade, then fielded a swing from the war-machine's giant cleaver on his shield. There was no way he was going to win this. Even through the guttering flames of his berserker rage he knew it. But…

"But I can do something heroes can't, Mister Schprinkler," he said, as his thumb found the rune on the grip of his sword.

A gold-toothed rictus grin was his answer.

"Is it *die?* I really hope it's die!"

Eddie shrugged.

"Perhaps. One day. But for now… it's *this*."

He let go all of the kinetic force stored up in his shield in a single immense burst, channeling it through the cold iron of the sword. Eddie felt a bowling ball made of ice squeezing through the arteries of the left arm, through his chest, and down his right arm in a single convulsion.

Now, he had been careful never to let his shield touch the shimmering aura around *Unaussprechlichelangeweileklingdunkelheit*, so it still contained roughly the power of the runaway steam train Major Monkston had prepared earlier.

All that force was concentrated through the pommel of what Eddie henceforth thought of as Exclobberer, the unmagical sword. Hundreds of tons of pressure and kilowatts of energy, in an area the size of your thumbprint...

It booted Hans Schprinkler out through a stained glass depiction of Saint Paul, so hard and fast that a tiny thunderclap followed. Clear through the jagged hole he'd made, Eddie could see the Nazi sorcerer still rising as he cleared the Straits and sailed off over the city of Istanbul.

*Not that it would probably kill him. He'd said it himself. He was the* bad guy. *You didn't get away with just lobbing the arch-villain off into the night and forgetting about him...*

Eddie looked up at the black iron war machine as he swung back on his lamp chain and dropped to the floor.

"I can be a cunning, underhanded bastard," he said. A fistful of 38-mm cannons spun and clicked as they aimed at his head. "And I can definitely *run away!*"

Eddie turned, and saw exactly what he'd spotted mere moments before, reflected in the gleaming silver of Hans Schprinkler's blade. It was Fyodor, behind the wheel of an immense armoured automobile, gunning the engine so that blasts of fire came licking out of twelve sawn-off exhaust pipes.

"Well, dinnae just stand there!" shouted Connor the Beige, popping up from a Vickers machine-gun turret atop the beast. "Let's get the hell oot o' here!"

Eddie looked back for a second. The demise of its master hadn't done anything to sweeten the mood of the Nazi war-engine. It stomped forward, ducking in under the dome of the great museum, its guns tracking around even as Eddie leaped up on the running board, and slammed the driver's door with his shield.

Fyodor gave him a smile. Or at least, a lot of teeth.

"I'm all for an egalitarian utopia of the proletariat, and the equal distribution of wealth without the artificial scarcity caused by excess," deadpanned the Russian vampire, who (and no surprises here) was now dressed in an immaculate black racing driver's speed-suit, complete with red-tinted goggles. "But I am *bloody* pleased to note that this is a Rolls Royce, comrade Weatherfield."

Fingers wrapped in black calfskin slammed a huge, crooked, eight-ball-topped gear shifter into first. Connor the Beige unleashed a billowing cloud of what looked like ink from his staff, blotting out the sight of the Nazi colossus. And the Ross-Royce leaped forward like a stallion with a wasp stuck somewhere uncomfortable, its great slotted headlamps raking the night. Fire popped from twelve exhausts as it burst from the Hagia Sophia, clearing a flight of marble steps with a roar.

"I reckon that might hae only pissed yon scunner off," hazarded the little wizard, holding onto his hat with one hand. Behind them, 88-mil cannon fire chewed up a swathe of ornamental shrubbery. "Got another steam train up your sleevie, Major?"

The muffled response from inside the armoured car seemed less than gentlemanly.

They went belting across the cobbles, under an ornate arch hung with vines and flowers, and into the city streets. Istanbul never really slept. Certainly, it got to that point where sleep was on the other side of another bottle, or another smoldering hookah full of hashish, or, indeed, a well-placed truncheon to the back of the head. But despite the late hour, there were plenty of people on the streets – up to and including, noted Eddie (as they took a corner on two wheels) the obligatory fez-wearing porters shifting large wooden crates full of fruit and vegetables.

It's a universal truth, acknowledged everywhere, that the natural enemy of the watermelon stand is the common car chase.

The Rolls-Royce blattered through a whole street of vegetable kiosks and market stalls, sideways, Mrs Hazelwood arising at the controls of that turret-mounted Vickers gun like a blue-rinsed fury.

"Eat British lead, you filthy great bugger!" she shouted, her headscarf flapping in the wind. She unleashed a stream of bullets, cackling like a harridan[21].

Now, the Vickers gun is quite a thing. Water-cooled, belt fed, accurate and stable, it's effectively a kind of remote bandsaw. So long as you have ammunition, you can use its evil stream of bullets to carve things to bits. Most of the back of the Rolls was filled with loops and

---

21 Section M employed two actual Harridans, a kind of half-medusa, half-vampire creature, invariably female, who hailed from the Transoxanian Mountains in central Asia. While the snakes on their head are purely decorative, the Harridan's most fearsome attack is its complaining and nagging, which bores into the psyche of the victim, revealing all those menial tasks as yet unfinished around the house, yard or office. For obvious thaumaturgical reasons, this turns the victim's brain to stone. Both of Section M's Harridans – Mrs Pinchworth and Mrs Shover, resemble English grannies with immense bat wings and large straw hats. They use their innate knowledge of chores and boring tasks to run the Labyrinth's janitorial department. As this is largely made up of small golems and poltergeists with no corporeal brains, the nagging is rarely fatal.

coils of ammunition, but it seemed that no matter how much fire Mrs H rained down on their pursuer… Well. At least the ricochets were pretty. Sparks lit up the night as the war-engine lurched forward, like a mime leaning into an invisible wind. It might have the gait of a three-legged spider, but it was gaining. An answering fusillade of shells blasted apart a small bath-house and a swathe of cobbles as Fyodor sawed at the wheel, making the tyres wail.

Inside the car, Connor, Patience and Major Monkston were arguing.

"Magic? We cannae just hit it with *magic!* First off, I'm near as oot of puff, pal. And second…"

"There's an *elf* inside that thing. Bonded to *iron*, Charlie." This was Patience, and for the first time, Eddie could tell she was afraid. "I can feel it. Every shred of its being wants to do what they always used to do when touched by iron. Disappear back to Tirfeynn."

"Which isn't there," snapped Monkston, as the whole Rolls-Royce took a corner, describing a perfect hairpin turn as if on ice-skates. Further melons, honeydews, tomatoes and a very angry chicken were swept from the armoured windscreen with a squeak of overtaxed wipers. "gone to… to *you-know-who*, bloody centuries ago!"

"Exactly," said Connor. "Cunning Nazi buggers, ain't they? Look like they're making a fine wee deal with the Queen, but all along…"

"You can't make a deal with the… the *things*," said Monkston. But there was a slight hesitation in his voice. "That would be *insane*. They don't even have what you could call a mind – just hunger and cunning glued together with hate!"

"Did Hans Schprinkler *look* like a reasonable man?" asked Patience.

The Rolls-Royce lurched into a higher gear as they crested a rise, and Fyodor aimed its armoured nose down a long, straight road. Not a second too soon – a wild blow with that massive cleaver pared paint from the car's bumper as the war-engine lurched behind them. The impact sliced clean through the lock on the Rolls' trunk, making it pop open in the slipstream. Inside, Jesus Christ and the Compte de Saint Germain were wrestling over the spear of destiny.

"Look, I know I must have met you somewhere before, but I'm telling you it's *mine!*" said the erstwhile Son of Man, his patience sorely tested.

"And I'm telling you that falafel was *humming*, mate! By rights, I should have got a refund for the donkey, too!"

The pair of them were sitting amongst a tangled nest of belt-fed Vickers ammunition, which slid and coiled around them as

Mrs Hazelwood continued to rake their pursuer with thoroughly ineffective fire.

"I don't like to pull rank, soldier, but it looks to me like you're a corporal, and I'm *the bloody messiah!*"

"Oooh, typical! I'll have you know that I'm a *Count*, you Nazarene pillock!"

"Well, you're only one letter wrong..."

A hatch popped open, and the horrible, sideburned mug of Lucky the Leprechaun appeared. A pair of hands with more scars between them than the international all-pirate crocodile-wrestling team shoved them down into the ammo.

"*Duck*, you pair of imbeciles!"

And not a second too soon. Fyodor jinked left, scraping up alongside an overloaded charabanc, and the iron monstrosity's cleaver whistled past, *just where their necks had been.*

They came up fighting, all hands on the spear. Up above, Mrs Hazelwood let loose another blast of machine-gun fire, hammering the Nazi war machine as it stomped after them, its striding legs crushing carts and tents and stalls as it came. Bullets spanged and whined. The Vickers chattered, steam belching from its water-jacketed barrel.

And the belts of ammunition wrapped around Jesus Christ and the Compte de Saint Germain pulled tight.

Suddenly the spear of destiny was the last thing on both of their minds. Jesus gagged as a serpentine coil of bullets cinched around his neck. Saint Germain had it worse, as a further loop wedged itself between his buttocks like the world's least comfortable bathing costume. His eyes bulged out, in a fair imitation of the common chameleon.

Lucky made a valiant grab, but in these situations, there's always some malicious little part of the universe which is in the wrong place at the wrong time. In this case, it was an errant watermelon, taking revenge for literally hundreds of its brothers and sisters which had died to punctuate this car chase.

The front wheel of the Roll-Royce hit the melon square. The whole car shimmied and bumped as it slid to the left. And the spear – the Lance of Longinus, inset with the nails of the true cross – spun end over end into the slipstream.

Only to be grabbed by a figure on a motorcycle, who came roaring in at the last second.

It's not just the good guys who get to make those game-changing, last-ditch efforts.

Hans Schprinkler looked like he'd crawled through a cesspit while on fire[22]. His uniform was a mess, but his eyes burned with triumph as he gunned the motor of one of the Wild Hunt's fallen bikes, leaving a trail of spectral blue flame in his wake.

"*I'll* just be taking that!" crowed the evil sorcerer, his pentagram monocle flashing red. "And now… perhaps… for you, the war is over!"

"Eddie!" shouted Major Monkston, playing what was probably his last card.

"Major!" shouted Percy, up in the passenger seat.

"*O, der'mo!*" shouted Fyodor, noticing exactly what Percy was on about. In Russian, that pretty much summed it up.

There were tanks on the road ahead. Ones which the Turkish army had cobbled together out of relics from World War One. Now, this might mean that they were antiquated, and under-gunned, and no match for a rampaging progeny of Nazi super-science and occult jiggery-pokery. Like the one which was even now stomp-scrabbling its way toward them.

But they *were*, all three of them, based loosely on the immense MK1 Land Ship, and had been outfitted with bulldozer blades, extra armour and no small amount of spikes. A Rolls-Royce hitting them at full chat would have the life expectancy of a snowman in blast furnace, magical top-hat and carrot nose included.

"We may be in a wee bit of bother, aye?" asked Connor the Beige, understating the situation valiantly. He produced a small flask of whiskey from the pointy bit of his hat, took a long swallow, then offered it to Patience.

Major Monkston leaned out of the window, one hand gripping his topper.

"Weatherfield," he said, in a voice as calm and frosty as that of a cryogenically chilled butler, "I'd be *awfully* obliged if you could fetch that spear."

Eddie gulped. He looked down at his hands, where they gripped the side of the Rolls. Things didn't look good. All the berserker magic had dropped out of him, and he was back to his normal size.

"Ummmm… well, Sir – I don't really know how to turn it on, and…"

Monkston closed his eyes for a second. There was a definite sense that he was counting to ten, very slowly.

---

22  This had actually happened. It had been a bad day for Herr Schprinkler

"You know, I saw that Nazi bastard shoot you in the face, back there. And I reckon if you let go, right now, the impact with the road will break pretty much every bone in your body."

Eddie gulped again. This time, his heart slammed up against his ribs like a blowfly in a bottle as well.

"*Really* not helping, Major..."

When Monkston opened his eyes, there was a light in them which Eddie found a little too familiar. He'd last seen that calculating, determined look on the scarred face of Hans Schprinkler.

"*Pain,* Weatherfield. The pain makes you angry. The anger makes you strong. So all you have to do… is let go."

Patience was beside him at the window. Her look of concern did nothing to make Eddie feel any better, but it did make him feel like a twit for doing nothing at all. Instead of leaping heroically into action he settled for flapping his mouth open and shut like a surprised goldfish.

"Couldn't you just use a kinesis spell?" she asked. "If I had any vitae left, I could grab that spear right out of his ha -"

Monkston cut her off with a scowl.

"I'm afraid I've used the very last of mine saving all of our sorry buttocks," he said. "Darrin and his lady friends should be arriving just… about…"

Eddie looked up as a familiar black shape came scudding in across the rooftops, trailing a sonic boom which shattered windows, pot plants, coffee cups and small ceramic ornaments in its wake. The *Black Buzzard* pulled into a turn which made it stand on one screaming wingtip, something huge and heavy swinging below it on a reinforced chain.

"Now, Weatherfield!" barked the Major. "We've only got one chance!"

Eddie looked down at the speeding cobbles. He gulped. They looked awfully real and very, *very* solid. He looked deep into his soul to screw up the tattered rags of his courage… and found it was conspicuously absent.

Hans Schprinkler must have seen it in his eyes. The Nazi sorcerer laughed with triumph, brandishing the Spear of Destiny.

"You see, Monkston! Not even a has-been! A *never was!*"

And then the *Black Buzzard* was on them, and the world turned upside down.

The thing dangling from beneath the belly of the arcane warplane was a magnet, salvaged from some immense scrap-yard crane. Lightning flickered around it as it swung like a colossal pendulum, plucking knives and spoons from tables in the houses on either side, wrenching nails from wooden planks and knobs from doors.

Time slowed down. Eddie looked up, and saw Lotte peering from a hatch in the *Buzzard*'s underside, working a set of levers.

The magnet swung wide around the colossus, but it recoiled away, staggering and falling. It went down hard, tumbling through a whole row of houses in a spray of brick dust and plaster.

*Because there's a reason elves hate iron.*

Tirfeynn, their lost world, swallowed up long ago when the Netherspawn stopped by for dinner, *didn't have a magnetic field.* Van Allen belts of pure magic protected it from cosmic rays, and the solar wind of an alien pair of suns. Magnetic flux tore through Elvish minds like a high-test dose of the baddest LSD, blotting out reason, and sight, and taste, and smell, plunging the poor creatures into a world of sensory horror.

Confronted by this abomination, the poor vivisected elf inside Schprinkler's war machine burst through the restraints which pinned it down. Its instincts kicked in, and it slipped sideways, between the cracks in reality, into the place where Tirfeynn should have been.

And, doing so, it opened up a hole in the world.

Hans Schprinkler nearly lost the spear of destiny as the magnet swung overhead, but he managed to keep a white-knuckled grip on the thing, even as his spectral motorbike was lifted six feet off the cobbles. Behind him, the colossus exploded, shattering as if it was made of glass. From between the slivered pieces of of iron, tentacles burst forth. Whips of claw-studded darkness lashed in every direction, hungry and mindless. They reached for the motorbike as it came crashing down, but Schprinkler gunned the engine, jinking left and right to avoid their grip. Whole buildings on both sides of the road were diced as those glistening tentacles raved, eyeballs and mouths budding open along their lengths.

And the Rolls-Royce *flew.*

The magnet struck home with a clang which almost made Eddie lose his grip, and all four wheels left the ground. The car rose up over the roofs and chimneypots, clipping a weathervane, spinning slowly as Darrin's gremlin flight crew jammed open the throttles.

Down below, Eddie watched Hans Schprinkler dodge into a maze of side streets, ducking under washing lines and hanging baskets. But the colossus he'd created…

*Was gone.*

Instead there was a wound in the world, a jagged-edged fissure through which black lobster claws and tentacles and whip-like antennae bulked and writhed, steaming cold.

"I really wish," said Major Monkston, in a sad, small voice, "That you'd just listened to me this *once*, Eddie Weatherfield." He popped open the hatch atop the Rolls as it ascended, holding onto his hat with one hand. The tails of his opera coat popped like pennants in the wind rushing past. "But oh well. Can't have one of the Netherspawn devour Istanbul on my watch. That would be a diplomatic incident, you know. Lots and lots of paperwork."

They were almost a mile high now, and rising fast. Hidden mechanisms were winching the airborne armoured car up toward the belly of the *Black Buzzard.*

"Wait!" shouted Patience, grabbing at the hem of the Major's trousers. He didn't.

"Apologies, young lady. Duty calls."

And with that, he leaped from atop the car, arms and legs spread wide, his fingers crackling with magical power.

*"Charlie!"* yelled Connor the Beige, leaning out of the hatch. "You daft southern bastard! What are ye *doing?"*

But the answer was horribly obvious. It hit Eddie between the eyes like a cold bucketful of sick. He was *being a hero.*

The tiny little figure fell, outlined in magic. Not enough to slow its descent. Not enough to make its impact anything less than fatal. But enough to steer its course, so that when Major Monkston took off his top hat for the last time and held it out in front of him, it was aimed right at the biggest, gnarliest knot of tentacles – the one in which a red-pupiled eye was even now blinking, bloodshot.

At the last moment, the brim of the hat flared out and contracted in at the same time. An event horizon bloomed, sharp as winter, black as villainy…

And the gap in the world turned inside out. Tentacles were sucked back through as the hat devoured the rip in reality, blurring everything around it into tangled quantum spaghetti.

There was a sound like custard being forced down a plughole. A shockwave rippled out across Istanbul, turning small objects into other small objects, some of which quickly crawled away to hide.

And, to those who had the sight to see, a battered, burning top hat came to rest on a patch of cobbles which had, against all probability, turned into strawberry pudding. Then it popped like a soap bubble and vanished.

Eddie almost let go, then. His fingers didn't feel like part of his body. His face was grey, his eyes hollow holes.

Patience grabbed him. She hauled him in the window as the armoured car clanged up against the *Black Buzzard*'s undercarriage, locking tight. A second later, she slammed home the big lever in the cockpit – the one with all the skulls and crossbones painted on it for the semi-literate. A whole coven's worth of grimoires flashed into sorcerous ash, and the world blurred, knocking Eddie out cold.

But not before he saw the look on her face.

The one which was all pain, and loss, and worse – *blame*.

The one that said he was a coward.

# Meanwhile, elsewhere again...

The Queen of the Fae didn't really belong in a forge.

It was hot, and smelly, and smoky, and just about the least appropriate environment in which to wear white silk, satin and lace.

None of these things had stopped her. Titania would have looked stunning rising from a skip bin full of medical waste, such was the blowtorch force of her glamour. Still, she held herself in a manner which suggested that the air itself here was too filthy to breathe, and wore an expression like a Victorian-era nun at an adult lifestyles expo.

"Is it hot enough, yet?" she asked, a note of petulance entering her otherwise heavenly voice. "Some of us don't have all day, you know..."

Vulkan arched one prodigious eyebrow as he hobbled around the forge, giving the bellows a pump with one immensely muscled arm. The hunch-backed little God could not have been more different in appearance to the Queen, but here, he held the power. And he knew it. He scrubbed at his charred beard, popping a louse.

"You just worry about delivering that uranium you promised. It's going to be the coming thing, you know..."

He gestured with one shovel-sized hand at a row of huge silver rockets, standing like pillars in the vault of his factorium. "Good for a few prayers, those bastards. Make that business with Sodom and Gomorrah look like a slap fight."

Vulkan hopped up on top of a wooden stool, and dipped one finger into the crucible atop the forge. Of course, he couldn't burn. The God of Weapons rubbed molten metal into his gums, and smacked his lips approvingly.

"All good! Lovely trace minerals! Now - where are the articles in question?"

Titania's hands had a definite tremor to them as she produced a rosewood box inlaid with runes. These seemed to crawl and sizzle as if trying to slink away into everybody's peripheral vision.

"Of course I can't touch them myself, dear. Stars alone know how much power I'm wasting just to shield myself from all this iron..."

The Fae Queen turned away as the Erl King opened the box and rattled out three long, corroded nails. They seemed to glisten with a sheen of phantom blood. Vulkan rubbed his hands together, with a sound like sandpaper.

"Excellent! Consecrated metal is always in demand somewhere, you know. Won't you reconsider? I could make these into a sword, or a nice axe, or..."

When Titania turned back, her face had lost its mask of beauty. It was a porcelain white deaths-head, blazing with frustration.

"Just destroy them! *Utterly!* You know who'll come back when you do, and you owe them. Remember that party at your place in Pompeii?"

Vulkan scowled.

"You never got the cleaner's bill, love," he said, hefting the nails in his palm. "But you're right. The lads did me a few favours back in the days. I'd like to see 'em back together."

Titania looked over his shoulder, at the massive workbench where Vulkan spent most of his days. A yellowing, dog-eared poster dominated the wall behind it. It was an ancient woodcut of a band of musicians in armour, posing on a mountaintop while lightning exploded all around them.

THUNDERBEARDS – FLEDERMAUS OUT OF HADES TOUR

Below the picture, down in the corner, was a smaller inscription.

*Odin, Oberyn, Dionysus and Mithras use and recommend Vulkan Brand instruments and amplifiers.*

Vulkan's craggy face cracked like fresh-cooled lava as he smiled, remembering past glories. Your average wood nymph wouldn't give a hunched, scarred old apparition like the God of Weapons a second look on a good day. But it was remarkable what wonders could be worked by the simple words 'I'm with the band...'

Plop, plop, plop.

And sizzle, and gloop, and bubble…

And the Nails of the True Cross were gone, swirled away like so much soy milk into a hipster's latte.

Titania felt it first – a ripple of power moving through the world, subtly re-writing the story of everything. She watched it pass through Vulkan, and watched the pattern of scars on his crusty old face shift and twist into a new configuration. She watched as it billowed through the Erl King, and he turned, hands reached for a space on the wall where, in the way of tool sheds everywhere, someone had marked out the outline of something loaned or missing. In this case, it was one of a set. It was a flying-V shaped electric guitar.

Titania smiled, even as her huntsman stared down at his armoured fingers, wondering just what the heck he was doing.

"Excellent work, petal," she said, patting Vulkan on the cheek. "My dear old husband will be *so* pleased. He so wants the band back together. And who knows? They might just send you some VIP tickets, hmmm?" Her raised eyebrow was as sharp and curved as a sickle.

Vulkan - the entity responsible for cluster bombs and land mines disguised as children's toys - actually blushed. But only for a second. Two of his sausage-sized fingers plucked Titania's hand away, gently, but with the force of hydraulic pincers.

"I heard your pet Nazi has been messing with the lost world. *Your* lost world. I'd caution you to..."

"And how do *you* know about that?" asked the Queen, through a brittle smile. The Erlking had come crying to her about this very matter not so long ago, after all.

"I'm the God of Weapons, dear, and *there's a bloody war on.*" for a second, Vulkan looked exceedingly weary, as if he'd had to hammer out every bullet and shell personally. "Just remember, it was magical war which lost you that place, my Lady. Same as the magical war which cost the Dwarves their Eldernholm and the Goblins their..."

This time, Titania cut him off with the full power of her smile. It outshone the red glow of the forge, and the golden bubble and swirl of the molten metal.

"Oh, you silly little man! I'm here to *finish* this war, not keep it going! If I were you, I'd be more worried about those uranium rockets of yours. You don't get a lot of prayers from cinders. Or have you forgotten that part of the big Pompeii blowout as well?"

Vulkan scowled, and pulled a huge lever set into the floor. A trap door rattled open, unleashing a belch of sulfurous fumes and a tongue of green fire. Deep, deep below, magma swirled.

"Just remember, Queen of the Fae. Three tons of the finest uranium, here within the week. You know the penalty for failure."

To punctuate his point, the crippled God plucked the crucible from the forge with both hands, and tipped it out into the abyss.

Titania kept her composure. Composure, to a creature like her, was nine-tenths of reality.

"Oh, I'm not planning on failing. And neither will my human allies. You've seen the weapons they're developing. Jet engines. Missiles.

Better bombs, bigger tanks – and they want a world ruled by the beautiful and the pure." She laughed, then, a sound like tiny crystal bells. It set Vulkan's teeth on edge. "I will give them their 'master race'. It will be *us*. And your old friends will provide the soundtrack to a new age of mythic darkness. One where the Netherspawn are bound with this *science* the humans have invented."

She swept out of the forge in a flurry of crystal-studded lace, leaving behind the smell of dead flowers. But the Erlking stayed, for a moment. He sidled up to Vulkan, and whispered behind one armoured hand.

"The… ummm. The guitar. Do you know where..?"

The God of Weapons sighed. He'd seen this coming.

"I sold it years ago, pal. *You* said it was defective. *You* wanted your money back. So now… ahhh, to slag with it!"

The hunched-over little deity scrawled some details on a scrap of paper, and thrust it into the Erlking's hand.

"Just don't say I didn't warn you both! This business with Tirfeynn and all, well -"

A high-pitched whistle came from the corridor. The Erlking winced, the metal of his helm creasing with a sound like tinfoil. Then he turned and trotted away after his mistress, leaving Vulkan alone in the firelight, suddenly thinking that three tons of uranium might not be quite enough.

The worst part about being a guard on a submarine, mused Gunter Braun, was the food.

No, wait… not the food itself. Though the cans of horrible unidentifiable mush were pretty bad, it was what they *promoted* which was worse.

Unless you've been trapped in a metal tube, underwater, with twenty other men, all of whom are farting day and night, you don't truly know the horrors of war. Gunter just knew that it wouldn't sound very heroic when he came to set down his memoirs, but the smell inside U-666 was a crafty and relentless enemy.

It was also the *only* one, if you didn't count the snoring.

Because, of course, there was a *good* part about being a guard aboard a submarine – especially the Black Sun's very own high-tech, super-powerful, ultra-secret one. When you're plowing through the darkness at the bottom of the Med, clipping 35 knots, there aren't many intruders to point a machine gun at.

Despite being hired for his square-jawed Aryan looks and his bulging muscles, Gunter Braun was smart enough to know that out there, lots of other good German lads were facing a slightly more arduous foe than pressure-cooked flatulence. He farted contemplatively and shivered, imagining the eastern front. No thanks!

He never heard the hatch behind and above him slowly unscrew itself.

He certainly never heard the deliberate hush of a squat and muscular figure dropping to the deck with practiced stealth. But he certainly felt the muzzle of a very large pistol when it poked into the back of his neck. And he smelled something new, cutting through the fug of trouser methane like a bandsaw through tapioca.

*Tuna breath.*

"Now, you just turn around nice and slow-like," hissed the person behind him. "And put that nasty little automatic down on the floor. Goooood."

Gunter Braun had seen a few black-and-white cowboy movies in his time – that was how he identified the voice as being American. But his eyes, when they swiveled around to face his captor, didn't corroborate this evidence *at all*. What he saw was a powerfully built creature in aviator shades and an olive-green U.S. army helmet, clenching an unlit cigar between rows of sharp little teeth. The thing bulged with just as much muscle as Gunter himself, though – and here was the problem, and why he thought of it immediately as a *thing* – it was covered in pea-green metallic scales. Gills were slashed red across the sides of its neck. And while it was wearing a pair of soaking wet camouflage trousers, it was shirtless, and the scales across its chest and arms had been ornately scrimshawed with naval tattoos – tall ships and anchors, hula girls and torpedoes and crossed swords.

This was all just a sideshow, however, compared to exhibit A – the pair of gigantic gold-plated revolvers which the apparition clenched in its webbed fingers.

"Oh, you like those, do ya? Had 'em made special. Genuine Vulkan Arms peacemakers. They can shoot underwater, and break the back of a frigate. So don't try any monkey business, son."

Gunter nodded. He dredged up the two words of English his father had insisted on teaching him, back when he enlisted. Dad had been in the big one – World War One. Dad had a wooden leg and a not-quite-fanatical attitude toward *der Fuhrer*.

"I... surrender," he stammered, mesmerized by the two tunnels of darkness pointed at his head.

The face above those gun muzzles broke into a slow, wide grin. It was a broad and cheerful face, even if it was made up of innumerable tiny green scales. Nictitating membranes blinked across a pair of dark eyes.

"Well done, son. Smart move. Now, as per the protocol for these things, I have to inform you that you've been captured by Colonel Al Schwitzer, U.S. Department of Alleged Intelligence, Special Attache to Section M of His Britannic Majesty's Irregular Forces. Seeing as you fellas on board here are the Nat-zee equivalent, that should *not* come as a surprise."

Schwitzer spun one gold revolver on his finger and slipped it back into a holster. He quickly patted down his captive, finding nothing but an antique pocketknife.

"But now, here's what you're gonna do. You're gonna tell me where Hans Schprinkler is, and where the Enigma code machine is aboard this tub, and then I'm gonna tie you up. Or, we can do this the hard way."

Gunter gulped.

"Ze… hard way?"

Schwitzer nodded. He rolled the unlit cigar from one corner of his mouth to the other.

"Well, it's like this. The hard way involves a lot of blood, and there's nowhere for it to drain away to in one of these U-boats. You end up with a whole lot of wrung-out Nat-zee bodies, and the red stuff slopping all over your boots. Ever tried to get blood stains out of a good pair of socks? Or get new ones in England? These here are proper cowboy boots, just like the Great General Douglas MacArthur has, and if I have to get them all covered in blood, I will be *ever so slightly aggravated.*"

Gunter looked down at the boots. They were, indeed, silver-toed Texan examples of ornate manufacture. He sighed, and held out his hands.

"Surrender," he tried again, wishing all of this was over.

"Smart feller. Now, before I get to hog-tying ya…"

Gunter tried to stop him. But he didn't know the English words for 'fart' and 'danger' and 'don't light that bloody cigar, you silly yankee fish-person'.

A chrome zippo lighter sparked in Schwitzer's hand. He closed his eyes, anticipating that first lovely drag of hand-rolled nicotine goodness…

Later, when Colonel Al Schwitzer came around, he found that most of the crew had been either killed outright or knocked unconscious by the explosion. Tritons, however, are made of sterner stuff – those scales can take a real hammering, even from a firestorm of pent-up methane gas in a sealed environment.

He was not amused to discover that Hans Schprinkler was not on board. He was even less amused when he discovered the enigma code machine, and the little pile of deciphered orders on a spike next to it, now all charred around the edges.

The tough-as-nails old Atlantean could read enough German to understand what was written on that top sheet of paper. Alongside all the bright red stamps of deaths-heads and eagles and swastikas.

It was a list of troops, and ordnance, and marching orders. It mentioned magically shielded aircraft, and this submarine's sister-ship, the Black Sun's own U-667.

And it came with a very specific date, and time, and set of co-ordinates.

"Oh, shitfire," breathed the Colonel. "Somebody get me my bathtub..."

But it was at precisely that moment that U-666, running at 35 knots in pitch darkness with nobody at the helm, chose to ram directly into a sunken mountain just off the coast of Sicily. Clawing fingers of rock gutted the speeding submarine, letting the cold, black waters of the Mediterranean flood in, and sending it to the bottom.

Of course, this was only a minor inconvenience for Al Schwitzer, who had been born where the lava wells up between the continental plates, deep in the middle of the Atlantic Ocean.

But it meant that it was quite a while before he could get his hands on a radio.

And that would prove to be one of those little eventualities around which the whole world spun...

# Ten – The Doom of the Labyrinth

"What *exactly* are you doing?" asked Doctor Lawrence Jeckyll, peering up over a pair of thoroughly improbable brass magnifying goggles at Eddie Weatherfield.

It was a good question. The lad was standing in front of the Doctor's desk at full attention, holding out a sheet of paper in one hand. And on closer inspection, there was some evidence that he'd been crying.

Jeckyll took the view that, during a conflict in which thousands of people were bludgeoned, incinerated and blown to tiny pieces each week, it wasn't at all un-manly to have a good cry sometimes. After all, it was less expensive than getting passing-out drunk, and achieved a similar aim.

But something about Weatherfield was not quite right. This was apparent to the Doctor, even though his grasp of social interaction was on a par with a common woodlouse's grasp of particle physics.

"Oh dear. You've seen the big mural, then?"

He pointed at the words which took up one entire wall of his subterranean tin hut.

Eddie nodded. He wiped away a dribble of snot with his saluting hand, and proffered the paper again.

"Resigning my commission, Sir. Couldn't find any other officers that I know, sir. Miss Golightly said I was being silly..."

This was more familiar territory. Doctor Jeckyll beamed.

"Well, that's all right then! Easy fixed!"

"Really?" The paper was a bit soggy. It had been typed up on canteen letterhead.

"Yes, because, you see, you don't have one. You're drafted. Pressganged. Dragooned. In the military without, as it were, any choice. On account of the all the Nazis still left knocking about, I'm afraid. They won't thwart themselves, old chap."

Eddie deflated.

"But… but I let him *die*, Doc! I could have just listened, and he'd still be alive today, and we could have…" Tears welled up, and the poor lad's face scrunched up with red-hot guilt.

Jeckyll, as noted, was not a doctor thanks to his winning bedside manner[23].

"There there," he said, patting Eddie gingerly on one shoulder. "I should think it'll be all right. After all, Istanbul is still standing. That's a result."

"But… the rest of them. I've let them down, Doctor. I can't face them again. Is there some way I can get a transfer?"

Jeckyll considered this. He considered it so hard that he missed the little red lamp on his desk lighting up – the one which indicated something coming in through the water gate.

"Let's see now…" the doctor tapped his front teeth with a pencil. "I could get you onto the Section M cricket team, but we've got a heck of a match coming up against the boys from Bletchley Park. Signals Corps. Otherwise you'd have to talk to General Crowley, and he's… hang about, what's this?"

Another pair of lights were blinking for attention now. And from behind the door which led to Doctor Jeckyll's subterranean dock, Eddie could hear muffled shouting, and the sound of boots on concrete.

As if they knew they were being listened to, the noises suddenly stopped.

"You know the *funny* thing, Private Weatherfield," said the doctor, slowly standing. "It's that all of our secret submarines are out right now. Squad 5 are in Sicily. Squad 11 are up in the Baltic. And Schwitzer

---

23 His degree had much more to do with demonstrating to the board of crusty old men who handed out doctorates that he was a whiz with maniacal potions. Ones which made things alternatively explode, levitate, mutate, glow in the dark or fart uncontrollably. The academic term is 'it's better to have the mad ones on the inside pissing out, than on the outside pissing in'.

borrowed another one, to intercept the big German tub that brought Hans Schprinkler to Istanbul…"

Now came the sound of something scraping the metal frame of the door from the other side. Jeckyll plucked a slim bottle of green and glowing goop from the top pocket of his coat, thumbed the latch, and swung the door open.

On the other side, a small Nazi in full commando gear – painted face, webbing belts of weapons, black-on-black swastika motif – suddenly tried to conceal a crowbar. Behind him were massed another twenty or more soldiers, all looking similarly sheepish. When you're trying to break into a secret base, it looks silly when the occupants open the door.

"Yes?" asked Doctor Jeckyll. Well, come on! What do you chaps want at this time of night?"

The Germans looked at each other. One prodded the small commando at the front, who made a gesture of utter helplessness, then rallied magnificently.

"Ve… ve vere vondering if you haf heard ze good news about Jesus Christ?"

The rest nodded. This was absolutely the kind of thing people knocked on your door at strange hours to ask you.

The doctor grinned.

"Yes, thank you. He's doing just fine. I had to stitch up a nasty little cut on his leg, but I gave him a lollipop, and he was a very brave boy."

He slammed the door right in the confused soldier's face.

Eddie Weatherfield had seen it all, over Jeckyll's shoulder.

"Those were *Germans!* Enemy soldiers!"

"Yes," nodded the doctor. "You see what I mean about them not vanquishing themselves? Now, I need you to read the bloody mural, and stick to it, all right? Keep calm, and go to raise the alarm. These won't be the only Nazis we see tonight. If they're finally making a move, we must have them good and rattled!"

Eddie tried to stop the feeling of free-fall in his guts, the trembling in his knees, and the pounding of his heart in the back of his throat all at once. He nodded.

A knocking came from the door.

Doctor Jeckyll opened it a crack, and poked his head out.

"Yes?"

"Ummm… it's just that, perhaps we could come in for a second, for ze cup of tea and zer biscuit?"

Jeckyll slammed the door again.

"I'll hold them back here. Tell Crowley! Tell Connor the Beige! We're only at about half strength here, but that strength is formidable! The armoured fist of English magic!"

With that, he ripped the cork from his glowing green bottle, held his nose, and tipped the contents down his throat.

"Oooooh! I don't mind the radioactive isotopes, but does it always have to taste of sprouts?"

The change came suddenly. Jeckyll's clothes ripped and tore as he ballooned outward, muscle and bone doubling and redoubling until his body was pressed up against the roof of the hut. In accordance with the rules of these kind of things, he was left wearing the ragged stub of his lab coat like a vest, and a pair of frayed khaki shorts. He turned his huge head toward Eddie as he gripped the doorknob between two fingers.

"Are you still here? *Run*, you fool! Raise the alarm!"

For a third time, Doctor Jeckyll opened the door. Though this time, thought Eddie, perhaps he really *was* Mister Hyde. If his old granddad had been the mad scientist, couldn't he have been the monster too?

The Nazis recoiled as a face made up of craggy brows, mad little green eyes and yellowed teeth the size of cigarette packets leered through the gap at them. Then a pair of hands like power shovels gripped the door frame and tore it wide open.

"Come on in, lads!" rumbled a voice in deep, horrible Cockney tones. "One lump or two?"

Eddie ran. He hadn't gone far when all the lights went out, plunging the labyrinth into darkness. A second later an explosion rocked the floor beneath his feet, and then the lights came back on – all red and dull, the emergency power system firing up in some deep sub-basement. He heard gunfire in the distance. And *not* the distance he'd come from. Well, probably not. This was a labyrinth, after all, and he was sort of... absolutely lost.

A gnomecart whizzed by, carrying what appeared to be a pirate, a mummy and a man with his head on fire. Part of Eddie's mind yammered at him to follow them, mainly as they looked like they knew where the fighting was. Another, more traitorous part insinuated that this was a good argument for continuing in the exact opposite direction.

In light of recent events, Eddie was inclined to throttle that second little voice with both hands. He screamed, then set off at a run down a third corridor, this one beginning to fill with smoke.

It led to the hangar. And there were Nazis there, too.

Nazis with flamethrowers.

Eddie crashed through the doors and into a vast oven the size of several football stadiums, where black-clad figures in the distance wavered before a wall of flame. They had set fire to the conventional aircraft at the far end of the hangar. Spitfires and Hurricanes enhanced with invisibility paint on their undersides, with scrying wands bristling from their cockpits to see in the dark, and with strange weapons made of copper and crystals replacing their machine guns. They'd also burned a rack of broomsticks, and the magical discharge as they took flame sent pink and blue fireworks popping and sizzling overhead.

Eddie took this all in with a breath of crispy-hot air. And then he saw the *Black Buzzard*.

A squad of soldiers was advancing on the sorcerous aircraft, the pilot lights of their flamethrowers winking blue and purple. But as he watched, a blur came racing out from under the *Buzzard*'s wing, spun circles around the foremost Nazi, and sped away.

A very unhealthy gurgling sound issued from his flamethrower. A jet of something green and gaseous hissed from the tank on his back. The sturmtrooper performed that frantic little dance you do when a spider lands on you in the shower - but only for an instant. His mates hit the deck behind anything that looked like cover, and....

WHOOOMPH!

*Gremlins*, remembered Eddie, *break things*. Maybe even the girls could swing a monkeywrench, if it came to the pinch.

Which meant that his friends were in there, and horribly outnumbered.

Once again, a certain little voice wheedled in the nasty sub-cellar of his brain, suggesting that he should try to sneak away. The fire wouldn't hurt him. Not with his peculiar abilities. And then it was up the ladder, through the Botanical Gardens and off on his toes, probably to a nearby pub. These fellows were part of a *secret* war, not the proper one. London wasn't full of gas-masked fiends in coalscuttle hats and swastika-brand athletic wear. Just this insane little underground part of it.

The voice was compelling. It was reassuring.

*It could bloody well shut up.*

Eddie cast about for something useful, and found it. His fingers closed around the handle of a panelbeater's lump hammer, even as his lips pulled back in a slightly mad grin.

Across the hangar, a bold Nazi peeked out from behind a crate, waving a machine pistol. A blur of pink and red tore across the scaffolding above him, and a mounted spotlight fell, squashing him like an insect.

"*In case of emergency, break glass...*" chuckled Eddie, in a way which would have disturbed old Doctor J.

Then he hauled off and smacked himself in the head with the hammer, just as hard as he could.

*He saw dragons.*

Not as he'd seen them in the moonlit air over Britain, but *as they really were*, in their own world. A world, he now saw, which the dragons had sealed off from Earth in the dawn times. When they had risen above the other giant lizard-creatures, forging a civilization based on sorcery. Visions of cities crafted from hollowed-out mountains rippled through his mind. Great winged beasts inscribed potent spells on plates of iron by lava-light...

And they'd *fought*. Oh, yes. Eddie felt whole aeons of war shudder through his living cells. He saw entire nations of warrior dragons blackening the skies. He saw dinosaurs harnessed to great arcane siege weapons. Mountains falling. Magics unleashed. Reality growing thin and pale, until claws began to slit it from outside…

It hadn't been a meteor that killed them.

A huge mass of rock hadn't come down from space to wipe the earth clean. No. *It had been torn from the planet*, wrapped in layer after layer of magic, and twisted away to a place where the Netherspawn couldn't follow. To give Earth a chance. To leave it to the snuffling hedgehog things and curious rodents who would inherit it, and grow, and change, and develop opposable thumbs, and plowshares, and best bitter, and the Model T Ford.

All this he saw, before the pain had a chance to travel like treacle down the axons and dendrites from his scalp to the centre of his brain.

And when it erupted, silent and hot and velvety, he saw the creature which had saved him.

"*Ahhh. You again.* You know, you really didn't have to hit yourself with that hammer. I felt that too, and it was bloody unpleasant."

Eddie pulled his mind together through the slow billows of agony. They raced out toward his fingers and toes like ripples through custard.

"*You…* what… what happened to the bony old Viking?"

The dragon huffed, a little jet of smoke escaping from the corner of its mouth.

"A thousand years underground, and he only had one thing on his mind, lad. *Glug glug glug.* Bit of a boozer, was old Foesbane. Now he's in Valhalla, where they have a big giant goat for all that. Udders full of beer. Lasts forever."

"A big giant goat? Not just… I don't know, a bottomless cauldron or something?"

The dragon contrived to look amused. This is difficult when your face is twelve feet long and covered in armoured scales.

"Don't look at me, human. It's *your* religion. I'm just here as a… whatchamacallit. Quasi-anthropic personification of your internal angst, or something. I'm me, but I'm basically here to tell you what you already know. And a big giant goat makes *far* more sense than a bottomless cauldron. At least there's a precedent for goats providing liquid refreshment."

The pain had reached the end of his fingers now, and was surfing back along the electro-chemical pathways of his arms and legs, raising goosebumps.

"So – why now? What do you need to tell me?"

The dragon grinned. Whole massive switchboards of primeval dread lit up in Eddie's brain. It was a grin which made your feet run away before your legs got the memo.

"*Fear*, Eddie Weatherfield. And Pain. At the risk of sounding like one of those insufferable demons, pain makes you change because *pain is pure*. It makes all the other little voices in your skull shut up. Fear, for example. Being brave isn't all about facing up to huge monsters, or massive odds, or suicidal situations. It's all about hearing that little voice that tells you to run, *and telling it to sod off.*"

Eddie could see the real world blurring back in around the edges now. The great scarred, scaled, ruby-red visage of the dragon began to waver.

"Easy for you to say, pal! I *like* being alive!"

The dragon shrugged.

"Keep listening to that voice, and you're not really alive at all, though, are you? Just anxiety with pants on. You know what else is pure, apart from pain? What my old mate Foesbane used to use. He'd think of something more important to him than being alive. *Then think about those bastards who were trying to take it away.* Worked every time. Got close to full thaumo-morphic manifestational transference, once or twice. But listen to me going on..."

There was a definite sense of hangar-ness happening now. Agony bounced around the inside of Eddie's skull like a demented blowfly.

"That's it?" he slurred – and he heard his own voice. "*That's the secret? What've I got… got left though? They all think I'm…*"

The dragon's eyes were the last to go, fading away with what seemed suspiciously like a wink.

Darrin Oakenbeard chose that precise moment to notice him.

"Eddie!" shouted the dwarf, ducking out from behind an overturned gnomecart. "Thank Grumnaar[24] you're here! They've taken all of levels three through six, and now they're trying to get through to the armoury!"

Despite rejecting the culture which had shunned him, Darrin had quickly reverted to his 'olde folkways' when trouble came knocking. He was wearing an iron helmet with a flip-down welder's mask, and carrying a hammer whose head was a solid lump of blue steel the size of a cinder block. Eddie noticed that he carried it *one handed.*

"Hey nazis!" shouted the erstwhile dwarf. "You're in trouble now! That's a dragonsblood berserker, that is! Between me, him, and the girls here, we're gonna g'zrakarza the h'zukk out of you b'zhar-zhun g'hrakkaars!"

A whole hangar full of Black Sun sturmtroopers turned to look at Eddie. He waved feebly, grinning a wobbly grin. There was a welt throbbing on his forehead the size of a hard-boiled egg.

"He hit himzelf mit der hammer, ja?" asked a very large Nazi soldier, carrying what appeared to be a small howitzer.

"Ooooh yeah!" chuckled Darrin. "Mad as a barrel of badgers, this cove. Show 'em, Weatherfield!"

Three tiny red-tufted female gremlins had also stopped their motion-blur assault to see what would happen next. Ilse was armed with a pipe wrench twice as tall as she was. Lotte carried a tyre iron. And Mica had equipped herself with a length of motorcycle chain. Eddie couldn't help but think that his little hammer looked a bit pathetic by comparison.

---

24 Grumnaar is the Dwarvern God of Drinking and Hitting Things with a Big Hammer, while Gragniir is the Dwarvern God of Hitting Things with a Big Hammer and Drinking. They are the twin brothers – or possibly sisters – in the dwarf pantheon, alongside Toki, God of Inappropriate Pranks, Snorr, Lord of Gold, Kur-Kazrak the Thunderer Below, and the deified hero Gavynn, who stole the secret of beard shampoo and conditioner from the Ice Giants.

"Raaarh!" he tried. A small Nazi turned to the howitzer-carrying thug, and scratched his helmet.

"Do you think zumthing was supposed to happen?"

"Maybe he needs to hit himzelf mit der hammer again?"

Their leader popped up from behind a row of barrels.

"Nein, this is the idiot Schprinkler told us about. He belongs with that soppy *hexen* girl and the horrible old Scotsman we captured earlier."

"Raaargh?" tried Eddie, with all the ferocity of a damp kitten. Then the man's words sliced in past the throbbing pain, past the embarrassment, and into his brain.

They had Connor. *They had Patience!*

Eddie had heard that the Nazis practiced unimaginable tortures. Unfortunately, his brain could imagine tortures all too well. And with all that practicing, they were probably pretty good at them by now! The image of Patience chained to a stake, with flames kindling around her toes, came unbidden to his mind.

*She thinks you're a loser, Weatherfield. She thinks you're a coward. A slimy little thing that isn't even worth stepping on.*

**Yes**, said a part of his brain with scales on. **And if she dies thinking all of that, you'll never get a chance to change her mind. Or any of the others…**

This thought made him quite angry.

In fact, on the scale of being catastrophically miffed, titanically peeved and world-manglingly cheesed off, it was right up there with a horde of vikings finding out that their bottomless beer-goat has been run over by a speeding truck.

Vast and leathery wings unfurled inside his head.

And *kept going*. Clothing tore, in ways which Doctor J would totally understand and sympathize with.

"RAAAAAAAAAAAAAAAAAAAARRGH!" said Eddie, as his horns – yes, there they were, stumpy and coal-black – scraped the scaffolding above.

And then the screaming started.

+++

There's a persistent belief out there that humans aren't magical.

Well, not by those new-age types who keep too many cats and smell of lavender. But you know. By *scientists*. People who 'know better', often for a considerable amount of money each semester.

This is a fib on the same scale as the moon landing or the death of Elvis[25], but it's one which Section M would really, really like you to keep believing.

The fact is, the so called 'magical races' have to suck down plentiful amounts of the stuff we produce in order to stay phased into our reality. A failure to do so would see them blurred back into those worlds of their own which they have lost – the realms now under the thrall of the tentacular, cold and utterly alien Netherspawn.

Humans churn out magic at the same rate they exhale carbon dioxide.

Apparently it's a product of how our minds work. The average human can only hold onto a semblance of sanity by believing in several utterly contradictory things at once. Belief, as your average God will tell you, is *power*. In fact, belief, in a saturated thaumic environment, is what makes the Gods and their fractious soap-opera families real in the first place.

The net result of Joe Sixpack, in Elk Scrotum, Idaho, believing in Bigfoot and Aliens and Jesus and Love and Death and the hopes of his favourite football team all at once is a great unfocused cloud of magic, spun into cyclonic whorls and thunderheads by the Earth's magnetic field.

Long ago, a few clever humans discovered this, and found ways to bend the background thaumic radiation in twisty ways, by using mental discipline, funny-looking mushrooms, illicit herbs and bizarre rituals. They were the first Wizards and Witches.

Of course, this put them in conflict with the elves, Dwarves, Goblins, Gnomes, Centaurs, Pixies, Merfolk and others who were refugees here on Earth – people (to use a very broad term) who needed all that sweet plentiful magic to stay alive.

But magic isn't just a fuel, like high-octane gasoline.

Magic is a fuel - like highly unstable uranium.

It's a catalyst. It *changes* things. And the flavour of the belief which helps create it subtly alters how those changes manifest.

Jesus of Nazareth was already finding this out, the hard way, as

---

25 All the rockets and so forth were just window dressing. The good old US of A got to the moon the usual way, with a pentacle of teleportation. Powered by Elvis, the inheritor of the guitar of the late great Robert Johnson, who, as we know, got it from the devil. Where Lucifer got it from is a whole other story, but it involves a garage sale, a box of mummified fingers, a single potato and a 1916 model T Ford.

he woke up in a red-lit Section M cell with the worst hangover in recorded history. For the last 2000 years his blood had literally been one hundred percent communion wine, and now it was just plain hemoglobin and plasma. His holy headache manifested itself as a jagged blur around his head, not unlike a crown of broken beer bottles.

And, in a hangar under Kew Gardens, a very, very scared and sorry squad of Black Sun Death Troopers were figuring out the same thing. They were stuck in a feedback loop. Because they *believed* in Eddie Weatherfield, the twice-human-sized, red-scaled dragon horror, the thing with sharp yellow teeth and one blazing eye a-boil with madness. They believed as fervently as a stick-thin old hermit prophet with a beard that is simultaneously his clothing, pillow, only friend and toilet paper.

Eddie drank it down like the *Black Buzzard* being fed on high-octane incunabula.

And that belief reinforced what he'd become - even as Darrin Oakenbeard charged, swinging his huge hammer. Even as Lotte, Ilse and Mica belted out the dreaded Gremlin Battle Limerick[26], and came in at knee-height, breaking shins with engineer-grade precision.

For a very, very short time, Eddie felt what it was like to be a demigod.

But his fuel was fragile.

The minds which built him up belonged to the brains he painted across the walls.

And so, as the flames were sucked in by his aura (and formed, for a second, the shape of mighty wings), his mind snapped back.

Tongues of fire turned to ice and trembled, held back from shattering by a moment plucked like a harp string.

The magic was cut off. The flames cracked and crazed.

And Eddie was glad someone was there to catch him.

+++

His mouth tasted like the bottom of a barbecue pit crossed with a

---

26 Once verse of which, to give you an idea, is -

*All our foes, on the magical spectrum*
*Think that armour and steel can protect 'em*
*But they never expect*
*To get recklessly wrecked*
*With a wrecking bar rammed up their...* well, you get the idea.

makeshift long-drop. His head felt as if it had been stuffed full of barbed wire and used as a football. Both his eyebrows had crumbled to ashes. And this was the good news.

Eddie could also feel the horribly slippery mess which dripped down his arms from the elbows. A none-too-thorough chronicler might just call it blood, and leave it at that. But that wouldn't account for the *lumps*.

He breathed in. He breathed out. Nothing seemed to be broken, fractured or leaking.

*That was a good start.*

And the rage was… contained. This time it didn't fill him up like flaming kerosene. It burned away in the background, but it was *controlled*. Shaped.

Eddie struggled to his feet, blinking a mist of red from his eyes.

When he'd transformed through pain, he'd lashed out mindlessly, at everything. Now he had a focus. For a terrible, stretched-out moment, every one of those nazis had been Hans Schprinkler. *The jolly, cheerful sadist who had shown him what he really was...*

Darrin Oakenbeard was staring at him, slack jawed. The hammer fell from his hand as he took a step backward. Around them, the hangar was cold and quiet.

No – not just cold. *Wintry*. Little fern-fronds of frost painted every surface, and the dwarf's breath formed a twinkling cloud of ice crystals as he exhaled.

"Geez louise!" said a small voice, coming out of a pile of rags. Lotte clambered out, shivering. "I didn't know he did *that*, Darrin!"

Ilse's head popped up from the pile, which Eddie now recognized as a hastily dumped mass of clothing, many, many sizes too small for a human being.

"You reckon the fox-fur, with the green overalls? Or the rabbit with the charcoal grey?" She blinked. "Yes, he does that. Though some kind of warning would be quite nice."

"I'm personally starting to miss the flamethrowers," put in Mica, emerging in a hooded fur coat, ski goggles and knee-high fluffy boots. "A girl can't get changed into something appropriate at supersonic speeds unless she knows what's happening with the weather."

Oakenbeard managed a smile.

"Well, at least all the Nazis are gone. You saved the *Buzzard*, lad, and that's good enough for starters. It's just… a bit shocking, seeing all that at once. The Major, Gods rest him, told us you were more of… well…"

Thinking about Major Monkston made the flame behind his eyes wobble. Eddie had a sudden premonition that it would be very, *very* bad to suddenly indulge in self-loathing right now.

"He told you I wasn't very good at it yet, right?" he sighed. "Well, I'm learning. The hard way, I guess."

Darrin rested a huge, callused (but not unkind) hand on his forearm.

"There's a war on, mate. Everyone's learning the hard way. These lads in particular."

Eddie saw the bodies. A crust of dirty ice didn't make them look any prettier. The fact they were Agents of Ultimate Evil didn't make them any less human, either. Several of the young Germans looked shocked and betrayed, as if having their heads twisted around backwards was the last thing they were expecting.

Which in a way, he supposed, it was.

"I don't even remember doing all this," he said. "What if I… I go too far? What if I can't stop when we're out of Nazis, and I…"

Darrin's already dour expression turned downright grim.

"You know how I know about you dragonbloods? We dwarves have 'em too. Very popular, you see. Sometimes, an oathbreaker, as it is, or a murderer, he decides the only way to atone is to give his life for the clan. Shaves off his beard and takes a big drink from the Black Chalice of Vengeance. They carve his name off the Clan Histories, and he sets off to fight the Netherspawn, or whoever the old Hammerjarl has beef with that particular week. And we know they can go wrong. Sometimes the dwarf wins, and he gets a nice funeral, and they melt down his axe and forge a new one to bury with him, see? He's been redeemed. But sometimes the dragon wins. And then we bind him up with collar and shackles, and very, very sadly turf him into a volcano. Berserk means *crazy*, Eddie. This thing's made you strong in the arm, aye? Now you have to be strong in here."

One huge stubby finger tapped him hard on the chest, right above his heart.

Eddie pictured it in his mind – a sad little procession of dwarves, down miles below the sunlight, ready to push a chained-up, frothing figure into a red-lit crevasse. He shuddered.

"I'll try, I suppose. It's all I can do. But – what's next? They've got Connor, Darrin! They've got *Patience!* And…"

"And we've got a clear route to the armoury," grinned the dwarf. Three pairs of hands clapped enthusiastically.

"Does that mean we get to..?"

"Are you finally going to give us the…?"

"And all the electrical tape and string we can…?"

The gremlins' faces glowed with frightening glee.

Darrin Oakenbeard smiled too. It was hard not to.

"Very well, ladies. Me and my mate Eddie here are thinking of going for a bit of a walk. Why don't you see what you can rustle up for a bit of firepower?"

+++

Elsewhere in the Labyrinth of Kew…

It was not going well for Ernst, or the rest of his kill-squad.

Laden down with hex-proof armour, sprigs of holly, bulbs of garlic and blessed rune-stones, he and his men had penetrated deep into the subterranean base. Clattering. Slowly. But *penetrated*, nonetheless. Kommandant Schprinkler would be proud of them!

At first, the Englishmen had panicked, and had run away. This was good. This made it easier to shoot them in the back. Ernst and all his *totenkommandos* carried MG42 machine guns mounted to their exoskeletal armour, and whole coiled drums of ammunition on their backs.

Then things had started to go wrong. The lights had gone off, then come back on, red and dim. The corridors had seemed to twist and shift, doorways appearing and disappearing where they shouldn't be.

*And something had started picking them off.*

Heinrich had been peering into a yawning elevator shaft when several lengths of yellowed bandage had sprung out like cobras, wrapped him up, and pulled him, screaming, into the depths.

Horst had sniffed the air - and asked if anyone else could smell wet dog - before something invisible and huge simply bit him in half at the waist. His legs had tottered backwards a few steps before they, too, were sheared in half again by great unseen jaws. All that was left was the anti-hex charm he should have been wearing around his neck. Someone or *something* had untied the knots.

Karl sunk into the floor, the concrete turned suddenly to quicksand.

Friedrich let off a burst of fire at an apparition of a man with too many arms, wearing a turban, who shimmered out of thin air waving an unlikely number of middle fingers. The bullets went straight through – and then a storm of cutlery slammed into the poor soldier from behind, razor-sharp cake slices, spatulas and kitchen knives making his back into a culinary pincushion. He gurgled as he fell to his knees. A bloody teaspoon fell from between his lips as he died.

Which just left Ernst.

A very heavily armoured, very heavily armed Nazi super-soldier, highly trained, full of the divine will of the Aryan race, and shitting himself.

There! Was that a noise? Some kind of supernatural horror waiting to carve him into…

No. Just a piece of paper blowing along the corridor, a kind of bureaucratic tumbleweed. Ernst sighed, sagging back against the wall. He ran one hand over his face, collecting a fair amount of sweat. What he wouldn't do for a cold beer and a whole packet of cigarettes right now…

"Oi! Bum-face! Down here!"

Something tugged at his trouser cuff.

Ernst looked down, expecting all kinds of terrors. What he didn't expect was a garden gnome in a pink floral dress, its beard curled and blue-rinsed. The creature wore a tiny pair of butterfly-wing spectacles on a purple ribbon. It was carrying a metal cylinder bigger than its own red pointy hat.

"Yeah, that's right pal! I'd ask you how the weather is up there, but the forecast isn't looking too feckin' sunny…"

Ernst made a valiant attempt to bring his huge machine gun around, but the gnome moved so fast it was just a blur of lavender and red. Oh *gott in himmel!* That big metal cylinder must be a *grenade!* And now the thing was *climbing* him! Up his trousers, up the inside of his shirt, out his collar…

Miss Golightly leaned back on the Nazi's chest, one hand hanging onto his collar, the other popping the cap off of what turned out to be an aerosol can of spray paint.

"Open wide and say aaargh, you lanky bugger!"

The aerosol hissed. A choking cloud of paint haloed Ernst's head. Miss Golightly dropped to the floor.

The luckless sturmtrooper looked down at his hands. They were bright red. More red paint dripped from his nose. His uniform was crimson from the shoulders up.

"What… what did you do that for?" he asked, more confused than afraid now.

Unfortunately, this was a state that wouldn't last.

Miss Golightly put two fingers in her mouth and gave a piercing whistle.

"REGINALD!" she shouted. "Coo-eeeee! I've got something for you to play with!"

Ernst swallowed, hard. It was a long corridor. Very long indeed. And in this one, the lights were flickering, pale white interspersed with darkness. Little splotches of red paint dripped around him like fresh blood.

Then something horrible came around the corner. Something huge and leathery and horned, with a gold ring through its nose and massive hooves the size of dinner plates striking sparks from the floor. Something which *bellowed*, in a tone that made Ernst's spine try to wriggle out of his body and escape.

It turned its head. *It saw him.*

Ernst remembered that old saying about bulls and the colour red just in time for it to not matter worth a damn. Then Reggie the minotaur hit him so hard he was reincarnated as a vegetarian.

+++

General Crowley was holed up in the armoury, along with a ragged and mismatched group of Section M soldiers. They'd barricaded themselves in behind a set of thick iron blast doors, but an angry dwarf engineer knocking with a hammer as big as a motorcycle engine tends to get results. After all, the enemy didn't have any dwarves at all, which sort of proved Darrin's credentials.

The General was shouting into a radio transmitter, clicking the dial between frequencies and rattling off orders, a grim look on his face. Wizards are supposed to be ancient, but the so called Wickedest Man in History looked just plain *worn out*. There was an open decanter of what smelled like very fine old whiskey on the desk beside him, next to an unsheathed sword and a large automatic pistol.

"Good. You brought gremlins," he said, as the little group from the hangar trooped in. Darrin told him the situation. Ilse, Lotte and Mica filled in details, with quite descriptive hand gestures. Eddie just looked sheepish. The power had damped down, letting him deflate to normal size again, and the remains of his clothes had to be held up by hand to prevent any kind of accidental nudity.

General Crowley nodded.

"Right. Then we evacuate everyone we can. They don't know that we've isolated the hangar, or punched a hole through their cordon. Sargent Goldbaum, Corporal Set-Ho-Tep? Put together a squad and relieve the administration level. Lance Corporal Singh, you and Private Three Rivers do the same for those in stores and inventory."

"But – we can take 'em, Sir!" shouted a voice from the back of the crowd. It turned out to be an immensely tall soldier with spider-web tattoos all over his face and hands. "Sodding Nazis, coming here! We'll stomp 'em flat!"

This raised a chorus of agreement, and no small amount of snarls, howls and animal noises. It was a fairly diverse bunch. Private Three Rivers, for example, appeared to be a full-grown Sasquatch in a tin helmet.

Crowley favoured them all with a sad, proud smile.

"That's my bloody lads! But I'm afraid that this time, discretion, better part of valour and all that. These Black Sun bastards are just the advance guard. There's *elves* coming. And we have to protect the writer. For the Accords."

Darrin looked ill.

"You mean… he's not gotten out? I know I'm not on great terms with the Hammerjarl, Sir, but I know this much. If we can't promise all those things in the Accords – the change, the *re-forging*, he calls it – then it's war. Elves on the German side? That means dwarves against them, sure as iron is iron."

Crowley grimaced.

"And what if we don't want them on our side?"

"I didn't say they'd be on *your* side, General. Just against the elves. The dwarvern under-empire are a side all of their own." He shrugged. "Sometimes more than one side. Sometimes they fight each other, just to stay in practice."

Crowley downed his whiskey in a single swallow.

"Then saving the one who's crafting this… *re-forging* is of paramount concern. Mister Oakenbeard, you and the ladies get the *Black Buzzard* ready for takeoff. I've sent one of our best squads to secure the writer, but I fear that I can't reach them on the radio. Hans Schprinkler will be going after him too. And those elves can't be far behind…"

"Surely they'll have locked themselves in the Null Vault?" piped up a small wizard, his face all but obscured by an immense and bristly ginger beard. "Let the elves come! We'll wipe them out with a counterattack. He'd need a whole lot of magic to crack that nut!"

Eddie thought of Patience and Connor the Beige, captured and tied up. He thought of the horrible, leech-like sword *Unaussprechlichelangeweileklingdunkelheit,* and how it sucked the sorcery out of whatever it touched.

"Erm…" he began. Not a great start to an explanation, but by the end he certainly had General Crowley's full attention.

"I see. Desperate measures, and such. Famous last stand, and all that. Seeing as I'm logos of the bloody aeon, I'll lead from the front. Weatherfield, you're with me. You too, MacNally, Hammersmith, Sudbury, Newchurch, and Boot Hill Bill. I'd love to have old 'Wrath in a Bath' Schwitzer here for this one, but he is, alas, still all at sea.' He picked up his pistol and sword, straightened his shoulders, and the years tumbled off him like snow from a roofline. "Churchill would probably have a rousing good speech about now, but you all know your business. And we have a bit of an advantage that jolly old Hans doesn't know about…"

He gestured with his saber to the racks and racks of weapons marching off into the darkness behind them. Tommy guns and brens, pistols and claymores, mortars and flamethowers, pikes, halberds and suits of armour. If it was dangerous, deadly, sharp, nasty or went 'bang', it was here, in this barrel-vaulted concrete cavern deep below the gardens of Kew.

"Ladies?" he said, holstering his pistol and throwing a crisp salute to Ilse, Lotte and Mica. "I understand you have some ideas about armaments?"

Three bright-eyed grins said it all.

*"Sir! Yes Sir!"*

"Then, Quartermaster?" he turned to an elderly gent in a tweed version of an army uniform, wearing a pair of ornate brass goggles. "Show them where everything is. And don't spare the electrical tape or string."

# Eleven – The Vault and the Vulture

Through the dripping shadows and the mist they came.

Long-limbed, lithe and fierce. Darting quicksilver through veils of drizzle. Appearing from the dark places between the trees. They unfolded like black umbrellas, all membranous clothes and many-jointed fingers. Pale faces, opal eyes and sharp little teeth. The sound of tiny bells preceded them, along with the smell of frost and blood.

The Gardens of Kew had elves tonight. And the things which His Majesty employed to keep the supernatural borderlands safe had a fight on their hands.

The ways into Fae are twisty and wild. They come out in woodlands and copses of trees on moonlit hills, not because the elves love nature, but because they hate civilization, and the children who live there, and what they have been made to believe[27]. When you're a proud, sadistic warrior of an elder race, dreams about fairy tea-parties *hurt*. Like eyedrops made of acid.

The creatures which stood guard on Kew Gardens had come forth long ago, when the loss of Tirfeynn had brought the elves to this reality. They had been dreamed up by Wizards from the dawn time, and their hatred of the Fae had not faded over a mere ice age or two.

As the invaders slipped through the shadows, eyeless wooden faces turned to follow them. Certain trees rose up from the soil on writhing roots, their branches curling into massive knotted arms. Fists like stumps and bunches of cudgels swung. Limber coils of greenery flicked like whips and nooses.

But there were too few of the Forestborn. The elves laughed as they

---

27 If you think adults have to believe in lots of contradictory things to stay sane, then consider for a moment that early part of your life, when you have *actual reality* to contend with. Kids can't be so easily fooled by their own brains, and can see clearly that the world is full of the magical, weird, wicked and wonderful. Children generate magic like tiny humming dynamos, and convincing them that the elves were flower-hugging inch-tall butterfly people did more damage to the Fae than a hurricane made of broken glass, or a comprehensive audit. To an elven warrior, the complete back-catalog of Rupert the Bear is more debilitating than a polonium and morphine sundae.

danced between the murderous swings and strikes of the trees, and they thrust with poisoned daggers of copper and black glass. Some of the defenders were overtaken by mould and decay, shuddering to rotten slivers in an instant. Others caught flame, screaming in wavelengths other than sound as they thrashed and died.

Now came their herders, roused from their sleep beneath the earth. Long-dead Shamen who had turned their flesh to petrified timber, wearing masks of bone and jade. With them came others – strange beasts bound by pacts and sorceries, things from tombs and catacombs, far-off jungles and frozen wastes.

The elves did away with stealth. They manifested with their vicious glamours boiling the air around them, painful and bright to behold. Humankind have long known about the arrows of the Fae – there are even some who believe we stole the secrets of archery from the fair folk. Things like jaguar-headed angels and four-armed, warthog-tusked warriors were pierced through as they joined the fray A winged baby corkscrewed through the arrow storm, unleashing a cone of purple fire from its lips. elves were blown away to ashes, their copper weapons splashed molten to the ground. Instants later, a black-fletched bolt skewered the deadly cherub. It was replaced by a storm of moths, bearing up a bearded and turbaned man. By a levitating coffin chained shut, crackling with lightning. With a pulsing cloud of crimson smoke, in which naked and voluptuous forms writhed.

Bizarre energies lashed out. Skeletons with swords sprouted from the earth amid the succulents and cacti. An ornamental stone grew a maw filled with diamonds, and pulped an elven archer with its teeth. It's a funny thing, but elf blood is blue. That might be where the saying about the arisocracy comes from, but the truth is, *there's no iron in the Fae at all*. They bled, and fought, and cerulean spray painted the leaves and pattered across the manicured lawns.

But they were ready for Section M's defenses. A chantry of Elven magi walked through the slaughter, their white robes untouched by the carnage, their bare feet an inch above the ground. It was suicidally dangerous for them to hammer the background magic here into their own wild sorcery. But suicidal danger blasted and raved all around them. They raised their voices in song, and the sound which came out was like glass resonating as it slowly cut through flesh. Harmonies built and meshed and bent the world, until reality began to blister outward in front of the chantry, their hands linked, their eyes dripping sky-blue blood…

The air crystalized before them in a great hissing sphere. One by one, the defenders reflected in that glassy orb flickered and blurred. It rolled in place, tethered by unseen forces, and now inside the tenebrous crystal *shapes* could be seen, hammering fists and claws against the glass. They had been swapped with their own reflections, leaving behind transparent, two-dimensional ghosts. Then the sphere collapsed in on itself, twisted through sickening dimensions, and was gone. The ghosts faded into motes of light, accompanied by the sound of far-off screams.

Now the elves pressed forward, led by their elite cavalrymen. Their horses were completely insane, bound up with sorcery and made vicious by long exposure to the borderland realm of Queen Titania. Strongest, cruelest – their glamours flickered and twisted at the edges, for these creatures were old enough to remember the Shakespearean Wars. Many of them had been affected by the Storybombs and Narrative Shear unleashed by the Bard back in 1595, and had narrowly avoided being mutated into twisted, suffering wrecks, frozen in ice in Titania's stasis tombs.

So it seemed that butterfly wings and the scent of flowers alternated with copper sickle-swords and spiked leather armour as the elves came on, breaking through the gap in the defenders' lines and racing toward the great glasshouse at the heart of the gardens.

With Nazis rampaging below, there were few mortal soldiers left to mount a counter-attack. Sporadic gunfire cracked and popped. Bullets were bent off course by the power of the Fae. Those which hit plucked riders from their saddles, spraying sky-blue blood. An anti-aricraft cannon popped up from a trapdoor set in the turf, and its four great barrels began to chew across the cavalry line, before the chantry focused their wyrd song and it folded up like origami, collapsing down to a flat square of metal. Blood came oozing out from its edges.

Voices soared in savage joy. There was nothing between the elves and the glowing glass building now.

Nothing but a single figure in what appeared to be a dirty dressing gown. He had a book in one hand and a hefty length of cactus in the other. But what was more amazing was the halo which flickered above his head. It stuttered and popped like a broken neon tube, illuminating an orbiting ring of glass, all slick and reflective.

The figure took a big bite out of the cactus and threw it away. It burped. It winced.

"Allright. Allright. Time for the big song an' dance, I 'spose. Now…

where's the... you know... ahhh, yes!"

The elves grinned as they bore down on the raggedy little man. Their ranks closed in, so that an arrowhead formation of horses galloped at him pell-mell - eyes rolling, mouths foaming. The cream of the Fae's aristocracy, or whatever other nasty chunks had risen to the top.

The figure found a bottle of headache pills and popped the cap off with one thumb. He poured the entire bottle into his mouth and chewed. He made a face like a cat who has just licked a nine-volt battery. Then he swallowed.

"STOP!" he said, and the word rang like a gong the size of a football stadium pummeled by Thor's hammer. He held out a hand. But the elves didn't stop.

Unfortunately for them, their horses did.

Each one of those mad-eyed mounts left four furrows in the dirt as their hooves locked into a skid. In accordance with the laws of physics, everything on their backs just kept going. There followed a series of thumps, crashes, rattles and bangs as twenty-three very surprised, angry and above all *heavily armed* elven lords hit the turf, hard. It's not best practice, vis-a-vis health and safety, to dive off a galloping warhorse while carrying a lot of sharp and pointy metal. Some of them didn't get up again.

But Duke Ilithrae, the Queen's Executioner did. He was big for an elf, bulky around the shoulders in a way that suggested that (if he was of a less lithe and graceful folk) he'd have no neck, and spend his days looking for opportunities to rip his tank top in half. He stomped up to the slightly wobbly figure in brown, vibrating with indignation.

"Just what in the *hell* are you playing at?" he growled, limbering up his sickle-sword. "How *dare* you presume to stand against us? Against *me!* I am the Lord Duke Ilithrae Shandaeran, right hand of the Queen, bearer of the sacred blade Dawnsplitter! Name yourself, and die!"

That grubby halo flickered on, illuminating a face which would have been handsome, some time last night. Now it looked like the visage of a man who had spent more time staring into a toilet bowl than is mentally healthy. Eyes like poached eggs focused, bloodshot little veins twitching. It grinned, through a tangled mess of beard.

"Wotcher. How's it going."

The man reached out with both hands and gripped the Fae Lord's pointy ears, in a move almost too quick to follow. It looked as if he was going to administer an old fashioned head-butt, but instead a ripple of magic jangled through the air, and Ilithrae gasped. He turned purple.

Not choking purple, but a rich, burgundy-and-violet shade. He opened his mouth, and a foaming torrent of pinot noir came gurgling out. That was just before he collapsed and died.

"Pleased to meet you. I'm Jesus bloody Christ. And I'm having a bit of a bad day."

"What… what did you *do* to him?" stammered another elf, backing away a step.

"Funny thing. Funny thing. The human body's mostly water, right? So is yours, mister bloody Elderflower or whatever they call you. And I can turn water into wine." He hiccuped. "Despite… I might add, *despite the best efforts of your bloody queen to ruin everything!*"

Now quite a few of the Fae foot-soldiers had caught up. Nothing motivates an arrogant ass like the possibility of looking bad in front of the help.

"Stand aside, peasant!" commanded another high-helmed elf lord. "We know your name. We spit on it. You have been *diminished*, and soon you will be nothing but another mortal for us to play with. Perhaps it will amuse the Queen to keep you as a pet. A mad godling, all broken and screaming."

Jesus grinned.

"I kind of hoped you'd say that. See, for the last couple of thousand years I've been forced to be a *very* nice guy. But you've caught me at an interesting time. Your meddling bitch of a Queen has pulled the rug out from under me, right enough. But right here…" he gestured around himself, at the darkened horizon of blacked-out London town. "Right here I have a bit of power stored up, as it was, for a rainy day. Just out there, there's the church of St Mary Magdalene, the chapel of St John the Divine, we've got St Lawrence over on the London road, and let's not forget the Russian Orthodox cathedral in Chiswick." He cracked his knuckles. "And I have this book."

He brandished it like a weapon, and indeed, the front rank of elves staggered back at the sight of the pale pink dust jacket.

"Don't like it, eh? Miss Harriet Juniper-Windlemere's magnum opus for the tiny tots, this is. *The Bumper Jolly Almanac of the Little Flower Folk.* A signed first edition. They kept it in a sealed lead box submerged in scorpion venom and lemon juice, because apparently it's so sweet it'll rot your pearly whites."

A few of the more enterprising elves nocked arrows to their bows. But all of them were mesmerized. The brightly painted watercolour on the cover seemed to mess with their glamours, sending out little snaps and static sparks. It depicted a troupe of good-naturedly brain damaged sprites with butterfly wings and floral clothes having a tea party with a bunny, a hedgehog and a mouse in a top hat.

Jesus opened the book. A low groan went up from the crowd. They tried to run, but their feet seemed rooted to the spot.

"Here's a lovely excerpt from chapter three – '*Princess Twinkly-Toes and the Magical Unicorn Fairy-dust Ballet Shoes*', grated the Savior of Man, in the same tones most people would use for 'this is a fully operational nuclear device'. "Read in my best impression of dear old dad's Voice of God."

Many of the elves were crying now. Some were trying to dig holes in the ground with their bare hands. The lord who had insulted Jesus reached up with a dagger, intent on sawing his own ears off.

"Now now, none of that." The dagger wobbled. "I said NONE OF THAT!" This time the words were scripture. They came out in an old English font, in capitals. The dagger dropped to the ground.

"Now, where was I? Oh yes... **Princess Twinkly-Toes had absolutely nothing fancy enough to wear to the King of Plum-Pudding's fabulous dandelion ballroom dance...**"

+++

Earl Kingsford, former taxidermist and current leader of the Wild Hunt, was hammering down the Chiswick High Road in Gunnersbury when the Cathedral of the Dormition of the Mother of God and the Royal Martyrs[28] lit up like a lightning rod off to his left. He gritted his teeth behind his faceless helm and cranked the throttle of his motorcycle wide open. The racket and roar of his hellish crew rattled the windowpanes as they followed.

A scrying globe lashed to the instrument cluster of the Brough Superior with copper wire began to pulse and chime.

"Arrrgh! Always when I'm driving!" He prodded the offending crystal with one armoured finger.

It was, of course, his Queen.

"The outer wardings are down. Dear old Herr Schprinkler is confident that he's about to win the war single handed. *Now it's your turn.*"

The Erl King chuckled.

---

28 Try saying that ten times fast

"Schprinkler seriously thinks he's going to get out of there alive?"

Titania preened. It was one of her principal skills.

"Of *course* he does. But he's outlived his usefulness. Right now, Jesus Christ is wasting the last of his power on some of my more dim-witted followers. The ones who questioned the necessity of a new World Order."

The Erl King nodded. He was not going to miss old-school elven snobs like Ilithrae and Eldrarion and Vaenar. William Shakespeare had messed them up, and they were stuck in the past. Better that they should have gone into the Winter Halls with the other casualties of the Storybombs…

But then again, he wasn't supposed to know about that.

"No, my diversionary forces are *meant* to die. *You* are the one who will stop these pitiful Accords in their tracks. Bring me the Author. Kill Crowley, and Schprinkler, and anyone else who gets in your way. And when you return – I have a present for you."

The view through the scarred-up crystal ball was not the best, but Kingsford could almost taste the dread artifact which his Queen held out to him. It was a flying-V electric guitar, black as a starless night, strung with seven silver strings.

He managed to choke off a gasp of pure desire.

"Yes, my Queen! I will not fail you!"

The crystal blinked off. The great cavalcade of bikers leaned left, roaring across the bridge over the Thames, two hundred strong. Of course, thought the Erl King, those others were idiots. Of course *they* were the diversions, the suicide squads, the necessary sacrifices. The stage-dressing for his triumphant return to the spotlight…

And in a place just on the other side of West London's shadows, Queen Titania turned away from a perfect crystal globe set amid sprays of white flowers. She reverently put down the guitar she'd been holding, feeling the eyes of a god burning into her back. A very self-important, very old, and above all very *male* god. The form she'd chosen left nothing much to the imagination (except for a cigarette afterwards), and neither did the dress she'd materialized. It was heavy on the spider-silk-lace and just about nothing else.

"So there you have it, Dion," she purred. "We're definitely getting the band back together. Even your old rhythm guitarist is *more* than keen."

Dionysus was in character – which is to say, he had put away enough top shelf liquor to embalm a shipload of sailors. He was dressed in what may have been the height of rock and roll fashion once, and may well have been set to become so again – yellow leather, a tasselled jacket, bell-bottomed trousers and a headband which made him look like a certain kind of pirate.

"Well, I see what you mean about him, love. But then again, he was *always* pathetically up for just about anything. That's why we split in the old days. Creative differences."

"You mean drugs, I assume?"

Dionysus looked up from chopping a line of something expensive on top of something antique, with something sharp.

"Well of *course* we mean drugs, y'ladyship. We always do. Satan gets the credit, but who's busy with a cheeky little long-range plan on the burner down Columbia way? Wine isn't the only thing that gets the revelers… y'know. *Revelating*. Fancy a hoot?"

Titania shook her pretty golden locks. She'd seen the kind of things Dionysus liked to snort. Often when they'd still been attached to various magical animals.

"Still, that's him, you, my husband.."

"*Ex* husband..."

"*Estranged* husband, and getting less estranged with every bloody word that silly little Nazarene speaks. We just need the big man, and the drummer. Any chance you know where he is?"

Dion sucked on his teeth. This was partly to see if he could still feel them.

"Weeeelllllll..."

Titania arched a perfect eyebrow.

"You know, I ground up the holy grail yesterday. Right in that pestle and mortar over there. There's bound to be oh, one, two, maybe *three grams* of it left. Fine as dust. Potent as Medusa's drano."

Dion's bloodshot eyes lit up.

"Hot damn!"

And then there were three…

+++

'Eddie Weatherfield. Not very good at war.'

That's what they'd put on his tombstone, if they ever bothered to get him one. Certainly, most of the other people – *ex people*, he supposed – they rushed past in the red-lit gloom of the labyrinth didn't look like they were set for the old dreary sermon followed by ham sandwiches. Possibly a mop and bucket.

Most of this infantry-combat business seemed to be about running. And carrying. The weapons which Ilse, Lotte and Mica had made were certainly fearsome – Eddie had pulled the trigger once, when something had moved down a side corridor. The recoil had thrown him backwards like a boot to the stomach, and bits of that unfortunate corridor were probably still on fire, underneath the rubble. But you couldn't say that the weird conglomeration of barrels, magazines, drums, fuel tanks and aiming reticules was *light*.

General Crowley set a cracking pace. He seemed to know exactly where he was going, and Eddie, bringing up the rearguard of the little squad, was pleased to note that he had no time for heroics. The General grasped a short baton in one hand, and any Nazis unfortunate enough to encounter him soon felt its power. With a snap of the wrist Crowley threw black-clad bodies left and right, squashing them against the concrete walls like cockroaches. Sometimes his offsiders, Newchurch and Hammersmith, would step out around a likely looking corner and unleash a broadside from their massive gremlin-forged cannons. Newchurch seemed to be made from three normal-sized men, and sported a huge handlebar mustache. Hammersmith wore a sailor's hat, had a belly like a steel keg, and arms like four more.

All through that mad, racketing descent into the bowels of Kew, Eddie was worried about one thing. If they *did* meet some real resistance, how was he going to change? Hitting himself with a hammer had worked a treat, but he'd foolishly let the gremlins borrow it, and now he had none. Getting shot was a proven tonic, but pointing the horrible hybrid weapon he now carried at his own head seemed more like suicide than strategy.

Then there was the matter of *food*. Eddie felt like he could not just eat a horse, but also make a sandwich out of its saddle. They'd passed crispy and unidentified remains which were still smoking, and Eddie was ashamed to report that he'd thought about bacon.

But there was clearly no time to stop for a snack. General Crowley halted his little squad just outside a huge round metal door, of the kind that usually lurks in the darkness underneath banks.

"Right, lads. This is it. Inside here is the Bard's Residence, and inside *that* is the Null Vault. You're going to see some things which I'll advise you are definitely real. You're also going to see a lot of things which you'll deny ever existed, until your dying breath, so help you whatever bleedin' deity has time for you. Understand?"

Eddie really didn't, but there was a lot of nodding going on, so he joined in.

"Arrrgh graak c'khrrr smhrmmmn?" asked Boot Hill Bill, who was a skeleton dressed in a long cowboy's duster, stetson hat, bullet belts and boots. He had no less than six pistols strapped to his bony hips.

"Astute question, William," replied Crowley. "And yes, there will indeed be a cadre of elite Nazi sturmtroopers in there, likely with hostages, likely in the company of Hans Schprinkler. We don't really need any prisoners."

Sudbury – the one covered in spiderweb tattoos – chuckled. McNally cracked his knuckles, then kept going, his fingers stretching like rubber. And the General gestured with his baton, making the big wheel at the centre of the door spin and the bolts slam open.

The vast hunk of steel swung out.

Inside was… well, it was one of those things which Crowley had just promised would be quite real. It shouldn't be. In fact, it made Eddie's eyeballs itch. But it *was*.

The door opened onto a meadow, which dropped away down a gentle slope toward a small brook overhung with willows. There was a copse of poplars in the middle distance, and stone walls criss-crossed the fields away to the horizon. The sky was blue, the air smelled of new-mown hay and wildflowers, and amid this all sat an absolutely impossible building.

The bottom storey was a cottage – a medieval cottage, by the looks of things, with stone walls and a corkscrew chimney and windows made of tiny bubbled panes of glass. Above this came a floor of Tudor wood and plaster, overhanging on every side with a profusion of dormer windows, steep gables and diagonal beams propping it up.

But the third storey was even wider. It appeared to be a baroque model of a castle, and it burst out on every side, giving the whole edifice the appearance of being built upside down. In some places the cupolas, turrets, observatory domes, spires, minarets and battlements overhung the ground-floor cottage by as much as twenty metres. A water wheel, as tall as the entire building but spidery and thin, dipped into the brook as it burbled past.

*"But there was no time to muse on geometric impossibilities"* said a voice from out of nowhere. *"Because Hans Schprinkler had posted guards among the hedgerows!"* It was a lovely voice, like the insinuation of mahogany and treacle. It sounded as if its owner owned at least one vintage pipe and a selection of tasteful cardigans.

"What was that?" asked Eddie, looking around in fright. The same velvety, deep voice echoed his own.

General Crowley motioned everyone to get down.

"Narration. The Bard's Residence was written by Shakespeare and actualised by John Dee. In here, everything's fictional."

***"Said the General. But it was too late. Hans Schprinkler's soldiers had seen the plucky little band of rescuers, and they opened fire!"***

The disembodied voice was right. Shouts rang out, followed by a rattle of machine-gun fire. Bullets spanged off the great round steel frame of the door behind them.

"Stealth's out of the question, then," harrumphed the Wickedest Man Alive. He fiddled with the brass rings which banded his truncheon, and Eddie watched the little clenched fist at one end extend a single, very naughty finger. "You know what you're doing, lads. Take 'em out!"

***"Meanwhile, Patience and Connor the Beige heard the sound of gunfire from outside the Residence. She turned to the old wizard and..."***

"And you can shut up as well!" snarled Crowley. "I don't know how he got any bloody sonnets written with you wittering on in the background all day!"

Then he rolled to his feet, pointed his one-fingered stick at the nearest Nazi, and shouted a word that seemed to have sharp edges and corners. A ball of bright purple fire whistled on a corkscrew path through the air, trailing black smoke, and the luckless German exploded. For an instant there was an after-image of a glowing blue skeleton, then that faded away to nothing.

The others came up firing, too.

Newchurch and Hammersmith were large enough to grip one of the gremlins' cobbled-together hell-guns in each hand, and they raked the foliage and hedgerows with everything from small missiles to musket balls, sending Nazis alternately sprawling, flying, screaming or in one case running away with his bum on fire.

Spider-tattooed Sudbury clapped Eddie on the shoulder and grinned.

"Flank left with me, lad. Old Bill can hold the centre, and the General and MacNally can take the right. We'll have the bleedin' pen-pusher rescued in two shakes."

Then he opened his mouth, and a spider crawled out. Followed by another, and another. Soon a torrent of scuttling arachnids was foaming out between the man's lips, as his tattoos blurred and shimmered with magic.

Thankfully, Eddie was not actually afraid of spiders. There are not many poisonous ones in New Zealand, for a start. And after the past few days, watching a man's eyes roll back to the whites as he was hefted up by a walking carpet of creepy-crawlies was almost normal. Sudbury turned his head, grinning, and one last tiny black widow popped out of his nose.

"Come on lad! They won't leave any for us if we're late!"

He needn't have worried.

Eddie executed a crouched-over run behind the tide of spiders, hearing bullets smack into the trees and stone walls around him. There were screams and curses in German off to the right, then the sound of a roaring wind cut them off. He popped his head up over the top of a shrubbery to take his bearings, and found that they were halfway to the Residence already – but that about twenty sturmtroopers had thoroughly fortified Shakespeare's potting shed.

Oh well. There was nothing for it.

Eddie couldn't for the life of him take control of the power which bubbled away in the back of his brain. *There was too much going on.* He was worried about Patience, and Connor, and if they'd actually be pleased to see him, even if he did come to rescue them. He was worried about getting out of here alive. In fact, he was worried about the twee unreality of this place under London, this little slice of fictional Tudor England with its snow-globe horizon and that silly voice…

At that moment, one of the stray ideas which bounced around the inside of the Bard's pocket universe ricocheted off the blue-sky painted ceiling and tunneled through his skull at 87.3 percent the speed of light. It was a largely painless process, and one which happens to most of us at least once a week. In cartoons, it's depicted as a small light bulb appearing above the cranium. Of course, out under the open sky, many of the stray ideas which sleet through the Earth come from aliens, and thus involve novel new cocktails based on liquid helium, or avante garde fashions for people with nine tentacles and one leg.

Sudbury wasn't waiting for Eddie Weatherfield to have ideas, though. The problem with his power was that, in his current state, his IQ was that of the smartest spider in the heap, divided by the number of spiders. The sum total of his intellect was devoted to herding the beasties to where their natural inclination (scuttle, bite things, look menacing) could do the most damage.

He came up over the potting shed roof, spread-eagled on a tide of little black legs, and engulfed the first two Nazis before they could drop their roll-up cigarettes. Enough venom went into those two in a heartbeat to pickle a blue whale. He held out his hands in the now-famous 'mummy's curse' pose, and tarantulas leaped from his shirt-sleeves, sinking their fangs into the faces of a further luckless pair.

"Come on!" he shouted. "A little help would be nice, berserker boy!"

Eddie took a deep breath.

"He wasn't sure if this was going to work at all, but he *was* certain of one thing," muttered Eddie through his teeth. "The narrator's voice was not used to being bossed around by silly little human wizards. It was going to narrate *something*, and so..."

**"*Hey!*"** said a bad stage whisper, as the sound of whimpers, screams and general punching drifted over the potting shed wall. ***"That's my job, kid!"***

It was the silky-voiced invisible narrator.

"… realised Weatherfield, who was just on the verge of turning into a great big dragonfire-powered monster and smashing a few Nazi heads together," said Eddie.

***"No! No! I'm supposed to do that!"***

"Then be my guest, said the handsome young soldier, who would definitely get a kiss from Patience after this daring rescue..."

***"Oh, come on! Look, leave it to the professionals!"***

"He could feel his muscles embiggening[29] and his funny-looking eye blazing with… umm… how do you spell eldritch?"

The voice sighed. There was a definite impression that if it had a palm or a face, they would have come together at that moment.

***"All right. All right. We do it like* this. *Bloody amateurs!"***

Time stopped. Little motes of dust twinkled in the perpetual summer sunlight. Behind the Potting-Shed-Upon-Avon, Sudbury's fist was frozen at the exact moment of breaking a sturmtrooper's jaw, a hail of bloody teeth glittering in the air like pearls.

***"Eddie Weatherfield shut up. But as he did so, he felt the tiny flame inside his head ignite, sending ripples of power through his body. Inside the Residence, Patience turned her head and smiled, despite the pain. Hans Schprinkler felt it too, and he stepped back, eyes wide.***

"The fool can *control* it? Impossible!"

***There was fear in his voice. And rightly so. As Sudbury went down under a pile of spider-covered, swearing Nazis, the potting shed exploded, and a muscular brute came shouldering through, one eye***

---

29 It's a perfectly cromulent word

*blazing red and yellow..."*

"You're pretty good at this," admitted Eddie, cracking his knuckles. The transformation hadn't hurt, this time. And it seemed to be like a creaky door or a rusted gate. Each time it went a little more smoothly. This time, like the last, he could almost taste and smell the dragons, in all their leathery, sulphurous impossibility.

His fist seemed to be tattooed with scales as he brought it hammering home, and a Nazi soldier went literally flying through the air. He grabbed another by the straps of his backpack, scattering ammunition, and launched him through the remaining wall of the potting shed, spraying bricks like shrapnel.

Now they noticed him, but it was too late. One managed to sink his dagger into Eddie's bicep, but it melted down to the hilt in the time it took for him to headbutt the man's cranium flat as a dinner plate. Another raised a pistol, thought better of it, and ran away. Eddie picked up a brick, took aim, and threw it so hard that it broke the Nazi's skull, sending him cartwheeling in a rag-doll confusion of limbs.

"Took your time, mate?" grinned Sudbury as he pushed his way clear of a pile of black-clad corpses. Some foamed at the mouth, others had turned a nasty shade of purple. Spiders flowed up from them to form a cape around the British soldier. "Still, good job. Now, on to the..."

But he never got to finish. Because at that moment Eddie saw something reflected in his pale white eyes. An instant later, Sudbury pushed him to the ground, using the combined strength of his own muscles and several hundred thousand spiders.

It was a crack in the air, like black lightning, skittering across reality (or whatever the Bard's residence occupied) - quick as bad news and twice as sharp. It sizzled through the space where Eddie had been standing, neatly bisecting Sudbury through the chest.

He coughed. Blood dripped from his mouth. The part of him above the crack was curiously out of phase with that below, as if he was merely a reflection on two panes of glass…

Then the places where the cracks met up fell away. The darkness inside was something which Eddie had seen before – in that terrible sucking vortex which Major Monkston had given his life to close.

"Bloody hell," said Sudbury, his eyes rolling back to show wide, terrified pupils. "Tell old Crowley that w..."

But it was too late. Horrible pale tentacles came out from those cracks in the world, studded with teeth, steaming cold. They ripped through Sudbury's body, little lamprey mouths biting and stretching his skin. Then they all pulled tight at once.

There was a very damp explosion. There was a horizontal rain of blood, and worse. There was a sound like broken glass being ground against concrete.

Eddie was very glad that he had closed his eyes.

But only for a second.

"Unmages!" roared the General, somewhere off to the left. "Boot Hill Bill! Now would be a good time, old fellow!"

Eddie poked his head up over a hedge, and saw exactly what Crowley was talking about. Outside the door of the Bard's Residence stood a trio of black-robed men, wearing golden swastikas on thick chains. If this – and the miasma of greasy sorcery which swirled around them – didn't mark them out as the architects of poor old Sudbury's demise, then the fact that their faces were on upside down would have. That, and the fact that their hands were burning skeletal claws.

The trio began a droning chant, and cracks skittered across reality, blooming and closing as the pressure built. Their target was striding toward them now, trench coat blowing in a non-existent wind, hands twitching over his massively laden gunbelt. Despite having no lips or lungs, Bill was smoking a cigarette.

"Weatherfield!" whispered a voice right by his ear, making him jump nearly out of his boots. It was the General, and he sounded like a man in serious intestinal distress.

"If you're still there, this is the play. I'm holding back those bloody Black Sun chaps with everything I have. Bill will try to shoot them down, but there's no guarantee I'll be able to deflect everything they throw at him. If there's one left, he's yours. Newchurch and Hammersmith didn't make it, lad. It's all on you."

He didn't give Eddie time to politely decline. Because at that moment the dark aura around the Unmages flared, and reality itself seemed to crinkle at the edges like burning paper. Boot Hill Bill cracked his bony knuckles. The leader of the Black Sun coven leveled a single charred finger.

And six pistols levitated from their holsters, whipcrack fast. Bill's skeletal hands twitched as he fanned all six hammers at once, and a fusillade of massive lead slugs followed. Even as a bolt of black lightning corkscrewed through the air toward the undead cowboy...

Crowley screamed as he deflected it. A portal opened in front of the magical blast, and it flew through. Three fields away it scorched back into reality and macerated an oak tree, scattering burning acorns. Then bullets ripped through the Unmage who had released it, throwing him back in a spray of crimson. A second Nazi let loose his blast, and Crowely just managed to summon a mirrored pane of nothingness in time. It knocked a hole in the artificial sky, from which blackened words fell like snow. This man, too, was cut down, his upside-down face blown to ruin by Bill's hand-cannons.

It was the third one who got him. General Crowley had nothing left in him, so he threw his baton to intercept the final blast of unmagic – the raw stuff of the Netherspawn, leached from doomed Tirfeynn. It spun through the air, middle finger upraised, and disappeared in a pop of flaming sawdust and molten metal. The bolt was weakened, but it hit Boot Hill Bill right in the skeletal chest. All six guns were severed from the air. The light went out in his eyes as he was folded into two dimensions, then a single black line, then a dot… then nothing.

"Go, you fool!" came a pained whisper in Eddie's ear.

Eddie experienced a full-body twinge, then, like someone plucking a single nerve in one of his molars. Along with the horrid sensation came an overwhelming urge to run away, and keep running until his boots spontaneously combusted.

But then he remembered the look in the eyes of Patience as the pair of them had hung, gently spinning, over the streets of Istanbul. He remembered the sad little smile on Charlie Monkston's face as he fell away into the slipstream.

So he snarled, whispered *anxiety with pants on*…

And charged.

The last of Hans Schprinkler's hideous crew had been preparing a bolt of sorcery to burn General Crowley from the face of the earth, thereby reducing the background wickedness of Britain by a good eight or nine percent. However, as this would also substantially reduce the chances of His Majesty's Government winning the war, Eddie was having none of it. He barreled through a section of ornamental shrubbery with his head down and his fist cocked back, ready to smash the upside-down-faced blighter into next week.

But just as the hero game was looking up for young Weatherfield, time seemed to slow to a sickening crawl. And who should step out from behind that black-robed horror than someone even less inviting...

No points for guessing.

It was Hans Schprinkler.

Or rather, a clockwork-filled, clattering automaton, with a glass cube atop its shoulders... and the face of the Black Sun's mastermind inside.

It carried the sword *Unaussprechlichelangeweileklingdunkelheit* in one robotic hand, and a huge cannon in another, complete with sizzling glass balls and copper armatures and a trumpet-shaped muzzle. A huge cog in its chest was blazoned with a glowing green swastika, and pistons thumped where its heart should have been.

Now, this might have been perfectly acceptable, if it were not for the fact that it was possessed of *four* arms, and that it held Patience in the other two. One bound up her hands, while the other was a claw clenched around her throat.

The unmage turned as Eddie tried to backpedal, and his mouth contorted into what may have been the world's first ever actual upside-down frown. A ball of seething darkness spun between the man's skeletal fingers, dripping little runnels of ink.

"Oh yes. Destroy him," sneered the robotic Schprinkler, its face moving in a jerky blur of static. "This one is *far* too fond of surprises, hmm? I think I'll have his head mounted. Above. My mantelpiece, now that he has those cute little horns and all..."

Patience kicked and thrashed. She met Eddie's eyes for a second, and was obviously trying to tell him something.

He supposed it was something terribly noble like 'run, save yourself', or 'there was nothing you could do'. But at that moment, he didn't want to hear it. Staring down the barrel of that dark fireball as the unmage raised it high, all he could see was the flame in his head, billowing up like a bonfire, filling his mind like the light of an oncoming train in a very narrow tunnel.

Then something flickered behind the unmage. The crook of an umbrella (shaped like a humorous flamingo) hooked around his ankle and pulled him off balance, making the blast of sorcery loop off into the air. Then the rest of Mrs Hazelwood appeared, spinning her crystal ball on one finger like a basketball player.

"Alley oop, Lucky!" she shouted, flicking the ball skyward.

The leprechaun appeared in midair, rising like a bad hangover from the ornamental begonias. At the top of his leap (reaching out in the classic slam-dunk pose) he grabbed the crystal ball and brought it hammering down with all his quite incredible strength.

There was a purple explosion. There was a smell of unwashed robes, burning. And with a sad little farting noise, the unmage of the Black Sun simply ceased to exist.

Hans Schprinkler's mechanical doppelganger was viciously quick. He swung his cannon around to snap off a shot at Mrs H, but suddenly Percy was there, gripping the Nazi's arm in his nightmare jaws. CHOMP! The weapon clattered to the ground, still clenched in a set of chrome fingers.

Schprinkler swung his sword the other way, where he held Patience at arms length. But it was met by a shimmer in the air, which resolved itself into the Compte de Saint Germain's rapier. With the flick of the wrist, he locked up both swords, then dashed the enchanted blade to the flagstones.

"Wotcher, ugly! Let's see what a few centuries of fencing lessons will get ya, shall we?"

"Stop!" shouted the leader of the Black Sun, brandishing Patience like a rag doll. "I can still crush the life out of her! One more step, and..."

The three shots came almost one on top of the other. You would have had to have possessed the reflexes of a very demon to work the bolt on a 1918 Tankgeschutz heavy rifle that fast. Or, indeed, those of a Soviet vampire sniper. Bullets designed to pierce the engine blocks of tanks sliced precisely through the ball joints at the robot's elbows, dumping Patience unceremoniously to the ground. Another collapsed its chest like a cheap tin can, and threw it back against the wall.

Eddie was there in an instant.

Now, it's never polite to tell a lady that she looks terrible. But there was certainly a pale, *drained* look to the young witch's features, as though she was coming apart at some fundamental level. He risked a glance over at the glowing *Unaussprechlichelangeweileklingdunkelheit*, where it had lodged itself in the stone pathway. A sword should not have been able to smirk, but this one managed. Eddie promised himself, then, that he would give the bastard thing some quality time with Darrin Oakenbeard's anvil. Or possibly just give it to Ilse, Lotte and Mica to play with.

Patience's eyes flickered open. She smiled.

"I thought you'd never get here, Weatherfield," she managed, a trickle of blood dripping from the corner of her lips. "And I see you brought the others with you?"

Eddie, never on the best of terms with his own feelings, was on the verge of telling her the whole, entire, quite long-winded truth. But

Lucky got in first.

"Oh aye, Miss Patience. We were supposed ta evacuate, like, with the rest of them. But, well, you know. What with him a-chargin' in here, and tagging along with old Crowley himself, and all..."

"We would have looked the right pillocks if we didn't help out one of our own," finished Fyodor, leaning nonchalantly on his huge cannon.

Eddie caught a little smile and a definite wink from his Sergeant.

Patience tried to stand up, failed, and let Eddie help her to her feet.

"I thought I told you to be careful, you silly boy," she said, softly. "And by the way – you look terrible!"

There came a scraping, grinding noise from the door of the Residence. What was left of Hans Schprinkler's double had managed to lurch itself upright, sliding up the medieval stonework and leaving a slick of oil behind it.

"Oh, ja, ja, this is all very touching, of course. But also. Completely. Useless." His face was a blurry ghost inside the cube of glass atop his shoulders. "Now, you may be wondering why I didn't come here in the flesh, for my glorious victory..."

"Pretty bloody glorious, you wanker," countered Lucky. "What with how I'm about to kick yer bleedin square head in, like..."

Schprinkler's eyes glittered.

"Now now. Temper temper, mein Celtic chum. Shouldn't you let good old Eddie do the honours?"

The seven-foot leprechaun mused for a moment. Then he tipped his hat in Weatherfield's direction."

"How about it, private? Do you want to do, as the rotten bugger calls 'em, 'the honours'?"

"Though perhaps, if you would *let me finish, you degenerate. Whiskey-soaked. Dumkopf! Yes!* There is of course, much more to my evil, genius plan. Seeing as I am, with no need to be, how you say, blowing the trumpet, an *evil. Fecking. Genius!*" Schprinkler's face, through the thick, green-tinted glass, was contorted into a rictus of self-congratulatory glee. "You see, the Wild Hunt are coming. I knew that they would try to betray me. So I used this wonderful little device of mine to speak to you from all the way across Europe. And to carry with it a bomb with a *very special* payload. Twenty MegaAlbtraums[30]

---

30 A single Albtraum, as discovered by Black Sun sorcerer-scientists, is enough of the stuff of the Inside-Out to inspire one bed-wettingly horrible nightmare. Twenty thousand times this level, unleashed as a blast, is enough to terrify the laws of physics themselves, causing up to become yellow, Tuesday to become sideways, light to

of antithaumic energy, direct from Tirfeynn! Enough to blow your precious writer out of his silly. Tweed. Trouser-hosen, yes? And with him… the Accords are *dead und buried!*"

Part of the automaton's ruined chest unhinged. There, behind the chrome-steel ribs and turning gears, was a glass tube, seething with malignant fire. Wires and hoses connected it to a big brass alarm clock.

"Look!" enthused Schprinkler. "I even did the bit with the clock, so you have the terrible sword-of-damocles type decision to make! Destroy my doppelganger, and kaboom! Instant meat confetti for you all! Or try to escape… before the relentless grinding of the second hand ticks away the final! Moments! Of your pitiful…"

The knobbly end of an old-fashioned bog-oak shillelagh came whistling out of the shadows to shut him up. The impact of wood on glass was followed by a prolonged coughing fit, as Connor the Beige appeared, in the company of a distinguished-looking professorial man, who (despite being in the middle of a war zone) was smoking a briar pipe with obvious enjoyment.

"And you can shut up too, you infernal wee collection of fiddly bits," said the Scots wizard, squinting at the members of his squad. "Nice work with the chameleon watchermacallits. I knew old Darrin was onto something with those. Now, did yon scunnerous bag o' bolts say something aboot a bomb?"

Schprinkler laughed.

"Four more minutes, you horrible little damp wizard! Then…"

The man who had come out of the Residence with him had opened a vast, leather-bound book, and was scribbling away with a fountain pen.

"This is jolly good stuff! Jolly good! I don't know if it's in the correct heroic idiom, but still…"

Connor snapped his fingers. A circle of purple fire appeared in mid-air, and a skeletal hand passed him the handset of a field radio through it.

"Tell Jeckyll it's time for plan Icarus. Now. The Residence. I'll stabilize the transfer. Oh, aye. Crowley's all right. A bit knocked about, and having a wee snooze in the geraniums, poor sausage." He let the

---

become spaghetti and sausages, entropy to tie itself in a ribbon around the bunch of camellias which was, until a second ago, the second law of thermodynamics, and everyone within a ten mile radius to go so utterly insane that this description makes perfect logical sense to them.

radio disappear, then turned to look up at the artificial sky.

"Your Bardship, we might need some help here, ye ken?"

***"Oh, all right,"*** came that silky smooth narrator's voice. ***"But if it's raining out there, you'll owe me!"***

"That voice… is the *Bard*? William actual *Shakespeare?*" asked Eddie, quite aghast. He'd said some rather uncharitable things about the old fella during his school days, after all.

"B.A.A.R.D." replied Connor, as the sky split open along hidden seams, and a huge disc of it rumbled away, revealing the spotlight-crossed night air of London. "Bio Alchemical Artithmetic Reckoning Device. He's a clockwork artificial brain, haunted by the ghost of old short-trousers. Doctor Dee got Galileo over to do the maths, see? Excuse me a minute."

The little wizard sketched a circle out in the dirt with his shillelagh, then motioned everybody to stand back.

"Any second now… and if I could just get you to write down that this definitely works, y'r honour..."

The circle flared white, then blinked paisley. There was a sound like an alpenhorn filled with bubbling custard, and mist boiled up, condensing into the shape of Doctor J in his monstrously large form. He carried Major Charlie Monkston's Talbot-Largo special under one arm, and an immense broomstick under the other.

"One minute left, chaps. Nick of time, heroic way of doing things and all that, I see!"

"Well," said the writer, "There really ought to be a dragon if we're going for *true* heroism. But I gather that this bit has nothing to do with the Accords in any case. Call it non-canonical."

"*Fools! Imbeciles!*" ranted the robotic Hans Schprinkler, as the good Doctor and Lucky bound him securely to that giant broom. It was one of the Demdike Mark Twelves which was designed to punch the *Black Buzzard* almost into orbit. "Your Accords are *finished!* I read what this poxy old hack wrote in '37, and it was *silly!* Little short people and drugged-up wizards and stupid songs! No wonder the Queen wants none of it! But you'll never stop us! I have the..."

"Thirty seconds. Patience, would ye care to light the fuse?"

This time Eddie didn't have to hold her up. The Revenge of English Witchcraft made a gesture with one hand, and purple sparks sizzled through the air.

"When you get to hell," she told Herr Schprinkler, "See if it's frozen over yet. There's a young man from 1804 who's waiting for me to call him back."

The immense broomstick shuddered. Squad 27 all took a cautious step back. A crackling and rustling came from the thicket of bristles tacked on behind the thing as the hands on Schprinkler's clock swung around to midnight.

"He's not going to hell, though, is he?" asked the Writer, looking up from his tome.

"The B.A.A.R.D. back-traced his signal, didn't it?"

Connor gripped the brim of his hat with both hands.

"Awww, you're nae supposed to *tell* him, ye daft scrivener! Now he'll know we're..."

But there was no time left for words. The Demdike Mark Twelve took off like a gigantic firework, whooshing up through the crack in the sky on a pillar of blue and white smoke. Little blips and motes of magic settled like powdery snow, crackling as they touched Eddie's skin.

Doctor Jeckyll had carefully placed the Talbot Special right-side-down, and now he was deflated back to his regular size, all swaddled in the remains of a torn-up lab coat.

"Don't worry about it, please, Mister To... I mean J.R... I mean *John.*" His eyebrows waggled conspiratorially. "Just hop in the car. We're about to be visited by some very nasty elves, and I'd like to get you and the General tucked away somewhere safe. Like Section W's secret base, which isn't very secret to me, seeing as my cousin Alfred is chief mad-science officer there."

The Writer snapped his great big leather-bound book shut and squared his shoulders.

"You know, I *did* serve in the last war, Lawrence old chap. Give me an Enfield and I'll help you see these rapscallions off!"

"No, sorry" came a croak from behind a box hedge. General Crowley staggered to his feet, covered in dirt, half blackened by sorcerous backwash, and with a potted geranium on his head. "Too valuable. In the car, old sport. And as for you fellows..."

He turned a gaze on Eddie and the rest of them which could have set blocks of frozen nitrogen on fire. Forget curdling milk – this look could have curdled solid steel. Some people say they will stop at nothing to achieve victory. This was the face of a man who would merrily drive off the curve of reality with his foot welded to the floor, if there were some Nazis to run over on the other side.

"*They blew up my base*, Connor. They tried to stop the Accords,

Patience. They killed my men, and ruined my breakfast, and for all I know they've gone and got rid of Jesus Christ, who was a bit of a pillock but a *damn fine adversary*, morally speaking. Now, we're taking (ahem) *John* here, and finishing the job. The Accords will be signed in two days time, in Switzerland. By that time, you'll have crushed Hans Bloody Schprinkler like a cockroach."

He smiled, like a row of tombstones by moonlight. Little crackles of magic crawled over his bloody knuckles.

"You're the last ones left, Squad 27. You'll do what must be done."

From outside, where the Labyrinth of Kew still burned, came the sound of motorcycle engines. The Wild Hunt was coming. Somewhere high above, an explosion lit up the sky over London, unfolding in a great glittering dandelion-clock of sparks.

The last thing Eddie saw of the Residence – or of Kew, for that matter – was by that flashbulb green and orange light. It was a tiny little green man carrying a suitcase bigger than he was, sprinting out of that impossible cottage like his bum was on fire. As the Talbot spun its wheels and slewed around in a fishtailing skid, the goblin leaped into the trunk, dragging his luggage behind him.

*"Master! Master not leave us here! We goes where you do!"*

"I wonder if that little fellow will make it into the book?" asked Fyodor, as much to himself as to anyone else.

And then it was time to start running.

# Meanwhile, elsewhere by about a vertical mile or two...

As the Demdike Mark Twelve solid-fuel superbroomstick powered up into the darkened skies, Hans Schprinkler tried to cut the connection between himself (seated on an ornate rosewood throne, in a castle in Germany's Black Forest) and the automaton his mind inhabited.

Unfortunately, the occult science which enabled him to command a four-armed robotic killing machine across the distance of half of Europe was more powerful than it was exact. Pentacles flared and torches guttered, but the signal remained clear and bright, a thin silver cord stretched tight across the magnetosphere. Another little secret stolen from the Queen of Spring, that one.

Hans Schprinkler felt gravity fall away as the great broomstick coughed out its last few gasps of sorcery. London was spread below him, dark and jagged under the blanket of the blackout. Beautiful, for a moment.

But while the dislocated mind of the Black Sun's commander contemplated the dapple of moonlight on the Thames, he didn't see the V-2 rocket powered bomb which was falling in toward him with the inevitability of gravity itself. Its trajectory had been predicted and plotted by some of the people below – those section P-for-Parapsychology boffins working in the conveniently P-titled sub-section PISCES.

It would have interested them greatly to learn that this was a very special missile, with a very special payload, and the code number 00000.

Then again, Parapsychologists say that traumatic events leave echoes backwards in time as well as forwards. So there might have been something to the fact that this particular V-2 rocket bomb smashed into an occult Nazi robot riding a gigantic broomstick just as the bomb inside that robot's chest unleashed the equivalent of twenty thousand screaming mad nightmares from a containment vessel the size of a regulation cricket ball.

The shockwave from the blast rippled out through the skies over London, causing all kinds of strange entanglements. Those on its very edges woke from their slumber, with images in their heads of kamikaze pilots and explosions and sadistic SS officers and sentient electrical hardware, and in one case, a hamburger that ate people. Dogs howled and cats hissed across the metropolitan area. Rats nibbled their own tails in anxiety. King William, the ancient, near-torpid boa constrictor of immense size who lived in the sewers under Westminster, rose from out of a manhole cover to take a peek, and shocked a trio of nuns into hysteria.

By the time the sparks had faded, it was all over. A few sad little bent and broken gears pattered down over Croydon, and a robotic foot lodged in a hollow oak tree west of Slough.

While somewhere in the Black Forest, Hans Schprinkler rose unsteadily from his throne and beckoned to one of his black-robed acolytes. His voice was the rasp of a man who has just woken up from a three-week bender to find that he has, inexplicably, swallowed a miner's boot full of marmite.

"Get me, in this order - a stiff drink, a new sword, another drink, a strong coffee, some fresh *underhosen* and a direct line to the Fuhrerbunker. They're coming."

# Meanwhile, elsewhere for what we promise is almost the last time...

It was raining at the crossroads.

This, in and of itself, was something to be remarked upon, because it had been hot enough to fry the roadkill on the ol' country blacktop this past week or more.

The clouds had rolled in off the bayou like a bruise-purple promise, shot through with veins of lightning, and everything sane and reasonable had hunkered down indoors, hoping that this wasn't tornado weather. When the rain came down it was like an ocean with holes in it, and even the insane and unreasonable sought shelter.

But...

The lone crow atop the road sign that stood at the crossroads had to be there. It was a union thing. It wanted to be a magical familiar, and it knew a voodoo lady out in the swamp who was known to be hiring. Even so, it was hunched up into its own greasy feathers about as far as it could go, as it watched the two men down below arguing with each other.

They were both well dressed, like the gentlemen of these parts. That meant embroidered waistcoats, silver-toed boots, natty dark suits and wide brimmed hats. They seemed to have both been going for the same look – that of a slightly louche preacher, or a card-sharp down on his luck. Both, inexplicably, were carrying guitar cases. One case was purple, and skinned in what the crow could tell was not exactly leather. The other was black as nightmares, and inlaid with swirls of silver.

"... And I'm telling you, they were talking about that bloody valley in Wales, mate. Your idea's just plain stupid!"

"It's all in the semantics. Prophecy's an oral tradition."

"I've got a bloody oral tradition for you right here, pal! *I* made this appointment, and you're trying to..."

"Trying *nothin'*! This is clearly part of my mythos, you jumped-up little quasi-demiurge! I have big plans resting on this thing!"

"Resting on the mispronunciation of some garbled bit of elf nonsense, and a cheap guitar?"

The first man (the one with the peacock-green waistcoat) was tall and slim, with a braided ponytail of fire-red hair dangling from under his hat. His eyes were blue as sapphires, and he wore a bolo tie sporting a golden bull's head.

"Well?"

"I assure you, this instrument is *far* from cheap. As the young man who's on his way will find out, through a story of truly legendary twists and turns, sure to have dire implications for the moral turpitude of humanity." His interlocutor was shorter, but stockier across the shoulders, with dark sunglasses on - even in the rain, even at night. Something red smoldered behind them, and he wore a neatly trimmed and waxed goatee to match his switchblade-thin sideburns. "Anyhow, my opposite number's in some strife at the moment, so I figured the time was ripe..."

Both turned, scowling, as they heard the sound of a car approaching. Headlights appeared in the distance, blurred in the rain.

"I don't suppose you'll be a good sport and just bugger off, then?" asked the man in the peacock waistcoat.

"No more than you would, friend," grinned the man with the wicked facial hair. "Rock paper scissors?"

But then, with a lurch of compressed time, the car was right next to them. It pulled to a stop with a creak of brakes and a hiss of rain evaporating on its hot chrome grille. It was a long, black 1938 Cadillac, with whitewall tyres and smoked glass windows. It was not at all the kind of vehicle either man was waiting for.

They shared a look at each other, of the kind which is full of questions. Top of the list – 'who exactly have you pissed off, then?'

Then the front doors opened, and two more men emerged. They wore identical black suits with white shirts and black ties. They wore identical black fedora hats, and black, thick-rimmed sunglasses. Even in the rain. Even at night.

They were clearly Dionysus and Vulkan, however. This was apparent by the fact that one was a scarred and hunch-backed gargoyle of a man with arms like hams stitched together with electrical cable. And the other was puffing a glass pipe made up of several coloured bubbles, which issued forth rainbow smoke.

"Ahhhh, there he is! Mithras, you old dog! You old plonker! You old… what do they call those things with the tentacles, and the handle on the top, and the little plastic wheels?"

Vulkan spat.

"They call it *lay off the pipe*, you poncy git. But still," his face split into a craggy grin. "Good to see you, Mithy old boy. Who's the lad with the chin-fuzz?"

Mithras – the waistcoated one – did not look one hundred percent pleased to see his old companions. "I have a feeling it's the prince of…"

The other man made frantic 'don't go there' motions with his hands, while grinning like a barracuda.

"Easy does it, folks. I'm not high in the PR stakes in this neck of the woods, if you can dig that. I'm just… that old fella at the crossroads."

Mithras rolled his eyes.

"Which brings me to the question. What are *you two* doing at this particular crossroads, right now? It's just that I had a bit of a side gig on, where I was going to…"

"*Swap a troubled young man one immortal soul for amazing musical abilities*" chorused the other three, as if reading from a script.

"Just like that dopey git with the pan pipes back in Macedonia?" asked Vulkan. "Naughty naughty!"

Dion exhaled a cloud of smoke which contrived to form a chain of perfect rings.

"Here's the thing, right. We're getting the band back together."

Vulkan nodded.

"We're on a mission from… from *US*."

"What, were you the guitarist?" asked the bearded gent.

"The drummer." said Mithras. "But those days are gone. Though I am feeling like engaging in a bit of percussion right now…"

Vulkan nodded.

"She said you might say that. She said to tell you you're the last one. All the rest of us are in."

Mithras' brow crinkled with consternation.

"Even the big man? Even… *him?*"

Dion nodded.

"It's all going to be different, this time. They're ready for it. The *world's* ready for us. And we need someone on the skins who knows the rhythm of the celestial clockwork, man. We need the old sun-god at the centre of everything…"

The man with the beard had finally put two and two together.

"You're… and he's…. Oh. My. Arch-nemesis! *Thunderbeards!* You were all the rage when I was an up-and-coming dark lord! What did you call that music of yours?"

Dionysus looked back over his shoulder as he climbed back into the Caddy. He peeked over the top of his ray-bans and smiled.

"Despite these costumes, it wasn't the blues, mister. We didn't call it *anything*. It called us, perhaps."

Mithras slung his guitar case in the back seat and slid in next to it. Despite the rain, he was absolutely bone dry.

"Good luck with the young fella, then. I hope he's everything you planned for."

The door slammed. The engine revved. And with a thunderclap and the smell of burning tin, the Cadillac disappeared, becoming nothing but a receding pair of red tail-lights in the rain.

The words 'can I get an autograph' died on the stranger's lips. He hefted his guitar case, and frowned. Somewhere off to the east, he could hear a rackety old model-A truck approaching, and behind the wheel burned the soul of a man who was ready to change the world. Not for himself, noted the strange dark spirit with the oil-slick goatee. Not for himself, but for his son, the twin who'd survived, the one who was too shy to sing but who loved music.

It was amazing, he thought, as he put on his best salesman's grin and leaned up against the signpost, what people would give for their children. As for him… well, he hadn't seen eye to eye with *his* daddy in centuries. He'd make the deal. The kid would get the guitar. And eventually…

"The heck with it. Those stuck-up boys want to have their silly little band, I'll take credit for the music!"

He didn't notice the colossal streak of birdshit down his back until the next morning, by which time the crow was long gone, the course of history changed, and the suit ruined forever.

Then again, it had smelled far too much of brimstone, anyway.

Meanwhile... look,
we assure you
that whoever has
been doing these
has been fired. In
the interests of
completeness, and
because of some
kind of union thing,
this will be the last
one, though you
can skip it and go
right to the bit with
the explosions and
the arms and heads
coming off and
the gritty heroic
monologues if you
like...

General Crowley had been called many things in his long, long life. Longer than people would have believed, in any case, and longer than certain beings of the planes immaterial would have liked, by half. He'd been called wicked, satanic, vile, crazy, loopy, mad, deluded and prophetic.

But he'd rarely been called a racing driver.

What was not widely known (and was even less widely talked about) was the fact that in the 1920s he had lived in Italy, and had been kicked out by Mussolini for reasons involving (allegedly) a bunch of bananas, a live conger eel, a pair of fisherman's waders full of grape jelly, and the fascist dictator's mistress. But in 1927 he had returned, heavily disguised, and had contested the inaugural Mille Miglia in a car of his own design.[31] If it hadn't been for a chance encounter with the same mistress, a penguin, a paddling pool full of vanilla custard and a hairdryer, he would have blitzed the field. That car – the Fnord Poltergeist Phaeton Supreme – had been quick, but the General was almost certain that Charlie Monkston's Talbot Special would have given it a run for its money.

The Writer peered out of the oval back window as the little car made a powerslide into a street of bombed-out houses, flames spitting from its exhausts. Up front, Doctor J hung out of the passenger window, a Thompson automatic in his hands. As the Talbot fishtailed through a row of dustbins, tyres squealing, he rattled off a blast of bullets, then dropped the drum magazine to the kerb.

"They're still behind us, Sir," he reported, in his usual jolly bedside manner. A new drum was slapped into place, and he leaned out to sit on the window frame, raking the slipstream with lead.

"I don't know why you couldn't have gotten one of the other chaps to do this part," said the Writer, who Crowley was doing his best to ignore. The fact that the man had produced, against all odds, another full pipe of tobacco from somewhere upon his person during their escape did not help one iota. "Wheatley likes this magic stuff more than I do, and Fleming's a better shot. They both popped over from intelligence last week, and..."

General Crowley frowned.

"*And they have their own jobs to do for the war effort,* old chap. Just like you do. Wheatley's got some ghastly thing going where I play a mad monk or some such. Going to muddy the waters about real magic

---

31 Which would go on to become the inspiration for the fictional character Dick Dastardly and his 'car double zero' in the television series Wacky Races

for a generation. And as for young Fleming… he's going to convince the world that England is not to be messed with."

They shimmied through an alleyway, across an allotment, through someone's shed, and down onto a towpath by the Thames. Behind them, Crowley could hear the war-whoops of feral elves riding spectral motorbikes. Things were not looking good.

"How far to Section W again, Sir?" asked the Doctor, ducking his head back inside just as the Talbot skidded around a corner, spraying gravel. "It's just that I'm out of bullets, and those bastards are gaining!"

Crowley gritted his teeth and pushed the accelerator hard down to the floor. Up ahead was the gaping maw of a drainage pipe, leading down into London's brick-lined underworld. Under the hood, the big Rolls-Royce engine devoured fuel and breathed out fire, pistons hammering and valves blurring. Into the living iron of the block had been cast a fragment of a magic sword, made by Merlin himself for an ancient king (in the days when a mighty kingdom was still big enough to walk across between breakfast and tea time)[32]. Among other things, this meant that every single little gasoline explosion was augmented with sorcery, and that excess heat was offset not through the radiator, but through a dislocationary spell that shunted it into a small area of the dry valleys of Antarctica. That engine sang. The Talbot *flew*.

But a Brough Superior enchanted with the predatory magics of Tirfeynn was no slouch, either. As the Talbot roared down the pipe and into a disused section of underground railway, the Erl King was right on its bumper, and his huntsmen were not far behind.

"What we need," mused Doctor J, "Is a distraction."

"What we need," opined the General "Is bloody divine, pardon my french, intervention!"

"*Whats yous neeed,*" came a muffled voice from behind the back seat, "*Is to goes faster! Gagrat hates nasty elfies! You not want to know what they do with poor innocent goblin!*"

The Writer folded down the arm rest between the back seats and rummaged in the trunk with one hand, finally fishing out a tiny green man, apparently clad in rags and garbage. His nose was long and pointed, as were his ears, and he smelled of musty old cellars and mushrooms.

"And what do you think the *humans* do to goblins who slow them down?" he asked. The goblin grinned. His teeth were like tiny bone

---

32 In this case, the King of a certain valley in Wales. He was known for his lute-playing prowess and his immense, luxurious sideburns.

needles.

"Dimplomatic imm-myooner-tea! You taught uss! Yess! I am messenger of the Mountain King, under flag of truce! You can't do nuffing!"

The Talbot slid right, bumped up a flight of stairs, and roared along an empty train platform. In the back of the car, rags, tweed, goblin limbs, books and pipe smoke were thoroughly blended.

The Writer emerged from under a pile of papers, holding Gagrat at arms length. It's worth noting that he could not do the same for the goblin's smell, which was another passenger in its own right.

"Then again," he said, in that far-off, dreamy voice which means someone is either having an epiphany or an overdose, "maybe I *can* do something with you. Remember what we'd been working on?"

Gagrat nodded.

"King's special program. Hush hush. Goblins gonna be taken *seriously* in new century of progress an' promisss, right?"

The writer shuffled his papers, and re-lit his pipe.

"Well, if you're keen to help us, Mister Gagrat, we can give it a test, right now."

Gagrat nodded, and rummaged through the assembled parchments and books.

"This one! What does it say?"

The Writer grabbed it away as though the goblin was holding a live grenade.

"*That* is written in what is called the *Burz Ta-Folun*, the language of darkness, and it is indeed the one we are looking for. I'm not going to ask exactly how you knew, because we don't want a diplomatic incident."

"We're going to have one any second!" shouted Doctor Jeckyll, throwing his empty tommy gun at the pursuing hunters. It smashed an elf in the face and he cartwheeled away, bike flying to pieces at the touch of iron.

"Here! Take the little fellow. And when I say 'NOW!', you throw him out the window."

"Yess! Out the… wait, *what?*"

There was a scratching of a pen on parchment.

"….dot the i's, cross the t's…"

"Really, master, yous don't have to throw Gagrat out of the actual window, I'm sure he was jussst…"

"NOW!"

Doctor J threw the wide-eyed and terrified goblin as hard as he could, while at the same time knowing that no matter how many times he washed his hand, it would still never be truly sterile again. A cry of *"Diplomatic emmm yoou nit eeeeee!"* was torn to ribbons by the wind as Gagrat hooked one clawed finger around the rear bumper.

And then there came a thunderclap of noise. The car slowed down as something huge and green climbed up over the boot, over the spare wheel, and onto the roof. It *roared*, and General Crowley watched the elves in his rear view mirror flinch. Now the Talbot came screaming out into the docklands of London, dodging lorries and longshoremen and sailors in their navy uniforms. They, too, saw the thing perched on the roof of the car, and began to scream and run.

Doctor J risked a look in the wing mirror, which he tilted to get a better view. Gagrat was gone. At least, the two-foot-high, wiry little green bugger with the athlete's foot and body odour was gone. In his place was a thing like a cross between a rugby forward and a silverback gorilla, green and leathery, clad in spiked black armour and rags of chain mail. It had a flattened nose, an underbite of yellow tusks, and the tiny red eyes of an unhinged psychopath. As an incautious Wild Huntsman came blattering up alongside the Talbot, the thing reached out with a long and muscular arm, then grabbed the luckless elf by the head. It *squeezed*, and something cracked, horribly loud. Then it used the limp body as a flail, unhorsing two more of the Fae.

"Come on, ya skinny gits!" it bellowed "Why's you waitin' for a fight? I got plenty fer yez allll!"

"My lord!" said the Doctor, as the huge creature unslung an axe from its belt and waved it menacingly. "You had a spell which could turn one of *them*… into one of *those?*"

The writer looked up over his spectacles.

"This is stage three in the Accords. Post-ironic transference with popular cultural feedback. I based quite a lot of it on those young fellows who like to punch each other in the face regarding football."

The axe swung in the metallic blur, ending with a gurgle and a thud and a whole lot of blue.

"What exactly do you call it?"

"An *orc*. It was Gagrat's idea. He says his King wants to fight, but that goblins have their limitations."

"Good God, man! We don't want an army of those beasts let loose here in England!"

The Writer shrugged.

"Not here, no. They're going back to their own world. The Netherspawn seem to have underestimated our small green friends. As have we all. In the spindly little chests of those snot-hoarding goblin cowards, beats the heart of... well, look at him go!"

The orc had leaped off the back of the car now, and he was effectively forming a one-monster roadblock to the Wild Hunt. There was no way Gagrat could win, or even probably survive. But he was laughing as he clotheslined four bikers off their saddles in one massive shrug of his arms, then punched the Erl King to a standstill with a single cinder-block fist.

"They're perfectly happy to be seen as the bad guys. As stupid, or crude, or even irredeemable. But for them, all the big questions of life and destiny will be answered. They'll fight the Netherspawn, and take their world back, and if you kill one, more will grow to take its place. That's all they asked for in the Accords. Future generations will think of the green-skinned race, and imagine *these*."

Soon the apocalyptic punch-up behind them faded into the distance. Gagrat, the world's first orc, had bought them enough time to escape. And as the Talbot-Largo Special rolled in through the secret entrance to the Battersea Power Station[33], General Crowley saw that it may just have been enough for the others, too. A streak of light sliced across the clouds above, heading south-east toward the far-off dawn. Squad 27 were on their way to Germany, and to the headquarters of the Black Sun.

Not the great castle at Wewelsberg, where the SS played dress-up and the *Ahnenerbe* squeezed funds out of the Reich with convincing farces. But that even more secret crag of solitude and darkness deep in the black forest, built in the age of Barbarossa and blessed by the great Antipope, Paschal III.

The Vulture's Nest. Schloss Bad Schickehosen.

Crowley sincerely hoped that they had all packed a change of underpants.

---

33 The original power station – with just two chimneys – was designed by Sir Giles Gilbert Scott, who is also hailed as the father of the red telephone box. Mathematicians have found that the same correlations of numbers, regarding angles and lengths, can be found in the traditional red phone booth as can be found in the Great Pyramid. Some say that this proves that measuring pyramids is nonsense, and the Egyptians didn't know as much as we think they did. Others say that this proves something about Sir Giles Gilbert Scott that he wasn't letting on.

# Twelve – Operation Vengeful Mongoose

The south of England lay under a smothering cloak of darkness. Tiny villages huddled in blacked-out silence as Squad 27 flitted by overhead, skimming the cloud tops. There was no moon, just the cold glitter of the stars, and this time, not even horrible ready-to-eat rations for supper.

The reason why was currently the centre of everybody's attention.

"...and so I woke up in Charlie Monkston's car, and he showed me the thing with the eye, and then… well, pretty soon after that I was on the boat to France with you all," concluded Eddie Weatherfield, slumped back in his seat amid an avalanche of empty ration packets. The dry food had tasted somewhat like sawdust, but it had filled the ravenous void in his belly – for now. "How about you, Saint Germain?"

"Oh, it's a famous story," said the old alchemist. He, too, was strapped into one of the passenger seats of the *Black Buzzard*, as a trio of gremlins and one very angry dwarf coaxed the machine up past the speed of sound. "The bible tells it wrong, of course. See, I happened to be minding me own business, selling a few knick-knacks up at crucifixion hill – that's Golgotha, in the old Hebrew – when I see all this fuss about one of the lads up there on 'is stick. There's women weeping and fellas in robes making speeches and a lot of Romans looking worried. So I figure, they might be in the market for some authentic crucifixion-day souvenirs, like. And I get up close with me tray, and I see that someone is having a laugh, and that the nails are just stuck in between his fingers, and it's ropes holding him up.

Mrs Hazelwood leaned across, offering a bag of hard-boiled sweets[34].

"So what did you do, dear?"

The Compte sighed.

"I only went and told the centurion, didn't I? And then J...J... the woodworking fellow from Nazareth, he's effing and blinding, and

---

34 One of the strange properties possessed by every old granny is the ability to produce a selection of 1930s style hard boiled sweets from somewhere about her person at a moment's notice. We don't know why grannies have evolved this ability, however, it may once have distracted large predators.

his disciples are getting shifty looks, and WHAM! He hits me with everlasting life. Just like that! Without so much as a by-your-leave, guvnor. Two thousand years of boring, boring life. Until I met you folks, that is."

Now the whole planeload of misfits scooched around in their seats to stare at Patience, who had been silently occupied with some witch business involving a small notebook, a crystal pendulum and some string. She looked up, all mock-innocence.

"Who? Me? No, I wouldn't want to bore you. It's not much of a story, you know."

She said it with a little smile, though. Percy couldn't help but nudge Eddie rather un-subtly in the ribs. Lucky grinned.

"Oh, sure and it's the way you tell it, miss. We Irish are reckoned to be fine storytellers, and I'd judge your technique to be, oh, at least twice as good again as that of any Englishman alive."

Patience sighed. It was sort of obvious (to everyone except Eddie Weatherfield) that this rendition of her story was pretty much just for him.

"They were burning witches in the 1600s," she began. "Well. They *thought* they were. What they were doing was burning old ladies who knew about herbs and suchlike, which is one of the reasons there was a lot of plague about in those days. If you go around setting fire to the only people who know how to cure things, and resort to praying instead, it's not long before bits of you turn black and drop off."

"Urrrgh!" said Fyodor, shuddering. "No offense, Percy."

"None taken," chuckled the zombie, who was busy sewing his fingers back on. He had used his own chin as a pincushion.

"Anyhow, it had gotten somewhat embarrassing. The true witches of England had always worked around the Church, with little concessions here and there. Sometimes a witch really *did* go bad, and we needed clerical assistance or a knight or two to help put her down. Sometimes the Archbishop found out that one of his priests was taking… well… at the time we would have said *'certain liberties'*. And it's so much better if he just gets spirited off into oblivion than the alternative. It can do things to the morale of a whole village, if they have to hang their local vicar. Our way, he simply vanished. So… Cromwell was a bastard."

"Hear hear!" shouted Lucky, Irish to the core.

"But Hopkins, his so called 'witchfinder general' was worse. Mad as a hyena in a concrete mixer. And *we* were getting blamed for the wholesale incineration of most of England's old biddies, who are, as you'd know, a vital part of the social order."

"Exactly," beamed Mrs Hazelwood, her false teeth and an improbably large lemon gobstopper wrestling for control of her gums.

"Anyhow, even after Hopkins died of tuberculosis – which any one the ladies he'd murdered could have cured for him – the silliness didn't subside. Charles the Second continued to break the covenant between English magic and the Crown which had lasted since the Merlinical Age. So we decided to do something about it."

Patience's face had slowly changed as she got deeper into the story, growing grim and sharp-edged as if underlit by fire. Now she looked up, and her eyes were the glittering deep purple of a pair of amethysts.

"We saw what was coming. Saint Germain, you knew Newton. You alchemists were on the verge of creating science, and ushering in the industrial revolution. The wilds would become parklands and curiosities. Magic had to be made intrinsic to what England was becoming, so we made our plans accordingly. In the year that young Isaac invented the calculus, we struck."

"Only because we let ye," huffed Connor the Beige. "And even then, only because Charles the Second was a pillock."

Patience gave him the old '*if you don't mind*' with one perfectly sculpted eyebrow.

"*As I'll explain,*" she continued, "the plan was threefold. First, arrange for a group of witches to be 'caught' by the authorities. These were all *real* witches, who provided ample proof of their powers. The witchfinders' eyes all but popped out of their empty little skulls. None of the other ladies they had burned had been able to do anything quite so magical, of course. There were five who sacrificed themselves that year, being 1666, a number which vexed the puritans no end. On the first day of Autumn five very carefully selected villages surrounding London had pyres lit. They formed a pentacle, of course. And the flames did not burn any of my sisters at all. At the height of the blaze, the Witch of Oxted, Mother Greycap, was heard to laugh and say *pyle ye on more logges, thou lazy soddes, this do butte tickle!*'.

She smiled, as if remembering something from just yesterday.

"The magical transference eventually popped them all sideways out of reality, though. A body can only take so much. But they'd harvested enough flame to create a truly unquenchable fire, which manifested exactly in the centre of the pentacle. We'd been aiming for a big monument, but what we got was a bakery next to London bridge.

Burned the whole city down."

"The great fire of London..." breathed Eddie.

"The great *rebuilding*, really, was what we were after. We had an agent in with the Natural Philosophers, and she'd just completed one heck of a psy-op for us. Margaret Cavendish was her name, and in one stroke she'd inspired Hooke and Wren and the lads to be utopians, and invented something which would keep magic alive in the age of science."

"So she gave them a plan for how to build modern London? I always thought there was something interesting about the layout of the streets and all..."

"Well, she *helped*. A few nudges here and there to get certain ley lines and roads and things lined up. We tuned it all over the decades by getting in obelisks and statues to harmonize the flow. Turned the capital into the biggest generator of usable magic in Europe. Hence the Empire and all. You don't rule most of the world from one little island without a heck of a lot of magic at your disposal. The bigger picture was that she wrote down a few of her adventures in the other realms, and invented science fiction[35]."

"But what about you?" asked Eddie.

"Well, I was found after the fire tore through the city. One of the watchmen wrote it down. A baby, found all alone and birthday-naked, amid a landscape of charcoal. The souls and powers of five witches had converged on that place, and fused together, and here I was. It didn't take long for the sisterhood to figure out what had happened. I'd been a normal baby, I suppose, who would have died in the fire otherwise. They bundled me off to a convent of nuns who were not really very Christian, and I was raised there by the Sisters of the Articulate Misconception. The title 'Revenge of English Witchcraft' sort of stuck, because I'm the last one left who does the old type of witchery. At least, without some assistance."

"And because ye personally eliminated one hundred and thirty-three European witchfinders, twelve renegade preachers, two executioners, and that creepy serial killer with yon eyepatch thingy," put in Connor. "There was that."

Patience rolled her eyes.

"Well, if you insist on being pedantic, yes..."

"So... you're ummm..." began Eddie. This was obviously a thought

---

35 This is another true fact. Her idea of a world within our own accessed via the poles is still out there today...

which was taking some time to circumnavigate the inside of his head. "Let's see… carry the one, adjust for fractions…"

Patience rolled her eyes.

"Why do they *always* get around to this eventually?" She cast about for some female solidarity, but found only the beaming face of Mrs Hazelwood, who was simply pleased to be in out of the cold and on the way to smashing more Nazis.[36]

"The number you're looking for is *275*. I'm 275 years old, Weatherfield. That's old enough to be your great granny's great granny. Pft! *Men!* I bet you'd never ask *Connor* how old he was!"

"Yes," put in Percy. "But then again, Eddie would never ask Connor out for dhmmm and hmmmuhhhnn"

Strangely, nobody got to hear the last part of what the zombie had to say, because Fyodor slapped a hand across his mouth, earning a wincingly painful palm full of pins and needles.

Eddie looked confused.

"No, that's not it at all. Someone very smart once told me a gentleman doesn't ask, in any case." There was a wistful kind of moment of silence. "Anyway, part of me seems to be a 20,000 year old dragon, so I'm more candles than birthday cake myself. What I meant was, right, if *London itself* is the big magical generator that you draw power from…"

"Is it safe for ye to go all the way to Germany, right now? When it's on fire, and all?" finished Connor the Beige. "We've *had* this discussion, I recall."

"You've had a big, overprotective rant about it," said Patience, not unkindly. "I've told you that when the ley lines join up, I'll still have just as much power in my fingernails as any wizard has in his silly little staff."

The whole aeroplane shuddered for a moment, and dropped like a brick for a few sickening metres. The lights flickered, fizzed, and eventually decided to come back on.

"No use asking if it's a good idea to go to Germany now!" shouted Darrin Oakenbeard, from up in the cockpit. "We're *here!* She's running slow, but those defense batteries didn't know what they were looking at when we blew past."

"If we'd bothered to pack some bombs, we could really make a mess of sooo much Nazi industry," sulked Lotte, peering down through an

---

36 Mrs H was not a witch, but a medium, which is a different guild entirely. She viewed the entire Third Reich as 'rude and ill mannered young men' who were filling the immediate afterlife with the equivalent of loud static

aiming scope. All three gremlin girls were back in serious one-piece pilot's overalls, their hair tied back with scarves.

"Huh! Listen to her! In touch with your masculine side and keen to break things, sister?"

"Let's just say that explosions are underrated by some of us ladies. And we'd be doing everybody a favour."

Mica zipped back into the cabin and swung from the tethered control panel which operated the *Buzzard*'s rear doors.

"Okay, soldiers! I've always wanted to do the big sergeant major speech, so..."

"Awww, come on!" groaned Lucky. "That's my job!"

Mica gave him a big-eyed look that could have melted glass.

"Come on! Please?"

The huge leprechaun rolled his eyes. Mica grinned.

"Right, you… umm… paramecium! You… Some kind of crawly insect things! You are apparently both a terrible disappointment to me, your sergeant, and also some of the roughest, toughest fighting men (And women. And zombies. And a ghost in a crystal ball) ever to defy good fashion sense by wearing a nasty shade of green into battle. But, even though the foe you face today has one of the most snazzy, cool, black and red uniforms ever, with all the neat little skulls and buttons and..."

She got herself under control with a deep breath.

"You're going to mangle them. You're going to hit them so hard their grandparents will feel it. You're going to make Hans Schprinkler and his goons wish they had never heard of Squad 27, or Section M, or war in general, or even the concept of organized violence in a more limited capacity!"

She beamed, still dangling from the control box with its glowing green buttons.

"How was that?"

Lucky tipped his hat in a polite little gesture.

"Lass, you did just fine. Now… Commander the Beige, Sir?"

Connor stood up in his seat. His horrible old corncob pipe was already lit.

"What she said. Make like yon local favourite sports team and hammer the bastards."

"For all those who died under Kew Gardens." added Fyodor.

"For the Accords, and peace," chimed in Saint Germain.

"For Charlie Monkston." said Eddie, possibly a bit wet around the eyes.

And then it was time, against all kinds of logic and common sense, for him to throw himself out of a moving aeroplane. Lucky had already gripped his tiny little hat and jumped out, as if he was performing a 'bomb' into a swimming pool. Mrs Hazelwood opened an umbrella, and shuffled off into space like a refrigerator-shaped Mary Poppins. Patience and Connor were tuning up rings of glowing runes on the handles of their broom and shillelagh respectively.

Eddie took a deep breath, looked at the bellowing void of darkness outside the *Black Buzzard*'s open doors, closed his eyes, and ran until he was out of anything to run on. Then, legs still windmilling in the hope of gaining purchase on several vast, empty cubic acres of night-time German atmosphere, he gave in to gravity and fell.

+++

Seth Gruber didn't notice the bubbles at first.

Privately convinced that he had the single best job in the entire Third Reich, corporal Gruber was playing a mean hand of solitaire and waiting for the kettle to boil, on a tiny camp stove inside the turret of his anti-aircraft *flakpanzer*.

It was a starry night, and a cool breeze insinuated itself between the massing ranks of pines as they bristled from the bare mountainside. It was a good time to be warm and cozy in his greatcoat, with the forecast calling for absolutely zero allied bombs.

Down below, he could hear the clickety-clack of his buddy Josef knitting something vast and shapeless with too many legs, possibly in the hope that he would one day adopt a baby shoggoth.

The pair of them were part of the perimeter defenses of Schloss Bad Shickehosen, a position greatly coveted among the Black Sun auxiliary for two reasons. Firstly, because the likelihood of any allied forces penetrating this deeply into the Fatherland was so remote that it ranked up there with Hitler becoming a Rastafarian. And secondly because neither Seth, nor Josef, nor any of the other front-line defense soldiers had to stay inside... *the castle*[37].

Seth shuddered. As a member of the Black Sun, he'd seen and heard a few things that would fair put the wind up the average man. But the

---

37 This should ideally be read as (pause) ze CASTLE (peal of thunder, flicker of lightning, mournful wolf howling in the distance).

Schloss, which seemed to loom over you on the point of near collapse *no matter which side you approached it from...* that was simply the worst. Sleeping in the underground barracks there – which still had big iron rings bolted to the walls, and suspicious stains everywhere – meant long nights of quivering anxiety, interspersed with an interminable parade of gibbering spectres, phantom nuns, noisy poltergeists and headless ghosts fumbling about for their missing craniums. You could hardly hear yourself whimpering.

No, this was the life. A nice four-barreled flak cannon, nothing to shoot at, hot coffee on the go and not a demented ghostly seventeenth-century baron to be seen.

Seth was just about to pour out a cup for himself when he noticed the bubble.

It drifted down slowly, spinning gently, rainbow sheened and filled with green smoke. Now he noticed more of them, then more, swirling on the night breeze as they descended through the pines.

Perhaps any normal soldier would have been a bit more suspicious.

But Seth Gruber had, as noted, seen some weird, wild, even *wyrd* shit during his tour of duty. In the area around the Schloss, where Hans Schprinkler's maniacs put reality through the mangle on a daily basis, fortean phenomena were so common that you could catch a nice fish dinner by leaning out your window with a bucket at the first sound of thunder.

Hence, it was far too late when a large and wobbly sphere popped on the end of his nose.

That's when he saw the turkeys.

The fist one was cheeky, peering out to gobble at him from behind a gnarly old pine, with its wattles bobbling absurdly. It was also roughly the size of a house. Tiny smaller turkeys orbited it, staring madly as they spun and bobbed. Seth giggled. More turkeys zipped and scuttled through the undergrowth. The kettle began to whistle, bubbling over, as hallucinatory fowl proliferated in the branches, eyeing him suspiciously.

There was only one thing for it, really.

Seth chuckled to himself as he dropped into the seat between the four big anti-aircraft guns, his hands slipping around the controls. There was good eating on a turkey. Especially one of those big buggers...

He never saw Patience land, lithe as a hunting cat, in the branches of one of the tallest pines. And he certainly never saw the little gesture of one hand which put a spin on her broomstick, a seven-foot length of timber falling in at terminal velocity. A long curl of wood peeled away from the tip as it spiraled down, sharpening itself like the world's biggest pencil…

There was a sudden meaty crunch. There was a moment of heavy silence, then a thump, followed by a sound like ruler held half off the edge of a workbench and plucked.

The turkeys vanished – mainly because the brain which had been hallucinating them was suddenly starved of oxygen-rich blood. Being impaled by a nigh-supersonic broomstick and pinned to a tree will do that to a person.

Patience threw a cord of spider silk over a beam of moonlight falling through the trees, and ziplined to the ground. She pressed her ear up against the side of the *flakpanzer,* and heard the unmistakable clatter of knitting needles within. Patience smirked. This much iron was a right bugger to magic through, but someone had left a little mailbox-slot view port open, probably so he could smoke a sly roll-up without suffocating.

She stood on tip-toes, cupped a hand around her lips, and whispered a spell which was all fuzzy edges and firelit mist in through the gap. There was a *clonk*, as of a helmeted head hitting the floor. There came a loud and rasping snore, the kind which says 'I can do this all night, pal, so you might want to invest in some cotton wool'.

Patience fiddled with a pentacle bracelet on one wrist, raising a feeble will'o the wisp glow.

"This is number three, reporting. Sentries neutralised at location B. Proceeding to… oh! Well, you could have said!"

This last part was due to the sudden appearance of Connor the Beige, who faded into view like the proverbial Cheshire feline, if that moggy was a one-eared, crooked-tailed veteran of Glasgow's lively alleyways. The little wizard was sitting on top of the tank's turret, smoking his foul corncob pipe and grinning.

"No need for all the military mumbo-jumbo, lass. This isn't what ye would call a properly sanctioned mission, after all. More along the lines o' some bloody revenge, in the old-school fashion."

Patience nodded.

"I think we're both sufficiently old-school to appreciate that. Are the rest of us on the ground yet?"

Connor squinted up into the sky.

"Oh aye. I'm old-school enough to be so old that there were nae schools at all when I were a lad. Learned a lot from a good kick up the arse, I recall." He realized he was on the receiving end of a certain pointed look. "Yes, yes, they're all boots tae the mud, all right. And don't worry. I have a feelin' yon squad of ours are a bit better at bloody revenge than they are at proper missions anyhow."

"Is that why you let Percy choose the name for this operation?"

Connor smiled, and a more disturbing display of yellowed ivory could not be imagined this side of Satan's harpsichord.

"How can you say no to those eyes? I mean, first off, because you dunnae know where he got them from. But ye have tae admit. Operation Vengeful Mongoose is pretty… ummm… what do they say these days?"

"Neat?" suggested Patience. "Groovy?"

"Naw. The American one. *Cool.* We've got this, lass." he dropped down to the ground, just as Lucky came stalking into the clearing. Mrs Hazelwood tottered out from between the trees in the other direction. Then Percy was there, and Eddie, and Fyodor, carrying his immense long rifle. The Compte de Saint Germain came last, absentmindedly picking his nails with a stiletto.

The little Scots wizard inflated his toast-rack chest until his heels almost left the ground. He grinned like a honey badger who has just seen something round and dangly come wobbling into its field of view. The smoke from his pipe spun out in coloured rings.

"Ladies. Gentlemen. So glad you could all be here. As I was just commenting to my lovely assistant Miss Patience, there's a lot ye can learn from a swift, hard kick up the arse. So..." and here he paused, to sweep the assembled misfits of Squad 27 with a sparkling gaze. "There's a lot of German lads up yon hill who are gonnae get an education tonight. Shall we go and spread some enlightenment?"

+++

Being a huge, craggy, intimidating gothic castle of the kind which would make Count Dracula fire his real estate adviser, Schloss Bad Schickehosen was not a place which rolled out the welcome mat.

This was *not* the sort of castle which would feature as a birthday cake, or be replicated in styrofoam at an amusement park. No magical princesses had ever sung to bluebirds from its battlements. It was the kind of castle which deployed hunch-backed coach drivers riding on skull-encrusted hearses to pick up travelers and bring them home for *dinner*[38]. Someone had sat down and had a good hard think about how to repel mobs of villagers carrying torches and pitchforks, vis-a-vis boiling oil, spikes, moats filled with horrible slithering things with too many teeth, and a drawbridge carved with a grimacing demon face. The Nazi party hadn't made it any more welcoming. Any girl scouts coming to offer cookies to the gang of uniformed murderers within would face a zig-zag gauntlet of machine gun nests, mines, barbed wire and flamethrowers. Not to mention the huge, spotlit swastika flags. These tended to be a tad more effective than a tatty piece of cardboard advising people to 'beware of the dog'.

That being said, Squad 27 had their own vampire.

And one thing which the Children of the Night know about castles, is that any self-respecting European aristocrat with a taste for type-B-positive and opera clothing always, *always* builds a secret escape tunnel.

And another thing, too. *Vampires are not very imaginative.*

It was the work of mere moments for Percy to sneak up on the two fairly dim guards who were posted outside the castle's graveyard, in a little valley beneath the crag. Neither of them really wanted to be inside the unhallowed ground, where the ghosts were so thick they were floating through each other in a kind of ectoplasmic bouillon. In deference to the fact that they were both very young lads and clearly already on the edge of gibbering terror, the zombie simply clonked their heads together with his undead super-strength, sending them down for a nice kip in the long grass. Then it was a quick hustle through the ranks of phantoms (who parted like the guests at a wedding when they felt the aura surrounding Patience and Connor) to a tilted marble mausoleum. Its lintel bore the coat of arms of the old Baron Von Schickehosen.

Eddie peered at it intently.

"What's that unicorn doing with that pineapple? And is that a..."

"I think It's supposed to be a tower and two hills," said Patience, blushing slightly. "Definitely. Or a humorous vegetable."

Connor pushed past, and rapped on the marble door with his shillelagh.

"Open ye dread portal, all wards and snares unbind, sort of thing," he muttered, squinting. A sputter of magic flared around the edges of the stone block, and the door yawned open.

---

38 Mwaaaa ha ha ha ha haaaaa (peal of thunder)

"See?" said Fyodor. "Predictable. The Count was one of the old firm. Opera capes, pointy teeth, haircut in the shape of a big bum, and a secret tunnel that comes up in his own bloody sepulcher. I bet he even went around spelling his name backwards as a secret identity."

Saint Germain ran a knobbly finger over an inscription on the wall.

"What? You mean he'd pitch up in the local pub with an iffy fake mustache callin' himself Giwdul Derfnam Gnagflow nov Nesohekcihcs? Were they all mentally slow around these parts?"

Patience smirked.

"I think they all got it, all right. It's just that he was a – pardoning your company, Fyodor – bloody *vampire*. You don't point out to someone who can rip your arms off like wet spaghetti that they're acting like a three-year-old."

Fyodor chuckled.

"It is a bit silly, isn't it? You can be sure we vampires are quite pleased with what the Accords have in store for us. Suffice to say, we're going to get a *lot* more attractive to the ladies. And we'll be able to live in normal apartments, instead of places like this." he looked up at the castle. On cue, a flicker of lightning wreathed its towers. "Still, though. There's a real sense of theatre about doing it the old fashioned way. That's why I brought a change of clothes."

"You're not going to..." said Lucky, deadpan.

"*That* old trick again?" said Percy.

"Well, I'm not waiting," said Mrs Hazelwood, tottering past and down into the gloom. A flight of stairs curled off into the bowels of the earth down there, illuminated by flaming torches that burst into life as soon as the tiny granny got near them. "A body could catch a death of cold hanging around in Nazi graveyards at this time of year. And me with my rheumatism..."

The rest of the squad shared a look. There was a brief miniature thunderclap as Fyodor changed his costume, emerging from a cloud of smoke in an immaculate 17th century nobleman's most foppish dinner jacket, cavalry officer's trousers, and a cape as black as night.

"Come on!" he said. "If I don't get ahead of her, this isn't going to work! And I spent ages on that gold braiding..."

Up ahead, up a long, long flight of winding stairs which straggled across the side of a bat-infested cellar wall, Mrs Hazelwood had reached a door. A person who was trying to follow her progress would be surprised at how much ground the squat little granny had covered, what with her compression stockings, sensible flat brown shoes and a walk which looked as if it was powered by clockwork. But anyone who has ever borne witness to a half price sale in the apron and hair-curler department of a large department store will tell you that the average old nan is slick as a hot-buttered ninja, and often twice as tetchy.

She rummaged in her immense wicker handbag, the amount of wrinkled face visible between her wax-fruited hat and her overlong football scarf crinkling into a grin.

"Come on, our Roger. This is the fun part, so it is. More Nazis to smash."

She extracted the crystal ball from within its nest of tissues, hankies, boiled sweets, old till receipts and bingo tickets in a bowler's grip. The face of Roger swum into focus, mustache quivering.

"What's that dear? More young people giving you trouble?"

Roger had been dead for some time, and had hardly perished at a ripe old age. But he had always been the kind of gentleman for whom walk shorts, thick socks and sandals were the height of fashion. He was *born* 65, and his body had simply taken a few decades to grow into his mind. Death had done nothing to improve his opinion of 'the youth', who, in Roger's opinion, had far too much life energy, and went around wasting it on things like football and singing and now, apparently, wearing jackboots and trying to establish the superiority of the Aryan Race.

He'd never admit that he loved a good punch-up. But then again, that was because the term 'disembodied spiritual vampirism' was as meaningful to Roger Hazelwood as a sushi menu written in Sanskrit. All he knew was that there was no single malt scotch on the far side of the Mortal Veil, but that squashing the ruffians who annoyed his lady wife gave him a similar pleasant glow.

Mrs Hazelwood opened the door and tottered into the underground barracks-room beyond, absentmindedly sucking on her false teeth and humming. A great many Black Sun sturmtroopers, in varying states of undress, were suddenly very surprised to find a tiny little old lady amongst them. She carried her purse in one hand, and a faintly glowing crystal ball in another. Her eyes glittered like glazed currants in a very wrinkly bun.

"Rise and shine, dearies!" she trilled. "On with socks and hands off… well, I certainly hope that's a salami, Fritz, or your mother would be *most* disappointed."

The very embarrassed Nazi wearing the 'Fritz' monogrammed pajamas turned bright red, and hid behind a hastily pulled up bedsheet.

He may very well have been wishing that the ground would just open and swallow him up, not realizing what was about to happen.

It took a second or two for the assembled troopers to remember that they were soldiers, this was a war, and that anyone speaking English was likely to be the enemy, (even if they did look more like they were here to tidy up a bit and cadge any leftover sherry and port). Hands found guns, and receivers snicked and clicked.

"*HALT! Dieser bereich ist für alte damen verboten!*"

They were met with a broad and slightly crooked smile.

"Now, now. Is that any way to make a poor old granny feel welcome? And me with me aching feet, oooh, and me dicky pancreas, and me lumbago and all..."

Mrs Hazelwood made a great display of hobbling infirmity, but only until she was absolutely sure she was right in the middle of a ring of very nervous Black Sun soldiers.

"Right, our Roger. *Let's do this thing.*"

With a click of her fingers, Mrs H sent the crystal ball whizzing forward. The first Nazi saw a grinning little man's face zoom up toward him before the lights went out once and for all, accompanied by a cartilaginous crunch, like someone snapping a bunch of celery in half. Then the commando gran dropped down into a perfect splits, while bullets racketed and roared above. The ball glowed purple and rang like a bell as it fielded several shots, causing them to ricochet with uncanny accuracy. Before that first unfortunate soldier could collapse to the floor, the front of his face now horribly concave, she'd performed a spinning three-sixty and allowed Roger to pull her back upright. Twenty-two sturmtroopers had caught each other in a perfect circular crossfire. Smoking holes quite ruined their uniforms as they gurgled and toppled over.

"You shouldn't go playing with guns, now, should you," muttered Mrs Hazelwood as she tottered away, picking her way between the corpses. "Someone will put their eye out, that's what I always say! Isn't that right, Roger dear?"

"Yes dear. *Of course* dear."

There came a low whistle from behind her.

"Where did you learn moves like that, Mrs H?" asked Lucky, popping through the door with Squad 27 behind him.

"I wasn't *always* an old lady, Sergeant," she said, with a chuckle. "Truth is, I was a burlesque dancer back when Victoria was on the throne."

"Henrietta!" The face in the crystal ball flushed beetroot purple with indignation. "Well I *never...*"

"Oh come *on*, Roger. You always used to come in after work for a nice cold pint and a bit of a sit-down, as I recall. Remember that evening in '88?'

Connor the Beige pushed past his gangling great sergeant, scowling.

"*Remember?* I was the one who got ye the job, lassie. Back then they called us the Black Ministry, but we always took an interest in those with *certain talents.*" He gestured with his pipe stem. "Percy, we dug ye oot of the mud and wire at Ypres, because a combination of poison gas, electric shock, a huge bloody explosion and an ancient curse on your family meant that ye conveniently forgot tae die. Between you and M'sieur Le Compte here, ye could hold off a small army." He nodded at Lucky. "When the Irish came to build Brunel's bloody railways, ye turned up in England, and you foolishly wished you were a little bit taller, Padraig. Eddie just crashed his plane intae a big daft lizard last week. But the two of ye, well… I've seen the charge of ten thousand armoured knights, one bloody day in a place called Acre. That's how hard you two lads hit. Fyodor got lent to us by old Uncle Joe, on account of his disregard for the nobility, but there's few better men with a long rifle. And, as noted, our former burlesque queen Mrs Hazelwood is also aboot as accurate as hell's own tax department." He waggled his eyebrows. "Ye get it? Section M, and the Black Ministry before them, and the Chamber bloody Praxis Occultis. They had a strategy. The Rule of Eight. Every squad ever formed for the purpose of magical warfare has followed it."

"They never told *us*," said Percy.

"They never had time! I'm not, as yer may have noticed, the most disciplined of wizards. Lucky has what they call…. What do they call it, lad?"

"Poor impulse control," said the leprechaun, repeating the words as if he'd heard them far too many times.

"And Patience tends to put the wind up them other witches, ye ken? There were…"

"*Incidents,*" she said, with a raised eyebrow. "I'm not going to cultivate warts just because some traditionalist hags from the eleventh century think that using moisturiser is 'letting the side down.'"

Connor sighed. He wrung his sporran between his hands.

"What I mean to say, lads, is that we three got busted doon to lookin' after the recruits. Charlie Monkston was me own probationary officer, right enough. Ye were supposed tae get training. Ye were supposed tae get encouragement. But..."

Eddie nodded, remembering the look on poor old commander Sir Horace Stackpole's face, when those orders came in from fighter command.

"In the end, the enemy were right here with us, and a spoon's better than no knife at all, right?"

Connor nodded lugubriously.

"Still, ye have promise, at all that. Some o' the least likely warriors in His Majesty's service, but the spit and bloody image of the Rule of Eight."

"Ummm… can I ask… what exactly…?" began Percy.

"Imagine a chess board," said Patience. "Two rooks, to defend the flanks. With the power of sheer resilience." she looked Saint Germain and Percy in the eyes. "Two knights, to charge ahead, dodge the enemy's foot soldiers, and deliver an unexpected crushing blow." This time she looked at Eddie and Lucky. "Two bishops, who can kill from right across the board." This time it was Fyodor and Mrs Hazelwood. "Then a Queen in the middle, for witchcraft, and a King, for Wizardry. If you ever wondered why chess seemed so strange like that, with a queen more deadly than the king, remember that *the queen should have pointy hat.*"

"Well, it's nice to know we're not pawns," said Eddie. "But are you sure it's going to work against a castle full of Nazis?"

Fyodor swirled the cape he'd brought with him around in a dramatic gesture.

"We've always got plan B! See, I'll tell them that I'm..."

Connor pinched the bridge of his nose.

"Vampires and their silly assumed identities! No, we'll go with the nigh-suicidal frontal full-on assault, thank ye. If I'm gonnae be obliterated, I'd rather have a bit o' dignity to drag wi' me intae the next life."

At that moment there came a great hollow booming from the double-doors at the far end of the barracks.

"Hello? Came a tremulous voice. "Insidious traitors of the Allied Powers? Are you in there?"

Everybody froze.

"Ummm… perhaps!" shouted Lucky. "Who's asking?"

There was a moment's scuffling and some pointed whispers from behind the doors, which were of the old fashioned 'hardened oak, banded-in-iron' school of architecture.

"Would you believe… singing telegram?"

A consensus of shifty looks among Squad 27 revealed that this was as unlikely to be bought as a spinach and anchovy sundae.

"What does it say, then?"

There was a pregnant pause.

"Ach… what is the English idiom?" came a horribly familiar voice. "I think it goes. Something. Like… KABOOM!"

A moment later, it did.

# Thirteen – The Battle of Bad Schickehosen

The great military historian, Doctor Odysseus Suet, once said that the art of warfare was like trying to thread a thousand needles simultaneously while wearing boxing gloves, inside a tumble dryer, with several enraged baboons. Then again, he said it while attempting valiantly to break the world record for the largest amount of two-dollar *Chateau Urine des Chats* imbibed for free at a faculty luncheon.

A far more accurate an assessment of conflict was recorded by the otherwise unknown centurion Quintus Latrinius, who memorably said, at the battle of the Teutoberg Forest;

"War's a bugger, but I'll be buggered if I let the other buggers bugger me first!"

Neither of these historic luminaries was there to witness the Battle of Bad Schickehosen, but both of them could have used it as an example of why their theories were spot on.

It all started when Hans Schprinkler's men fired off a small howitzer to demolish the barracks doors. They had stood since the time of old Antipope Paschal, and were probably heritage listed, but you don't get to be the bad guy by caring about antique timber fretwork. Three Nazis manhandled a field gun into place, put their fingers in their ears, and pulled the string.

But...

Anticipating just such a sneaky move, Connor the Beige chose to forego the doors, and simply demolished the entire wall.

The howitzer shell hadn't quite kissed the iron-studded oak when it was evaporated by a boiling fireball, hotter than the core of suns. Connor's opening salvo tore loose hundreds of heavy blocks of stone, sending a very historic swathe of castle flying to pieces. Cannon, crew and all were blown away in a hail of rolling, bouncing masonry, flaming splinters and red-hot hinges. A humourous gargoyle doorknocker embedded itself in a far-off Nazi's face, a great iron ring clenched between its sizzling buttocks.

But all this broke around the figure of Hans Schprinkler himself, resplendent in a full SS uniform of midnight black, trimmed with red and silver. Brightly polished *totenkopf* buttons winked in the flamelight as he gestured with a plain steel staff, parting the maelstrom into twin catherine-wheels of destruction. He sent these arcing up over the walls, dissipating them into sparks. Of his cannon crew, reduced to shreds of cloth and windblown ashes, there was little left. Some half-melted wheels and a splash of molten steel revealed the fate of their gun.

"Bravo, Herr Connor! Bravo! Such bombast! Such *passion!* Hauptmann Schmidt? Where is the very large victrola which I ordered? With the Wagner, and the valkyries, and the suitable warlike idiom? Hmmm?"

The smoke blew away. Searchlights on the gaunt, dark towers swung around to fix on the gaping hole in the wall. Behind Schprinkler, hundreds more troops hustled into position, setting up tripods, hefting anti-tank rockets onto their shoulders, and in some cases drawing black, double-edged swords. Unmages lined the battlements, upside-down features contorted with concentration and hatred. Just to keep in with the Fuhrer's favourite theme, there was even an honest-to-goodness Tiger III tank parked in the middle of the citadel, its great 88mm cannon pointing like an accusing finger. A very small Nazi in a very big coat scuttled along behind Schprinkler, setting up a folding card table, then winding the handle of a brass-horned antique record player.

Inside the breach stood eight figures. Silhouettes, slowly taking on features and form as the smoke cleared. Eight against an army.

"I might hae put a wee too much sauce on that one..." muttered a truculent voice.

"On my order!" screamed Hans Schprinkler, red lightning sizzling around his staff. Its tip was a cube made of swastikas, beaten out of copper. "Schmidt, make with the opera! The rest of you... *Deliver them to hell!*"

But there's a thing about being outnumbered a thousand to one. It's not actually that much worse than being outnumbered ten to one, in terms of bastards who can get their hands on you. And if you don't expect to survive, every enemy you take with you is a cheeky bonus...

It's also worth mentioning at this point that Patience had done something rather naughty. Something which, had General Crowley known about it, would have ensured that she was busted down to teaching little old ladies in the Home Guard how to crochet blackout doilies until well after D-Day.

The Revenge of English Witchcraft had set the route for Darrin and the girls aboard the *Black Buzzard*. She'd followed the web of ley lines which criss-crossed the earth, linking places of power together like a great geo-thaumic telephone switchboard. And, with every other allied witch out of action, she'd gone ahead and routed all of the power generated by the blitz-damaged, defiant, battle-scarred city of London down through a series of henges, barrow graves and hallowed groves, until she'd struck the raw, concentrated narrative shear effect of the Black Forest.

The Brothers Grimm had tried some pretty crafty thaumic warfare here, back in the day. When it looked like the Turks would come steamrollering through via Vienna and introduce Christendom to fire, the sword, reasonably priced kebabs and see-through trousers, in roughly that order. Not as finessed as Will Shakespeare's work, but the storybombs they'd unleashed left echoes.[39]

Those were not very nice fairy tales. A witch of the old school, who borrowed power from the land itself, could cast some long and powerful shadows with them. Plugging London's power directly into the Black Forest was like throwing a three-bar electric fire into a bathtub.

So it was that Patience had an almost painful compulsion to build things out of gingerbread and enjoy a children-and-mustard sandwich as she drew power up through the stones of Schloss Bad Schickehosen. But she also cast a huge and jagged shadow, pointy hat, hooked nose and all, in *the opposite direction to the floodlights*. She cracked her neck left and right, unfurled her fingers, and unleashed a rush of earth magic so potent that it made moss erupt from the stones around her in a quiet and verdant wave. It sounded like someone politely trying to open a bag of potato crisps during a movie, multiplied by ten

---

39 The Grimms had militarized the folk beliefs of most of central Europe to combat the supernatural vanguard of the Ottoman empire, made up of sundry eastern sorcerers, magi, djinns and efrits who, it's safe to say, were just not ready for the horrors inflicted in a jolly bedtime fashion on the minds of generations of European children. When cannibalistic witches, possessed bloodthirsty puppets, ravenous werewolves and mass-murdering evil queens are the stuff you save for the little kids, what comes out when some hard-bitten Thaumaturgical mercenaries with the surname 'Grimm' set to work is enough to curdle kerosene. Subsequently, clean-up teams had damped down the overspill, making the current versions of the surviving wild stories slightly less horrific.

thousand. Wooden beams twisted and dripped sap.

And great invisible skeins of power wrapped around her seven friends as they charged, turning them into legendary versions of themselves.

Time slowed to a crawl. Thousands of Nazi fingers gripped triggers, and clenched white-knuckles around the hilts of swords. Hauptmann Schmidt finally got the needle in the groove, and crackly, thunderous Wagner erupted across the courtyard. Muzzle flashes blossomed in a rippling wave, sending a wall of horizontal lead flying toward Squad 27.

Who came snarling and leaping and howling and rushing forward to meet it.

Not a single bullet hit St Germain, far out on the left. The little alchemist and semi-professional botherer of deities *changed* as the wash of magic bound him up, his uniform becoming a beautiful seventeenth-century dandy's satin coat, dripping with brocade and pearls. His cane-sword swept out with a sound like a wet fingertip on crystal, and the very shockwave of it severed bullets from the air. Then his silver-buckled shoes were running on the inner wall of the castle, and he was laughing, his immense and silly wig rising up to battlement level like a horse-hair thundercloud. Unmages spat their curses and flung inky darkness, but the sword stitched among them like hard lightning, and they fell.

Clear across the inner ward, on the right flank, Percy caught a twisting blast of magic too. Muscles erupted inside his clothes as if someone was blowing bubbles in his skin, and he lurched for a second, growing and changing even as his tin helmet wavered and blurred away, becoming a tall silk top hat, daubed with a stylized skull. Huge, black-clawed hands erupted from the sleeves of a dinner jacket almost bursting at the seams. But his face had become an indistinct darkness, from which two sizzling red eyes burned like coals, above a grin so wide and full of teeth that it looked like that of some deep-abyssal fish. Black Sun sturmtroopers emptied clip after clip into him as he came on, bounding across the courtyard in a great loping stride. Clots and spatters of darkness flew out behind him, scattering graveyard dirt. But he healed as fast as he was hurt, stitches looping themselves together and pulling tight. And when men looked into that horrible absence of a face, what they saw was *themselves*, two weeks dead, all maggots and meat. They were screaming long before the chewing started.

Fyodor's disguise (which, let's face it, had just been a rather sad old opera cape) was suddenly transformed into the wings of nightmare. He swooped up out of the smoke and descended on a panicked knot of soldiers, immaculate in full evening dress, complete with a widow's peak you could tell the time by. Rifles and machine-pistols fell from trembling fingers as the enemy were mesmerized.

"Behold!" he shouted, in a deep, dark baritone. "It is I! Master of..."

"Holy crap! It's old Giwdul Derfnam Gnagflow nov Nesohekcihcs from down the pub!"

Fyodor shrugged. His smile was a wry and comical grin, and at the same time a horrible display of sharp enamel. Sometimes you just have to roll with the classics. He gripped the ends of his cape in both hands, raising them up above his head.

"*Blah blah!* You *beloooonnnk* dead!" he shouted. "I hate the fact this feels so *right!*"

The shadow of bat wings rose up to snuff out the light, as a score of Nazi soldiers quailed back, their screams cut off by a noise like the whistle and crunch of a guillotine. Blood painted the castle wall halfway to the battlements.

Mrs Hazelwood didn't change at all as the stones under her feet erupted with grass and flowers. She tottered along with her immense handbag clutched up under her chin, humming a half-forgotten Victorian vaudeville tune (which may well have involved a naughty milkman). Hundreds of guns were aimed at her. Thousands of bullets sliced through the smoky air, as teeth were gritted and night-vision goggles flashed green under the brims of coal-scuttle helmets.

None of it helped, of course. Because Roger Hazelwood was back, and he was not happy. Normally, the amount of background magic conjured up by Henrietta did nothing but pop open a little keyhole, through which he could possess her hovering crystal ball. Now, however, an overspill and backwash of thaumaturgy sizzled around the ball in a purple cloud, sending streamers of pink lightning crawling across every surface. Roger, there at the threshold of the Mortal Veil, usually only had his old missus for company. Now, if he looked over his ghostly shoulder, he saw that there were thousands of ghosts behind him, attracted to the blaze of sorcery like moths to a gigantic spotlight.

Roger absentmindedly reached out with finger-filaments of lightning, stopping a sleet of bullets in midair. He looked at the spirits who crowded up around him, and nodded. Many of them were young men in army uniforms. The freshly deceased, during wartime, often are. They wore the colours of the Polish and the Free French, the Russians and the British, the Australian and New Zealand ANZACs, and the Canadians and Americans too.

"Wotcher, lads," said Roger. "I can't help but notice you don't seem too pleased to see our Nazi chums here. Would I be right?"

A murmur of ghostly anger rippled through the crowd. There really was no seeing all the way to the back of it.

"Well, don't tell the missus, but when I were a lad, we used to scrap with the boys from over in Peasegarden Street, and we had us a bit of a saying for times like this..."

Roger had spent most of his life, and all of his afterlife, being as respectable and middle-class as humanly possible. But some of the anger which sloshed through the spirit world made him decide, here and now, that it was time to get back to basics.

"What's say we batter the bastards, eh?"

Time came swinging back, like the most merciless and razor-sharp pendulum a mad torturer could ever dream of. Thousands of bullets dropped from the air, clattering to the ground. Henrietta Hazelwood paused, cocked her head to one side and tutted.

"Language, dear!"

Then Roger did away with the keyhole, and kicked in the door. A radial shockwave rippled out from the crystal ball in every direction, complete with a blur of contorted, wrathful faces. It slammed through the ranks of Black Sun troopers, throwing them backwards, making sparks sizzle and blip from their fingertips and the toes of their boots.

When they rose again, it was with the jerky, tottering motion of the possessed. White and empty eyes turned on former allies as hundreds of freshly stolen hands hefted whatever weapons were available…

Mrs H was only just able to wrestle the crystal ball around in time to deflect a shot that came howling in from her left; from that mean old Tiger III. Shrapnel and smoke blew past her as the tank stared her down, hidden mechanisms clunking and sliding within its turret as another shell was loaded.

"You got this one, Lucky?" she shouted. A few more bullets spanged off the crystal ball. And striding out of the smoke came her answer.

It didn't take long for the crew of the Tiger to latch on to this new and imminent threat. Lucky was resplendent in green, from his long moleskin trousers to his little waistcoat, and for some reason a t-shirt advertising the as-yet-non-existent Delorean Motor Company. He advanced like ice-age glaciation in fast forward, relentless and fixated, his fists meting out great cracking blows to any soldiers who stood in his way. Bullets which seemed sure to cut him down flickered into rainbow detonations an inch from his skin. Some evaporated. Some turned into butterflies. Some splattered to the ground as custard.

Now he came to a huge block of fallen masonry, tumbled across the courtyard by Connor's magic. He began to hum a tune as he climbed up atop it, peering into the skies. Then he nodded, smiled, and clicked his fingers. A wide circle of Nazi soldiery flinched back, but nothing seemed to happen. Lucky pointed, with a digit that looked like it had once lost an argument with an industrial pencil sharpener.

"Right, you bloody gobshite little bastards in the tank. You want to be shooting at a poor old lady, do you? Let's have some manners kicked into you, then!"

Every muscle in Lucky's huge wiry frame tensed like industrial cable. His hair bristled, lifting his tiny comical bowler hat an inch from his scalp. And he leaped forward with a battle-cry unheard in all of Western Europe since the days when the *Fomhóraigh* were driven from Eire, at the bloody field of Mag Tuired.

The machine gun mounted to the front of the Tiger had barely enough time to aim before it was gripped between a set of scarred and gnarly fingers, then twisted into a pretzel of steel. A pugnacious uppercut rocked the turret as the main gun was bent like a banana. Then the horrified crew felt a huge impact, and saw the imprint of four knuckles hammered into the inside of the Tiger's armour.

Another came, and another, but though the thick plates of metal buckled, they held.

The tank commander grinned. It had been the same all over. Nothing could batter its way through that steely hide. He popped open a tiny hatch, no bigger than a letter box.

"Ha ha! You can't get us! Go away and try to ruin someone else's tank, you silly Irish *dumbkopf*!"

He seemed more than a little smug. Even despite the fact that the gunner had definitely peed his pants when that first blow landed.

Lucky put one eye up to the hatch, then the other. Then he stepped down off the tank, dusting off his hands.

"Oh, don't worry about me, fellers. That was just a bit of test, and all. I reckon your real problems are about to start right… about… *now*."

He tipped his hat and backed away a very precise number of paces, grinning in a way which made the tank commander feel horribly,

horribly insecure. That was when he heard the whistle, coming closer. *Falling* closer, he clarified, like one of those dive-bombers with the huge big siren on the -

One thing that most people know about the average Leprechaun, is that they have the ability to summon a whacking great cauldron full of gold coins. Some will tell you that the gold is an illusion, and that it will vanish before sunrise. No one is very specific about the ephemeral nature of the cauldron itself, though in some parts of Ireland, especially in medieval times, a whole lot of gold was just likely to be trouble, but a nice big cauldron was something to hang on to. The gold, it seems, is part of a tribute paid by Oberyn himself to the magical folk who already inhabited western Europe at the fall of Tirfeynn. While the price was obviously not worth the cost, in the end, the rulers of the elder folk, the *Tuatha De*, decided to keep the gold safe so they could one day return it. Probably as a suppository, considering.

Lucky was no exception. He had often found a hoard of magical gold pieces a great comfort, especially when in the presence of innkeepers with more whiskey than fiscal sense. This time, however, he'd manifested a great big black iron cauldron, the kind you could use to stew up an entire goat, stuffed it full of gold, and brought it into existence - in low earth orbit.

The cauldron had been plummeting toward the ground for the entire time the huge leprechaun had played with the Tiger tank. The forces of friction and speed which tortured it as it ripped through the atmosphere did their work, developing a blazing orange plasma sheath around the belly of the pot itself, and eventually heating the iron through red to white and then to a molten state. Drag attenuated the entire seething, glowing mass as it arrowed in toward Germany, spin forces forming it into a three-part cone; pure, sun-hot fire, a drillbit of spinning, blazing iron and a liquid centre of molten gold. For a brief time it was the fastest thing in the world, covering miles in a heartbeat, trailing a sonic boom like the flatulence of God.

When it hit the Tiger tank, square from above, the effect was like some cosmic thumb squashing an insect. Sections of tread blew out sideways, along with a selection of carrier springs and iron wheels. One of these whickered across the courtyard like a shuriken, neatly decapitating both a statue of the old Baron and the nazi hiding behind it. The turret was obliterated, the main gun left pointing up into the sky. The engine was ejected forcibly from the rear, crushing a machine-gun crew and scattering other soldiers like bowling pins. Not a single person in the entire castle remained standing as the shockwave tilted the towers and cracked the ancient stones.

In the silence which followed – the kind of ear-ringing, post-rock-concert silence of slack-jawed wonder and horror – Lucky sidled up to the shell of the tank. He popped open the hatch with one finger, looked inside, and winced.

"How… how does it look?" asked Fyodor, pausing with a very drained-out sturmtrooper in each hand.

Lucky shook his head.

"Wellll - if they were going to hand out one of them academy awards for most surprised dead Nazi this year, they'd have four statues to choose from," he said. Little drips and puddles of molten gold were still trickling out from under the tank.

"Don't just stand there, you fools!" shrieked Hans Schprinkler, caught in a stuttering flash of raw magic, his staff held high over his head. *Destroy them!*"

He swung the metal rod down in a blurring arc, but it was met by Connor of Anstruther's shillelagh, and a blaze of light and sparks detonated like the expiration of suns. Left, and again he was blocked; right, and this time the old wizard came in close, delivering a non-magical but very solid hobnailed boot to the shin.

"Your destroyin' days are done, pal! Why not make it easy on yeself, and just explode right now? At least we won't have tae hear any more of your daft villainy bollocks…"

The twin staves blurred again, sending sheets of magic boiling across the battlefield like razor aurorae. They locked up, grinding together, the swords of embattled knights. Connor and Hans grimaced at each other, noses mere inches apart.

"That is where you are wrong, my little Scottish fool. I have assembled here a force of *two thousand* of the most magically. Potent. Soldiers in the entire Reich!"

Connor pushed with all his out-of-proportion strength, throwing Schprinkler back. Then he unleashed a crackling fireburst from the knot of his shillelagh, striking the Nazi sorcerer like the stream of a flamethrower. A red, swastika-shaped shield of energy bloomed around Schprinkler, fading as the fire sputtered and died. He strode forward again, unscathed, his staff whistling through the air to crack against Connor's bog-wood weapon with a sizzle of sparks.

"Your precious two thousand men are dying, Hans. And you're next!"

The Black Sun's kommandant raised one eyebrow, and smiled.

"I never said *precious*, Mister the Beige. Just *potent*. You know how magic comes from belief, of course? Well, these poor boys *believe*. In all that *scheisse* der Fuhrer rants into his microphones. In all the garbage they preach at Wewelsberg. About the supremacy of the master race, and the power of the. Divine. Aryan. Will. They are not here for *me*, old chum. Ach, no..."

Connor gritted his teeth and spun his staff through a blurring combo of strikes which would have made a samurai proud. Nine out of ten failed to connect, blocked by the steel rod in Hans Schprinkler's hands. But the tenth caught him a solid blow across the chest, with an audible crack of splintered ribs. The Nazi slumped, still grinning, blood dripping from between his teeth. Connor bristled with rage.

"You'd even sacrifice your own men? Ye damned old monster! Monkston was right aboot ye, boy. The world will be happier without ye scrofulous arse upon it!"

"Oh, *now* who's doing the big bloody recital, hmm?" Schprinkler's eyes narrowed, even as three feet of solid bog-oak rose above his head like an executioner's blade. "Tell me, Connor the Beige, what do you know about *full thaumo-morphic manifestational transference?*"

Connor's eyes went wide, even as he brought down the staff in a crashing blow. Hans rolled deftly sideways, cackling.

"You mean... they're all just *food?* You scunnerous wee bastard! How are ye gonnae control it? And *then* what? Do ye own a bloody circus?"

"You will never find out, alas. Or you will find out far too late. You see, the Accords will not pass. And my little friends the elves and their lovely Queen most *definitely* wish to betray me. I need the science and industry of the entire Third Reich to enslave them. And what better way to seize that power... than to become *the new Fuhrer!*"

Now Connor was on the back foot, parrying a storm of blows from Schprinkler's hissing, spitting steel staff. The swastika runes at its tip glowed red-hot.

"I willnae ask how, ye mad bugger, for fear ye'll go on all night! But
—"

At that moment, the immense background surge of magic flowing into Connor was sliced off, as if someone has flipped a massive, Frankenstein's-castle-issue electrical switch. He heard Patience scream in horror, just as a pair of very strong arms wrapped around him from behind. Schprinkler leaned in, grinning gold and gruesome, until the sizzling head of his staff was right in the little wizard's face.

"Easy und also peasy, as you horrid Britishmen say. I have the assistance of some very wonderful allies here tonight, who know all about your English *hexenkraft*. And who remain. Frankly. Unimpressed."

Connor looked down at the thick, brown-skinned arms which held him in a vise grip. Although clad in a Nazi uniform, they boasted hundreds of red-inked tribal tattoos and hands with long, sharp black fingernails. A face, recently unmasked, pressed up next to his own, eyes rolling to stare at him with tiny yellow pupils on black.

"The Tcho Tcho cannibals of utmost Burma!'[40] Which means..."

"Your magic will not work on them, keeper of the flame," grated Hans. "They worship the devourers of sorcery. *The Elder Ones.*"

Connor spat in his face.

"Not *that*, ye windy old shitebag! I mean I know who betrayed us!"

Schprinkler wiped away the spittle with a hand that was ever so slow and precise. Then he proceeded to backhand the Scots wizard so hard his pointy hat flew off into the dirt.

"What does it matter? You were *always* going to be betrayed. It's that kind of war! What's important..." and here he leaned down, pinching Connor's chin between his leather-gloved fingers, turning his head around, making him see... "What is *important*, you pathetic little man, is that I will have a DRAGON. Let Adolf try to fecking explain *that* one away, hmm?"

Connor couldn't help but look. A little trickle of blood oozed from his split lip as he watched the focus of Hans Schprinkler's murderous show. Elsewhere, the battle was dying down, as thoroughly magic-immune Tcho Tcho and their traitorous allies swarmed Lucky, Mrs Hazelwood, Fyodor and all the rest.

But in the middle of the courtyard, where the spotlights beat down like the sun at high noon, magic was building. A crackling vortex, surrounding a form all red and hazy, fighting on amid a cloud of

---

40 The Tcho Tcho cannibals of utmost Burma, it's widely known, are a people brought low by their love of gastronomy as much by their worship of dark and gelatinous Gods with more face-tentacles than common sense. For one and all are addicted to the Bak Bon Dzhow, the forbidden black hot sauce which is served with human flesh. This unhallowed tracklement not only guarantees a taste for the 'long pork' of myth and legend, but also builds up an immunity to magic. The hot sauce is how the Tcho Tcho actively recruit – one dab of that delicious, addictive blend of spices and human brains on what you thought was a perfectly innocent sausage on a bun, and you're off to the jungle with a knife and fork, ready to join their merry crew.

electrical sparks where the impossible and the possible ground up against each other, like steel on steel.

He looked on Eddie Weatherfield, and he despaired.

Because the poor dumb bastard was *winning*.

+++

Things had taken a definite turn for the worse.

The Compte de Saint Germain had burst into a tower room, only to find himself confronted by a great grey-green stitched-together monster of a man, with a flat head, neck bolts, and an apparent immunity to being run through with a rapier. The creature had been ready for him, too. It was carrying a stinking hessian sack and a set of handcuffs, all inscribed with the name of a certain Jewish cabinetmaker.

Down in the courtyard, Percy sucked the last scraps of gristle off a Nazi femur, and turned his head just in time to see a barrage of animated bandages leaping toward him, dry as desert dust and implacable as steel. Fyodor felt the magic drain out of himself just as a huge and hairy shadow fell in front of the spotlights, accompanied by a far-too-theatrical howl.

"Bloody *bollocks*. Hello, Yevgeny..."

Mrs Hazelwood was quick enough to close her eyes as her own assailant let the turban fall from her head, revealing a nest of snakes. A beam of turquoise sorcery struck her crystal ball, splintering into filaments, piercing all of the possessed in a heartbeat. There came a grinding noise like tank treads on gravel, and a circle of Nazi soldiers became ornamental statuary. Then an old man with a cricket bat knocked the crystal ball out of the air, and the medusa caught it in a heavy rubber bag.

Lucky felt something tiny and fast scurry up his trousers, up through his shirt, and clamber up to face-height in a single sickening instant. His eyes crossed, as he looked into the mirrored aviator shades of a combat-ready gnome. The little bugger had a fist knotted in the ginger hair of both his sideburns, and his forehead struck like a tiny bullet, with an audible 'thunk'. The giant leprechaun went down like tall timber, measuring a seven-foot streak in the dirt.

While in the ruin of the castle's barracks, Patience was pinned up against the wall by something vile. A glistening knot of glassy, ghostly viscera hung before her, centred on a ring of silver with sawblade teeth. A metal mouth, gorging on earth magic. The pipes and tubes throbbed obscenely as vitae pumped within, turning in on itself, blackening, condensing frost from the air. Its presence *hurt,* like toothache rot and hangovers all at once.

"Do you like it?" asked the voice of something nearly as vile again. It was the plump young archmage Snetterley, once of the order of the Celestial Light, but now most certainly not. His robes hung in rags, stained with unspeakable stains, and his skin was freshly etched with line after line of red tribal tattoos. His teeth were black and filed to points. Despite all of this, he still looked like a horrible little public school bully-boy.

"I call it Snetterley Minor's Geomantical Injunction. A spell which can snip off a ley line like pinching off an artery. Do you know how long it took to do all the maths? Even after Daddy's friends brought me that thing in the middle..."

He sidled forward, gesturing at the great knotted abomination of wizardry and witchcraft combined. "If only your sisters were more forthcoming, it might have not been so difficult. As it was..."

Patience *definitely* knew what the little bastard was implying by that comment. She snarled, rallying what shreds of power were left to her, and came out of the corner swinging, spikes of ice forming a corona around her fist.

Snetterley pulled something from under his robe, and a silent explosion of force knocked her back like a rag doll. It was an axe, with an oak handle and a head all scarred and blackened by fire.

"I had hoped we wouldn't have to use it again," he said, with just a little wistful sadness in his voice. "He's still inside there, you know. In the metal. Mad as an electric turnip, but his *mind*..." Here Snetterley looked up, and his eyes were two pinpricks of piss-yellow amid oceans of glossy black. "Like a sharpened compass needle! So sure of purpose. I feel a bit like that now. You could too."

Patience knew exactly the provenance and history of the weapon he was holding. The axe of Hopkins, the Witchfinder General. They had always said he'd been bound up in when he died, choking out a stolen wizard's spell as his lungs turned to slime in his chest...

"What have you *done*, you stupid little shit?" she asked, all but breathless. The axe exerted a presence which was like the worst stench she'd ever smelled, mixed with tangible darkness. Like being suffocated in cess-pit velvet. "Did you forget about the war? The Nazis? *England?*"

The chubby little wizard crouched down beside her, and tilted his head to one side.

"This isn't the war, silly girl. This is just the curtain-raiser. Daddy told me what must be done. We will deliver this world to the Masters, and then we… *we*, the magically gifted, the *elite*… we will rule over the peasant masses. Just as it always should have been!"

Patience sighed. You didn't need to be able to see the future to know exactly what was coming next. Sometimes she wished she was just a normal girl, with normal things to worry about, like deciphering codes and building aeroplanes and overthrowing a stifling corrupt patriarchy. Instead…

"It doesn't have to be like this," wheedled Snetterley, reaching out to touch her cheek. His fingers were clammy and cold, naturally. "You're the most powerful witch left alive. We could… you know… *betray them together*. You and me. Rule this world, in the glorious darkness of the Netherverse, as king and queen!"

Sometimes it was horrible to be right.

"Would I have to wear one of those witch-queen outfits with the cape, and the high collar, and the big knee-high boots and not much else?" asked Patience, who had seen the covers of any number of terrible paperbacks.

Snetterley's eyes goggled. No matter how far gone you are with cannibal hot sauce, Elder Magic and vile ambition, if you're a teenage boy, the old hormones still have both hands on the steering wheel.

"*Cor blimey!* I suppose, yeah, and we could build a huge dark tower, and have thousands of slaves, and -"

Patience had heard enough. Having ascertained that the aforementioned hormones were working just right, she proceeded to kick young Snetterley very, very hard indeed, exactly where they were produced.

Sometimes magic is what you need. Sometimes it's just a women's size seven regulation army boot.

The teenage arch-mage's eyes crossed, and he gurgled his way to an undignified heap on the floor, adopting that 'oven ready turkey' pose so beloved of those who have been kicked in the plums. Patience pushed a strand of hair out of her eyes with one unsteady hand, then pushed her way up the wall and to her feet. She swallowed. There was no choice, really. With tentative hands, like someone reaching down a shattered-u-bend and into raw sewage, she fumbled for the axe…

Only for a big black boot to come down on the handle, hard.

Patience looked up, into a face which looked like Snetterley's, from a future where he was a chartered accountant. Waxy and thick of jowl, adorned with a neat little topiary mustache and a pair of gold-framed spectacles. And, it must be said, line after line of warping, seething tribal tattoos. Snetterley Senior's lips were black from an excess of the Bak Bon Dzhow, and now they pulled back from a row of teeth a shark would have been proud to show his dentist. It was, against all evidence, a smile.

"Stupid boy. So keen on betrayal, but so bloody cretinous! And as for *you*, young lady… well. When it comes to the backstabbing game, you might as well join the winning team, hmm? After all – *you're* the one who's just left all of London unprotected. Do you think our chums in the Luftwaffe are going to let that slide? When what's left of jolly old Section M finds out what you've done here, they'll think you were one of us all along."

He stooped, and picked up the axe one-handed. The look on his face was that of a maths teacher reviewing a very, very badly failed test. Not angry. Just *disappointed.*

"So. We can do this with all your arms and legs on, or without. It's a very old story, but never *once* do they say that the dragon cared about getting all the wings and drumsticks."

+++

This time there was no rage. This time there was nothing but clarity, crystal pure, tingling cold, as time dripped by like meltwater from a glacier.

Eddie felt Patience's burst of earth magic lift him up from behind, at once a wave and an electric shock. He felt invisible fingers push through his living spine, as if it was made of butter. The change overtook him as he ran, and it was easy as breathing. He closed his eyes on one world and opened them on another, in which all the silly little black-clad stickmen were either kindling or prey.

His clothes burst as red-scaled slabs of muscle swelled. Clawed feet popped his boots open like banana skins. Then his hands were closing around the necks of two sturmtroopers, and the explosions of blood were like the crashing first chords of a symphony. The part of Eddie Weatherfield which was concerned about socks and love and rules and aeroplanes and family – the part of him which *was,* in fact Eddie Weatherfield – was pushed back until he was just a passenger behind a pair of mismatched, blazing eyes. He watched those hands get bigger, until they were tearing men in half at the waist like paper dolls. He saw the shadow of huge wings flare out behind him, and felt the ripple and stutter as bullets bounced clean off them. Black-armoured knights with swastika and black-sun tabards swung their swords. Desperate men loaded and fired panzerfaust rockets. He felt himself exhale, and a jet of white-hot death scoured the courtyard clean before him, little matchstick scrawls ablating away to screams, to dust.

And still the magic built. Instrument after instrument swelled the chorus. His nerves sang like wires in a hurricane. Every cell trembled with the same will that had caused some ambitious flounder, aeons past, to head on up the beach and get evolving.

Eddie's mind sunk further back into his brain, wrapped in blissful detachment.

*And here was the world of the dragons again. A severed chunk of the Earth, floating in a rainbow bubble, its sky held tight by magic and bloody-mindedness. He saw mountains hollowed out like vast termite mounds, caverns carved with inhuman sculptures and runes, and everywhere the great wyrms, both torpid and awake. Some few dragons moved through the ancient corridors, or perched basking atop the crags. But only very few. This race was suffused with magic, and their waking minds sat on reality like a fat man on an inflatable sofa.*

A great scaly visage loomed up before him. Little sizzles of chemical fire dripped out between teeth the size of bananas.

"So *close* this time, Eddie," it breathed. "You took my advice, hmm? You're not fighting for your own soft skin anymore, are you? You're fighting for *them*. How very noble."

The dragon chuckled, even as Eddie watched his teeth rip through a Nazi soldier's chest. He had teeth like that? Spiked enamel butcher knives? He supposed he had to have; they were all that held in his big, forked, purple tongue.

"And each one of them is so full of lovely, sweet power! Ahhh, just a little closer! I know I mentioned it last time, Weatherfield, but did you ever work out what it meant? *Full thaumo-morphic manifestational transference?*"

Eddie would have shook his head, but something strange was happening. He felt all warm and comfortable, back there in his brain. But his eyes seemed far away, like two flickering cinema screens. The image of the dragon in his mind was more real than the battle raging outside. He realized, with a cold frisson of fear, that he couldn't shake his head. He couldn't control his arms or legs. He wasn't (to put a finer point on it), in control anymore.

"*Berserk*," he whispered to himself, remembering the look on Darrin Oakenbeard's face. "*Means crazy. We had to know how to stop them when they went too far...*"

The dragon arched one scaly eyebrow.

"It means more than *crazy*, Eddie. It means that you're going to take a little nap. We have business with the Accords, you see. My people could be *changed*, and come back, and feel real sunlight and wind on our wings again. We could certainly take care of those upstart Fae for you. But of course, no one believes in us anymore. Your fool of a Writer was going to keep us as big, greedy lizards with all the ambition of a gang of burglars. Sleeping on piles of gold while everyone else gets on with things! Pah!"

Now Eddie felt it. Silvery lines of force went flowing past him, bridging the gap between himself and the image of the dragon, like so many filaments of spider silk. They grabbed his imagined wrists and ankles. They lashed around his neck like strangling fingers. And they pulled him toward a ripple in the air, like a vertical pool of water, seething with little sparks.

"No! They need me! You can't let them die out there!"

Frantic, now, as the tips of his toes broke the surface. It was cold, like clear air on a winter's morning, and beneath it, Eddie felt nothing at all. Behind him, his empty eyes looked out over a massacre. His body roared as its neck grew several more vertebrae. His spine arched as his wings and arms grew, his ribcage attenuating with a series of sickening pops.

"Oh, Weatherfield! What is their little sacrifice, against that of my people? We, who gave up an *entire world* to save it from our power? You *owe* us, human! You, and your ancestors, all the way back to those horrible little hedgehog things that used to get stuck in my teeth!"

He turned his face away for as long as he could. But first one cheek, then one eye, then his nose went under. There was nothing but white light, and utter cold, and the sound of static.

"Promise..." he hissed, saving as much of his last breath as possible.

But the wisdom and sincerity were gone. All that was left, on that inhuman face, was triumph.

"I promise *nothing*, human. Except this; you will have your body back, once the Accords are done. How dare they not invite me? *Me!* Vauragath the Crimson, ambassador to the Heart of Fire!"

Eddie Weatherfield closed his eyes again.

And out in reality, out in the courtyard of Schloss Bad Schickehosen, Vauragath the Crimson opened his.

The great dragon saw little humans running here and there, some of them on fire, some of them leaking, almost all of them screaming at cross purposes. Some of them had been captured and tied up by others, but little details like uniforms and flags were beneath the regard of Vauragath. He exerted a tiny fraction of his magic, feeling it flex against reality like a talon against some prey-beast's skin.

**STOP**

They had no choice but to obey. Deep in his skull, like an itch he couldn't scratch, Vauragath heard the tiny human, Weatherfield, raging and crying. But the spell had bought him some peace and quiet on the outside. Weapons fell from hundreds of hands. A thousand terrified eyes looked up with what the Ambassador counted as proper reverence. *Of course.* They had never seen a Dragon, these fools. Not a real one, in the flesh, potent with sorcery. Not for a thousand years. The undead things in their barrow-graves were to Vauragath what a fart is to a thunderstorm. What a match-strike is to a volcanic eruption.

He cleared his throat. Little puffs of smoke escaped.

"Right then. That's better. Now, I don't care at all about your silly little human war, but I *am* slightly peckish. So if you all just shake hands and make up, I'll be wanting about thirty head of cattle, a big barrel of your finest house red, and..."

Weatherfield was still screaming about something, down in some gristly part of his brainstem. Something *not quite right.* But for the great crimson wyrm, concentrating on individual humans was like a human concentrating on individual ants.

"A pinot noir would be lovely, but a cheeky drop of..."

That's when he saw it too. A pair of humans who seemed unimpressed by the huge, furnace-bellied lizard which had appeared among them.

*They were not bowing! The temerity! The arrogance!*

Vauragath felt that an example should be made, and a part of him which was more pride than intellect stoked up the fire in his gullet, letting it out as a kind of orgasmic burp.

The east wing of Schloss Bad Shickehosen turned to horizontal magma in that instant. A tower, shorn off diagonally like a vintage calligraphy brush, slid down on a gooey trail of its own molten rock, then collapsed into the darkness beyond. Which was not quite as dark as it had been, thanks to a rapidly spreading forest fire.

*There. That should be dramatic enough.* Dragons used wholesale destruction as punctuation.

But the two humans were still on their feet. Perhaps he should nibble on them a bit? No, decided the part of Vauragath's brain more evolved than the rest. *There was something about these two.* Nictitating membranes (made to see in spectra so far beyond the visible that they bent all the way around into the imaginary) slithered across the great wyrm's eyes. They told the truth. The one on the left, wearing the remains of a cloak covered in dirty stars and moons, was quite utterly mad. He currently believed himself to be a tea-tray full of rubber ducks, for example. But the other one…

"*Just give it to me, you daft old fool…* ahem… Greetings, your excellency! And might I say, what a pleasant swathe of destruction you have wrought?"

Vauragath narrowed his eyes. The second little human was dressed all in black, and he had wrestled something like an oversized silver crown from the hands of the mad one. His mind was very much like that of a dragon's, thought the Ambassador. His thoughts were not the fizzing plasma-globe of hopes and dreams of these other little apelings. No – they were sharp and cold and hard, streamlined to a point. Vauragath cleared his throat, and leaned down.

"Well met, then, human! It's good to see that at least one of you still has deference to your betters. Now… as to the Accords. We will, or course, demand a seat at the High Table," he chuckled 'or at least a very big pile of gold to lie down on, heh, heh. And some kind of delicious crunchy sacrifice would be fitting, I think. Now, let's get back to that pinot…"

Hans Schprinkler didn't wait another second.

"Your Immensity, perhaps you do not understand *exactly* who I am. This is the Schloss Bad Schickehosen, the most evil castle in the most evil part of the black forest, in the most evil part of the entire Third Reich, who, if you were to listen to quite a lot of the world, are not a pleasant bunch of chums enjoying jam sandwiches on the seaside, ja? I am widely considered to be the most nasty, malicious, devious and spiteful member of the Axis high command, a bunch of villains so black-hearted they would wash down a puppy sandwich with the tears of orphans on Christmas morning! To put it simply, I am the *bad guy*, and your talk of Accords and tributes and other such nonsense is as meaningless as the, how do you say… *fart of a hamster*, yes? Because, while you have just doublecrossed my old friend Eddie Weatherfield, **I have more treachery in mein little pinky finger than you do in your whole big scaly body!”**

With that, he threw the silver circle in his hands like a discus, sending it whickering through the air in a nimbus of magic. Before Vauragath had time to react, the thing had snicked open, displaying an inner surface made up entirely of teeth. For it was, of course, Snetterley Junior’s Geomantic Injunction; or as the double-crossing leader of the Black Sun liked to call it, a collar of enslavement. It snapped tight around the dragon’s neck with a clang like crematorium doors slamming shut, and the beast convulsed.

*“No! Impossible! You utter little bastar….”*

“Thank you, und goodnight!” cackled the Nazi sorcerer, holding his hands high as Varagath collapsed to the ground, greenish foam bubbling from his lips. The dragon’s eyes rolled back to pearly whites as his limbs twitched, pedaling air. Schprinkler turned to Snetterley, just as the English wizard’s son came tottering over as well, one hand massaging his tender fruits.

“You see? *That*, my friends, is the power of villainy made manifest! When you embrace your role as the villain, *everything* becomes part of your convoluted, twisted plan. The power of London, the ley lines, the witch, the collar of enslavement – why, it even turned out that we didn’t have to deal with Herr Weatherfield himself.” Hans smiled contentedly, tipping his head on one side to regard them through his monocle. “And now, I suspect, *you* suspect I’ll have you. Both. Shot, hmm?”

Snetterley Senior chuckled.

“Of course, old bean. You’re the *bad guy*. But then again, I’m a traitorous wizard with a squad of turncoat monsters and a small army of cannibals behind me. I reckon I’m pretty bloody wicked in my own right. You may want to reconsider.”

Hans pulled a luger pistol from his coat and dropped it to the ground. It was a prissy little gesture; he gripped the gun between two fingers like a butler handling a cat turd.

“True, I suppose. Shall we go and do some fiendish gloating together, then? We have oh so many prisoners, and now - we have a dragon, too! The Accords are… finished!”

Snetterley wasn’t about to be outdone. He joined Schprinkler in a bout of unhinged laughter.

“Decimated!”

"Ruined!"

"Buggered!" chimed in Junior, striking a villainous pose. The other two looked at him in contempt for an instant, then went back to laughing.

"Bwaaahahahahahhaaaaaa!"

Above them, lightning cracked the sky above Schloss Bad Schickehosen.

It seemed that the bad guys had won.

# Meanwhile, in flagrant disregard of the memo from Section M H.Q. telling us not to write any more of these...

Famously, there was once a lamp-post just inside the borderlands of Fae. It was often depicted as standing in a snowy forest, incongruous and alone, lighting a patch of frozen ground among the trees.

Times had changed, as a little of the world beyond leaked into this parasitic set of non-euclidian co-ordinates, bringing a kind of progress with it. Now the lamp-post had been joined by a red telephone booth, a post box, a rubbish bin which was always half full of beer bottles, and a small amount of pavement, straggling off into nowhere. Sometimes, when the mathematics lined up across the gulfs of space and time, a very confused Egyptian architect would pop into existence inside the phone booth, thanks to its special measurements and properties. There was a note on the wall in Third Dynasty hieroglyphs telling them what number to dial for a ride back to their own time and space.

There was also a little house there, right on the border. You could get here from many places; by walking sideways between two aspen trees in Yorkshire, for example, or by falling asleep near a standing stone in Wales. Where you *went* from here also depended on how you came. There'd been some embarrassment when an ill-advised carpenter made a wardrobe out of one of Oberyn's sacred oaks, but it had all been sorted out diplomatically.

Now there was a horde of motorcycles parked outside the house, which appeared to be a quaint little suburban number, of the kind they were building out in California. There was a Ford five-window coupe in the driveway, a white picket fence, and a little birdbath in the shape of a scallop shell. elves clad in leathers, copper armour and skulls milled about in the yard, making sure to keep off the flowerbeds. The reason why could be seen through the kitchen window.

King Oberyn had not been too pleased to see his old bandmate the Erl King. He'd always been suspicious of the little bugger, ever since his ex-wife had abducted him and made him into something the elves couldn't be – a hunter armed with steel. He'd been a gambit to try and turn the tide, but turning the tide isn't something one man can do. As many thoroughly sodden and embarrassed kings can attest.

Still… he was bound by honour to at least break bread with him. Old rules, and all that. It wasn't his fault if his new missus had taken 'breaking bread' to mean having to sit there awkwardly and pick around old times while she made one of her legendary apple crumbles.

"So it's going to be quite a show," concluded the Erl King, nodding to the guitar case which he'd casually leaned up against the pantry. "We've got all the lads together, and you know… one last bash, and all that? Before they sign the Accords, and all this kind of thing goes south."

Oberyn grumbled.

"Oh, you say that, yes, I hear you. But it's *her* idea, and I know it. She just wants the old days back again, with the running about killing people, and the tricks, and the clever plots and all. I could never keep up, really. Better that we get changed into something different, Earl. Better that we move with the times."

The Erl King leaned forward, armour creaking.

"So what? Let them change us. I don't mind either way. I'm not of the Fae, and I've seen what they've got for me. Riding around on a motorbike is good fun, and there's talk of a flaming skull helmet and even… being a *good guy*." he conceded this last point in a half-mumble, as if it was a bit of a shameful secret. "But one more for the road! One more for history! *Let's give them the music*, and see what they can do with it when we're gone!"

This lit something up in Oberyn's eyes.

"Well, that at least was never hers, eh? I can feel the power sloshing around, where she's taken that poor old Israelite out of the picture. It would be a shame not to use it. This way, I'd be using it for something she doesn't want. I don't think Titania has any respect for my powers of self-control."

Behind him, his wife chuckled. Self control, it seemed, was a rare commodity in the Oberyn household. She turned from the oven, holding a hot pan of apple crumble with a pair of plaid oven mitts.

Eris, Goddess of Chaos, was said to have existed before the universe began, and would be there to light the fuse on the next one, when the last star winked out amid the particle gazpacho of utter heat death. In her present form she was a five-foot tall blonde with an hourglass figure, a button nose smattered with freckles, a cute little gap between her teeth and eyes the terrifying, blazing green of a nuclear disaster.

"Well, *I* think you should go and have some fun with your friends, Obie-kins," she said. The Erl King tried not to laugh at his sovereign's pet name. He was glad he was wearing a faceless helmet as Eris went on.

"Your poor old ex thinks she's very cunning, but trust me, duckie, I didn't just write the book on clever plots, I swindled the publisher out of all the rights and burned down the printer's for the insurance money as well. Go and play. Even if she tries to ruin the Accords for the humans, well… what a backdrop for your music! Fire, explosions, buildings burning, people screaming…" she clapped her oven-mitted hands together with a little shiver of delight, then yanked Oberyn's face up to hers by grabbing his beard. "You come home straight afterwards, and tell me *all about it*." She planted a kiss on his forehead. Oberyn blushed.

"Yes dear. *Of course*, dear." he tried valiantly to rescue the sinking ship of his royal dignity, grasping for some old-fashioned idiom. "We will smite them mightily with our… ummm… tunes, and such. Yes. Mightily!" Oberyn fished around inside his robes, until he found a key attached to a Ford badge and a tiny stag's-skull keychain. "I'll see you over there, lad. A show like this deserves proper threads, and there's a feller in Shoreditch I know who can still make me look good in leather trousers."

The Erl King sucked his teeth, and gave a little shake of his helmet.

"Not the best idea, squire. London's unprotected, so they say. I have a little business down those ways before we head off to the gig. Barely a stitch of magic left to stop us, so the Queen… that is to say Ti…"

Eris gave him a warning look before the name could come cut. It was the kind of warning that normally shears about three feet off the front of a battleship. Earl Kingsford gulped.

"*Sh…she* told me to get down there and carve up what's left. Knock over a few obelisks, burn some churches, kinda thing. Keep her pet human, this Schprinkler fellow happy. At least until she betrays him."

"Lots of that going around," purred Eris, neatly handing him a paper-bagged portion of crumble.

The Erl king nodded.

"They say it's that kind of war," he managed. "I tried to tell her that the Nazi was going to betray her first, but, well," he appealed to Oberyn. "You know how T… I mean the q… I mean *she* is."

Eris slung a plate of apple crumble and custard down in front of her husband.

"That's settled, then. You go on and do whatever mortal things you have to do, and I'll find something in the cupboard to make Obie's legs look less like sad old chicken drumsticks."

The Erl king was quite pleased to get out of there the same shape he'd gone in. He rounded up his posse of Fae bikers and gunned it off into the winter sky, disappearing with a grumble of thunder.

Meanwhile, as Oberyn struggled and swore and tried to suck in his prodigious belly while giving several pairs of antique trousers a whirl, Eris opened up the top drawer next to the oven, and pulled a slim black folder out from beneath her pile of dog-eared old cookbooks. It was the kind of file which normally has a title such as 'The Abraxas Protocol' or 'The Damocles Initiative'. Cocking an ear to make sure her husband was still in the throes of constrictive sartorial combat, she opened it a crack, and riffled through the contents.

Everything in the folder was invisible. Each piece of paper was immaterial, noticeable only by the crackle of red lighting where her fingers touched it, hinting at edges, postmarks, seals, ribbons and gilded foil. Eris, it has sometimes been noted, has a thing about not being invited places. To be fair, there are plenty of events – christenings, ship dedications, nuclear power station ribbon cutting ceremonies – where the avatar and essence of creative chaos is not first on the guest list. But these… these were all the events which she had pointedly and deliberately not been invited to, for very specific reasons. Their anti-imprint in spacetime was potent enough that she could reach out and pluck them from the swirl of randomness and probability that those fission-green eyes saw *all at once*.

This one, for example, was an anti-vitation to a very exclusive little makeup and beauty club, just for goddesses. One which Isis, Eostre and Ishtar had attended, not so long ago. She'd written a telephone number on the back, and now she slipped out the front door, breath steaming in the cold. She looked both ways for straggling elves, then went to the telephone booth, high heels clicking on the frozen pavement. She picked up the handset, and dialed a very long number that did not exist yet. A number with an Israeli prefix and mobile phone code.

Eris smiled, with a twitch of her adorable freckled nose.

This was going to be *fun*.

# And Meanwhile, finally...

Jesus walked into the telephone booth just as soon as he heard the phone start ringing. They'd given him a funny look when he came staggering into Saint Paul's in a bathrobe, pulled up a chair and drained the baptismal font of holy water through a straw. But it hadn't half worked. He felt almost human, now, rather than like an animated curry stain on a foul old bathroom rug. He'd picked up a book of hymns and inhaled the scent of musty old faith, his lungs filling with the scent of incense smoke, beard oil and lavender water. When he put it down, every page was blank.

The priest had tried to stop him when he popped open the cupboard behind the altar and started chowing down on communion wafers. *Dad* that had tasted good! One look into the feverish eyes of a bearded, thin fellow who looked unspeakably familiar had sent the poor cleric running to lock himself in the vestry, where he was still chewing on a small cassock.

To put it simply, Jesus was feeling more than a little angry when he heard the phone start to jangle. It was an empty booth on an empty street, but somehow he *knew* the call was for him.

He had not been disappointed.

"*Really,*" he said, beard bristling. And...

"*I see,*" he said, in the tones of someone who was definitely going to either strangle somebody or explode in the near future.

"*Right,*" he said, with just a hard-edged little hint of Gospel creeping into the inflection. A spider, who lived an otherwise blameless life in the eaves of the phone booth, legged it away as fast as it could.

Jesus hung up the phone, with a deliberate little guillotine click. He looked at the door of the phone box, opened it, looked up and down the street, closed it, snapped his fingers, then opened it again. A little nova of holy magic blossomed in silence.

And the door opened onto the car-park of what appeared to be an American diner. One of those ones built entirely of polished aluminum, with recessed pink neon tubing all around so they look like a robot's birthday cake. A stuttering neon sign, in a similar hue of pureed flamingo and candy, read 'Gabriel's'.

Jesus squared his shoulders, focused very intently on a point about three metres in front of his nose, and gave it the full Genesis.

"Let there be… a Matchless G3/L with white-wall tyres," said the Son of Man, unleashing a sizzle of his old man's power.

And here's the thing about Gabriel's. The little diner, off in its reality-adjacent sideways-space, on a cliff overlooking the universe, may have featured a selection of horses tied to an old-west style hitching post a second ago. But now, there had *always* been a row of classic motorcycles instead. There was a Triumph Speed Twin in shining white, all pared back and chopped until it was as lean and fast as possible. A BSA M20 in military camo, which looked as if it had slogged through every festering post-battle charnel-field in Europe and then been left outside of the shed to rust. An Ariel Red Hunter in (predictably) red, complete with a huge, gold-plated MG42 machine gun in one saddlebag. And finally, a Vincent Black Shadow. Every part of it, from the spokes to the fuel tank to the exhausts – even the faces of the wing mirrors – were utterly black. Somebody, however, had tied a pale grey plush toy pony to the handlebars.

Jesus pushed through the glass doors and was far from surprised to find that there were only five people present. Four of them were clustered around a booth table, and the fifth was behind the bar, buffing an already-perfect milkshake glass.

"Evening, y'r honour," said Gabriel, nodding politely. He was all golden curls and blue eyes and cheekbones, this one, even if he was kitted out in the costume of a soda-fountain jockey. "Aren't we a bit early?"

Jesus raised one eyebrow.

"Couldn't say as to the time, Gabe old chap," he drawled. "Looks like your clock is on the blink."

Indeed it was. The only clock in the joint – and a big, chromed, neon-wrapped monster it was – only had one hand. That hand was set at two minutes to midnight. Under the clock, like a blunderbuss on a country tavern wall, hung a long golden trumpet.

"Nevertheless, you know what your old man said, JC. *They* don't get to do the big curtain-dropper 'til he's ready. Which, if things go on like they are, is going to be tomorrow, about teatime." he shrugged. "Can I interest you in a banana split, in the meanwhile?"

Jesus looked at the *they*. They were playing cards amid the ruins of what appeared to have been the mother of all fry-up dinners. Four figures in robes, though the red one had accessorized with piecemeal armour, all plated in gold. The sickly green one looked like it had been dragged backwards through the toilets after a rugby game and then rolled up in the corner of a student flat for three semesters. The white one was made of latex, and was as form-fitting as a drinking straw. And the black one… well, the black one looked like it hadn't been woven out of any mortal fabric. It looked as if a very long, very thin slice of interstellar space has been cut out with a scalpel, then knitted into a shroud for silly concepts like 'hope' and 'aspiration'. The King of Kings leaned over the counter, pushing his sunglasses down to the end of his nose.

"Well, here's the ineffable thing, Gabriel. You're an angel. Guardian of my Dad's word. But, thanks to this whole trinity thing, *I'm Him as well.* Not to mention the fire of the Holy Spirit, which is legendarily good at convincing people to do my bidding. So, here's what's gonna happen. I'm going to go over there and preach a very short little testament to those guys. And you're not going to even *think* about touching that flaming sword under the counter, yea, even verily the one you got off Uriel in that game of poker back before Eden was bad real estate. For the purposes of this visit, I'm pulling the trinity card, and acting as the old JHVH himself, right?"

Gabriel nodded slowly, moving his hand away from the as-yet-unlit four foot long gladius he had gaffer taped under the bar.

"They won't do it, mate," he said, trying to be all chummy and conciliatory. "Not without all the other bits. Oceans of blood, plagues of locusts with weird little baby heads, the whole cake shop. The only four angels neither sanctified or fallen. Vessels for God's wrath."

Jesus pushed his aviator shades back up over his eyes.

"Well, I'm feeling a bit tetchy right now, as it happens," he said. "Thoroughly peeved might cover it. Wrathful, though… well. Not yet. By the way, Gabe, if you were thinking of trying anything, remember that He Who Raises His Hand Against The Throne Shall Fall. Not my rules. *His.* Well… trinity thing, you get it. You'd be taking a dip in the lake of fire quicker than you could say 'asbestos soap on a rope.'"

Gabriel looked like he was about to protest, but Jesus pushed himself away from the bar, spun around, and marched over to the table where the four card players were just finishing another hand.

"…shall see thy two paire, and reply with… ummm… how much is the one with a sword through his head worthe?"

The red robe groaned.

"Damn it, Plague, you always… hang on a second. Looks like we've got company."

Three apparently empty cowls turned to face Jesus. Then three pairs of hands pushed them back. The one in the black robe just leaned back on his chair, cool as you like, hood up. Something – no, *two* somethings – glittered deep inside, like coins at the bottom of a well.

"Didn't expect you this early," rumbled Red Robe, now revealed as a horribly scarred-up man in an army helmet. His face looked as if it had suffered through an explosion in a wood chipper factory, then been repaired by blind seamstresses. Each of his teeth was a sharp little copper-jacketed bullet. "Not til' teatime tomorrow, he said."

"And you're supposed to have your costume on," said White Robe, through lips as emaciated as two dried-out strings of chewing gum. He seemed to be all mouth, this one, and skin stretched over accentuated, pointy bones.

"Face made of gold, six wings, sword for a tongue or something? Didn't sound terribly practical." This was whispered in a hiss like putrefying gases leaking from a corpse, by a man who appeared to have been made of rotten meat, then left in the sun for a few days. His eyes were bubbling pools of something that looked like custard.

Jesus spun a chair around and sat down, his arms folded across the back.

"War, Hunger, Plague. There's been a change of plans."

Now the other one leaned forward. Elbows on the table. Now darkness seemed to loom up with a bass rumble, pitching half the diner into midnight.

"We ARE the change of plans," said the Angel of Death, whose face was a pale and perfect mask, transparent as glass, over a bleached skull. His eyes were still the shimmering silver of two coins the ferryman had dropped overboard. "And now is not our Time."

Even Christ himself quavered a little before a being who could put a capital T so emphatically on that word. Arguably, a being *for which that word existed*. But he was here on a mission. He forced himself to smile, something only an entity who had met Death before and lived to tell about it could have done.

"I appreciate it. Totally do. It's your job, all four, to be the vessels of God's divine wrath on a world sorely in need of judgment. I get it. It's just that… well, someone beat you to it."

There was a collective intake of breath. Well – three intakes. The

Angel of Death considered breathing to be something his customers failed at, nothing more.

"You *what*, mate?" asked War, injecting the question with enough belligerence to launch a thousand football riots.

Jesus shrugged.

"Queen Titania, Empress of Spring, Mistress of the Fae, Lady of Tirfeynn and treaty-sworn Parallel Principality, has sent out the immanentizers of her Armageddon, I'm afraid. So I came to tell you that no matter what happens at teatime tomorrow, you might as well pack up and go home. The whole thing's been outsourced."

They all took it in different ways. The table under War's fists began to smoulder as his armour heated up to red-hot. A cloud of flies burst, buzzing, from inside Plague's robes, haloing his horrible head. And Hunger's hiss of anger turned his chair so brittle that he fell right through it, leaving a pile of paper-thin shards. Death just frowned. That was more than enough.

"Where exactly are they going?"

"London," said Jesus. "Middle of the biggest empire in Christendom. Definitely home turf, but like I said..."

"And what are they *doing*, pray tell?" bubbled Plague. "I liked London. Nobody did bubonic catastrophe quite like London. Then there was..."

"Shut Up," said Death, capitalizing again with malice aforethought. "What *are* they doing, Christ Child?"

Jesus tried to act nonchalant.

"Oh, you know. Riding forth in the sky, spreading terror, making mortals wail and gnash their teeth, bringing fire and destruction, the usual. So you can take the day off, I suspect."

"... show me another city in the world where you can choke people on the fog..." muttered plague truculently.

"That's totally *our* bit! I bet they even have cool-looking horses," hissed Hunger, unfolding to his feet like an origami nightmare.

Jesus tried not to grin. Oh, he had them now.

"No, no. Not horses. They said that was old fashioned. They've got, well... kind of..."

Death rose up like a Tsunami in the gene pool, his robe crackling with lightning bolts which were both tiny and light-years long at once.

"*Show Me*," he said, reaching out a hand toward Jesus.

And the human part did. It had no choice. It showed the image of wild riders over the Straits in Istanbul, wheels on fire, headlamps burning across the clouds. The Angel of Death grinned, both with his ghostly face and the skull beneath (which really had little choice). He pointed, with one sharp and bony finger.

"Where do we procure such… devices?" he asked. The other three nodded, leaning in closer. Jesus took a step back.

"Funny you should ask, see, because I kind of saw a few parked right outside. With your names on 'em, as it were."

There was a thunderclap. Something long and black came arrowing in through the roof of Gabriel's in *exactly the right place* for Death's hand to close around it when it struck the floor. It was an eight-foot long staff of blackest night. As his skeletal fingers gripped it, a blade hinged out with a sound like a finger on the rim of a wineglass. It was the Scythe. *That* one. The Endmaker, Soul-Severer, the Ultimate Mowing Machine.

"It is settled then," he said. "We Ride." The capital R clanged into place like a dungeon door.

Gabriel did his best. He looked quite angelic, despite the stupid little paper hat and the apron.

"Guys! Guys, come *on!* I'm gonna get in *so* much trouble for this! You can't go and start the Apocalypse before time!"

Death pushed past with that famous imperviousness to barriers which has made him a byword for breaking and entering. The others followed in his wake. Plague stopped to prod the angel in his chest.

"*Nobody* upstages the old guard," he bubbled. "So we won't touch your precious mortals. But we will show these young bastards how it's done."

Jesus was the last to leave. He straddled his Matchless, strapped on a pure white helmet with a golden halo floating just above it, and gave Gabe a jaunty wave. Then they were off, five streaks of fire and wrath blazing across the sky with a single purpose.

Gabriel took comfort in some very un-angelic swearing for a minute or two. Then he noticed another new arrival. A celestial postman's van pulled up outside the diner, and another angel got out, lugging a scroll the size of a Turkish carpet. It was adorned with seven large and jewel-encrusted seals.

"Package for Mr Gabriel?" asked the angel, who was, by his number of wings, eyes and general aura of sanctity, a low-level cherub from signals and dispatch.

Gabriel sighed. His shoulders slumped. Not for the first time, he wished he had a less demanding job, like cleaning up after the weird, mutated creatures who flew about the Throne all day, singing.

"You're a bit late, mate," he said, pushing the door open with one hand. "But can I offer you a milkshake anyway?"

# Fourteen – Year of the Dragon

Eddie Weatherfield awoke in his attic room, in the creaky old homestead of Brokenwaters Station, and realized it had all just been a dream.

Well, it *had* to have been. Obviously.

Because here he was, tangled in sweat-stained cotton sheets, in a room which smelled of lanolin and old socks. There were his model planes, hanging in a dusty constellation. There was his crinkled-up old poster with its picture of the All Blacks, ranked up in rows, all mustaches and sideburns and stolid fortitude with their shiny boots and their bulging muscles.

Eddie sighed, and unfolded himself from bed. Downstairs he could hear his mother bustling about in the kitchen, and out the window, he knew, the shearing gang would be out on the porch of their bunkhouse, enamel mugs of hot tea steaming. There'd be Colin, the drover, rolling up a foul bent cigarette from last night's leavings. Roger Rushbrook, with his arms like sacks full of hams, pulling chin-ups on the pipe from the water tank. Sideways Malcolm shaving with a straight razor in a shard of mirror, with a prospector's pan full of water to catch the foam. Even the master shearer they'd brought in to school the young bucks, old Bill Richards, who fancied writing a book one day. They'd be...

It was at that moment that a vast and terrible anger gripped him, like a bolt of lightning running from head to toe. Unbidden, one hand scrabbled for the washbasin beside his bed, and picked up his own mirror, a little round chrome thing that had once belonged on the passenger side of an Armstrong-Siddeley.

He brought it around, just as he heard footsteps on the stairs - and just as some traitorous part of his mind sketched in the smell of honey and pancakes.

He looked into a red and yellow nightmare of an eye, and threw the mirror against the wall, where it smashed to pieces... and stuck.

*"Well, I thought we'd have problems. Just not quite yet,"* grumbled a

voice from behind the wall. The pieces of mirror snicked back together again with a glassy little grating noise that set Eddie's teeth on edge. "Smart one, you are. Too smart, probably."

"All this is from my memories, isn't it? It's all fake."

The voice sighed. It resolved itself into a red and scaly shape, which pushed itself through the mirror and hovered in mid-air, magpie-sized, little wings blurred like a hummingbird's.

"It's all I had to work with, really. Not too bad, is it?"

Eddie scowled. He wished he had something real, and above all *solid*, to throw at the tiny dragon.

"Except for the fact that my Dad would be shouting the house down if I was still in bed on a shearing day. And that honey and pancakes was strictly birthdays only, or if you broke you leg, or something else important. That, and..."

Eddie showed the dragon his arms and legs. Despite being clad in bright tartan terrycloth pajamas, there were plenty of cuts, scrapes and bruises on them. Ones which definitely came from being a vibrant and engaged member of World War Two.

"The body remembers, I'm afraid," said the tiny wyrm. "I'd hoped you would just plaster over the cracks in your so-called reality, like most of your kind do. Because I've got a bit of a problem out there."

Eddie raised an eyebrow, in unconscious and utterly perfect imitation of Major Charlie Monkston.

"Let me guess. Hans Schprinkler betrayed you, did he? Trustworthy looking fellow like him? What's the Third Reich coming to?"

The dragon bristled, smoke puffing from between its teeth.

"Global domination, I'd say. In between all-out thaumaturgical warfare and the inevitable devourment of the Earth by things with more vowels in their names than the Welsh phone book."

Eddie stood up, pretty much on autopilot. He crossed to the big wicker laundry hamper where he kept his only-slightly-soiled clothes and began to get dressed.

"I suppose you'll want my help, then? If you've been so... wait a minute. How *did* they outfox you, anyway? Aren't you a gigantic, bulletproof, fire-breathing dragon out there?"

The dragon - the little miniature Vauragath - covered its eyes with one scaly claw.

"Do you mind? I really didn't need to see *that* on top of all the... well, if it'll make you put some trousers on faster, I'll admit there was some doublecrossing. I... erm... that is to say..."

Eddie hopped on one leg, looking exactly as annoyed as a person can when trying to put his socks on.

"*After* that. Which we'll discuss later."

Vauragath preened a little, a draconic sign of extreme embarrassment.

"Well, I'm not really out there, see? It's still actually you. Just... you know werewolves, right?"

Eddie nodded.

"I've read a lot of pretty bad comic books, and seen a lot of pretty awful movies, you know. That's why... for goodness sake, '*it was all just a dream*'? You really thought I'd fall for that old cop-out?"

The dragon blushed a slightly deeper red.

"It's like the werewolf thing," he said. "Full thaumo-morphic transference. You go too deep into the berserker rage, you become more dragon than man. And seeing as *I'm* the dragon, well... you get it. I sort of get to drive."

Eddie was already tying up his bootlaces.

"Go on..."

"Well, it means that we've got the same thing about silver. Very disruptive metal to the thaumic currents, silver. The Dwarves used to know about the... well, we call it the loophole, if you must know. They made great big spiky silver collars to take control of any of their kind who went too far. Where they got one from, I don't know."

Eddie's mind sometimes let him down. Sometimes it was by forgetting exactly where he'd put a pencil which he'd just been using. At other times, like this, it was by being a suspicious, paranoid little bastard of a thing. He remembered Darrin Oakenbeard, back in that hangar full of burned and snap-frozen Nazi soldiers. About how the dwarvern engineer had known all about his 'condition'. Who knows what a Nazi, who knew just what he was looking for, could have looted from the Labyrinth of Kew?

"So," he asked. "How do we get it off?"

Two little sparks of fire shot out of the dragon's nostrils.

"We *don't*! Don't you get it? That's why I wanted you tucked up nice and snug in dreamland! They're going to make us *do* things, Weatherfield, and if we don't it'll get tighter, and it'll *twist*, and if we disobey too often - *pop!* Off comes my head! *Your* head! Our collective bloody cranium! It only comes loose if we die!"

Eddie stood up and pulled open the door. A kind of pencil-sketch of his mother was there, half drawn in, with a stick-figure child's drawing in the middle and layer upon layer of paper-thin memories filling her up. He pushed past and rattled down the stairs, into the frozen-silent kitchen, just as his brain caught up with itself.

"What kind of things?" he asked, his voice a rasping whisper. Vauragath the Crimson flitted past to perch on top of the tea kettle.

"The kind you don't want to see. Your mind breaks and *pow*, no way back for me, is there? I'm stuck as the remainder of a diminishing sum in an equation that wants me *erased from this particular plane of existence*. No, no, matey. You have to stay sane. Can't have you... *urk!*"

This last syllable was squeezed out as Eddie's hand closed around the little dragon, his knuckles white. Hans Schprinkler was the bad guy. Bad guys lived in stories. What happens in a story when the bad guy had his very own dragon, and a pack of captured enemies?

"*What kind of things*, lizard? Does your arithmetic diminish faster if I stuff you in that kettle and throw you down the number three long drop?"

Vauragath tried very hard to look smaller.

"...probably eat people..." he coughed, sulphurously.

Eddie shook him, none too gently.

"What?"

"I said they probably want you to *eat people*. You know. Ravage the land. Burn some thatch-roofed cottages. Put swathes of, you know, tracts of... thingy to flame and all that. Big, convincing dragon stuff."

Eddie could imagine exactly who Hans Schprinkler would want him to gobble up first. If the rest of Squad 27 were his prisoners, then he'd not miss the opportunity to dispose of them in the most villainous way possible.

"So we only get loose if we die, eh?" he mused, pushing open the kitchen door and walking out into the farmyard. Motes of dust hung frozen in the hard, flat sunlight. A pair of blackbirds were apprehended in mid-air, trying to stuff grass into the exhaust stack of an ancient diesel tractor. "Dragon, I have a stupid, stupid idea. One from comic books. But we need to tell the others..."

Vauragath wriggled free from Eddie's fist, and flitted around his head, hissing steam.

"Oh no. No no *no*. I'm here in your head with you, and I can see all the things that are wrong with *that* particular idea. It's silly. It's asinine. It's like something from a very badly written novel! The kind where they have pictures of us on the cover with tiny little wings too small to get us airborne!"[41]

But Eddie was in the dragon's head too. He caught the edges and angles of the idea Vauragath was trying to poke under the metaphorical kitchen carpet with one yellowy claw. He grinned, understanding dawning across his face like a treacle sunrise.

"Patience is a *Witch*. She's psychically attuned. Mrs H as well. Probably Connor has a little bit of it too. They're like radio masts for thoughts that are big enough. All we have to do is think… very… BIG."

Eddie broke into a run.

In this imaginary version of Brokenwaters Station, there was a wide, low building made of corrugated iron just past the hay barns. Eddie threw open the doors on their rollers, revealing a shape which was all wires and angles, yellow cloth pulled taut over wooden bones. In his imagination, the Le Rhone Avro looked like it wanted to leap into the pastel-blue dome of the sky, screaming. Strapped to its belly were the big tanks of fertiliser dust that his brother had been working on.

"That's one silly idea each, Dragon," said Eddie, as he swung up into the pilot's seat. The smell of warm leather and engine oil wrapped him up, and he found himself smiling. "But yours first, eh?"

It should have been impossible for Vauragath the Crimson to be afraid of flying. He'd been catching thermals over primeval volcanoes since before the human race decided to lose the prehensile tail. Nevertheless, he hunkered down on the passenger seat, digging in with all his claws.

"Tell me when we get to your bit, and all we have to do is die," he groaned, as the engine sputtered and roared into life.

The propeller blurred. The wheels moved. The sun hit those bright yellow wings, flaring to gold…

And Eddie Weatherfield flew.

+++

Patience had woken up in worse places, but this was only because 275 years afforded a lot of scope for getting extremely drunk.

It's also worth noting that a good 220 of those years had been experienced in an Olde London Towne with the sanitary characteristics of a flooded cesspit. So, by those standards thing were looking up. There wasn't any kind of manure in her hair, for starters.

---

41 You mean, like on the back cover? [ED]

Then again, she *was* tied to a stake.

Witches, on the whole, are used to this kind of thing. It's standard practice, really, and girls with talent in the field of witching are given handy self-defense training fairly early on, such as how to undo knots and slip out of chains. The advice 'if all else fails, pee on the kindling' was only half a joke.

Patience rolled the clicks and aches out of her neck, therefore, and didn't struggle mindlessly against what she discovered were very, very good shackles indeed. Lined with silver, and cut with certain runes that prickled against her skin like nettles. Instead she stealthily opened one eye and took in her surroundings.

These were less than appealing.

Despite his constant whining about the Fuhrer not sending him enough money, Hans Schprinkler had hollowed out a sizable Alp. Either that, or the immense, cavernous space (with its pillars in the shape of bat-winged ghouls) had been carved out by someone else, back in the kind of dim antiquity when people would worship anything that could make up a name from the leftover bits in a scrabble set.

It was echoing, dank, shadow-haunted and filled to the brim with riveted steel machinery.

In fact, it seemed as if Schloss Bad Schickehosen itself had just been the cherry atop a maggot-riddled cake. Everywhere Patience counted Nazis in black rubber suits and gas masks, trundling canisters of glowing liquid, wheeling little carts full of tools or simply fussing with clipboards and pencils. The reason for all of this industry was apparent when she dared to tilt her head up a little, and peer through a straggle of hair at what lined the far wall of Hans Schprinkler's cavern.

At first, she thought they were more pillars. But no.

They were *rockets*, shaped like the infamous V2 bombs, and similarly chequered black and white, with big red swastika roundels and Black Sun emblems all over. However, these rockets were the size of cathedral towers; like u-Boats turned up on end, the bell-shaped muzzles of their thrusters big enough to dwarf the poor Sturmtoppers who were cleaning them out with mops. And it got worse.

Loaded into the mid-section of each rocket - they were hoisting one now, with the aid of cranes slung from a spiderweb of over-hanging gantries - were copies of the black colossus which had killed Charlie Monkston. Brutal iron tubes, their cannons and cleavers and tentacle legs tucked away. But there was no mistaking the design. Or the warped aura which surrounded them, indicating that a very uncomfortable elf was wired and strapped inside.

Patience tried the manacles again, just to be sure. It was no use. Hans might be committed to villainy, but he'd gotten this part right at least. There'd be no easy escape from...

*Hang on a minute... What was that buzzing noise?*

Patience knocked her head back against the wooden stake, trying to shake loose what sounded like a very large and angry mosquito. But the whine just got worse. Like a lawnmower far away, or a two-stroke motorboat, or...

She was interrupted by a leather-gloved hand, grabbing her roughly by the chin. The smell of old whiskey and very expensive cologne struck her in a nauseating wave.

"Wakey wakey, fraulein Goodhallow! It's time for, as the Americans. Charmingly. Put it, *dinner and the show*. So glad you could all join me for my moment of triumph!"

It was Hans Schprinkler, of course, in full Black Sun Death Korps uniform, from the top of his skull-encrusted cap to his silver-toed boots with their pentagram spurs. As Patience drew herself up against the stake to stare him in the eye, a lackey approached with a small ebony box, and the Nazi sorcerer produced from it a set of false teeth, which he popped in with a flourish.

"Spare me the amateur theatrics, and get to the bonfire," snarled Patience. Schprinkler waved a schoolmasterly finger in admonition.

"Nein, nein, my dear. It's *all* about the showmanship. Proper villainy has a rhythm. It's a dance! A brilliant, meticulous waltz of spite and vengeance! The power of being truly rotten doesn't come to those who cut corners on the old *sturm und drang*." He grinned. His teeth, glistening gold, now bore the jewel-encrusted words 'Seig Heil'. "So. Here we are. An old fashioned witch burning. Toasty! But what shall we use to light the fire, hmmm?"

Patience looked to either side of her, where six other stakes stood planted in the granite of a raised dais. Chained to them were Connor, all bruised and ragged, Lucky, with a black eye the colour of a thunderstorm at dawn, Percy, Fyodor, Mrs Hazelwood with her raffia basket chained across her chest, and the Compte de Saint Germain, looking bilious green thanks the altar-cloth stuffed in his mouth. If she could just...

But here came that whining noise again, sawing and insistent. It was like a dentist's drill inside her skull! *Perhaps she'd been hit on the head? Perhaps being hit on the head again would make it go away?*

She could see Schprinkler's mouth moving, as he wrung his hands together in glee, gesturing to the traitors of Squad 27 where they waited by a smoking pit in the floor. But there was no other sound. Snetterley junior gave her a sad little wave as his dad threw a giant lever, making the whole cavern vibrate. Nazis tending the rockets scattered and slipped. Hans did the full scenery-chewing, hands-in-the-air wicked laugh.

And Patience saw the aeroplane.

It was transparent, unreal as the reflection on a soap bubble. But it was *there*, bright yellow and blurred, flitting in from the corner of her peripheral vision. As she watched, it pulled into a sharp ascent, turning it into a loop with a wing-twisting dive. Smoke was pouring out behind it, leaving a shape in the air.

P

Now the tiny aircraft performed another roll, stitching the air with cursive. Up, then across, then down, and a flick of the tail to puff out a tiny dot. The smoky letters hung right in front of Hans Schprinkler as he ranted, but even though he put his finger clear through the second 'a', they seemed invisible to him.

Patience I have a plan

It was only as a gigantic steel cage rose up from inside the pit that Patience put two and two together. The words unfurled across her mind as another, more remote part of her took in the swept-back horns, the rows of jagged teeth, and the dripping chemical drool which burst into blue - green flames where it splattered...

That part of her saw the dragon, and desperately wanted to crawl under something made of asbestos. The other part of her saw Eddie Weatherfield, and nodded.

"Allright. Tell me," she whispered.

She just hoped there was enough of him in there to make all that scaly bulk obey...

+++

The sky was as flat as a watercolour painting, blue as eggshells, and as real as an idle daydream. Eddie jammed the throttles open and pulled the nose of the Le Rhone Avro up, heading for that invisible barrier with every intent of bursting through. In the passenger's seat, Vauragath the Crimson closed his eyes…

They hit.

And outside, in a cage, before a dais carved with knights and swastikas, Eddie Weatherfield opened his.

The first thing he noticed was the sense of power.

Vast, nigh-limitless power, radiating from the blast-furnace in his belly to the great lumbering engine of his twin hearts, then down his veins like magma. He was a storm of steel claws, an armageddon of flames. He was a *dragon*, fully manifest, a member of a race who wore the might of High Magic like a halo around the sun. This cage may as well have been made from paper. This mountain may as well have been gossamer and matchwood.

But the second thing he noticed was the agony around his neck.

The collar bit into his flesh with hundreds of teeth so sharp they were half invisible; blades of sorcery which carried the essence of silver. It *hurt*.

But it was still far less annoying than the fact that Hans Schprinkler was bang in the middle of one of his villainous monologues.

And that his audience were Squad 27, tied to a row of stakes.

"You see! *An Imperial Great Dragon!* And it's all mine! Let's see Adolf try to explain that one away when it lands on top of the Reich's chancellery! Between my dragon and my army of the Fae, nothing will stand between me and complete. World. *Domination!* Bwaaahahahaaaa!" A small Nazi handed Hans a towel and bottle of water after that effort.

Lucky groaned.

"Oh, here we fecking go..."

"But do you know what needs to happen first? It's an old covenant. A spell which binds the beast to one master, and one alone. Surely you've heard of it? No? Well, what we do..." and here he spun across the dais like a dancer in a silent move, silver spurs twinkling, to lean up against Patience's stake. "What we do, is feed the dragon a nice. Tasty. *Damsel in distress!*"

Patience arched her back against the chains and made a solid effort at biting his nose off. She settled with spitting in his face instead.

"How's that for distress, you disfigured ape?"

Hans smiled a twitchy little smile. He applied the towel judiciously.

"I'll forgive you, my dear, but only because of what comes next," he said. Then his monocle blazed with power, and he held out his hand. His metal staff with the swastika-cube rune on top came sizzling in from out of the shadows to smack into his palm. *"Showtime!"*

"You will nae get awa' with this, Schprinkler!" shouted Connor the Beige, red in the face.

"Your opinion is noted. But I *will*, you know. I'm the *bad guy!* DRAGON!"

Eddie tried to resist. But the collar flared arctic cold, frost crusting its surface and spreading tendrils across his scales. In his head, Vauragath moaned in horror. Inch by inch, against his will, it brought his head around. It was as if invisible hands were clamped on each side of his draconic skull, with fingers sunk down to the bone.

Hans Schprinkler smiled, gold and rubies flashing. Squad 22 looked on, hungry and gloating – all except Snetterley Minor, who looked somewhat unconvinced.

**"Dragon – devour that damsel!"**

The compulsion was like nails through his forehead. Like wires binding him up. The front of the cage fell away with a riotous crash of steel, and Eddie knew he only had once chance. If Patience hadn't got his message, then it was curtains for the lot of them.

Draconic instincts made him rear back his serpentine neck, swaying like a king cobra. It was all he could do to hold back the fire which brimmed in his throat as his eyes focused on Patience.

"Yes! *Do it!* Become my slave!" roared Schprinkler, who had retreated to the edge of the dais, in expectation of over-splatter. The collar squeezed tight, ice choking Eddie, blurring his vision…

And he let it loose. He *struck*.

At the same second that something hotter even than dragonfire flared inside Mrs Hazelwood's raffia bag.

At the same instant that Percy, who was only held together with thread and staples, pulled his hands up against the shackles so hard that they popped clean off.

The crystal ball was airborne as Eddie's mouth gaped open, all sharp enamel and strings of incandescent drool. Percy opened up his own mouth halfway around his head and swallowed it, even as he completed a perfect dive and roll to stand in front of Patience.

"Ever so sorry, old bean," he said, "but this is going to taste *awful…*"

Jaws the size of an excavator bucket closed around the zombie, and gobbled him up. It was instinctive. SNAP! GULP! SWALLOW!

And…

Eddie felt Percy get stuck in his throat. The undead soldier always carried a horrible big trench knife with him, along with a barbecue fork two feet long. The blade jammed into the inside of the dragon's esophagus as Eddie recoiled in horror, mainly at the predictably awful taste. Percy had been singed a little on the way down, and the flavour was like a casserole of socks and roadkill. It was only going to get worse, however…

Vauragath screamed inside their shared cranium. Eddie reared back, front claws scrabbling at his throat. But it was no use. This was the only way. A hand with preturnatural strength sliced through his neck *from the inside*, precisely where the collar of enslavement clasped shut. Eddie's vision narrowed down to a black tunnel as he choked, his vast body failing. Hands with blue-black fingernails scrabbled for the catch as blood spurted. He convulsed, wings unfurled, and collapsed, smashing the cage to pieces. Purple starbursts fizzed inside his eyeballs.

*It was no use. There was no air.* He had no more fight left in him. Control was slipping away.

*Well, if not one way, it would have to be the other…*

Patience gasped. Hans Schprinkler screamed.

And Eddie Weatherfield died.

He felt it all, as his spirit broke loose from his vast and transformed body. Vauragath's spectre was torn away, as if by an invisible wind, sucked down through a twist in space-time to where his real form lay torpid in the realm of dragons. With his flesh now a soulless husk the collar released its grip, sprung open, and fell to the ground to shatter into a million frozen pieces.

Each glittering shard tumbled… slowed, gravity cast aside…

And *stopped*.

Eddie had a brief glimpse of infinity, his place in it, and how he was both mind-blowingly important and totally inconsequential at the same time. The same effect is sometimes experienced just between finishing a pint of absinthe and one's head connecting with the pavement. It was over in an instant.

Then he was standing on cold marble, before a frame made of bones, surrounding a door carved from starry darkness. There was a humorous letterbox in the shape of a rude gargoyle on it, and a plaque which read 'DUNLIVING. No hawkers, pedlars or evangelists please'. For some reason, as the door cracked open, Eddie heard the sound of motorcycle engines and smelled high-octane petrol burning.

The Angel of Death poked his head around the frame, hastily tucking a motorbike helmet behind his back.[42]

---

42 The angel of Death can (and indeed *must*) by definition, be everywhere that life ceases to function, at once. This still means, however, that he'd rather not concentrate on the boring ones, and focus more intently, say, on kicking ten bells of shite out of

"Yes? What is it? I'm sort of busy ushering in the Apocalypse right now, so if you could just hurry on through, we can dispense with the paperwork, and..."

"Er... *herm*."

Eddie and the Angel looked around at what was perhaps the politest little cough in recorded history. If coughs were coloured, this one would be tweed.

It was Roger Hazelwood, in a natty brown three piece suit, with a little pair of gold-framed glasses on. And – worryingly – a clipboard in his hands.

"Who are *you?*" asked the Final Judgement of Worlds, in a voice like tectonic collapse.

"Roger Hazelwood, sir. I'm his attorney. And it seems there's been a mix-up with the forms. Special, last-minute circumstances, and all."

The Angel frowned, his ghostly face twisting above the sharp contours of his skull.

"I AM special last-minute circumstances, Hazelwood! Your human law has no place here!"

Roger *tsked*, tapping his very full clipboard with a yellow pencil.

"No, no, squire. Celestial law, this is. Very numinous. See, the subject, that is to say soul article 4) (b) sub-clause III, was slain while possessed by an entity from one of the territories classed as..."

Death reared up, filling the doorway, his hands clenched into bony fists. Wings made of oil-black feathers fanned out, quivering.

"Look, I don't have all day, you know!"[43]

"Well, it's easy, innit? Just take this form *here*, sign here, initial here, take it down to processing, then this one in triplicate to HR, then another waiver here for the draconic possession, that needs to be countersigned by a seraph of grade 6 or above, then we can schedule the meeting with..."

Death seemed to deflate. His vast raven-black wings furled in again, becoming a dark and dusty cloak.

"Look, is there any way we can kind of just... make this go away? I mean it's just one soul, after all. Armageddon's getting started. Soon they'll be coming through here like prunes through a sick goose."

Roger tapped his nose conspiratorially.

"Say no more, guv. Say no more. Just so happens I have a transplanar

---

the Erl King in a thrilling aerial motorcycle battle over London that's not really in our special effects budget.

43 As noted above, he really does.

portal on my person for just these eventualities. Call it a near-yourself experience, then?"

The Angel nodded, producing his motorbike helmet and peering back around the edge of the door. Inside, something whizzed by and exploded. A bubbling, sick voice yelled 'Choke on this!"

"Fine, fine! Call it whatever! I'll owe you one, Hazelwood, if you just take all that paper and burn it!"

The door slammed shut. Eddie and Roger stood there, both slowly fading away.

"Good thing, of course, he never looked at it. All receipts for lager and crisps, actually. Best I could come up with on short notice..."

Eddie tried to shake his hand, but his phantom fingers went right through.

"Thank you!"

"Out of interest, what exactly were you going to do if I didn't show up?" asked Roger.

Eddie managed to look sheepish, with only his smile remaining.

"I was going to tell the Grim Reaper to look out behind him, then push him back inside and slam the door."

Roger shook what was left of his head, even as it dispersed to smoke.

"Young people these days! I hope you have a better plan for..."

Then something complicated happened down on the level of quantum entanglement, possibly involving super-strings and variously flavoured quarks. People like Connor the Beige were much more comfortable calling it 'magic', so that's what Eddie thought of it too... a sensation like static electricity traveling under his skin from head to toe, as he was folded out flat and posted through the infinitely narrow letterbox of eternity.

Back into his body.

Back into his giant, were-dragon body.

Back into the sizzling, clicking control room of his brain, without Vauragath the Crimson as co-pilot and backseat driver.

Back, in fact, through the crystal ball, which acted in this case as a sort of revolving door to the afterlife. Exactly as Eddie had hoped it would, in his B-movie heart of hearts.

For the last time that day, he opened his eyes, and beheld madness.

Hans Schprinkler was kicking him. This was about as effective as a cockroach assaulting a panzer tank; the Nazi's silver-capped boots bounced off his scales and did nothing but hurt his toes.

"Nein, nein *nein!* You aren't supposed to die! You were my ticket to the big leagues! The little mustache and all the nice shiny uniform! YOU!" he rounded on Squad 22, who quailed back from his finger, knowing exactly what it could do with malice aforethought. "*Traitors! What have you done to my lovely dragon?*"

Eddie shifted his head just a little to see what was going on. A ripple of fear went through Squad 22 like a mexican wave as Schprinkler advanced on them, black flames boiling from his monocle. All of them except Snetterley Junior, who was inexplicably missing.

"Not us!" wailed the elder Mage of the Celestial Light. "I had a much better doublecross figured out! There was going to be custard, and a penguin, and everything!" His cronies nodded. Eddie shifted his head on its long prehensile neck, sweeping his gaze around to the dais. Six tightly chained figures leaned forward, almost palpably radiating hope.

That was when something horrible happened down inside Eddie's stomach. Or one of them, anyway. A whole lot of the autonomous functions of his dragon brain were taken up modulating the twisted chemical works in his guts, which contained more deadly chambers than the Wu Tang temple. Nevertheless, something was knocking politely on the inside of one of them. Eddie gulped, stifling a belch.

*Oh good gods! Percy!*

Eddie had no idea how to operate the more subtle nuances of his body. So he did the equivalent of mashing whole panels of switches, causing himself to rear up, fire jetting in rainbow colours from his nostrils, wings spreading wide enough to almost span the cavern. A superheated fart toasted several Black Sun scientists, who cowered behind a tanker full of liquid oxygen.

And, as Hans Schprinkler turned, his face a mask of demented glee, Eddie found the right cluster of nerves. He pulled the ganglia like a mad bellringer.

For those of you who have never thrown up a live zombie, the experience is not to be recommended. At least a dragon's neck muscles are specially designed to expectorate high-velocity balls of burning chemicals. This meant that Percy's trip from Eddie's stomach, and back out through his mouth, was at least a quick one.

Well, that might be an understatement.

Actually, the zombie was coughed up like a living hairball, at a speed which would definitely get you a ticket from most highway patrolmen.

"It lives! It **lives!** It's... *oh mien gott in himmel!*"

That was all Hans Schprinkler managed before Percy, covered in dragon bile and slime, hit him in a flying rugby tackle at 65 miles per hour. The pair slithered and slid and rolled until they reached a square concrete shaft cut into the floor. For an instant it seemed as if they'd fall, but Hans managed to lash out with his staff, bracing it sideways to stop them. Percy was smoking, and still missing both of his hands. As Eddie watched, a bubble rose up from his toast-rack chest, swelling his neck, then completely filling his head. Whatever the undead soldier was stuffed with, it didn't seem to be bones.

It was, in fact, Mrs Hazelwood's crystal ball.

"Quite sorry about the inconvenience, of course," said Percy, as his horrible tooth-studded mouth unzipped nearly all the way around his head. The glowing purple ball popped loose and hung there for a second, thrumming like a bass string several miles long. "But what with you being an evil bastard and all that... *not terribly.*"

Percy leaped back. His boot lashed out, connecting with Schprinkler's crotch with a sound like a bag of celery in a washing mangle. The Black Sun commander's eyes crossed. Then Roger Hazelwood used the crystal ball like a drop-hammer, smashing him end over end down into darkness.

Up on the dais, Patience was very surprised to find a pair of hands unlocking her manacles. Not that she was surprised to find a pair of hands getting the job done – it's just that she had expected the disembodied hands of Percy, which had spider-crawled across to the nearest post after popping their stitches, and had already nearly freed Lucky from his chains.

*These* hands belonged to Snetterley Junior.

"I couldn't let them do it! I mean, being evil is all fine and good, but there's a *limit*, you know! Father said that you would be mine, and although I appreciate a good doublecross as much as the next man..." he looked up at her, expectantly, his piggy little face sheened in sweat. So horribly, horribly full of self satisfaction. "We're meant to be together, you and I!"

Patience did her best impression of a swoon (largely taken from black and white films) as she felt the locks come free.

"My hero! You saved me... *from the bloody stupid predicament you got me into in the first place!*" Sarcasm sloshsed about in the second half of that sentence like hydrofluoric acid in a teacup.

Snetterley took a step back, as violet fire ignited in his paramour's eyes. Her hair blew back in an invisible wind.

"But... but..."

"Don't shit on the carpet and tell me it's a bunch of roses," snarled the Revenge of English Witchcraft, landing a right cross to his jaw that spun him three times in the air before he hit the dais with one pudgy cheek. His spectacles exploded. Actual, factual tiny stars and planets spun around his head. The little goon was snoring by the time Patience knelt over him to take his keys.

And now Lucky was free, and he snapped off Fyodor's stake with his bare hands, and Connor was pulling his shillelagh out of some alternate dimension that smelled of old tobacco and flatulence, and Squad 22 were leaping the barricade and charging. From a side-door to the cavern came a horde of Tcho-Tcho cannibals in Nazi uniform. From another, actual Nazis in traditional Tcho-Tcho costume, just to be fair and balanced[44].

"Stop where you are!" Shouted Snetterley Senior. "You're surrounded! You'll never get out of here alive!"

Connor the Beige pushed forward, just exactly as pissed off as a Glasgow wizard can be. This, of course, is so far off the scale of regular peevishness that the little needle melts and the dial turns to tapioca pudding.

"*You!* You big southern gobshite! I call on the powers of the unmanifest and all the realms celestial to witness! I challenge you to a duel of wizardry, one on one, and..." here he grinned a horrible, horrible grin, the kind that usually is only found on the business end of certain abyssal eels... "I'm gonnae kick you from arsehole tae breakfast time, ye six-foot streak of pish!"

"Last chance," quavered Snetterley, taking a step backwards. "Surrender! you're totally outnumbered!"

Lucky cracked his knuckles and adjusted his little hat.

"Seems like we are, and all," he spat. "But you're forgetting a big fecking point, my lad. You're *outdragonned.*"

Eddie didn't miss his cue. He stopped retching and trying to wipe his tongue with both front claws, and rose up to his full height, tail whipping back and forth.

"Ahhh. Yes. About that..." said Snetterley Senior.

Then it came. The little moment when the bar full of angry bikers

---

44 This consists of a cloak made from woven bark and grass, a loincloth with a hollowed-out gourd as a codpiece, lots of warpaint and bugger all else. Obviously it's not at all funny in context – i.e. when you've just realized that the big black pot you're in is not in fact a welcoming spa bath, and that the carrots, broccoli and spices are not to aid in younger-looking skin.

is held, frozen, tension twanging in the air. The second when the protesters are face-to face with the snarling riot police, and everything turns to liquid crystal, *waiting for it*. Waiting for that one berk to yell something about someone's mother from the back of the crowd. Waiting for someone to snap, and throw that billiard ball, or big glass jug.

Waiting for a Nazi, dressed as a cannibal, to try and throw a spear at Mrs Hazelwood, in this case. It missed by a good three feet. But...

"Right! *That's it!*" said the little old lady, her crystal ball slicing through the air to slap into one wrinkled palm. "It's time to take out the trash!"

Soldiers, tribesmen, magical monsters, witches, wizards and sundry other bastards let out a massive war-cry all at once, surging forward from all sides. Somewhere, poor old Hauptmann Schmidt had found his gramophone, and bombastic opera music belted out as the battle was joined.

Eddie was aware he wouldn't be like this forever. Somewhere, a clock was ticking down, slicing off the seconds until the universe realized that he wasn't supposed to inhabit seventeen tons of dragon-shaped fury. It would probably hurt tomorrow morning. But for now...

He sighted down between his nostrils, flaring them like turbo intakes, and squared up a whole squad of machine-gun toting cannibals. This time the flame came naturally. Toasting cannibals seemed fair, after all. *You could call it a victimless crime*. A lance of superheated plasma blew them away to ashes, each one popping like a sausage in the oven. A sweep of one huge talon, and Sqaud 22's lumbering frankenstein went flying, impacting with the cavern wall twenty feet up.

Yes, it was probably going to hurt tomorrow.

But today... *it was going to hurt them more*.

+++

What can be said about the Second Battle of Bad Schickehosen, amid the horrors of a whole world at war? On the grand scale of that mighty conflict, it was only a little thing. Just as the games of cat-and-mouse between submarines and u-boats under the ice of the north Atlantic were little things, or the desperate last stands of tank commanders in Libya, or bayonet charges in the jungles of south-east Asia.

Or, indeed, the bizarre spectacle which was unfolding over London this night, as a horde of little green sparks clashed with five sizzling comet-tails of light; red, green, gold, white, and what people afterward could only describe as *'the other one'*. Hitler had dispatched his bombers, but one look at the blasts of raw energy dancing across the cloud-tops had convinced most of them to just go and drop their payloads in the North Sea and call it a night. Those who pressed on never made it back to base to accuse the rest of cowardice...

So, on the larger scale of things, the battle which erupted inside Hans Schprinkler's hollow Alp was hardly a blip on the graph. If the Angel of War had not been busy slicing through renegade elves from the back of a motorcycle, high over Brixton, he wouldn't have even bothered to write it up in his big, red, leathery tome of conflict.

But little things are often the hinge upon which the whole world pivots. And, when it comes to important events, it very much depends what end of the dragon you're on. From a detached, floaty place, deep in the cushions of his own brain, Eddie watched the walls turn red. Quite a lot of the mess was probably his fault.

He watched The Compte de Saint Germain behead Squad 22's medusa, six Black Sun sturmtroopers around him turning to stone, as her gaze splintered through one of his foppish pieces of costume jewelry. He watched Snetterley Senior prepare incantations and circles of subtlety and power, filling the air with sparks and pentacles, before Connor hit him like a shaved badger on adrenochrome, battering him to submission with his horrible old shillelagh. Lucky went toe to toe with the frankenstein's-monster man[45], and copped a pummeling from the thing's bolt-studded fists before he put it down forever, with a punch so hard its head spun around eight times and came right off. Everywhere was shouting and strife, desperation and violence, as Section M's finest took their revenge.

They say that in a fight, it's often the one who can go the distance that walks away. Feeling a bit tired, in such mortal circumstances, often means you'll kip in a coffin. But when Eddie started to flag, he didn't slow down. He just began to *shrink*.

*Down from full thaumo-morphic conversion size, to a mere twenty-foot-tall ogre of a thing, with a face like a crocodile that had run into the*

---

45 It's probably polite to point out that this particular monster, sewn together from the bodies of the strongest, biggest, meanest dead people its creator could find, was not actually a Frankenstein ™, but an off-brand attempt made in an allotment shed in Swansea, by an aspiring young mad scientist named Bellingham Wallace. 'Bellinghamstein' was considered a bit too silly, however, so the monster passed himself off as one of the original batch.

*back of a bus. Down to a hulking, red, scale-skinned man who at some point had regained his pants...*

Doctor Jeckyll had written a very large and complicated scientific paper about this, positing a parallel space-time which contains things like trousers when a body changes shape. The mathematics were curly and the implications were disturbing. All Eddie knew was that one minute he was scaly and naked, throttling a frantic Tcho-Tcho in each hand, and the next he was wearing a ragged pair of cut-off khakis and holding his shield and sword again.[46] Can we describe the feeling of growing mammalian testicles all at once, during a pitched battle, in a sleeting cloud of magic? Probably not. It was thoroughly unpleasant though, which just made Eddie Weatherfield angrier.

*Anger gave him focus. Anger burned away the spots before his eyes, the leaden feeling in his arms and shoulders...*

This proved very handy indeed when a blast of wild magic knocked him flat.

Hans Schprinkler rose up from out of an oily maintenance pit before him, bloody and bruised, levitating in a cloud of swastika-shaped sparks. He carried his staff in one hand, and an unmage's black longsword in the other, little curls of blue fire licking up the blade.

Was he pleased to be back?

Was he *shit*...

"Weatherfield! *You!* I always thought it was going to be Charlie Monkston, you know? The *good guy?* But it turns out it's *you*." He levitated closer, his feet touching the ground with a pair of prim little clicks. "You pathetic. Sniveling. Lemming's-fart of a person! Last minute escapes, half-arsed plans working out at odds of a million to one... all the tiresome trappings of a bloody *hero!*" He spat this last word with all the vitriol a half-dead Nazi wizard could muster. It was more than enough. "And I fell for it, too. Brought you to my. Inner. Sanctum. Gave the big speech about my plans. Arranged the elaborate doom for you, involving making you kill your friends... ach, the story, it unfolds the same way every time. Unless – *you control it!*"

With this, Schprinkler unleashed a flare of sorcery from his staff, arcing like red lightning. Eddie caught it on his shield, and felt it push him backward across the floor, the hobnails of his boots scraping Yes – they were back, too.

---

46 Even if your arse becomes the size of all outdoors when you change, Jeckyll's Third Law of Sartorial Transmogrification states that it's just the lower legs of your pants that will be shredded when they come back.

And Schprinkler, true to form, wouldn't shut up.

"It doesn't *have* to be you, you see."

Another blast. Another frantic block.

"Monkston's not dead. Nothing can truly die, out there."

Another, and Eddie could feel the grips of his shield heating up.

"You know *where*, of course? The other side. The *Netherverse*. I'm sure if we brought dear old Charles back, you'd be relegated to a bit-part once again. Your death would simply be… motivational."

This time, Eddie felt his skin crisp and blister, even though he knew he was immune to fire. The pain was in his mind, but his mind was all too real. Down there in the core of it, a little voice was yammering at him to *run*.

*Damn, but he was tired of doing what he was told.*

So Eddie did exactly the opposite. He pressed down on the runic hand-grip of Exclobberer, and charged.

"Shut the HELL UP for once, you stupid Nazi *prick!*"

The red-hot shield smashed into Schprinkler's face, mercifully making him do just that. A wild blow with the sword was parried, then another, steel skirling and grinding. But Eddie was desperate, and desperation gave him strength. He pushed in, swords locked, and delivered a headbutt with those evil little horns of his. He felt the Nazi's nose pop, and blood spatter wide. An instant later he had to jump backwards, as three feet of black metal hacked at his belly, scoring a line across the scales. Schprinkler grinned gold.

"You *owe* him, Weatherfield. He went into that abyss for your cowardice. Who knows what torments he suffers, there in the Inside-Out? Defeat me, and you might be. Able to. Bring him back…"

Eddie followed Schprinkler's one good eye, then. The other was a ruin of jelly and gore behind a shattered monocle. He saw the workstations, and the blinking lights, and the webwork of cables which fed into the Black Sun's rockets. He saw a glass dome, crusted with hoarfrost, and under it…

Charlie Monkston's hat.

Another parry, and a blow from that sizzling-hot staff against his shield.

"How do we get inside the Accords? Inside your general Crowley's great wardings and runes? *We fly through the Inside-Out!* We navigate a deeper darkness! And what better way to do so, than to use the tortured soul of my enemy as my guide?"

Eddie gritted his teeth and mounted a final, last-ditch assault.

His sword came down like thunder, notching Schprinkler's blade, carving long curls of swarf from the edge of his staff with a sound like screaming angels. He drove the mad sorcerer back. He howled, an animal bellow, and forced Hans Schpinkler backwards over the console, where an invitingly large red button glowed next to granddad Barnabas's silk top hat.

Hans laughed, his face a mask of blood and ruin. He dropped his sword, and fumbled in his pocket for something else. A medallion, inscribed with a snake eating its own tail.

"Choose, Weatherfield! All I have to do is speak the word, and this amulet will transport me back to Berlin. I have my own suite in the Fuhrerbunker, you know. Very tasteful." He giggled, an unhinged sound. "So *choose!* Kill me, or save the poor Major! You only. Have. Time. For *one!*"

Schpinkler's good eye twitched across to that red button. He was sheened with sweat, burning as if with a fever. Green sparks crawled over the amulet in his hand as he took a breath…

Eddie considered his sword, held high. He considered the button, just out of reach. If there was a chance he could save Charlie Monkston, then he had to take it. He rolled left, letting Schprinkler go, and hammered down on the console with his fist.

All at once, three things happened.

Hans executed a backwards roll and tumbled over the workstation, coming back to his feet with a cackle of laughter. Red lights and klaxons filled the hall with sensory overload, painting every surface crimson. And a voice echoed out above all this, in cool, calm, German.

**"Starten, Starten. Raketen aktiviert. Bitte ziehen Sie sich auf einen mindestabstand zurück."**

"Or, you know," said the leader of the Black Sun, shrugging. "You could just launch my assault on the Accords for me, like the idiot you are…"

Down at the far end of the chamber, the first rocket ignited. A lance of superheated flame, more potent than any dragon's breath, speared down into the concrete pit beneath, blazing up again from holes in the floor. It rose, smoke billowing out to choke the cavern, and as it did so a portal opened in a ring of copper and steel above it, revealing a sky speckled with unwholesome stars. *The Netherverse.* As Eddie watched, aghast, the rocket slipped out of reality and on its way.

"No! Not after all of this! You don't get to win!"

The second rocket roared into life, waves of pulverizing sound blotting out Eddie's snarl as he leaped the console, weapons thrown aside. Hans Schprinkler laughed, holding up his amulet…

And a shot plucked it from his hand. Eddie heard bones crack and blood fly as the bullet hit home, sending the little disc of gold spinning off into the smoke.

*Fyodor could see in the dark...*

Eddie struck him an instant later, as the third rocket went up, then the fourth and the fifth, sending pillars of raving fire dancing across the cavern floor. Every shaft, hole and pit down into the undercroft beneath had become a furnace mouth, spewing white-hot flames.

*"You don't get to win! Not after all of this! Not after everything I've had to do..."*

Eddie's hands picked him up by the neck. Schprinkler barely weighed anything at all, but he was still laughing.

"Don't you see, Weatherfield? You can't kill me! I'm the *bad guy!* You're a nothing. Not even a has-been. *A never was!"* The words came out as a bubbling croak. Eddie could feel blood trickling over his fingers.

"Better a never-was, than a never-should-have-been," he growled, reaching down deep for his courage.

Eddie knew, on a certain level, that despite the pain, he was immune to fire right now. Millions of years of evolution yammered at him from all the other levels that he wasn't.

His mind screamed NO, but his clenched fists sang out YES, with a sound like choirs of angels. So he took two steps forward, eyes screwed shut. And he plunged Hans Schprinkler into a torrent of flame.

The pain came, raving and clawing, like hot barbed wire under his skin.

But along with it came the sheer, primal satisfaction of watching Hans Schprinkler finally lost for words. All that came out of his mouth, as his hair caught fire and his skin bubbled and crisped, was a long and unbelieving howl. Eddie held on while the Black Sun's kommandant thrashed and struggled. He held on as long as he could, while his nerves broadcast agony on every wavelength, but his scaly hands remained untouched. Then he dropped Schprinkler, watching him fall into emptiness as the last rocket escaped into the Inside-Out, as the fires guttered and died.

He watched, until that blistered face blurred into shadow.

Then there as nothing but smoke, and echoes, and a little cinder of satisfaction crushed out, as he slumped to his knees and realized that he'd failed.

*All that muscle. All that power. All that strength. Combined with all his uselessness.*

He hardly felt their hands on his shoulders as they came for him. He hardly saw them waving various numbers of fingers in front of his eyes, or heard the echo of gunfire and radio chatter. Somewhere, beyond a twist in space and time, the dragons waited.

But out here, there was just Eddie Weatherfield.

*Has-been. Never-was. Shouldn't-have-bothered.*

Perhaps all of the above.

+++

Now see the *Black Buzzard* descending through the illusion of a mountain-top, underslung Demdike Mark Twelves angled for vertical landing.

Watch Percy sew his hands back on, careful spiderwebs of black thread pulled tight.

There's Doctor Jeckyll and the General, calculating trajectories and times through a twisted un-space on a vast, two-level Cambridge chalkboard.

Eddie Weatherfield, numb and human-sized, hot water running down the scars on his back as he showers on some un-named airbase. His fingers trace a new scar on his neck, where he knows an undead hand was pushed clear through between his vocal chords.

On a battered old chair outside lies a fresh new uniform. New orders. One last chance.

In Switzerland, at an alpine resort as opulent, distant and cold as the scene in a snow globe, they are already arriving. Black Mercedes and Rolls-Royce limousines ferry odd-shaped dignitaries to their lodgings. Chefs sworn to utter secrecy prepare dishes both outlandish and unspeakable.

Here is the silhouette of Winston Churchill on the telephone, a cannonball-headed and stocky shape against the windows of Whitehall. Cigar smoke drifts as he speaks a few fateful words.

The Angel of Death breaks the seal on a huge golden scroll, and frowns.

"Very well. We will, as you say, *stand down*. But we made those bastards run, didn't we?"

Patience sits on the top of a set of military bunk beds, trying to scry the future with a saucer full of ink and lamp-oil. With a shock, the porcelain cracks; the ink catches fire.

And under Schloss Bad Schickehosen, a horribly burned hand claws its way out of a pool of water, deep in some subterranean grotto.

As is the rule with scenes like these, phosphorescent fungi paint the scene in hues of green and blue. An arm follows the hand, then the dome of a blistered and peeling head, little more than a skull.

Hans Schprinkler hauls himself up onto the subterranean shore, and opens his one remaining eye. He is very surprised to find that he is being watched.

Here, miles below the surface, there is a great stone sarcophagus, carved from the living rock. It's heavy on the skulls and crosses, along with scenes of young women without much on. The lid is pushed back, and a man all in black and white is perched on the edge, his face sunken and hollow, his eyes a shocking red. His haircut, many centuries out of style, looks rather like a big bum.

"You *total* pillock," says this apparition, shaking its head. *"Vot haf you done vith my castle?"*

Hans struggled to his knees, with a herculean effort of will.

"*Your* castle? What have *I* done? Do you have any idea who you're talking to? I have defeated death! I am..."

A hand with three-inch fingernails, crusted with gold and ruby rings, shushed him.

"Oh, come on now. Ve haf all heard zat speech before, yes? Ve haf all… *monologued.* But you don't get it, do you? What is the *name* of this castle zat you have made such a bloody mess of, hmm?"

Realization dawned, and Hans Schprinkler grinned.

"Oh, I get it. Yes. What a lovely plot twist. We all know how this is going to go. Because you can't kill me, you see. *I'm the bad guy!*"

Baron Ludwig Manfred Wolfgang von Schickehosen rose up to his full height – a tall and lanky seven feet – and *hissed.* His teeth were fangs as long as fingers. His shadow seethed with busy darkness. Centuries of myth and legend crowded behind him, tweaked to madness by the Narrative Torque and Shear of the Brothers Grimm.

"Oh, *really?*" asked the vampire, as he reached out with both hands...

Down in the dark, there was a sad little click of breaking bone. Then a sound like a milkshake being drained, down to the last drop.

Then silence.

# Fifteen – the Unmanifest Accords

There was no room in all the realms and worlds and parallel semi-detached dimsensional-loft-conversions of creation big enough to hold the High Table.

It was as big around as a cricket oval, empty in the middle to leave room for a huge dais with three judicial-looking lecterns, and polished to such a sheen that one could easily see the screaming skeletal faces frozen into wood-grain. Some said that it had been hewn from a fallen branch of Yggdrasil, the world-oak. Others opined that it was the thirteenth task of Hercules, the single biggest piece of flat-pack furniture ever invented.

Today the High Table stood in the centre of an alpine meadow, cupped in a bowl of snow-capped mountains. A scattering of edelweiss painted the hillsides, and green grass lapped up around the table's stumpy legs like a tide. There were hundreds of chairs arranged around the circle, ranging in size from the tiny (held up on pillars of stone) to the gargantuan. Each one would have made a perfectly serviceable throne for a moderately-sized kingdom. Each one was occupied, and most also had a small crowd of creatures milling around behind it, making with some sharp elbow-work to stay up near the front.

Here were the movers and shakers of the Unmanifest, from factions who were represented by a handful of creatures (the Sirens, the Centaurs, and the Minotaurs, for example) through to the leaders of mighty unseen nations. Here was the Hammerjarl, Snorlaf Skaraldsenson, a cube-shaped dwarf in gilded armour, carrying a war-hammer almost the size of his torso and a beer stein slightly bigger. His retinue of mining engineers, warriors, soothsayers, scribes and other lackeys had actually pitched tents behind his ornate seat, and were already cracking open barrels of ale. Across the table (so as to discourage outright slaughter) was his erstwhile foe, the Mountain King, Zaric Grulgrak. The leader of the fractious green-skinned tribes was a goblin in name only, as he was more than the size of a man. Most of this was made up by his belly, which was borne up by several smaller goblins with fat-herding prongs and forked sticks.

Here, too, was the Alpha Ultima of the Werewolf clans, a gaggle of the Eldest of the Vampires, the Queen of the Gnomes with diamonds in her beard, the High Shaman of the Yetis, the Supreme Biggest of the giants, and the kings of races as disparate as the Tritons, Efreets, Oni, Kobolds and Ghouls. Lucky's lord and master the High Chief of the Leprechauns was there, seated next to a tarantula the size of a small van. They were sharing a sly drink of something which made the spider hiss and chitter with laughter.

In the centre of the table were the humans.

General Crowley looked positively hot and uncomfortable in the ancient robe of Merlin. Rather than being the billowy, star-spangled confection people might have imagined, this was a no-nonsense dark brown woolen garment packed with hidden armour. The extent and depth of its many pockets was still unfathomed.

Next to him on the dais sat the two other most senior practitioners on Earth; an African man so old and gnarled that he looked to be carved from leather, and a tall, pale Oriental woman in a jade-green dress and golden cape. A smaller table below their lecterns held the Writer, still in full professorial tweed, Doctor J, a massive tome the size of a paving slab, and, under its own glass dome, an item of magical power so potent that it generated its own twisting rainbow aura.

This was the True Quill, a pen with a nib of meteoric iron and a shaft made from the feather of a phoenix, bound with sorcery so that it resembled both a peacock's plumage, in purple and orange, and a snap-frozen flame. When people spoke about the pen being mightier than the sword, *this* was the pen they were referring to.

"Well, it looks like about time. Where are the biscuits?" asked Crowley, mopping his forehead with a large monogrammed handkerchief.

"More to the point, where are the *elves?*" asked Quentin Adebayo, the octogenarian African demon-slayer. "Not like them to be late. And very much like them to be troublesome."

Chiharu, the elementalist, frowned across at him.

"You boys worry too much. If the Jarl and old tubby there aren't fighting each other, we're off to a great start. It's not like they're going to vote us down, in any case. Too many reasons to love the new Accords."

"Pure bribery," agreed Adebayo, lighting up a long, thin cigarillo. "And of course, none of us want our world to go the same way theirs have."

General Crowley just massaged his aching eyes. Out of the human contingent, *he* was the only one who knew what was coming. A very ragged band of defenders were waiting for it all to go wrong.

But it seemed that the elves being late was not going to be an issue. Even as the General groaned to himself, eliciting raised eyebrows from his fellow Wizards, the great Gateway at the far end of the meadow flickered, and trumpets rang out. The Herald of the Accords (at short notice) was Reggie the Minotaur, and when he blew reveille (the only tune he knew), people several hundred feet away had their haircuts ruined. It was trumpets, plural, because the gigantic bull-man blew into a bouquet of them, welded together.

"Announcing – the Royal Courts of the Fae, Autumn and Spring. For the Autumnal Court, His Majestical highness, King… what? He's *where?* Well, Allright then, who do I…" there appeared to be a small scuffle around the microphone. "ALL RIGHT THEN. AHEM. Representing Autumn, the lawfully wedded and most definitely invited to this occasion wife of King Oberyn… *do I have to read this bit? Oh, very well…* The Ineffible One, Dame Fortuna, Lady Luck, Supreme Incarnatrix of Entropy Imponderable, Eris, Goddess of Chaos."

A rippling murmur went through the crowd, as creatures turned to other creatures and expressed their varied amusement, shock, outrage, indifference or outright fury at a celestial being stepping onto the sacred turf of the Accords. As far as the exiles of the unmanifest races were concerned, there was only so much magic to go around, and the Gods were competition. But Reggie, true to form, just bulled on.

"And representing the Court of Spring, the Rightful Queen, Once and Future lady of all Fae *(hey! You wrote that in just then!)* Titania, the Eternal!"

The two ladies and their gigantic entourages came through the gate like the rivals at a boxing match weigh-in, almost visibly arcing with animosity. Sometimes two cats can stare at each other for hours in mutual loathing, concentrating their hatred to a point so focused that you can hard-boil an egg between them. As Eris swept down the red carpet, barely four feet away from her husband's ex, that sticky, electric feeling was multiplied by a billionfold.

It only got worse when they were forced to sit on massive golden-wood thrones next to each other. Their entourages glowered daggers, while the ladies both smiled, trying to outshine each other with radiant opulence. Eris was clad in a toga which seemed to be woven from strands of mother-of-pearl, and she was wearing enough Athenian-style gold jewelry to sink a trireme. Around her neck on a chain that could anchor another ship was a solid gold apple, inscribed with a diamond-studded letter K. That toga did little to disguise more dangerous curves than a glass formula-one raceway, and her eyes blazed radioactive green, a match to the egg-sized emeralds she wore in her crown.

Titania was not to be upstaged, however. She'd gone for a sky-blue outfit finished in silver, long black hair, and the stolen glamour of no less than three goddesses piled on top of her own. Right now, Isis, Ishtar and Eostre were wearing Titania's patented combination foundation and smoothing masque, with the added twist that all of their reflected beauty was channeled through the silver circlet that bound up her tresses. Every male creature around the table suddenly felt about five degrees too warm. Things that were only nominally gendered at the best of times felt a bit hot and bothered. The combined quad-barreled cannon of glamour lashed out like a lighthouse beam, causing a peculiar constriction in the trousers, and almost blistering the varnish on the High Table.

Chiharu wasn't having any of it. At six hundred years old, she'd manipulated a lot of libidos to get her own way, and she felt that both the Goddess of Chaos and the Queen of Spring were being about as subtle as a jalapeño enema.

"So where *exactly* is the King?" she asked, shutting down the hubbub around the table with a smack of her gavel. Eris smirked and gestured to Titania, who fielded the question with the aplomb of a veteran attorney.

"Check your programmes, ladies, gentlemen, and others," she purred. "Right before the signing of the accords. You'll notice that there's a line marked 'entertainment'. He's part of that."

More than a few of the assembled dignitaries worked out what that might mean, all at once. Upon noting the absence of Titania's huntsmaster, the Erl King, that supposition was redoubled. A sussurrus of excitement rippled around the table, as those old enough to remember the 'good old days' gave each other certain nudges and winks.

*"Preposterous!"* started Crowley. "We never agreed to Thun… I mean any kind of musical interlude!" Deep down inside, the general was thinking about the mess those bearded bastards had made of Pompeii, and quietly chewing the corner of his armour-plated robes.

Outside, he was all jowl-quivering defiance.

"Thankfully, you didn't need to," smiled Titania, as radiant as a small supernova in the glow of her own assured victory. "It's customary at these things to have some bards, or other such merriment. I'm afraid that the previous troubadours were… indisposed. Thankfully, replacements could be found. We just did the job for the sub-committee on light entertainment."

Halfway around the table, the representative for the Medusae gave a none-too subtle thumbs-up to the Queen. It's amazing what a little bit of publicity and a half-pound tub of moisturizer can buy you in politics.

Crowley didn't like to think too hard about that 'indisposed'. But Titania, while ambitious and preening beyond most human imagination, was not entirely evil. The Welsh folk quintet who were supposed to fill the spot were simply laid up in a cheap hotel room in Zurich, suffering through a bout of supernaturally bad food poisoning.

"Be that as it…" began the General, but Titania cut him off.

"Quid pro quo, Mister Crowley," she said. "What authority does *England* have to call a change to the accords, when humanity is at war with itself?"

Adebayo spread his hands in contrition. He looked about as sorry as a cat holding half a budgie sandwich.

"In this case, by way of a pre-existing arrangement. The groundwork for this change to the Accords was tabled in '37, with everybody relevant present. This is simply a final ratification. It's not our fault that the leaders of German, Italian and Japanese Wizardry and Witchcraft seem to have had some trouble with their respective governments."

"They were deliberately excluded!"

"Switzerland is *neutral*, Your Majesty, in case you forgot. They could come here if they were allowed to. Being stuck in a concentration camp puts a crimp on your business travel schedule, however, or so it would seem."

"Then why not…"

Crowley didn't let her finish.

*"Because whether the Reich likes it or not, Hans bloody Schprinkier is not his nation's ambassador to this assembly!"*

Titania radiated smugness.

"*You* mentioned him, not *me*, General dear. Though where he's gotten to, I just don't know. Like a certain silly old hen I know, little Hans has quite a bee in his bonnet about not being invited to things."

For the merest fraction of a second, everyone around the High Table could see the bones of everyone else, as if a gigantic x-ray flashbulb had gone off inside their heads. Then Eris calmed down. Her fingers were charred an inch deep into the arms of her throne.

"Better than a cooked goose, I'm sure," she managed, teeth welded together in a smile. It was a venomous hiss, meant only for Titania to hear, but it carried like a fart at a funeral. Down at three-o-clock on the sunny side of the table, the Hammerjarl hammered (of course) his massive, gilded beer-stein on the boards.

"I say! Can we get on with it, please! I'd really like to get this all sorted out and get back to Number Twelve Gallery, before they crack into that lovely new seam of sylvanite. Time is gold, as I always say!"

"Gold! GOLD! **Gold!**" came the chorus of Dwarvern voices around him, rattling their ceremonial weapons enthusiastically.

Crowley felt that it was high time he took back over as ringmaster of this particular circus. He stood and brought his gavel down with a resounding crack.

"Very well. Ladies, Gentlemen, and, as our friend the Queen so aptly put it... *others*. Without further ado, here is the Laureate Designate for this round of the Unmanifest Accords, to explain how the changes posited for each of the supernatural races will provide stability and, we might hope, *prosperity*, well into this new century of ours."

The Writer gave a small and professorial bow, first to the left, then the right. Doctor J helped him up on top of the table, as Quentin Adebayo made a series of mystic passes, materializing a very large blackboard from out of nowhere.

"Ladies and gentlecreatures," the Writer began, pausing a for a moment to fuss with his pipe. "The issue is not one of diminishing belief. After all, there are more of us *Homo Sapiens* than at any other time in history! No, the problem, it appears, is one of *quality...*"

A piece of chalk appeared in his hand. A wave of silence rippled around the table, fanning out left and right until it met its own tail in the middle. And in the hush that followed, the Writer made his chalk *dance*.

+++

For the second time in recent history, Eddie Weatherfield crashed an aeroplane.

This time it came down with a hissing rush, sliding on its belly across a field of parchment-pure snow. The General had explained that there was no point in trying to take off again from where they were going, and in any case, Darrin Oakenbeard had only provided enough sheets of rune-inked vellum for a one-way trip.

Crashing never got any easier, it seemed. It was still terrifying, and not just for him.

Patience had the good grace to look quite embarrassed when the sliding, bumping, snow-ploughing progress of the aircraft stopped and she was still screaming. She turned the tail-end of it into a series of coughs.

"Well, that went better than expected, Weatherfield. I can see how you got into this mess in the first place, with flying skills like that."

Eddie massaged the purple sparks from behind his eyes, and contemplated the fact that he'd have a big horrible bruise on his forehead *exactly* where the last one had been. Darrin had built this little version of the *Black Buzzard* in a matter of hours (thanks to the help of his team of Gremlins), but to save time he'd made it from the carcass of a stripped-back Spitfire. This meant that Eddie's hands and feet moved pretty much by themselves as he hauled himself out of the cockpit, the voice of Sir Horace Stackpole bellowing in the back of his mind. He perched on the wing and helped Patience climb down, making a step with his crossed fingers.

"It's a surprise I kept the blasted thing up in the air," he said, sliding down the wing to the ground. On the way past, he ran a gloved hand over the picture of a Gremlin girl in a yellow sun-dress and crossed ammo belts the ladies had painted on the side. The plane's name was the *Black Sparrow*. "We'd have been better off just hijacking one of Hitler's rocket bombs!"

"Well, at least you got us here. The Black Sun have been trying to find this place for most of the war. The Reich even funded some civilian expeditions. But you have to have a special kind of invitation. Lucky thing about the Major's hat, isn't it?"

Eddie waited for Patience, then began forging a path through the knee-deep snow. It was only after a few struggling minutes that he noticed that she was walking along on top of it, light as a feather.

"Not lucky..." he panted, resting for a second. Patience offered him a hand and pulled him up. "Probably not a co-incidence, either. Things are happening, with us right in the middle. Even *I* can feel it."

Patience nodded.

"Try being a witch when that kind of thing is going on. There's two different futures fighting to be the real one right now. And here we are, knocking on the door of… well… that."

For a brief moment the flurries of snow parted, revealing fold after crinkle after rumpled infinity of bleak grey mountains, capped in white. Just ahead of them, about as far away again as they were from the wreck of the *Black Sparrow*, was an ornate, oriental-style billboard, capped with a sloping pagoda roof. Two red lanterns burned at the corners, illuminating a sign in, against all odds, English.

**Welcome to the Plateau of Leng. Population, Nobody. Now, bugger off!**

Next to it stood a red London phone box. Sir Giles Gilbert Scott certainly got around. There was nobody inside, just a single light bulb burning, illuminating a selection of cards advertising 'adult entertainment' and a heavy black telephone.

"So how do we get in?" asked Eddie, arriving slightly later than Patience, who stepped down off the snowbank with effortless grace. "This doesn't look very much like a retirement village, or whatever the General said we were after. And, if I can remind you, some of us are freezing our boll… I mean or ars… I mean our *fingernails* off out here!"

Patience turned, one hand on the phone booth door.

"It's sweet that you think I haven't heard any swear words in 275 years, Eddie. But the main thing to remember is that those rockets will be landing right on top of the Accords any minute now. If we can't convince these old bastards to help… well, your arse and bollocks will be the least of your worries." She opened the door, looked inside, scanned the range of little cards on offer (Madame Prue, strict discipline, rubber boots and gloves provided, Thursdays and Saturdays only[47]) and beckoned Eddie within.

"Have you got the hat?"

A locked metal box on a leather strap rattled ominously on Eddie's back. It was there alright.

"Got it."

"Then remember your lines, and we'll get through this. Just think of them as very, very elderly people. No matter what you see, don't worship anyone. And don't actually put the hat on, whatever you do! Now… costumes!"

It's a well-recorded fact that certain superheroes can change into tights inside a telephone booth without fear of embarrassment. They

47 This was, in fact, and advertisement for a very stern and puritanical washerwoman, who was VERY confused by the kind of men who kept telephoning her

ought to try getting out of arctic survival gear inside one (while attempting not to look at a half-naked young lady you quite fancy), then putting on a complete tuxedo with a white bow tie and tails. Eddie Weatherfield, face mashed up against the glass, imagined that they should invent a new medal to award him for this gallant service to King and Country.

Behind him, he heard a rustle of silk and satin, then the sound of the rotary dial.

"You can look now, Eddie. And, if I may say so, you look *much* better in a tux than you do in half a pair of dragon-burned trousers."

Patience had changed. So had the scene outside the phone booth door. While the other windows of the little cubicle still showed a high Himalayan snowfield, the view out the door itself was into a pale peach lobby, with a fountain and several plastic potted palms. The Revenge of English Witchcraft, now clad in an evening gown as soft and silvery as a cloud, strode out across the swirly-whirly-patterned pastel carpet with supreme confidence. Eddie followed in her wake, trying to take it all in.

It certainly didn't *look* like the kind of thing he'd expected from the Himalayas. There were no monks, for starters, and no kung fu, no yak butter, no prayer wheels or saffron robes anywhere in attendance. Eddie read a lot of comic books, and not one of them had ever mentioned that the secret underground temple of the invisible masters smelled slightly of lavender and cat's pee, and was very much like the lobby of a slightly chintzy seaside hotel.

He followed Patience, trying not to goggle at the fake palms, the tacky fountain with its clutch of constipated mermaid statues, or the little carts pushed here and there by middle-aged women in pale green uniforms. He tried not to hear the smooth and half-unreal music which murmured from hidden speakers. After what seemed an eternity, they reached a large and well-scrubbed counter, behind which sat the single most imposing female Eddie had ever seen.

This vision appeared to have been constructed from one of those opera singers who famously come on last, then extended in the front, with gusto. Acres of starched cotton stretched tight across her mammoth bosom, taut as the sails on a square-rigged man o' war. The rest of her was conceived on a similar scale, from arms like the thighs of rugby players to a pair of massively curled plaits, stuck to the sides of her head like blonde pastries.

Eddie was not surprised that her name tag read 'Frau Hilda'. Though he *was* concerned that it seemed a little too German.

Patience was not intimidated at all, even though Hilda was literally four times her size. She flashed a bright smile and leaned against the desk, pretending to rub some life back into her aching legs.

"Don't get me started about aeroplane food, love," she began, as Hilda opened her mouth to speak. "Blinkin' six hours up there, and do we get more than peanuts? Do we *what?* I tell you, whoever books these package tours should be marched out the back and shot." Patience's cockney accent, even after 275 years of living in London, was as cod-pantomime as that of Mr Punch.

Hilda raised one massive eyebrow.

"I'm afraid you must have come to the wrong place, nevertheless, my dear," she said, with that peculiar combination of politeness and utter contempt which belies the long-time civil servant. "This is a private facility. No mortals allowed."

Patience laughed.

"Ahhh, pull the other one, Hildy old chicken, old stoat, old… what are those ones with the little antlers and the tail? Badger? We're the *entertainment.* This *is* the old Fred, innit?"

Hilda drew herself up, in a fair imitation of a volcano about to obliterate the townsfolk and preserve their customary arts and crafts for future generations of archaeologists.

"This *is*, in fact, the Friedrich Nietzsche Memorial Home for Gods in their Twilight Years, yes. But I know nothing of any entertainments. The Ladies and Gentlemen have nothing like that scheduled for, oh, at least another few weeks. They've all been quite happy watching the war."

Patience affected a queer squint, and tapped the side of her nose. Eddie realized, with horror, that she was trying to look conspiratorial.

"Say no more, say no more. And I bet you'd love to be able to take some time off and get down there, eh? Lots of nice battles happening. Lots of strapping young warriors taking the final bow before honour's red curtain, sort of thing."

Patience produced a plain manila folder from her handbag and slid it across the desk with one finger.

"I know how it is," she said. "You only took the job to keep an eye on the old boys… well, keep an eye on the one with one eye, mainly. But the *old* job was much more exciting. I get it. I was one of those flying trapeze girls before I was a magician's assistant."

Frau Hilda looked both ways before furtively opening the folder.

From what Eddie could see, it contained military records, and photos of several soldiers.

"Ach, it would do me good to send a few of these lads to Valhalla," said the Frau, in a wistful voice. Eddie was horribly unsure if this was a euphemism. "But - no. My duty is here, now. The Ladies and Gentlemen need me."

"Oh, go on," smiled Patience. "That's what we're here for, after all, innit? That's Barnabas Monkston's great great great... well, some kind of son. You know how much they like to see a bit of magic done the old fashioned way. You could pop out and be back before we were even finished sawing me in half upside down in a shark tank."

Hilda peered at Eddie. He waved. She settled back on her chair, frowning.

"Well, it is very much against regulations..."

"Buuuuut..." filled in Patience.

"But you only live once!" smiled the immense Valkyrie, who had indeed only taken the job of head matron to keep a close eye on her former boss. "Well, I say that, but some of these boys - ah! - proper hero material! They'll really enjoy the big giant goat, I'm certain!"

With that, she rose to her full height, bosoms swaying alarmingly, and snapped her fingers. One of the middle-aged women in pale green uniforms scurried over, the wheels of her little cart creaking.

"Show these good people to the day room, nurse. I have some... er... inventory issues to take care of. Page Miss Merrywhistle to take over here on the front desk for a while, would you?"

The silent, peppermint-sucking nurse led them through a maze of identical peach and fawn corridors, suffused with smooth jazz music and the smell of carpet shampoo. At last, they reached a set of immense wooden doors, hung with the sad remnants of tinsel from holidays past, and adorned with a cross-stitched sampler reading 'No Prayers Please'.

"'Ere you go," said the nurse, turning over that huge, bath-plug sized mint between her false teeth. "Nap time's at two, so you've got a while. Just refrain from anything that might angry them up. Politics, religion, that kind of thing. Anubis, especially, gets all incontinent when he's angry."

And without further preamble, she pushed open the doors, to reveal the realm of the Gods.

It was vast. It was pastel. There were horrible floral curtains with a pattern of camellias, and clear plastic sheets over all the furniture, making the whole vast room seem like a discount mausoleum. Here and there, nurses in starched uniforms moved between the ranks of recliner chairs which lined the pale pink carpet, their crepe-soled shoes bipping with static electricity. Some pushed trolleys, laden down with bowls of porridge and selections of desiccated cakes. Others silently changed the fat plastic leeches of I.V. bags, hung up on silvery poles. At least one, noted Eddie, was probing the crevasses of a recliner with a vacuum cleaner, trying not to wake its sleeping occupant.

In every respect, then, this huge, barrel-vaulted room, with its slowly grinding ceiling fans and its cork-boards of dog-eared, yellowed memos, seemed to be the very archetype of an old folk's home. The kind of place where they keep the Grim Reaper on speed dial. The kind of place where bingo night Tuesday is so hotly anticipated that you would think it was the Sodom and Gomorrah Grand Prix.

All except for two very important things.

The first of these was the row of picture windows which all those ranked-up recliners faced. Brown, beige, corduroy, mustard yellow and green, each overstuffed chair and its incumbent pile of shawls, doilies, pillows and hot water bottles was pointed at a wall of glass three storeys tall, broken into sections by ornate pillars carved all over with a mish-mash of cherubs, ladies with no clothes on, winged lions, Egyptians doing their classic pose[48], and Sumerian gentlemen with beards you could use to tell the time by. Each pane of the great window showed a different scene from around the world.

There were arguments in parliament chambers. There were naval battles, with explosions and plumes of spray and desperate heroics. There were fighter planes swooping through clouds of battlefield smoke. Pane after pane of, well, *pain*.

Eddie found himself feeling rather cross with the withered old husks who inhabited those endless rows of chairs. This was because, in no small part, he knew, bone-deep, that what was happening in those myriad, blurred images was happening *right now*. That if he opened any of those windows and slipped through, he'd find himself facing a

---

48 The classic hieroglyphic pose, now so well known to archaeology, is in fact the consequence of the world's first ever dance craze, devised by a groovy little quintet called Azuf and the Camel-Tones, some time before the first pyramid went up. How were they to know that, just after their single swept the charts, Egyptian civilization would adopt a fanatical adherence to tradition that was to span thousands of years? The closest parallel we have today is the holiday tradition of playing 'Snoopy's Christmas' in all shopping malls on an endless loop until young bagging clerks shove sharpened pencils in their ears.

bayonet charge on the Eastern Front, or bobbing about in the Coral Sea, trying to explain that he only knew two words of Japanese.

This was their *distraction*. The hidden powers didn't play games with the lives of men - they used them as light entertainment. Like those interminable radio plays about fractious rich families that his Mum liked so much. Soap operas. Movie serials.

Because that was the second thing.

The wizened, bleary-eyed, ancient horde who filled those chairs were definitely The Gods. Ones who had given up, Eddie supposed. Ones who had either lost so many worshipers that they were only known of by a few sad old professors who could never get a date to the Science Department Social. Ones who had had their temples paved over with basketball courts and car parks, or who had just caved in on themselves and stopped caring. There were *hundreds* of them.

Some had animal heads. Some wore painted wooden masks. One was entirely made of lightning, which is quite a thing to see wearing an adult diaper and a Liverpool cardigan. There were beings with too many arms and pale blue skin, beings with jaguar spots and serpent scales and auras of cold flames. One or two just looked like normal old ladies and gents, but with costumes heavy on the feathers, gold, halos, big silly hats and spiky armour. There was one up the back who was definitely part woolly mammoth. He (She? It?) was wearing a bobble hat, and a scarf wrapped around what was clearly a trunk.

As one, all the nurses turned at the polite little click of the door closing, and raised a finger to their lips.

"Shhhhhh!"

Patience gave an embarrassed little smile and a twinkly-fingered wave.

"Sorry! Sorry!" she stage-whispered, reaching into her handbag. It must have had properties much like Charlie Monkston's hat, because what she pulled out was definitely a gigantic Russian drum-fed RPD machine gun. She racked back the slide, and turned to face the wide-eyed gaggle of nurses, slinging it from one hip. "Now, everybody be cool, and hit the carpet with your hands behind your heads. This is a break-out!"

+++

The graphs on the blackboard collided, sending off fractal loops and lines on wild tangents. Between them, eye-watering strings of algebra proliferated between atomic diagrams, and what appeared to be some middle-Egyptian cake recipes. The Writer's chalk was a smoking nubbin.

"So you see – and special thanks to Mr Turing for use of his analytical machines, of course – the factor is not fear, or worship, or even, strictly speaking, *belief*. It's the amount of space you take up in the collective human imagination. I call this the I-Shadow, for obvious reasons."

Several of the female creatures present (the ones who wore makeup) giggled. The Writer pressed on.

"So, to ensure a healthy existence for all of you, without what the Ministry are calling Scenario Seven - i.e., complete loss of I-Shadow, and the vanishing of a species back to their own world in the Inside-Out – we can do one of two things."

He had their attention now.

"Vampires! This is a chart of your I-entanglement, from 1840 through 1940." The Eldest of that fearsome race, all sun-goggles, wide hats and parasols despite a spell of midnight which wrapped them in tenebous shade, leaned forward. The effect was of several well-dressed vultures attending a motor rally. The Writer snapped his fingers, and a large sheet of paper lapped over the chalkboard. It showed a graph with a line bumbling along near the bottom until about half way through, at which point it leaped like a salmon. "Look at this. You were *tanking*. Some peasants in the Transoxania and the Urals, some stories in Hungary and around the Black Sea. Then BAM. Bram Stoker publishes Dracula. As you've seen from the Accords, there's more to come."

The Writer paused, as the assembled bloodsuckers nodded. Bram had done wonders for their wardrobes, not to mention their appeal to young women in see-through nightgowns.

"The numbers don't lie, people. You try to extort belief out of people the old way, and with the population imbalance now, to get the right amount of I-Shadow you'll break the world. Cold calamari surprise for all of us. But if we can *grow* the human imagination, and give it an image of you to hold onto, you don't *need* to do things the old-fashioned way. You don't have to be feared, or even, strictly speaking 'believed in'. You just have to be in that I-space, and the returns, as our Transylvanian chums have seen, will be palpable."

Of course it was Titania who had an issue with this. She rose from her throne like a very pretty thunderstorm, pointing an accusatory finger.

"He wants us to be nothing but their *entertainment!*" she shrieked, somewhat losing her composure. Eris, beside her, smirked as only the embodiment of Chaos can.

The Writer was ready. Before General Crowley could bang his gavel and cry for order, he had held up a hand, stopping the Queen in mid-rant.

"Quite so. Have you ever seen a *motion picture*, your Majesty? Fascinating things. Just twenty-four photographs per second, and look at what they've done. Two centuries ago, if you asked the average person who was the fairest of them all, they would have at least *thought* of the Queen of Springtime. Now the whole list is made up of girls from rural America who hitch-hiked to Hollywood. Less and less humans have even *a second a day* to think of goblins or trolls or ogres. Their minds are filled up with the Lone Ranger and Superman." he spread his hands. "I'm just here to tell you to take what's rightfully yours. I can help you. *We* can help you. But only if you want to help yourselves."

The uproar which engulfed the High Table echoed back off the mountainsides.

If it hadn't, General Crowley might have heard the first little cracking sound, high above. He might have looked up, in time to see a hair-thin fissure skitter across the dome of the sky, like a fatal flaw through windshield glass.

Another followed, and another; lightning-bolt traceries fanning out and merging as something pushed on reality from the other side. High in the alpine atmosphere, an explosion was trying not to happen.

Unfortunately, it was losing the fight.

+++

Eddie finished off tying up the last of the nurses, and caught a Thompson sub-machinegun with his free hand. Patience Stood in front of the windows now, evening gown shimmering in the light of a hundred desperate battles, her hair unbound and her eyes glowing amethyst purple. Eddie had never seen anything so god-damned gorgeous in his life. This image, he was sure, would be burned into the back of his skull for the rest of eternity.

"Right!" she asked. "Where's Odin? Otherwise known as Julnyr, Langbardr, Old One-eye, Allfather, the Bloody-handed? I haven't got all day, so, the first one who can point him out gets..." she rummaged for a moment in her handbag - "… a selection of shortbread biscuits. Look, there's a little scotty dog on the tin, and everything!"

A green, scaly God in the front row, with little gold bifocals perched on the end of a crocodile's snout, raised one trembling hand.

"Sobek, miss. Lord of the Nile, eater of clumsy canoeists, all that. I think he's gone. Passed on. Gone to the other side."

Eddie groaned.

"You mean he's *dead?* But he's a *God!* You're all Gods! What are you doing here, like this?"

This prompted a chorus of wheezing, tutting, muttering and moaning from the assembled ranks of the Divine.

"He don't mean old Eyepatch i'dead, you mortal pillock," chimed in a nearby recliner-dweller, this one wizened and black, with immense horn-rimmed sunglasses, a tropical shirt, and a banana-yellow fedora hat. "He means e' gone back to the world. Ask 'is boy, why don't ya?"

Patience nodded, and gestured vaguely with her RPD.

"Allright. Fine. Thor Odinsson. Big feller, usually has a hammer. Where's he?"

A hand wobbled skyward in the second row, and Eddie rushed over to kneel beside the chair of a white-bearded geriatric, wearing a blue toweling robe over chain mail.

"That's me, miss. Are you the new matron? Because Frau Hilda always used to give me double porridge, and..."

Patience smiled, a brittle, this-side-of-madness smile.

"You *do* get the shortbread biscuits, Mr Odinsson. If you can tell me where your dad went."

Thor chuckled. He really did look every one of his two thousand years at that moment, with his wrinkled-up face and his wispy white beard, made all the worse because he was wearing armour too big for him and a helmet with wings.

"Two lads in black suits, black ties, white shirts and sunglasses came and got 'im. Said they were getting the band back together. Said they were on a mission from… well… *us*. Wasn't like I could stop them."

Eddie couldn't believe it.

"But – but you're THOR. Everyone's heard of you! Most of these other has-beens – no insult intended – are old news. But you were the god of thunder, man! The guy with the hammer! We learned about your legends in school, and they were great stuff! Ice giants, and battles, and heroic deeds!"

Thor looked wistful for a moment.

"I seem to recall some heroic deeds, once. Long time ago. It was cold, and everyone was very keen on boats. We've got a new hammer guy now, though. Started yesterday."

The wizened God pointed with a liver-spotted finger, and Eddie's hopes (already in the bargain basement) crashed though several subterranean floors.

It was Jesus Christ. Gone was his halo of power and his air of effortless cool. Instead, he was dressed in carpenter's overalls and a tool belt, and he was trying unsuccessfully to install a small shelf on the wall of the day room. When he hit his thumb with his hammer, he giggled mindlessly, eyes blank.

"Aww, Jesus! They got you too!"

The Nazarene turned and waved, a complete lack of recognition on his face.

Patience flopped down on the windowsill and buried her face in her hands.

"We're too late. They got to Odin. Obviously December twenty-fifth belongs to the elves again. And these people -" she gestured around her at the ranks of comfy chairs, bearing their senile passengers through eternity. "They're no help. Odin was our only way back, in any case."

"No." Deep in Eddie Weatherfield's despair, he found a little core of anger. It wasn't the dragonfire he'd been loaned. It had been with him all along. The stubborn, flinty little core of bloody-mindedness that allowed him to keep going in a world cut out for people who were a different shape and size to him. The bit that made him commit to stupid things, like going halfway around the world to find his brother, or flying a plane against the Nazis, or deciding, right then and there, that if they got through what was likely to happen next, he was going to ask Patience Goodhallow out for dinner and a movie. Perhaps. *Definitely.*

"What was that, sonny?" grinned Thor, his false teeth slipping.

"I said NO! That's not right! There's some mad bastards out there trying to destroy the world, and you're just sitting here *watching*? I don't think so."

"Ach, what can you do? Nobody believes in us anymore," said an old-lady goddess, with four eyes and a pair of dusty-looking wings. "So the world gets destroyed. We had a good run. I always wanted to see the giant snake eat the stars, anyhow."

"You daft, woman?" asked an elderly, bird-headed God next to her.

"It's not a snake eating the stars. It's a withering flood of molten metal. Got it on good authority."

Another God laughed, showering dandruff on his toga.

"You're all wrong. Time of the Fire Titans, so it is. They'll arise, see, and first thing they'll burn is..."

Soon the whole room was arguing. Thor beckoned Eddie closer.

"Silly old fools. An 'uge wolf has to eat the moon, then it's Ragnarok, and we'll all have a lovely big fight. Looking forward to it, so I am."

Eddie gripped the old God's hand.

"You're *all* looking forward to it, aren't you? The end of the world. Because you get to start over, don't you?"

Thor nodded happily.

"Worlds end all the time, boy. Whenever something dies, even the tiniest mosquito, a world ends. Worlds are a dime a dozen. Real good endings though… well, they're like chocolate cake Thursdays."

"Then let me show you all something," said Eddie, looking at Major Monkston's hatbox. He left Thor's side and peeled back the lid, lifting the black silk topper out between fingers that seemed suddenly very, very heavy.

Patience caught his eye as he held it up, and he saw a shock of fear go through her. But he strode to the front of the room anyway, up to the giant picture windows, still playing their endless loop of conflict and war.

"Charlie," he whispered. "I'm sorry I didn't listen to you before. But I hope you can hear me now. And if we we get through this, I promise I'll find someone worthy to wear this blasted thing."

Patience held out a hand to stop him. Time slowed to a blurred, shadowy crawl. Somewhere, far away, Eddie could hear a sound like a train rushing through the night, all hissing steam and thundering pistons and sheer, unstoppable momentum.

He reached out and pressed his palm to the window. Electricity crawled and snapped all the way up to his shoulder.

With his other hand, he gave a little vaudeville flourish.

And he put the hat on.

+++

"You've all seen phase one," said general Crowley, banging his gavel for order. "And while the precedent for a hole in thaumic space shaped like a Ring of Power is possible, it's also self-negating. The narrative clearly has said item destroyed in a bloody huge volcano. *I'm* satisfied.

And that takes a lot, believe me." He scanned the whole great circle of the table with his eyes, weeding out dissent. "In conjunction with his previous work, our friend here will release a trilogy which re-defines the roles of the unmanifest races in the human psyche. We anticipate that this, the first ever Class Thirteen Working, will fractalize exponentially after publication. Other authors will add on, there will be feature films, models, comic books..."

"Games," added the Writer. "Mr Turing, who I thanked earlier, has some ideas about simulating games on electric machines. There could be a few opportunities there. And we have a program to introduce games where people pretend to be members of your various species, for fun. There are lots of different dice."

One of the attendants to the Hammerjarl scoffed, spraying beer across the table.

"You're saying perfectly tall humans would want to *pretend to be a dwarf?* What would they do? Pretend to fight dragons?"

A huge, mottled-green ogre slapped the tabletop.

"And are we to assume that there'll be fair and just representation in these movies? I hardly think humans will accept an ogre hero!"

The Writer motioned for calm.

"You've seen the figures, ladies and gentlecreatures. I assure you they are quite correct. These three novels will set off a cascade in the human I-space that will self-perpetuate. You'll have enough magic to sustain yourself for centuries."

Crowley saw Titania drawing in breath to argue, so he struck first.

"Motion is called to vote on the ratification of the 37th Unmanifest Accords. All in favour, raise your right hand, in the manner customary to this assembly!"

The three gavels held by the three greatest human magicians came down as one. And around the table the hands started going up.

There were hands sick of being remembered only in fairy tales and nursery rhymes. Hands tired of being nothing but legends trapped in university libraries, or used as metaphors by self-important philosophers. Hands (and claws, and hooves, and pincers) which yearned to break free of traditions and rules laid down by people carving pictograms into stone, back when a loincloth was the first and last word in fashion. They'd read the Writer's trilogy, and they'd seen the graphs, and added up the figures. Some had even paid very expensive firms of human accountants to double check them, paying in ancient gold or gemstones that were only a little bit cursed.

A few hands stayed down. But only a few. There were some of the elder races who liked their place in the shadows. There were a handful who still clung to the idea of being feared, as though it was the same thing as being respected. And there were a tiny number who agreed with Titania.

"All against this insult!" she shouted, skin pale as ice, eyes blazing winter-sky blue. "All against this robbery, this madness, this *disgrace!*" She looked around, hunch-shouldered, fingers crooked into claws. "They dare to presume to change us. *Us!* We shaped their minds, and made them fit to serve! Now they want us to be their entertainment, and live off the scraps of second-hand belief! I say we take our rightful place! I say we should *rule* these human cattle!"

But the tide was against her. The Hammerjarl gave her a sad little shake of his head, as he held his ale-cup high. The Mountain King looked acutely embarrassed, but he, too, raised his hand, thinking of Orcs, and the future, and retribution. All around the table, creatures from a thousand lost worlds could not meet her stare.

She pulled herself together. She clawed back her composure. Her glamour flickered up and around her like a guttering flame.

"*Very well.* I see how it is. I see your cowardice. And I don't judge you for it. My fellow…"

"PASSED!" shouted General Crowley, cutting her off with a mighty thwack of his gavel. "Passed, and enacted as law, binding from now until eternity, or until such time this duly ratified, lawfully assembled council sits again in judgment to make the Accords anew."

"Passed!" intoned Chiharu and Adebayo, making notes in their great, leather-bound ledgers.

In the echo of the gavels, Titania started to laugh. It was a good one, this. It would have done poor old Hans Schprinkler proud. It began low and deep, with her hunched over the table, a cascade of inky-black hair covering her face. Then it built, her shoulders heaving, mad peals of laughter setting up wyrd reverberations, until she threw her head back, hair wild, and shrieked, unhinged, staring up at the empty bowl of the sky.

Well. Not *quite* empty.

"You think this is how you change the world?" she asked, still racked with mirth. "With little wooden hammers, and words, and stories about shortarses with hairy toes? I'll show you how you change the world, mortals. I'll fecking well show you ALL!"

Titania seemed to swell, then, sucking in light and heat, growing ice-shrouded and spindly and crazed with thorns, the very spirit of the spring frost that snuffs the life out of hatchlings in their nests and lambs by their mother's side in the fields. Her face was all black-needle teeth and horrible, gloating pride.

"Look, fools! Look there! Before you even sat down at this table of treason, I knew your cowardice and your fear. And I prepared my answer. Not *my* judgment, lords and ladies. Not mine. But THEIRS."

They all turned their heads up. They saw.

The cracks in the sky thickened, widened, *merged.* Flakes of blue and cotton-candy white fell away. Darkness leered in, stained with unwholesome stars.

And here they came. Falling out of the alter-night, the sideways, the busy dark. Thirty great steel rockets, rimed with frost, parachutes blooming above them like malignant flowers. Black suns and swastikas on every one.

Panic gripped the table. Creatures began to scream, and run, and fight each other in their mad rush to escape. But the runic gateway blurred and stuttered closed. There was no way to hide from what hung above them all, like a scar.

The darkness of the lost worlds.

The places they had all fled from.

The *Inside-Out.*

And against that starry abyss, something moved…

+++

There, above a valley in Switzerland.

There, across a row of windows, painting a room full of easy chairs in flickering monochrome.

There, inside the heads of the mad, and the souls of the insane…

The Writer saw it, and felt every dark thing he'd ever imagined spring up around him, inky fingers scrabbling. Crowley saw it and all the wickedness of his long, long life came rushing down on him, wings of sin and depravity spread wide. Quentin Adebayo saw it, and a lifetime's worth of demons came hauling their broken bodies out of the hells he'd sent them to. Chiharu witnessed oceans of flame, infernos of ice. Patience saw the souls she was born from coming apart. The pain and agony of five women burned alive while the puritans watched, slack-jawed and hungry. Eddie was paralyzed again, as scaly coils bound him up, squeezing everything that was human from him, crushing him until the sinews of his mind creaked.

The old Gods saw it, as something cold and ancient (even by their standards) heaved its shapeless mass to the threshold, and reached out…

+++

*P'thgan waagra fnaghl th'hi graaal shugnath gorg u'fpth krith grungrud nfwhierg tuejd g'than qerot waaaj oqwebh rtofui'nghrt* **his hands were moving** *thradosh nagur thup frop gruul dqwen pyopi'ii shuddith qupepp gthaarth awefwex klqehg* **one finger at a time** *qeroegh plurgh nup therrdhux fgjio wergnu ryl'othu blaghih thwod rasdl'ifhpawergn aerg* **frozen tendon by aching muscle, mind on fire** *aseropdf gwaaag theraf p'fghthhh aaaxux tjpok werjh qkwaagh kwaaall* **just one trembling inch further** *thwee fnar ghrahal thopruu g'hukk nuckok ryxudfg* **until…**

**Pok!**

Eddie knocked the hat from his head and collapsed to the floor.
*Reality.*
Yes. That's what they called it.
*Reality* warped back into focus as he went sliding down the window pane, all pale and boneless.
*The hat! Inside it! The horrible, gnaargling slorbs! The nuppers, the schleeg, the vorping nuprience!*
It rolled to a stop, all innocent-looking - except for the ice which crinkled around it on the carpet.

Eddie's breath rasped in his throat, as something cold and gelatinous still pressed up against the inside of his eyes, horribly intimate. He knew they'd seen it too. A lot of those adult diapers, whether they belonged to Gods or not, were full right now.

He felt Patience sling an arm around him and help him to his feet, nausea twisting through him like wire. Her head slumped against his shoulder, and he noticed that she, too, had been sickened and drained by – well, whatever that had been.

The hat lay there steaming, little threads of electricity crawling and arcing across its brim.

Next to it, on the carpet, the end of a black tentacle flopped.

"*There!*" gasped Eddie to the room in general, propping himself up against a convenient pillar. "*That's* how your world ends. Right now.

Out there. Sucked down the bloody cosmic toilet while you sit here worrying about crossword puzzles and porridge. That's not the kind of end that allows for a new beginning."

"Oh, sonny. Oh, we're sorry." said Sobek, literal crocodile tears trickling across his scaly skin. "We didn't know. But it's too late, isn't it?"

"There's not enough of us left to fight them," put in a bull-headed God, who looked as wrinkled and cracked as an old leather sofa. "I haven't had a human sacrifice to my name since Agamemnon was a nipper. What are we supposed to do?"

It was Patience that answered.

"You've all got *something*. You're just spinning it out thin, aren't you? If there was really nothing left of you, you'd be nothing but sparks and echoes on the wind. But there's something holding you all here, waiting for that second chance. A statue in a museum. A few pieces of paper in a library. Some runes on a standing stone. A folk story where they get your name wrong, just a little. Well. *Use it.*"

"Are you mad, woman?" asked Sobek. "Look at the new feller over there. That's what happens when you get down to the bottom of the barrel." he pointed one clawed finger at Jesus, who was still trying to fix his shelf to the wall. It was upside down now, and bristling with bent nails.

"You've seen the alternative," said Eddie. "So have I. And I'm just a coward, and a mortal, and a bit of a fool, but I'm going to fight. You?" he shook his head, disgusted. "You used to be *Gods.*"

It started as a low rumble, almost too deep to hear. But it silenced the room. Something was happening to Thor's chair. The I.V. bags were jiggling, the tea-tray vibrating until it fell to the floor. His magical hammer, Mjolnir, began to glow where it was jammed into a cup-holder. It took a few seconds for Eddie to realize that the ancient Norse God was *growling*. It was a sound that ran up and down the human spinal cord with cleats on. It was the sound of a grizzly bear right behind you, or an angry wolf turning to face its hunters.

"*Ragnarok!*" muttered Thor, his liver-spotted hand throwing back the blanket. Threads of grey shot through his wispy beard. His eyes were milky white, glowing from within. "They want to take the final battle from me, do they? Thousands of years of waiting, and collecting warriors, me and dad. Thousands of years, and they want to just switch this world off like a light?" His fingers grabbed the stubby handle of Mjolnir, and, with a sound like a rubber bands being stretched, his skin lost its wrinkles. Grey hair faded to blonde. Muscles grew under his skin, from what appeared to be shucked oysters on a piece of string to huge, corded slabs of meat. *"Well, bugger that!* If I'm going to be forgotten, I'll give them a battle that they won't soon… well, you know what I mean!"

The collected detritus of decades of elder care was swept aside as Thor stood up, tearing off his bathrobe. Pills, sweet wrappers and used tissues scattered like rain.

"Yes!" shouted Eddie Weatherfield. "*That's* the God they taught us about in school!"

Thor grinned, giving his hammer a few test-swings.

"Feels good to be young again, I have to tell you. I can probably sustain this for a few hours, you know, before time catches up. But there's a lot of arses you can kick in a few hours, yah?"

"Bugger it," said Sobek. "I'm in. I haven't tasted a nice crunchy human for centuries. Must be good for the digestion." The crocodile-headed God struggled up from his own seat, changing as Eddie watched. Soon he, too, was a frightening tower of muscle, though this time wrapped in Egyptian linen and carrying a huge golden mace. "Oi - Set, Anubis, Thoth! You and old budgie-face should tag along. Come on, get lively!"

All around the room, Gods and Goddesses were clambering up from the depths of assisted-living torpor. Out in the world, scrolls and statues and scholarly texts were mouldering, and crisping, and abrading away to nothing. But there was enough stored belief out there for one last hurrah.

Thor leaned down and gave Eddie a calculating look.

"I'm no fool, you know. I know who you work for, lad, and what they're up to. So, for services rendered today, I want my own comic book. That's the way of the future, so far as I see it. I've been reading Batman myself, but I reckon I'd look pretty good as a super-hero. You make it happen. Plenty of belief to be had there, and maybe, who knows? They might make a movie one day. Wouldn't that be something?"

Patience gave Eddie's arm a little squeeze.

"Just say yes, Weatherfield. The General can sort it out, if we manage to survive."

"Allright then, Mister Odinsson. Now, how do we get back to…"

At that moment the doors to the day room burst open. Frau Hilda was framed (but only just) in the pale pastel light streaming in from beyond, a look of pure unadulterated wrath written across her face.

"What is the meaning of this nonsense! You've all been very, very naughty! Get back to your chairs this instant, and don't think there'll be any pudding to – oh!"

The huge matron's tirade was cut short as if by a steam-driven guillotine when she saw Thor up and about, filling out his armour to the point where the rivets creaked.

"Never mind pudding, Hilda, dear," he said, striking a heroic pose with malice aforethought. "Seeing as Dad's gone AWOL, I've decided to bring Ragnarok up a bit on the schedule. All bets are off. It's time to put the old firm back in business."

*"Hot damn!"* said Hilda, her eyes alight (in a very literal sense) with the same thrill which now suffused the day-room. A legion of Old Gods, now looking not so old, crowded in behind Thor, ready to work some celestial mayhem. She grabbed hold of the fabric of her starched white uniform with both hands and tore it apart, as easily as if it were tissue paper. Underneath, Eddie was pleased to see that she was wearing full chain-mail armour, and a steel bodice which appeared to have been hammered out of two cauldrons and a section of anchor chain.[49]

"Has anyone seen my helmet with the horns on?" she asked, her face split into a very satisfied grin.

Thor clapped her on the shoulder.

"It's in the linen closet, next to the vacuum cleaner. Now, you can still do that rainbow bridge thing, can't you?"

Hilda nodded. She couldn't seem to keep her eyes off of Thor's rippling pecs.

"Then let's go and end some worlds," he said, gathering up Patience and Eddie under one beefy arm.

There was just time to pick up Charlie Monkston's hat and scoop it into its box before the cheering, heaving mob surged forward, carrying both of them with it.

---

49 Because the alternative was an amount of nudity that shouldn't be seen all on one person at the same time

# Sixteen – Thunderbeards Reunion Tour

The thing about Vulkan – the thing that made him the unofficial sixth Thunderbeard, in fact – was that he took care of the little details.

In this case, he'd taken care of how the band were going to make a suitably grand entrance, right in the middle of the Accords, as a big surprise to all involved. So far as 'little details' went, it was several hundred kilotons of brilliance.

General Crowley, anticipating trouble, had set up a series of very cunning perimeter traps, along with his own surprises for when Queen Titania did the inevitable and tried to doublecross him.

But he just hadn't thought *three dimensionally*. Firstly, because he knew about the rockets coming from the Inside-Out, which would make an assault via parachute a rare and explosive form of suicide. But secondly, because even Oberyn himself could hardly believe that the Forge-God and his army of kobold roadies could have excavated such a large cavern, and fitted it with a massive, fully rigged stage - *overnight.*

It was impressive.

The stage itself was the size of a football pitch, arched over with skeletal lighting rigs and pyrotechnic paraphernalia, smoke machines and even, for one memorable number, a giant inflatable dominatrix puppet operated by construction cranes. It was designed to rise up on hydraulic piston legs, shifting aside a massive swathe of turf which had been reinforced with steel. The king of the elves just hoped it would work. Kobolds, in his experience, were smelly and untrustworthy buggers who would just as often eat building materials as nail them together.

And still it was just the four of them.

Oberyn had been a peculiar mix of anxious and pleased to be back with the lads. Dionysus was still his wisecracking, half-cut self. The Erl King looked like he'd been pulled through a car compactor backwards, but he seemed happy enough as he fondled his jet-black guitar and checked his amps. Mithras was enthroned behind his ornate, triple-layered drum kit, his signature sun-emblazoned golden gong hanging behind him like a war-chief's banner. Oberyn himself was sweating in a pair of tight leather pants, his old Thunderbeards costume completed with a shirt of copper mail, massively spiked shoulder pauldrons, and a crown made of carved wood and thorns.

*A bit too much like the young middle eastern feller's, he supposed. Still, no point in crying over spilled divinity, and all that.*

They had a show to do. The old energy was there, palpable in the air. Little green sparks crawled up the strings of Oberyn's bass guitar as he tuned it, each peg a silver leaf. He checked and re-checked an array of effects pedals which did things to sound that should only be possible with hardcore mathematics and harder drugs. *And still that drama-queen the Allfather hadn't shown up.* Just like him to play the man of mystery, even after all these centuries. Probably stopped off for a pint. *Probably not a bad idea...*

That's when something huge and dark came clattering and flapping its way down from the lighting rig to perch on the end of his bass. It was an oversized raven, head tilted to one side, in that manner peculiar to certain birds and serial killers. From up in the back, amid the mountain of drums, Oberyn heard a yelp of surprise from Mithras.

"Bloody thing! That's not an eyeball, you daft goth parrot, it's the end of my gong hammer!"

And He was there. Rocking that capital H as if he was still top God. A click of his fingers and the ravens flew back to his shoulders. Oberyn wondered why the old charlatan never seemed to have shit all down the back of his jacket.

*But then - no. Odin Long-Stride, the Bloody-Handed, was all about* style.

Now, the rest of them had been up and about in the world, trading on what little bits of belief they could get down the decades  But Odin had packed it in and booked a seat at the Old Fred. Said he was stretched too thin.

He didn't look it, though. The figure who came stalking onto the stage, smoking a long thin cigarillo, was not the haggard ancient that Oberyn had expected. Instead he was square-shouldered and hale, despite his long plaited beard, held together with silver rings. His eyepatch was crusted with an unwholesome number of rubies. And his great axe-shaped guitar, hanging from his hip, seemed to buzz and jangle all on its own, without being plugged in.

"Lads. Boys. Brothers. We're all back together eh?" Something about his smile and that rich, whiskey-tempered voice got right past your innate suspicions and slung a metaphorical arm around your shoulder. "Back on stage, where the music lives!" And just like back in the day, the others listened to him. It was as if this part - the part where they forgot about their differences and pulled together as a band again - was an unlisted track on the album of real life. They were following music that wasn't music.

"Not a second too soon, either, or so I hear. Listen, fellers," Odin cupped a single hand to one ear, still smiling like a wolf in a butcher's shop. "They've started without us."

Vulkan popped out of a hatch in the stage, welder's goggles strapped to his forehead.

"He's right, you know. Those are explosions. *Screams*. Can't have you lads upstaged!"

Odin smiled even wider, and held out one hand. An amplifier cable looped in out of the dark like a striking snake, in exactly the right place to be pinched between his fingers.

"Alright then, Thunderbeards," he said, plugging in. "Let's lead off with one we all know back to front. *Howling Bloody Steel*, and we'll follow it up with *Ravaging the Underworld Domains*. You ready to make 'em go crazy, Dion?"

Dionysus took a swig of something smoking and purple to bolster his courage, then gave Odin a high five. He stepped up to the golden microphone in the centre of the stage, and shot Vulkan the signal.

**"One, two, one two three *four...*"**

+++

# WHAAAAAAAAAAAAAAAAAAA!
## (*kchunk!*) WHAAA WHAAAAAAAAAAAA!

Three almighty, crashing chords rung out as the turf split, and the stage began to rise.

The space encircled by the High Table lifted up and away on hidden mechanisms, toppling General Crowley, Chiharu, Quentin and all from their perches. Papers blew backward from the sheer force of massed speakerboxes. The Writer's chalkboard flew end over end, right off the mountainside.

It was undignified. It was disastrous. But by god, it was *loud!*

Cranes, lighting towers and gantries rose like a lost continent, followed by beetle-black cromlechs of amplifiers, all turned up to numbers with Greek letters on the end. The General could be forgiven for thinking this was part of Titania's attack strategy, because it blew him clean out of Merlin's robes, revealing brass-buttoned military long johns beneath.

And what the members of Thunderbeards saw, as they ascended behind a wall of sound, was indeed a battlefield.

Thirty great iron colossi had detached themselves from their rocket transports at the low end of the valley, sprouting a confusion of weapon-studded limbs. To make matters worse, the rockets themselves had come to rest on spidery legs, opening up hidden doors and flaps to reveal even more nasty toys inside. Tanks and self-propelled guns of the Black Sun's own secret regiment spilled out, manned by changelings in Nazi armour and gas masks.

The General rolled for cover, coming to rest under the table next to Quentin Adebayo. Now Mithras had cranked up his drum kit, and a pounding, primal beat joined the scream of Odin's lead guitar and the inhuman wail of Dionysus. It was the kind of music that pierced the soul, then tugged on the hooks. It was the kind of music which gave the middle finger to your higher brain functions, and poured your spinal cord a double. The wickedest man in the world heard all of his heartily mis-spent youth (not to mention his fraudulently invested middle age) in that confection of noise, and he grinned.

"Well, she's done it now. At least no one can say we were unprovoked. Bloody good tune, this."

Quentin raised an eyebrow.

"But you couldn't dance to it, old man! More importantly, do you think they got everyone on board yet? And can we do this without Monkston and his hat?"

General Crowley rolled over onto his back, and pointed up at the underside of the table. In between the inevitable blobs of pre-chewed bubblegum, it was carved with a vast circle of runes, sweeping off to the left and right.

"I reckon we can manage, old chap. Just follow my lead!"

About a quarter-turn around the great table, Titania now had a legion behind her. With their escape blocked, the delegates of the Unmanifest had tried to put the entire giant piece of furniture between themselves and the Queen of Spring, but it looked like a rather flimsy barrier. Titania hung in mid-air, suffused with power, flakes of ice swirling about her in veils.

"Yes! Hear the sound of your doom!" she yelled, eyes wild, hair whipped up by a spectral hurricane. The 'sound of their doom' shifted gears, upping the tempo and pitching into a fast-paced thrash, with double-bass drums. "I've *done it!* December twenty-fifth is *mine!*"

It was Eris who stopped her in mid-rant.

In the confusion, the Goddess of chaos had not even bothered to rise from her throne. She had, however, managed to procure from somewhere a large and tropical cocktail, of the kind that's overburdened with umbrellas, straws, cherries on a stick and slices of pineapple. She finished this with a very unladylike gurgle and raised her hand.

"'scuse me. Yep, you, the mad bitch with the bad hair? Why, in all the hells you so richly deserve, do you want *Christmas*, anyway? Asking for a friend."

This prompted a bout of unhinged laughter from Titania, who now stood backlit by a freshly-re-opened rune gate. elves in chantry whites gripped the frame, eyes bleeding blue. The image through it was of her own corner of the Fey lands, a pleasure-garden centred on a great, silver-banded obelisk of ice.

"You're really too stupid to see it, aren't you? Tell me, General Crowley. *I know you're here, cowering in the dirt with the rest of these freaks!* Tell me – what is the significance of December the twenty-fifth?"

On cue, the music from on stage dropped low and tense, a thrumming bass-line carrying the song. Crowley wondered if Oberyn could stop his fingers from playing, even if it was to stop his ex-wife's plan.

"It's the holy day of those buggers on stage!" he shouted, stalling for time. The plot he'd worked out with Quentin, Chiharu and Doctor J took a bit of logistical calculation. "Winter solstice, traditionally."

He sneaked a look, and immediately wished he hadn't. Thirty iron colossi, twice as many tanks, and two hundred changelings. Added to them were the delegates who supported Titania, and who had come ready for war. It was shaping up to be quite an army. But the mad Queen wasn't finished.

"Perhaps it was, back in 1595. Back when the Earth was flat, and that horrible, baldy-headed little scrivener of yours cursed my people. But you've made such *progress*, haven't you? Where was that feckless little trouser-fart Eddie Weatherfield from, again? Australia, was it?"

Quentin was scratching runes in the dirt with a long ivory needle. He looked up at General Crowley and waggled his eyebrows in a meaningful fashion.

"...ummm. New Zealand, actually. Nice place, or so I'm told. Lots of sheep."

Titania's laugh was definitely hysterical now.

"Of course! Can't forget the sheep! But you've gone and made it a *globe*, General. Just like the name of his grubby little theatre. That's the point. Gone and seeded all kinds of silly beliefs all around it, too. Down there, General, the twenty fifth of December is *Midsummer's Night.*"

"Oh, *shit.*" breathed the General, just as the band on stage wound down to a screeching racket of feedback.

"It's not everything, but it's enough! Enough for me to enact a little working I've kept over from the good old days."

It expanded around her, like in innards of a clock made of transparent amber, exploding in slow motion. Wheels within wheels, tined and forked and clicking. Razor-thin planes of runes folded through each other in ways that would make the inside of your eyes itch; reflections of themselves cast on nothing.

And *nothing* was exactly what the General could do. Everything he had – everything he could beg or borrow or claw down from the sky – was bound up in the sorcery he'd planned with Adebayo and Chiharu. So when Titania brought her hands together, with a grunt of effort and a thrill of static electricity, the working went off unopposed.

A ripple went through the world, like the coils of some vast serpent moving under a layer of ice. Things changed. Things *had always been* changed, all the way back to a point where the working was tethered, in 1595.

And behind the queen, through the rune gate, that obelisk of ice blurred. Rainbows outlined it for an instant, then it disappeared, replaced by a rather tasteless fountain. The buttons on Crowley's underwear went from brass to silver. Quentin Adebayo lost a scar across one cheek, and gained it on the other.

"Yes!" crowed the Queen of Spring. "*It is done!* Out there, in a million of your sad little libraries and schools, you'll now find copies of a play entitled 'Three Nincompoops of Sutton Coldfield'. A comedy, by one *William Shakespeare.*"

Chiharu paused in her modifications to Quentin's scrawl.

"Why does she care about the theatre, Crowley?" she asked. "That

Shakespeare fellow was one of your Englishmen, wasn't he?"

The general was ashen-faced. He tried to stand up, but succeeded only in knocking his head on the underside of the table. Shaking hands searched for a cigarette packet that wasn't there.

"The elves won't follow her. Not the modern ones. Not the *sane* ones. The ones who are with her husband, you understand. Oh no. She's *brought back the ones he burned*, back in the old days. The ones he reduced to *cuteness*. To fluffiness. If there's no Midsummer Night's Dream..."

"Any hour now," yawned Eris, still relaxing on her throne. "You really love the sound of your own monologues, don't you 'Tania?"

The Spring Queen pointed with one frost-blackened finger. Its nail was now a solid chip of glacier-green ice, two inches long.

"Oh, typical. Just *typical*. Can't let me have any fun, can you? You stuck up, apple-thieving, husband-seducing piece of ancient Greek *trash!* Very well. I'll cut it short." She gestured to the rune gate, sparks crawling down every filament of her hair, snapping and arcing from her jewelry. "It's time for these pathetic humans to DIE! And you're going with them!"

Behind her loomed a Midsummers Nightmare.

All the old lords and ladies of the Fae, the wildest, most cruel, most barbaric things to escape Tirfeynn. A whole horde of them, dripping venom from copper claws, clad in flickering glamours like aurorae chained to earth, adorned with feathers and bleeding scraps of fur and scales of gold. Their huge opal eyes were alight with the kind of mischief that ends in the funeral pages. Beautiful faces laughed, contorted with bloodlust. These had been the vanguard of the elven horde, back when Shakespeare had unleashed his narrative torque and shear. The first to be turned into sprites and fairies, or left half-way; mutant things which didn't know what size to be, or how many eyes or wings of arms and legs to have. Storyburn was horrific to witness, and it wouldn't heal. Some were broken in the flesh, some broken in the mind. Others were simply lost, singing merry songs and trying to skip and prance while jagged ends of bone and torn butterfly wings twitched them around in circles.

Now they were back.

They were whole again.

They were, to put no fine point on it, *monumentally* pissed off, and there was not a single line in the unremarkable 'Three Nincompoops of Sutton Coldfield' that could do so much was cause them a mild headache.

As the horde charged, tank treads rumbling, colossal steel feet stomping, mad elves singing hymns of carnage, Quentin Adebayo gripped General Crowley's arm.

"They mustn't reach the Quill, dammit! *They mustn't reach the book! It's now or never, you stupid old fool! SNAP OUT OF IT!*"

The old African grasped his hand. Crowley touched the underside of the table, nodding grimly. Chiharu took his other hand, and plunged one finger into the dirt.

"They'd better be ready to hold on..."

She opened her mouth, and spoke several syllables of precisely crafted silence. Not just a lack of words, but holes cut out of reality where words should have been. Quentin joined in, velvety anti-noise rumbling out from deep in his chest. Finally, General Crowley finished the spell, his rich anti-baritone falling like hot buttered tweed across the grass.

At first, nothing happened. A tide of iron and copper and grinning elven death still came roaring toward them. The delegates of the Unmanifest squared up to face their doom, or cowered behind their chairs, each according to their nature. On stage, Thunderbeards launched into the long, noodling opening sequence of their progressive masterpiece, *Dream Quest Through the Labyrinth of Time.*

Then, ahead of the onrushing horde, the ground cracked open. At first it was just a zig-zag fissure in the turf, but it yawned black as the earth began to rumble, and little flashes of sorcery curled up around its edges. There was a sound like a creaking door, magnified and looped back a millionfold. There was a smell of rust and blood and lavender. The chasm split wide, suddenly full of green flames.

And, as the elves in the front tried desperately to stop, and the elves in the back piled into them, something huge and grim and jagged-edged rose from out of the depths, all towers and turrets and wires, flags sizzling with St Elmo's fire (and the magical fizzlers of several other saints besides).

It was an entire Royal Navy destroyer, still dripping salt water, and it was forced up through the dirt with a mighty heave that flash-burned the runes under the High Table to dust. Above the valley, the sky convulsed, as the Things of the Inside-out scrabbled for the warmth and power of it.

Now twenty mighty deck guns turned, ponderous on their huge bearings. Now detonations popped off from the sides of the ship, where slabs of its armoured hull had already been partially cut through. Breaching charges borrowed from the British Commandos dropped those heavy panels of steel, sending them crumping down into the dirt, forming giant ramps.

Up on the bows, where the name *HMS Boleskine* had been painted on in dripping green, a lone figure in a full admiral's whites hefted a giant megaphone. It was old 'wrath in a bath' himself, Al Schwitzer, and even though this was all happening in a mountain valley miles from the sea, he was damned if he wasn't going to consider it a naval action.

*"Allright you motherlovin' sons of weirdness!"* he shouted, in tones which would have made General Patton proud, *"Let's pulverize these fashion-show Nazi bastards!"*

He suited actions to words, aiming a huge gold pistol with his free hand, and letting loose a round at one of the elven panzers. The bullet – one of Vulkan's specials – was made to ignore the drag of seawater at several fathoms, so it sliced the air like a sailor's curse. And the massive explosive charge in its nose crumpled its target, sending it spinning tracks-over-cannon to crush several changelings in its wake.

*"For the Allies! For Section M! For Victory!"*

And here they came.

Every survivor from the Labyrinth of Kew had been packed into the dry-docked *HMS Boleskine* on short notice, armed to the teeth with hastily Gremlin-designed weapons, and told to hang on tight when the signal came. They'd brought with them some allies from Section W, the Ministry of Mad Science, and even a small contingent from the Soviet Okultburo and the American Office of Alleged Intelligence.

Not all of them were front-line soldiers. Many of them had never fired a weapon in anger. But all of them were boiling mad, tooled up, and filled with righteous fury as the sides of the destroyer came down and they charged into the fray.

The elves recovered from their shock just in time to roar defiance and surge forward to meet them, glamour and diesel exhaust boiling over them in a cloud.

The deck guns spoke, and colossi fell, pierced and burning. Elven bolts and Nazi shells spanged off the armour of the ship, as its crew met the Fae lines with a riotous crunch. This was no modern war, no shooting skirmish between bombed-out buildings, or a game of cat and mouse in the hedgerows. This was more like a medieval battle, up close and personal, above which the colossi and the *Boleskine* exchanged withering blasts of cannon-fire.

There was Miss Golightly, at the wheel of a gnomecart armoured up with welded-on tea trays and kitchen knives. A whole horde of her brother and sister gnomes hung on to the thing's rollcage, teams of two working machine-pistols while yet others used their awful, disproportionate strength to reach out and whack elves with billyclubs and cricket bats. A team of stone golems, (like the ones which had 'tested' Eddie's powers) waded into the fray, hands dripping lava. The bearded lady from the canteen had found a claymore for her left hand, but still swung her giant iron soup ladle with her right, caving in Nazi helmets like it was going out of fashion.

And there were more. Half-naked succubi with scimitars and crimson bat-wings. Mummified creatures dressed in feathers and jade, wielding obsidian axes. A bark skinned tree-man, ironically swinging a chainsaw.

All along the line, misfits of magic and soldiers of sorcery unleashed their powers, wizards casting whirling spells of sparks and neon blades, tommy guns barking their rip-saw sound - while overhead the levitating and the winged creatures of Section M slung grenades, dropped aircraft-sized bombs, or, in the case of Mrs Pinchworth and Mrs Shover, the Harridans, let loose a tirade of supersonic nagging which literally drove the Fae rebels mad. Darrin Oakenbeard was there, clad in a suit of diesel-powered armour, wading in amongst the tanks to rip apart treads and twist guns from their mountings. His friends the gremlins moved in a blur, three streaks of colour accompanied by a trail of hideous cracking sounds; the evidence of wrenches and hammers connecting with Nazi knees and shins.

The elves fought back with equal ferocity. Lords of the Fae, freshly restored from the horrors of 1595, flung themselves into battle with feral glee, slicing left and right with copper swords, massive sickles, war-scythes and whips made from living thorns. Many a soldier found himself simply trampled by their wild advance, then grown over by the vines and brambles which sprouted from the ground behind them.

But now… yes!

Last out of the land-locked destroyer came Squad 27, battle-weary but grim with determination. This had gone far beyond being personal, and it was all about the war again. It was hard to say which was worse for the enemy.

As the elven horde threw themselves into the fray, Connor the Beige appeared with a clap of thunder among them, blasting a circle of foes from their feet. Before they could rise, his companions leaped into the melee. There was Lucky, swinging a huge cauldron full of gold on the end of a chain and screaming Gaelic poetry. Mrs Hazelwood unleashed her crystal ball to slice a scar through the elven lines, bowling changelings down in a rag-doll confusion. Then Percy charged through the breach, grabbing up a leather-and-foxfur clad elf in both hands and swallowing him whole. Fyodor levitated above the fray, his army uniform augmented with a black and red opera cape, and the thumb-sized bullets from his *tankgeshutz* tore through the air with a sound like knives through waxed paper, punching through armour to detonate fuel tanks, and crack engine blocks in two. Saint Germain's infamous immortality seemed to have remained, despite the unfortunate plight of Jesus Christ. He held off a trio of sixteenth-century elves with a yawn, his rapier everywhere it needed to be at once, parrying a trio of swords while he sipped absinthe from a cut-crystal goblet.

Elsewhere, the elves had the upper hand, though. Sheer force of numbers pushed back the Section M advance, as the Fae brought out abominations they had fashioned in the black workshops of Tirfeynn. The Erl King's warhounds were unchained, monsters the size of bulls with every shred of canine sanity beaten and burned out of them. They were nothing but raw muscle and hunger, thorny ribs bursting through their scabrous skin. A wedge of mad elven cavalry flanked the Okultburo special forces, and crashed into them with a splintering of lances and a churning of hooves and mud. The red banner went down, and didn't rise again. Everywhere across the field, the resurrected old guard of the Fae pressed their advantage.

Titania herself was a force of nature, hefting a pair of curved blades in her hands, each one a razor of ice. She cut her way through a swathe of warriors, heading directly for the *Boleskine* and Schwitzer, ready to silence its guns. Left, right, and uniformed soldiers were sliced in half, their bodies freezing in mid-air to shatter where they fell.

The Triton wasn't having it. He snarled, a sound like an insinkerator full of marbles, and leaped from the deck to block her path, landing so hard he formed his own little crater. The battle parted, swirling all around them, and he aimed down both his revolvers, the stubby cigar in the corner of his mouth fuming.

"You're a slippery bitch, I'll give you that. But try to dodge this!"

Twelve shots rang out. Twelve bullets that could hammer through the keels of dreadnoughts flew. And Titania's swords sliced every last one from the air, sending them ricocheting off into the melee.

"All right," said Schwitzer, with a shrug. "That was pretty impressive. How about… this?"

Sheer force of glamour meant that never before in her long life had anyone dared to punch Queen Titania square in the face. But old 'wrath in a bath' had eyes which could see right through her sorcery. Eyes, indeed, that could see in the abyssal depths of the ocean. His fist was like a wrecking ball wrapped in shark-skin, and it lifted the evil Queen off her feet, spinning her in the air three times before she hit the ground.

Titania came back up to her hands and knees. She cuffed away a trickle of blue blood from her mouth, smiling.

"Is that all you've got?' she asked, rushing to her feet in a single motion, blue light blazing between her fingers…

The blast simply froze the poor Triton solid. Al Schwitzer rocked backward slightly as a crystal of solid ice formed around him, moisture sucked in from the air itself to make his tomb. Inside it, the look of shock on his features was all too plain.

But Titania's triumph was short-lived.

*"Oi! You! The fairy wench with the stupid costume! Want to pick on someone who's not you own size?"*

It was the Hammerjarl, and he was steaming mad. There'd be no freezing this dwarf, with his giant war-hammer and his runic armour all crawling with orange sparks. Anti-magic wards wrapped him up, a three-foot tall bonfire of pure anger.

"No!" came another voice, as a gigantic axe split through the fray. "She's MINE! *Time for a taste of green, you unicorn-hugging hedgehog botherer!"*

And that was Zaric Gulgrak, Mountain King of the Goblins, getting the drop on the Writer's proposed changes by being just as big, mean and furious as the bodyguard who fought at his side; Gagrat, the world's first orc.

The pair glared at each other, then at the Queen, then back at each other.

"Rock paper scissors?" asked the dwarf.

"Ahhh, let's just both kill her, and tell everyone we did it on our lonesome!" snarled the goblin. "Gagrat, go bring me the head of one of those iron beasties!"

Titania smiled again, needle teeth dripping blue. She summoned her blades and strode forward, blocking a hammer high and an axe low, then parrying both with a skirl of steel and sparks.

"Come on, you weaklings!" she rasped. "Let's give you an ending fit for my legend!"

Around them, the fight raged on. But it seemed that the fight was being knocked out of the allies. One by one, the deck guns of the *Boleskine* fell silent, either blown apart by the cannonfire of the colossi, or simply flat out of munitions. Up on deck, General Crowley gripped the rail with both hands, once again wishing he had more power to throw behind his soldiers. Because, despite some heroic work by Reggie the Minotaur, (who had peeled open one colossus like a can and ripped its elven pilot shrieking from within), it seemed that nothing could slow down those black iron monsters. Arcs of power flickered between them and the rune gate as they healed.

"It's not enough! We never counted on her undoing Shakespeare's workings! *It's not enough, and it's all we've got!*"

To his left and then his right explosions raked the ship. Cannonfire tore away whole gun emplacements, shredding the towers, sending the flags fluttering and burning on the breeze. Despite the firestorm, General Crowley didn't move, didn't flinch. *This was the endgame, and all he could do was watch.* The colossi came stalking forward now, those armed with cleavers and mechanical flails and saws plunging their weapons into the fray, swinging them in bloody arcs through friend and foe alike. One of them smashed Darrin Oakenberard with a diesel-powered chain-flail, crushing his armour and throwing him clear across the battlefield. He struck the side of the *Boleskine*, where he stuck in a dwarf-shaped indentation, smoking.

*Mad machines, rabid with agony* - they butchered their way forward as the General watched. All he could do was summon the words of his death-curse, and hope that it would take a few of them with him down to Lucifer…

Then, off to his right, down past the stern of the *Boleskine*, where the valley sloped up into sheer walls of rock, light bloomed. Prismatic, shifting light, painting the air with jagged rainbows. A sound like miles of tearing silk and breaking glass rang out, overpowering even the band, who wound down in a haphazard fury of feedback.

"Hey! Shouted Odin, for once losing his cool. "That's *mine*, that is!"

And so it was. The Bifrost, the bridge of rainbows, opening a way between dimensions. Frau Hilda had found it, and a suitable amount of double-A batteries too.

Now the Gods walked the earth.

Or, to be more accurate, the Gods charged out onto the field like a pack of drunken football hooligans, some still wearing dressing gowns and pajamas, some wielding swords and sacred sceptres, others hefting walking sticks, or in the case of the Zoroastrian god Ahura Mazda, a toilet plunger.

There's no real word for the sound of a legion of cranky, irritable Gods crashing headlong into the midst of a swirling melee, but if you neatly stack a thousand cans of pet food and then demolish them with a sledgehammer, you might achieve a tiny percentage of it. Elves flew back from the impact like chaff before a combine harvester, and when some of the more enthusiastic deities reached the iron colossi the fun *really* started. Thor himself was right in front, swinging his hammer like a demented blacksmith. He battered a Nazi war machine down, blow by ringing blow, lightning sizzling through the air with each impact. Other Gods unleashed blasts of purple fire, rays of holy light, storms of spectral knives or, in the case of Sobek, a bite that ripped through metal like a pair of engineering shears through tapioca.

Behind the Gods came two human figures – Patience Goodhallow and Eddie Weatherfield.

The Revenge of English Witchcraft left a trail of blooming wildflowers in her footsteps as she advanced on the Fae, and nothing in an evening gown had ever looked so frightening. She fired her RPD machinegun from the hip until it ran out of bullets, then threw it away, pointing down at the dirt. A small tree sprouted instantaneously, with a sound like crinkling cellophane. Patience snapped a wand from its topmost branches. She cracked her neck left and right, as power came welling up under the ground beneath her, so potent that even Eddie could feel it.

"Switzerland. Hmmm. Still got some of that Grimm Brothers thing going on, I suppose. Let's see..."

She gestured like a symphony conductor, and uttered a word that was all sugar and sharpened curls. There was a sizzle of sparks...

And one of the changelings' panzer tanks turned to gingerbread, complete with a candy-cane cannon and biscuit wheels. Something tried to scrabble up out of the hatch; something with crumbly biscuit skin, and two gumdrops jammed into its sugar-frosted skull where its eyes should have been. It broke apart at the waist, and blue blood gushed out, along with coils of elven entrails. The top half kept screaming until one of the Fae lords' horses, riderless (just the remains of two smoking boots in the stirrups) bent down and ate its face.

"Right!" said Patience, with a sweet and utterly chilling smile. "Where's that mad queen of yours? I've got some red-hot glass slippers for her to try on..."

Eddie Weatherfield, however, realized he was running at full pelt toward a wall of swords and gunfire without any discernible powers at all.

*Funny thing*, he thought, but for a determined coward, he hadn't even considered whether he'd make it through the other side. The fact that Vauragath the Crimson was nowhere to be heard inside his skull seemed to confirm his suspicions.

*Oh well. This was what the military was all about, wasn't it?* Not dying for your King and Country, but making the other fellow die for his, and all that. It seemed a whole lot easier when you had an entire big giant V12 aeroplane between you and the enemy. It seemed even easier when you could reach down into your anger, and become vast, scaly and bulletproof.

But of course – Vauragath had just been using him. *Eddie Weatherfield – catflap to reality. The human revolving door. He should get 'no circulars, please' tattooed across his forehead...*

It was just as his MP40 ran dry, clicking on an empty chamber, that he remembered what the dragon had wanted.

*Vauragath,* he thought, closing his eyes. *You cunning red bastard! I know you're in there. Out there. Whatever! Well, I'm here at the Accords. You could have their attention. You could have whatever you wanted, really. Except for the fact that the elves have gone mental, and I'm about to get squashed...*

He cracked open one eye. A quartet of wild-eyed and warpainted elves were galloping toward him, waving copper-bladed spears alight with bright feathers and gold. The things they were riding on might have been unicorns, but they resembled the five-year-old-girl's-bedroom-wallpaper variety only in that they had gigantic spiral horns erupting from between their eyes. In every other way, they looked like skinned wolves the size of buffalo, with hooves and fangs sheathed in bronze.

*Vauragath? Any time now would be wonderful!*

Closer, and time seemed to slow, the ground ripped to shreds and clods by those pulverizing hooves, ropes of steaming drool whipped back from the black gums of the unicorns, and the rictus grins of the elves.

*Vauragath! You bloody well get here* now, *or I swear I'll get them to relegate you all to folk music and… and children's colouring books!*

At last, as the nearest of the Fae pulled back his spear to stab Eddie through the chest, he felt something like a great, rheum-crusted lizard eye crack open in his soul.

*Allright.* Partners. *But we've decided we like the music those guys are playing. We want dragons very, very much involved with that…*

The change rippled through him like nausea in reverse. Suddenly, a very tired, very haggard Eddie Weatherfield felt like he could take on the world. As that was pretty much what he was doing, he was pleased to see his clothes split at the seams, and watch vast muscles swell under skin turned all scaly and red. That elven spear met the palm of his outstretched hand, and crumpled. The shaft splintered. Eddie followed through by picking up the unicorn as it thundered by, executing a deft sidestep, and throwing both mount and rider twenty metres into the air.

*You'll get your dragon music,* he thought. *But only if we get through this!*

A roundhouse blow unhorsed the second elf, sending her sprawling. He gripped the unicorn by its great spike of ivory and slammed its head into one knee, knocking it out cold. The third took one look at what he'd become - balanced between man and dragon, a thick-necked, bat-winged gargoyle of a thing, ten feet tall and red as hellfire - and he sawed on the reins, turning aside with abject terror boiling up through his glamour. Eddie's claws missed him by a whisker as his unicorn clattered up atop a ruined tank and leaped away, whining.

Up on stage, the band played on. Oberyn couldn't have stopped if he tried. The music was a fever, and it burned in his fingers, sleeting in through the top of the old King's head and down his arms without his brain even bothering to object.

And it was *right*. This was the exact kind of accompaniment you needed for a battle between mad elves and wizards and gods and… was that a *giant*, laying about himself with a whole entire tank turret? Was that a huge spider, wrapping a stony-skinned troll up in wrist-thick webs? It had all gone mad down there, where Oberyn looked down over the burning decks of the *HMS Boleskine* and into the fray.

With one last thunderblast of noise, the song finished – *Raging Glorious Warfrenzy,* if anyone except Vulkan was still keeping track of the set list. Oberyn took the opportunity to stretch the kinks out of his fingers, which hadn't had such a workout in decades. He also risked a glance up at the sky directly above them, which was not looking at all healthy.

In fact, the once blue and breezy vault of heaven was looking downright ulcerated. Cracked through with spidery veins, split by dripping darkness – the King of the Fae was horrified to note a confusion of jellyfish-like tentacles questing down from within, as something heaved against a backdrop of stars. The something *blinked*, making perspective itself see-saw madly.

"Ummm, lads," he began, a definite quaver in his voice. "I, errr… that is to say, I've seen this kind of thing once before, and we should probably…"

But events had already taken a turn for the worse. The guitarists were arguing again, just like in the bad old days.

"… and I'm telling *you*, pick up that piece of junk and *play!*" roared Odin, beard bristling. "This is the time! This is the right place for it! The music must be reborn here, and *now!*"

"But your stupid boy's buggering it all up! We were supposed to *win!* Crush the Accords, seize the Quill, re-write that shameful defeat back in 1595. Be feared! Respected! Without that young skinny Nazarene in the way, you could be top God across all of the North! Don't you want that?"

That was the Erl King, his guitar propped up against an amplifier, and a sword in his hands.

"What I want," grated the Allfather, "is the intro to *Rage of the Firestorm*, and if you ever, ever insult my son again, so help me I'll…"

"You'll *what?*" anger flared off from the Erl King's faceless helm in a literal halo. "You'll stop me from doing *this*, perhaps!" He reached into a pouch at his belt and brought out a crystal ball – the same one that had so recently been wired to the handlebars of his motorcycle. "Riders, the time is now! Take them! Slaughter them! Feed these pitiful Gods to the Inside-Out, that our masters may claim this world!"

Odin, as good as his reputation, simply stepped forward, gripped the Erl King's sword arm, and nutted him. The old Viking's forehead was as hard as the prow of a longship, and had broken more noses than an entire firm of East London doormen. It met with Kingsford's helm with a sound like a temple bell ringing out for a funeral, and the champion of the Fae staggered back.

"You know, you little pillock, I had a *plan* here. Infuse our music with the essence of the most glorious, riotous, incredible battle ever to take place. Right there. *That one.*" He gripped the Erl King's head and turned him around by one antler. "All that lovely energy, all that vitae of violence. We've sown the seeds with a thousand kids at a thousand crossroads, to give this music to the human race. It was gonna be huge! And now, you've gone and set us back by *decades* with your silly little assumption that I *actually want Obie's batshit-crazy ex-wife to win?* Oh dear."

"They're coming!" chuckled Kingsford, even as blood – *red* blood – trickled out from under the lip of his helm. "Armed with the weapons of the Netherverse. The black arrows. The blades of unmaking. You can't stop my Wild Hunt now!"

Odin sighed, and looked down at his hands.

"No. You're right. I can't. But… by what right do you command them, Earl Kingsford? You, who were once known as Oengus the Red, chieftain of Crowfeather Hill? You, who wandered into Fae back when my people were still known to yours only as demons from beyond the Sea of Ice?"

Dionysus sensed the change in the atmosphere. It was both figurative and literal – frost began to spread out in radial patterns from both the Erl King and Odin, painting fronds and curls across the stage.

"Heeey, come on now guys! It's just a song, we could always play something el…"

He saw the look they both shot him, and stopped in his tracks. Out of his entire long, sozzled existence, this was the single most important time, he thought, to knock back a stiff drink.

*"By right of might, and trial by combat,"* grated the Erl King. "Do you really want to go there? Now?"

Odin nodded, grinning his wolf's grin.

"As challenger, I get to pick the weapons, sonny. Older laws than both of us."

Kingsford nodded too.

"I didn't think you were a fool. One slice with a blade from the Inside-Out and you'd be nothing but ashes, and a name we didn't quite remember. Oh well. What do you choose? Maces? Axes? Bare hands? A spear is very much in your idiom, isn't it?"

Odin swung his guitar around on its studded strap.

"This," he said, softly.

The Erl King's eyes went wide behind his helm.

"You're serious? You can't fight to the death with guitars, old man! You can't kill with music!"

Odin pressed his fingers gently to the fretboard, and sighed.

"Now who's being a fool? *It can cut you to the very heart.* Do you accept the challenge? Or do you forfeit the Wild Hunt to the four winds, and the dark corners of the Earth?"

The Erl King jammed his sword into the stage, and grabbed his jet-black flying-V.

"Very well. I accept. Let's make this quick, though. We have a world to conquer."

So it was, that as Titania battled her royal foes in an ever-increasing circle of dead henchmen, and the Gods hammered into the ranks of the Fae, toppling iron war machines and sending bursts of darkness up to pierce the sky, and the brave, exhausted warriors of Section M held back a tide of changelings from the decks of the *HMS Boleskine*, the Writer himself was all but forgotten.

The crescendo of dueling guitars rose like a tsunami, like demons in love and angels in heat. Sobbing, howling, scintillating sheets of noise all clashing and swirling together – it rung out over the valley, obliterating every other sound.

The Writer had served in the Great War, and he knew a lot about crawling through the mud while explosions and shrapnel happened just above you. Amid the cracked and broken no-mans-land in front of the stage (where part of the High table had been struck with a random blast of sorcery, and turned to lemon jelly) he saw his target.

Crowley was busy making a heroic last stand, which was silly. Adebayo and Chiharu had lost sight of what was truly important as well, standing with him atop their burning battleship, casting fury down as bolts of ice and hellfire. It was all just pyrotechnics. Wizards, as the writer knew, loved their fireworks.

He elbow-crawled the last few metres, and wrapped his arms around a dusty dome of glass. One wipe with a convenient scrap of tweed (he'd really have to find a new tailor if this battle nonsense was going to be a regular occurrence) and he could see through, revealing the frozen flame inside. The True Quill. Now all he needed was…

A shadow fell over him. A literal chill sucked all the moisture from the air, making it rasp, dry and icy in his throat. At the edges of perception, he heard the sound of tiny bells.

*"Looking for this?"* asked Queen Titania, cradling the great Book of the Accords in one arm. The other held a notched and bloodied sword of ice.

The Writer rolled over onto his back, clutching the Quill to his chest inside its protective dome.

"Actually, yes! If you'd be so kind, I'd very much like to – aaah!" his words were cut off with a swipe of that curving blue saber. It almost got his neck as well. Titania advanced, her eyes blazing, her face covered in scratches and dirt, her hair a tangled mess. What was left of her evening gown hung in strategically placed rags, thanks to sheer power of narrative.

"Give me the Quill, human. Let it happen. There will be so many more stories when we rule this place. Horror and comedy and tragedy all at once! Come, and you can be my bard in the realm of Spring. Write verses to my glory, and have every pleasure as your reward!"

The Writer squinted.

"Madam, I think you should look out behind you," he said.

Titania gritted her teeth.

"And here I thought you were good at making things up," she snarled. That saber of ice came up on the backswing…

And was pinched between two red, scaly fingers.

"He's also a bit too chivalrous for his own health," said Eddie Weatherfield, dragonsblood berserker. "However - I'm not."

And with that, he snapped the blade in two, and drove his fist into Titania's stomach with the force of a cannonball.

To be fair, the Queen of Spring could take a punch. She doubled over, dropping the book, but she came back up swinging, a new blade materialising in her hand with a sound like splintering glass. Its edge clipped the top off Eddie's stubby little left horn; had he been any slower it would have opened his throat. Then came a flurry of blows as the sword blurred, becoming a hissing, liquid thing. It assailed Eddie from all sides. It was all he could do to deflect it with the hard, scaled flats of his palms, backpedalling, falling away one step at a time before Titania's fury.

"You!" she hissed, "You've ruined *everything!* Or at least you've tried. How many of my faithful have died thanks to your meddling? And all for nothing! Look up, Weatherfield! The sky is breaking, and soon your new masters will be among us."

He snarled at that, railing against the truth. For the sky *was* breaking, and now thick droplets of darkness were falling, splashing in glutionous slow motion. Where they landed, the grass turned oily black and froze solid.

Eddie ducked a wild swing of the Queen's saber and hammered an uppercut into her jaw, following it up with a right cross. The Fae Lady's head snapped back, and she staggered, but she turned the motion into a smooth pirouette, coming back at him with another storm of cuts.

The tip of the blade scored through the scales on his chest, burning cold. He fought the darkness which crowded in at the corners of his eyes, bringing up his hands before him, but another strike slipped past his guard and pierced clean through his bicep, needles of ice ramifying down his veins and into his heart.

Eddie staggered. Titania placed a silver-shod foot on his chest and toppled him over backwards, where he sprawled in the dirt, struggling to rise.

He expected a killing blow, then. He expected the last thing he saw to be the Queen's opal eyes, slitted above a mocking grin.

But she wasn't done with him. The eldest Fae are a cruel people, and are renowned for liking to laugh and play. It's a good thing those old legends aren't too specific about what games they play, or what they're laughing at.

Titania spread her fingers, manifesting a brace of icy daggers. They flew quicksilver, piercing his hands, nailing him to the dirt. Frozen agony exploded from each puncture wound. Three, four, and his wings were pierced through, pinning him immobile. Titania stood over him, triumphant. Above her, the sky was peeled open like a wound, and something formless and grey was heaving itself through, spasm by spasm. Tentacles a kilometer long thrashed in the upper atmosphere. Eyes like crater lakes blinked, dripping.

"You're not one thing nor t' other, Eddie Weatherfield," gloated the Queen. "A pain in the arse, yes. A thorn in my side, certainly. But at the same time, both a weakling, a coward... and a *monster.*" She smiled. It was far from reassuring. "Well, never let it be said that I don't welcome the outcast and the hideous. We Fae may be beautiful, but we love the taste of human terror. We give a home to things which can harvest it for us. No matter how repulsive." She placed the blade of her sword over his heart, digging in with the point, twisting.

"So I'll give you a choice," she said. "I've *always* loved to watch your kind choose. You can be the weak little milksop you know you really are. The sickly child, the disappointment. The *coward.* And you can die clean, here, *now*, without seeing what your weakness has bought." Another twist, and ice wrapped its tendrils around Eddie's heart. "Or you can embrace the monster. Become the creature. Become rage, and terror, and pain. You can be *my* monster, and live in the new Tirfeynn I will build, eternal and strong."

A blowtorch of glamour seared into him, then. *The combined might of hundreds of years of controlling human minds, making them see what the Queen wanted them to see, making them believe what she wanted them to believe.* Eddie saw himself in that distorting, heat-haze mirror; a stick-thin little weakling, pitiful and cowardly. Without a scrap of courage or determination. A slave, who should be glad to receive the pain he so richly deserved. *If only to prove that he was still worth something's attention.*

Or - the other.

Behind the trembling wretch, Eddie saw the dragon looming up. Not the creature he was now – man-shaped, scaled and powerful. No. *The opposite.* A twisted amalgam of hand and claw, sinews exposed, human eyes rolling mad in a stretched and thorny skull, teeth so sharp and profuse they sliced his lips to ribbons…

"Who knows," purred Titania, her words curdling the illusion like milk in raw liquor. *"I might even let you keep your little witch as well."*

Inside Eddie's head, something snapped. Like his shaving mirror striking the wall, in Vauragath's dream. Like the crazed and broken dome of the sky above him. Something shattered like glass, shards springing apart only to twist, and reform, and click back into place once again.

Whole. Certain. Unmarked.

But *something else.*

There was a ripping sound as Eddie's arm moved in a blur, fingers hinging shut around Titania's neck. He'd pulled right off those daggers, leaving them smoking in the dirt. He exerted a little pressure, and felt Vauragath squirm, all the way through the veil in the realm of the dragons. A wide-eyed and frightened elven face was dragged inches from his own.

"You don't get to make me choose, your majesty. And you don't get to decide what the choices are. I'm Eddie Weatherfield, and *I* get to choose who I am. You can do what you want with the rest of the world, but I'm not yours." He bent her head back. He rose up, knives tearing through his flesh. The ice melted as fire jetted from the wounds. "See, I haven't always been strong. I know what it means to be weak. I know what it means to be *afraid.* And I see that terror in you, milady. I smell the stink of it. You don't like your chances against them up there, so you want to kiss their arses and hope for the best, eh?"

The sky convulsed. Great shapeless limbs slopped through, sucker-studded, jointed with too many knees and elbows, connecting with the ground and making the earth shudder. Titania gasped. Eddie just held on tighter.

"It's the same with those Nazis, really," said Eddie, now standing on his feet. The Queen's toes thrashed in the air, unable to touch the ground. "They know their masters are mad. But they're *afraid*. That fear makes them vicious. Tell me, do you hate yourself as much as they do? For what you've had to do? For what you're doing, right now?"

Titania's voice was a strangled croak.

"We had a deal. I give them the Earth. They give back Tirfeynn. You should have seen it, Weatherfield! The glory, the beauty! The *perfection*. You still could! Come with me. I will give you such power, such privilege..."

Eddie would wonder for the rest of his days if he really could have just closed his fist then, and popped the Fae Queen's head from her pretty shoulders. He would never know, however, because of three things that happened all at once, in a rush so fast it was impossible to follow.

First, there was a tiny little sound, expanded to fill all of time and space. It was the papery whisper of a book being opened, and the scritter of a pen across crisp, empty whiteness. Then a silence so profound it made the void before creation seem like an outdoor festival.

Something rippled away through the fabric of being, unpicking threads and re-weaving them. Eddie's whole body felt as if it had been folded and twisted like damp laundry, then pulled out taut again as reality snapped back, all sizzling electrons and rigid laws.

The Accords. The Writer had sealed them. He'd signed, for humanity.

The sound which came back, after that ringing, cotton-wool void, was the blurring scream of two instruments pushed beyond the limits of wood and wire. All eyes turned to the stage, high above the burning hulk of the *HMS Boleskine*, where Odin was bent back on his heels, guitar holding him off the ground in a haze of lightning. His fingers were a blur as feral energies lashed out across the stage, clashing up against a similar fury of sparks and decibels. The Erl King was hunched over his instrument, wringing a machine-gun torrent of chords from strings that were already nothing but a molten spatter of metal at his feet. What he played now were seven razorcuts of darkness, resonating with the power of the Inside-Out.

The forces ground up against each other, like a train wreck in slow motion, or tectonic plates colliding. A ball of crackling, eye-searing anti-colour formed between them, expanding with each riff and distorting everything around it. Amplifiers were sucked inside its event horizon, and flashed into infinitely long chains of probability and mass. Lighting gantries bent and bowed, lamps plucked from them by the inexorable force that still built, turning the flat stage into a funnel.

Eddie caught the moment when the Erl King slipped, but only just.

One bum note, and that entire sphere of force bulged outward toward him like an egg. He dropped his guitar, and it shattered like glass, before being sucked into the vortex. Then, with a sigh, and a rush of wind that knocked elves, dwarves, goblins, humans, sundry other species and assorted war machines sprawling, the sphere exploded. It turned into a solid rod of annihilation, which struck the Erl King and turned him, briefly, into the E l K g, then just the l K, then nothing.

This all paled in comparison, however, to the third and final happening in that fateful instant.

Because it had all been too much. The Accords were sealed, and the races of the Unmanifest would change - but it was too late. Too much sorcery had poured into the world, here and now. The sky above slit itself open, bursting with amniotic darkness. Whole panes of splintered blue fell end of over end, disintegrating before they hit the ground. And out of the broken hole left behind descended things like mountains of flesh and shadow, warped and swaddled in layered halos of impossibility.

*The hungry ones. The primordial lurkers. The Netherversians.*

The things of the Inside-Out walked the earth, and their birthing cry was a wail of terror from every creature left standing, friend or foe. Because they were here to claim the Earth, just as they had claimed the lost worlds of every magical race present. And all of those desperate refugees – call them that, in extremis – knew that there was no stopping them.

# Seventeen – Pure Grim Tentacle Horror

Eddie's mind didn't want to try to explain - or even consider - the three vast Things which descended into that little Swiss valley on that otherwise sunny afternoon.

In fact, his mind wanted nothing to do with them at all. His eyeballs slipped over them like fried eggs on a buttery skillet. His frontal lobes were unwilling to admit that they were there, having both poured themselves into reality and slowly descended from the hole in the sky in a series of stop-motion jerks. It didn't help that the entire valley seemed to skew on a different obtuse angle depending on which one of the Things he looked at.

On this, however, all his screaming brain cells were unanimous. *They were Things with a capital T.*

And despite wanting to simply hit himself on the head with a toy plastic truck, say 'wub wub wub' and think of chocolate pudding while soiling himself whenever he managed to focus on the trio, there were distinct and horrific features attached to each one.

The nearest – though terms like 'near' and 'far' were melting under their mere presence – seemed to be spiral tower of rancid seafood, equipped with thousands upon thousands of spider legs and lobster claws all around its base. For some reason, bat wings dripping with slime had been tacked on halfway up, and the crown of the Thing was orbited by a chain of eyeballs, which seemed to be on fire.

Behind it wallowed a mass which resembled one of those statues of a portly Buddha, except rendered entirely in gibbering, leering, gnashing mouths. What skin appeared between those toothy orifices was purple and warty, dripping yellow ooze. Its neck truncated in a stump, raw and glistening, while above it levitated a pyramid of riveted and rusty iron, its surface emblazoned with the crude semblance of a cycloptic face. This whole edifice rotated slowly, and was bathed in a nimbus of pink flames. Both of the Thing's arms were tentacles ending in preying-mantis claws.

Finally, Eddie beheld the last of the ambassadors of the Inside-Out; a shadowy presence veiled in smoke, tall and thin, surrounded by twisted thralls that seemed half man, half jackal. They flitted about it on dirty wings, playing a cacophony of bone flutes and bagpipes. The Thing's four arms were skeletal, roped with half-rotten skin and taut tendons, and it wore on its unseen head a vast straw hat, black as sin, adorned with wax fruits the size of houses and a veil behind which burned two guttering green flames as eyes. It carried a gigantic handbag in the same style as Mrs Hazelwood's, made of what appeared to be paisley carpet.

Looking at them made Eddie's brain hurt, as though his grey matter was a pair of poorly made underpants, and the fact of the Things' existence was a very determined sumo wrestler, trying to put them on. Beside him, he heard the Writer gasp.

"They're real! Really real! Old H.P. said things like this were out there, but I thought he'd been hitting the laudanum, you know! I looked them up, to see if there was any chance of working them into a story, but they were supposed to be *indescribable!*"

Eddie turned to him, the motion seeming to take far too long. His face felt like bubblegum, stretching and peeling off the surface of reality. The Writer's face was boiling, his eyeballs popping and rising like bubbles only to re-form in their sockets.

"I'm seeing them! My brain's describing them to me! *How do we stop them?*"

The Writer's lips parted, far too far. Inside, his mouth was a spiral blur of colours.

"Names. Nail 'em down. Collapse the field. Keep them in the wardings..."

He riffled through his pockets, and came out with an old envelope. He licked the end of the True Quill, and scratched the paper, with a sound like the millstones of God being fed a bag of marbles.

"Xaxarphoth, The Eternal Peckishness. He Who Summons The Dreamer To The Fridge At Three A.M."

There was a hissing pop. The first of the Things solidified, gaining three dimensions, a shadow, and sundry other laws of physics at once. It looked quite uncomfortable, to the extent that a mountain made of seaside offal can.

"Nglyarngylarschlup, He Who Is Unable To Be Spelled Correctly. Haunter Of Proof Readers, Curse Of The Obsessive Compulsive!'

The second creature from the Inside-Out screamed as it was hauled over the threshold into consensual reality. The sound was like purple Tuesday clockwise, times its own square root divided by custard.

"And Tsthagatha, the Dull Aunt Out Of Space. She Who Carries The Bottomless Handbag! Mother Of 10,000 Doilies!"

Now all three had been dragged into what was locally described as space and time, losing none of their outlandish horror in the process. If anything, the addition of a strange, cold clamminess in the air and the smell of burning wires made their presence worse. A gale howled from the hole in the sky, blasting up sheets of dust and dirt.

**"We are among you. We hunger. We will take this world, and bring it into our embrace."**

The voice of the Inside-Out was a chorus of screams, combined with a sound like a toothless grandpa gumming gristle. It screwed itself into Eddie's ear like a greasy finger, just as General Crowley, Patience and Connor the Beige came pelting across the no-mans-land between the *HMS Boleskine* and the stage, bent double against the wind.

The wizard and the witch were holding the general upright, as it seemed he was not in the best of shape. *Shape*, in fact, was the very crux of the problem. The figure which Patience and Connor supported was not really a figure at all. He'd lost one of his dimensions, and flapped about in only two, like a sheet of animated paper.

"Well, this is a fine business," said Connor, with typical understatement. He paused to tap out his pipe on the sole of one boot. "Yon thingies are definitely here, and the wardings round the Accords are all that's keeping 'em in."

"They can't hold for long, though." said Patience, who smelled faintly of gingerbread. She squinted up past the looming forms of the Netherversians, to where the hole in the sky continued to crack and split around the edges. "If any of you have ideas, now would be the time."

Titania *definitely* had ideas.

Mad ones, perhaps, but then again, everyone was off the edge of sanity now, and plummeting into the abyss like a frog duct-taped to a toboggan. The Fae Queen ascended to the very top of the stage, and perched on Thunderbeards' lighting rig as the Things of the Inside-out peered down at her. All her power, all her glamour - well, all that was left in that ice-prickle, frost-jagged form – looked like a sputtering candle flame before their aura of total insanity.

"Yes!" she crowed. "My allies! Mt friends from beyond the veil! I call on you to seal this pact! Take the Earth, and all who live here. *Give Tirfeynn back to its rightful Queen!*"

"Ummm. Dear?" came a voice from on stage. Oberyn hazarded a little wave. "I know it's probably a bit obvious, but these Things look a lot like the ones that…"

Titania cut him off.

"Not *now* Obie! Can't you see I'm *working?*"

Everything male within earshot winced and shook his head sadly.

The entities from the Inside-Out drew together for a moment. It was like watching a trio of mountains try to huddle. Then the one called Tsthagatha leaned down, green eyes blazing behind its colossal veil. It reached out with one titanic claw, and for an instant Eddie thought that the Thing was going to shake hands with the Queen of Springtime. But then that horrible, spit-and-gristle voice sawed through his head again.

**"We don't think so. Why not just devour both?"**

Skeletal finger and thumb snapped. Titania was flicked away from her perch like a spider from a shower curtain, screeching as she spun end over end, away over the wreck of the *Boleskine* and out of sight.

"Hey!" shouted Oberyn, dropping his bass guitar. "I know she was a bit mental and all, but that was my *ex-wife!* You can't just come waltzing into this reality without so much as a how-do-you-do and start chucking queens around as if they were common bloody baronesses!"

This time, there was definite menace in the way the Netherversians loomed up over the stage.

**"Whyever not, little King? Do you intend to try to stop us?"**

The unreality emanating from the trio really seemed to disagree with Oberyn. It was doing horrible things to the other Thunderbeards as well - even Odin, who for once in his long existence had lost his cool.

"Bugger this for a game of soldiers!" he shouted, as waves of warping energy messed with his thaumic signature, causing him to bubble and drip like a living cartoon character dipped in paint thinners. "Every god for himself!"

For a moment it looked as if King Oberyn was going to stand his ground and say something pithy and heroic like 'not on my watch' or 'come take your best shot'.

But at that instant something fell from the hole in the sky, spiraling down on the uncanny wind like a very strange sycamore seed. When it was directly above the stage, the tiny figure furled in the great sail of paisley fabric it was using as a makeshift glider. It fell, sketching out a human shape as it came closer, until with a great slamming detonation it landed. *Heroically.* Down on one knee, a single arm extended, fist pressed against the bottom of a crater in the stage.

"No, it said, head bowed, the ragged remains of a dinner suit with tails steaming where they hung in tatters from its frame. "I rather think *I'm* going to stop you, old chaps. Terribly sorry for the inconvenience and all."

"It isn't!" breathed Patience.

"It cannae be!" goggled Connor the Beige.

"Mwhhhthrnnn bhh!" attempted General Crowley, with a mouth that appeared to be drawn on with magic marker.

But Eddie Weatherfield recognized him immediately, even as that bruised and frost-rimed head came up to fix him with a twinkling gaze.

"Perhaps *this* time, Private Weatherfield, you would be so good as to snap to it, hmm?" said Charlie Monkston, the first person to ever survive in the Inside-Out for longer than the time it takes to tuck in a napkin.

Eddie reached for one of the straps which dangled across his body, and pulled it around to the front. *Of course!* He was still wearing that big old hatbox, lashed on like war-gear. The item of millinery inside was clattering and banging against the sides like a bat in a biscuit tin.

"Go on," encouraged Connor, giving him the nod.

"Yes, go on. None of us would make it," said Patience, giving his arm a squeeze.

Eddie squared his shoulders, gritted his teeth, looked up – and found out why.

The jackal-faced servants of Tsthagatha weren't the only minions the Inside-Outers had brought to the fray. Xaxarphoth had spawned slaves which looked like a cross between a cactus and an explosion in a bait factory. Nglyarngylarschlup had conjured up a horde of mushroom men, blue and yellow and red, their caps studded with eyes and stinging tentacles.

Now they clambered and slid down the lower slopes of their masters, dropping to the stage, where no trace of Thunderbeards now remained but empty mineral water bottles, cigarette butts and discarded instruments.

"Any time now would be lovely, Weatherfield," said the Major, his voice hardly wavering at all despite the madness which surrounded him.

And this time, it didn't matter if there was courage there when he looked. This time, Eddie just made his own up as he went along.

The battle was short, brutal and bloody. But to Eddie, it seemed to last an eternity. As he charged, bounding from stack to stack of amplifiers, the air became greasy and slippery, suffused with the scent of burning hair and hot metal. Writhing waves of force broke over him, the exhalation of the Inside-Out, and with each one he felt a little of his power bleeding away. Vauragath faded as he pushed on, uphill into a gale, punching and crushing, grappling and mangling the things of the Netherverse down.

They were poorly made, those things, or else they had only a tenuous grip on reality. Because they burst open like rotten fruit with every blow he struck, the fabric of them fraying as their innards splattered black and cold.

*But there were so many of them.* And Eddie could feel the change shuddering through him, robbing him of strength, diminishing him, until, at last…

He stood, chest heaving, heart hammering in the back of his throat. The Things from the Netherverse hung over him like thunderclouds of flesh, their malignancy so palpable it was like a hand pressing down on the tender meat of his brain. He was human again, saturated in icy black gore, stick-thin and wild-eyed, clad in nothing but the obligatory pair of torn-up khaki trousers.

And there were still ten of them left. Ten assorted monsters that should have been embarrassed to crawl their way out of a nightmare. Behind them, Charlie Monkston stood, carefully arranging the lapels of his ruined dinner suit. He looked through the shambling ranks, and *winked.*

**"We don't think so, tiny one! Your friend has no power. He is *nothing.* Those skulking lizards who aid him are far away, and now…"**

Eddie Weatherfield looked up into the blazing halo of eyes of Xaxarphoth, the cyclopean pyramid-face of Nglyarngylarschlup, and the hideous wax-fruited veil of Tsthagatha.

"And now, you can all *shut the feck up!*" he shouted, without a shred of his draconian might or authority. "I'm sick of the lot of you! I want to go home, and have a very large drink, and sleep for a week, and not ever, *ever* do this again!"

Then he gave the three Gods of Utter Madness a very rude gesture which might not even apply to their physiology, and made a dive for the Netherversian lines.

*Funny thing. He distinctly remembered, back in his horrible school days, thinking that being bad at rugby wasn't the end of the world. Now it might be. In fact, it almost certainly was…*

Eddie gripped the hatbox in white knuckles as he slid between the legs of a jackal-faced angel. He rolled to his feet and elbowed a fungal mushroom-man in what might have been its face, but could just as equally have been its genitals. The effect was similar; it fell back, shrieking like a steam-whistle, black blood spurting. A pair of cactus-cephalopod horrors lashed at him with slippery appendages, but he dodged left, then right, tangling them up together. Then it was just a single arcing dive, up and over a slavering, toothy beast, and he was there. He slammed the hatbox down at Major Monkston's feet and rolled to a slithering stop, his vision blurred with purple spots and his lungs on fire.

Which is why he saw what happened next sideways, and through a haze of sheer exhaustion.

The clasp of the hatbox failed spectacularly, and the silk topper within spun up into the air, only to be grabbed by one of Major Monkston's white-gloved hands. He flourished it, defiant in his artistry, and plunged his other hand inside.

Nobody knew what might be in there. Eddie's best guess was that he'd emerge with some kind of flaming magical sword, or a sceptre of power, or at least a big bazooka.

But instead, he drew his hand back from the warp beyond the brim holding a trio of oddly-shaped dice. They had twenty sides each, and he held the three of them between his fingers, splayed out, as if he was about to perform a magic trick.

Eddie wasn't the only one who saw this. Vulkan, down inside the half-ruined machinery of the stage, connected a pair of wires and nodded. Fat sparks sputtered. And the image of Charlie Monkston flickered into life on a giant screen, half the size of a football pitch, right atop the lighting rig.

Above it, the Things of the Inside-Out recoiled.

*Nobody* missed that.

The rag-tag remnants of the battle had utterly wound down, and now various survivors of the Accords – those not fleeing with a thoroughly defeated Titania – came sifting through the wreckage toward the flickering glow of the stage. It wasn't just humans who enjoyed a show. And none of these refugees had ever seen *anything* give the Netherversians pause. Not even when they were gobbling up their homeworlds with a knife and fork.

Sadly, it didn't last long.

**"Dice? Toys from a game of chance? You seek to threaten us with *these?* We, who existed before the primordial chaos?"**

Charlie Monkston nodded.

"Welcome to the Accords, ladies and… errr… assorted others. You'll find we've been expecting you."

Eddie groaned a little, and rolled feebly onto his back.

"We have?" he croaked.

Charlie gave him a wry little smile, then stage-whispered behind one hand.

"We *have*. It's not just the bad guys who get to do the dirty doublecross, Weatherfield. It's just that I thought old Crowley would take care of this part. What have you been up to while I was indisposed?"

Eddie grinned back. Black blood stained his teeth.

"Tell you later," he promised – just as the Netherversians started to laugh.

It was the kind of laugh that was definitely rehearsed, utterly without humour, and came accompanied with overtones of bubbling tar, and undertones of hundreds of teeth being strewn on a metal surface, then slowly run over by a steamroller.

**"Then you have been expecting to be *devoured*, little creature. In our mercy, therefore, we shall consume you first. You will not have to watch your friends perish. This is our gift to you."**

Monkston tossed the dice in his palm.

"I think not, Xaxarphoth. Level sixty Netherspawn. High strength, high resilience, woeful dexterity, plenty of magical power but… sod all intelligence. I could beat you right now just by rolling 18 or higher."

Eddie caught it out the corner of his eye. The Writer had slipped the piece of paper – the one with their names on it – into the great Tome of the Accords. Xaxarphoth must have felt something shiver through reality as well, for it quailed back, tentacles flailing.

**"What have you done to us? I feel… *wrong!* Diminished!"**

Monkston rattled his dice. All three Things shuddered.

"Well, old chap, you've come to Earth. Here, we believe in things so we can handle them. We make up stories, so we can make up plans. These people are smart enough to work with us." He gestured around him, taking in all the assembled dignitaries of the Accords, down in front of the stage, or perched amid the wreckage of the *Boleskine*. Some had even managed to find popcorn. "Others... not so much. I'm afraid you've been part of our narrative for a while, now. And now you're on my home turf. You are what I *say you are!*"

**"But we are mighty! We are the indescribable horror! The nameless fear!"**

"Nglyarngylarschlup. Level seventy-one! Impressive! Resistant to fire magic, and to cold. But ever so delicate when it comes to the colour green, humourous limericks, and swords made of brass."

The pyramid-headed Thing howled, thrashing the air with its mantis claws.

"We named you. We described you. You've come to fight on human terms, right here, right now. And what you are..."

**"We are existential dread!"** screeched Tsthagatha. **"The manifestation of your insignificance in a cold, indifferent universe!"**

"Yes. You've helped us quite a lot with that. Considering the vastness of space and time, and what a speck we are in all that cosmic soup – well, that can be a bit scary. But bug-eyed tentacle monsters? That's *easy*. We've been slaying those since Conan was still in fur underpants, matey. Soon all you'll be is an animated movie villain. A prop in bad fiction. *The monster at the end of a game.*"

The Major rattled his dice again.

The Netherversians seemed to cower and shrink at the same time. What had once been their alien, looming menace became silly, cartoon grotesquerie.

"Shall we roll for initiative, you pack of stupid bastards?"

The dice flew in slow motion, leaving rainbow contrails behind them. Patience, who had added this twist (and was quite proud of it), got a sharp little kick in the shin from Eris, who was standing right beside her. The Revenge of English Witchcraft noted that the Goddess of Chaos was also holding her fingers up to her temples, and had her eyes crossed.

The first dice landed with a sound life a rifle shot. BANG. Then the second, and the third, rolling and spinning to a stop. BANG. BANG.

Each one of them showed a perfect 20.

The Netherversians' howl of rage scrabbled its way up the scale from a bowel-rattling *basso profundo* to a dog-exploding treble in a matter of heartbeats. They seemed to warp and blur, stretching out life warm toffee, their colours running together as they were coiled and twisted into a single rope of ectoplasm. Tentacles and scales and claws and eyes churned in this pillar of liquid madness for an instant, before it was sucked back up into the sky, still screeching. Up into the hole, which, with a lurch that made a thousand assorted creatures wish they'd never eaten anything, ever, went into a sickening rewind, shards of blue and pieces of frozen cloud snicking together as the cracks between them were welded shut.

Eddie managed to lever himself up onto his knees as the first cheers broke out. All across the battlefield, dwarves and goblins, ogres and gnomes and kobolds, oni and sasquatches and yes, even the allied elves loyal to King Oberyn were celebrating. Things were hugging other things who had, until this morning, been murdering each other for generations.

*And they'd all seen what just happened.*

They'd all seen a human being, armed with nothing but three small pieces of plastic, defeat the creatures which had eaten their worlds.

"So?" asked Eddie, as Charlie Monkston slumped down next to him. "Do we join them, then?"

The Major shook his head. He took his top hat, and carefully set it in place atop his lacquered haircut, giving a contented sigh.

"No, Weatherfield. *I'll* be joining them. Now that old Crowley's no longer a sheet of paper, we've got some diplomacy to take care of. Did Connor and the lads catch up with Schprinkler?"

"Actually, I burned him to death in a rocket exhaust. He wasn't pleased. Said he was waiting for you."

Monkston chuckled.

"He never got it, did he? The good guy never comes into his power until right at the end of the story. And the bad guy never sees it til it's too late. No, you're not going to get to enjoy the party. You're going after the Queen."

Eddie looked into those twinkling eyes, and sighed.

"Does this make us even, then?"

Charlie clapped him on the shoulder, getting black gore all over his crisp white cotton glove.

"Let's just say you don't owe me that big kick in the plums anymore, for the golem thing, eh? Now hurry along, old son. I think you'll have some help on this one..."

+++

This time there were motorcycles waiting on the edge of Fae. The remnants of the Wild Hunt belonged to Odin by right of conquest, which, if he had to admit it, was his very favourite right of all. He'd done away with the tormented horseflesh and copper motif, and taken a cue from the four other riders who sat with him at the head of the hunt, resplendent in their red and gold armour, white polyvinyl lab coat and robes of utter darkness respectively. Plague couldn't have looked resplendent with a year long bath in Chanel Number 5 and a nice haircut, so he just slouched.

"Looks like these boys followed the huntsmen, to see who'd put old Earl up to his tricks," boomed the Norse God, back to his hale and muscular self. His son had been sent to deal with politics and build bridges with the delegates of the accords; Odin felt that a big bearded bloke with a hammer might just find a few new worshipers in the dwarf contingent. "Good idea about the look of the thing, and all that, even if they are from the wrong eschatology."

Eddie was still a bit dazed. Some of it was from seeing and experiencing all the madness which had crammed his life from end to end in the past few hours. The rest was from witnessing just how quickly a whole horde of multi-species politicians could brush aside a titanic battle with monsters from beyond space and time, and get back to wrangling over tiny percentages in trade residuals within a matter of minutes. All Crowley, Adebayo and Chiharu had had to do was get the big ruined ship out of the way, and dust off the seats around the table.

The Accords would go through. The world would change, in several billion human imaginations. And years from now, nobody would think of what happened, only what the races of the Unmanifest had become.

Here and now, though, there was work to finish. Eddie climbed aboard the Indian Chieftain motorbike which Odin pointed him to, and gingerly threw one leg across the saddle. He'd had more experience with planes, to be utterly honest.

"Why are there seven more?" he asked, as he looked up from the red scale paintwork and New Zealand flag airbrushed onto his fuel tank. Odin hadn't missed a detail. Heck, even his Wild huntsmen looked more like ghostly vikings than elves.

"Those would be fer us, lad." came a voice from behind him. Eddie turned, and saw Lucky striding through the rune gate, ducking his head under the frame. "Sure and if I'm going to be flying through the sky on a bleedin' velocipede, I'll be doin' it next to me mates and all.

Who else is gonna buy me a drink when I fall off?"

"Just like riding a broomstick, but with handlebars," said Patience, shooting him a wink and a little smile. Eddie's heart suddenly felt like a basketball made of marshmallow inside his chest.

"Och, I still dunnae aboot this," muttered Connor, kicking his own big Harley-Davidson gently with the toe of one boot. It was tartan, though, which made him smile.

"They say you never forget how to ride a bike, Sir!" said Percy brightly, swinging into the saddle.

"But did your tricycle *fly*, you stitched-up Southern lunatic?"

The Compte De Saint Germain had no worries at all. Immortal, and all that, of course.

"Well, if it all goes pear-shaped, I'll just go bat-shaped," said Fyodor, mounting his black and red bat-themed chopper. Mrs Hazelwood settled herself into the sidecar that lurked maliciously beside it.

Right at the front of the column, at the arrowhead, Odin held high his legendary spear. A flag unfurled from it, depicting a skull wearing a helmet with antlers.

"Gentlemen, if you'd be so kind as to fire them up! The four horsemen here will do the honours. We ride to capture the traitor Queen, and..." Odin shot a glance at king Oberyn, who was there at the doorstep of his little house to see them off, Eris at his side.

"Don't be too harsh with her, old chap," he said, with rather a despondent tone. "She's a bit mad, is all. Never really got over the transition to Earth. You know how it is. They say time's a great healer, but it's a much better executioner, and well… we're all immortal, us."

Odin nodded, as grimly as only the Allfather of the Norse can.

"I'll spare her life. If she'll let us."

Then came the roar of hundreds of motorcycle engines firing up, and Eddie heaved on his own kick-starter, sending a shuddering rumble through the big bike's engine block. A cough from the fishtail exhausts, and he was away, Squad 27 at his side, the Wild hunt all around.

Up ahead, Odin bellowed some kind of sorcery, and first the front wheel and then the back of Eddie's Indian left the surface of the road. Despite the rapidly receding ground, he could still feel the big whitewall tyres rolling, crunching on invisible tarmac as the whole Hunt ascended into the skies over Fey.

They rode through veils of clouds, ragged wisps whipped across the face of a huge and alien moon by the wind. Despite the snow and the darkness it wasn't cold up here, and Eddie wondered if this was part of the magic of Fey, or an enchantment of the Wild hunt itself. Below them, the jumbled, topographically dense little world of the elves flickered by, at once snow-globe compact and utterly vast. Bonsai mountain ranges, and trackless expanses of forests the size of a tennis court. Lakes like oceans in a thimble cup, vast moors with glowing trilithons and dolmen he could have covered in the palm of his hand, but which, he knew, would take days to hike across. Places where the mind could get lost, while the body was mere inches from salvation. Under the spider-shadow-silver of the Fae moon it was a confection of razors and sugar, darkness and glittering edges, beautiful and cruel and wild.

It didn't take long to catch up with the Queen.

Her ragged band were riding hard, horses foaming and failing as they crested a high ridge line and were silhouetted by the moon. The Wild Hunt surrounded them, hemmed them in, and brought them to a halt, lances bristling every which way between dead elves and living ones.

The Queen, for all her defeat, for all her raggedness, was proud. She stood in the stirrups as Odin leaned his great black Vincent motorcycle up on its stand and approached, planting his spear in the ground so the flag of the hunt unfurled.

"So, you've come to see how a Queen dies, have you? Usurper and forgotten God not good enough for you? Do you need to be a regicide as well?"

Odin shrugged.

"I've hacked the heads from Kings and Queens so often there's nowhere left to store the bloody crowns," he said, mild as you please. "But I promised Oberyn I'd spare your life. Come with us. There's a place for you at the Old Fred. Helga'll take good care of you, and you can have all the porridge you like."

Titania bristled with anger, her eyes flashing blue.

"Never! You think you have me beaten, Ravenfather, but you know me not! Here, on my ground, you will..."

Odin held up a hand.

"I had to ask. Obie's an old mate, and all. And you did help me get the band back together. I think that music's going to have some interesting echoes, in, oh, thirty years or so. When the Accords have really gotten settled in. You see, it's all about change, dear. You have to move with the times. I've got no more fleets of reavers in mail, hacking people to bits with axes. So I've adapted. My boy has too. Ha! Comic books! That's kids for you, though…"

Titania contrived to look even angrier. Her face contorted into a mask of shadow and rage.

"Stop your wittering, you one-eyed old fraud! You'll never change me! I'm the Spirit of Spring! The May Queen!"

Odin nodded.

"And I daresay some echo of you will still be spring-cleaning the hedgerows when I'm living off that music we've let loose. You, however. *Well.* Why do you think I brought some humans along with me?"

Titania's face changed in that instant. The instant when Odin's hand came away from the grip of his short Viking sword, and reached inside his coat for something much deadlier. The light of the True Quill shimmered on the snow, like upside-down aurora borealis.

"There's another kind of elves, you know. A kind that some of these strange, story-telling apes believe in, just once a year. Not your kind, with the terror and the music and the laughter in the woods. Not the new kind, all noble and bright and warlike, standing tall against evil. No. *The others.* All one of these people has to do is mention them. Then I'll write it down. Then… pop. It's all over for you!"

Titania was now as pale and sickly as a corpse. She waved her hands at Eddie and Squad 27 in a desperate gesture.

"No! Don't say it! Don't even *think* it!"

Eddie was stumped. He turned to Patience, who shrugged. Saint Germain rolled his eyes. Odin grinned at them, twirling the quill between his fingers.

"Let me jog your memory, folks. See, I'm famous for having one hundred and seven names. Names of power. Some I was born with, some I stole, some were whispered in my ear by the north wind and the spirits while I hung impaled on the world-tree. But here's two of them…"

Eddie saw the old God change, then – a subtle trick of the moonlight shivering through him as it became reality. Odin's beard was growing, long and white. His fur cloak turned from bearskin to a similar shade of cream, trimmed with red velvet.

"*Odin Julnyr.* Odin the Yule-bringer. The spirit of celebration in mid-winter, who brings the gift of new life."

"No!" stammered Titania. "Not that! Anything but…"

Odin's transformation was relentless, however. His armoured helmet became a warm felted cap. His gloves became white leather, and his tunic red-dyed wool, stitched with runes. His boots were big and black, crusted with snow, and around the tops were sewn tiny silver bells, like those the Morris Men used to bind and ward against the Fae.

"*Odin Langbardr.* Old long-beard. The one who comes to reward the good, and punish the wicked."

Eddie had gotten it now, but he could scarcely believe it. The Norse God looked at him and winked, a picture straight from a biscuit tin lid.

"That's right, son. Once a year, they still pray to me. They send me letters! They question whether they have fallen athwart my judgment. *Say my name.*"

But it was Percy who broke the silence.

"Sweet tea and crumpets, he's only bloody well *Santa Claus!*"

The ripple of recognition was audible as a sizzle in the air. Titania sawed on the reins, making her horse rear back, pawing the air. She spun in a circle, but there was nowhere to go. Her traitor Fae shrunk back from the great, bear-shouldered proto-Claus as if he was radioactive.

Odin smiled, broad and toothy.

"That's right. In these hard times, you have to adapt. You have to have a sideline. But answer me this." He pointed one finger directly at the Queen of Spring, who quailed as if it was a loaded pistol.

"*Who makes the toys?*"

Titania screamed as she leaped at Odin, twin blades of ice crackling in the air as they manifested from her fists. She flew up and over Squad 27, performing a perfect backflip, but the wily old longbeard was ready for her. As she somersaulted toward him, Odin wrote three runes on a tiny scrap of paper, and palmed it on one hand. Then he parried both blades with the Quill itself, and held out his arm, meeting Titania as she fell.

There was a flash of light and steam. The pen had indeed proven mightier than the swords, which had evaporated on contact. Then came a second blast, this one of raw magic. Eddie had felt its like twice before, as Titania's great working had rippled through the weave of the world, removing A Midsummer Night's Dream from existence, and then again at the signing of the Accords.

This time, it froze the Fae Queen in mid-leap.

Within the strobe-flash of the Working, Eddie saw Odin's hand pressed up against Titania's forehead. For a second, light played around her, green and red and silver. There was a sound, as of tiny bells jingling, far away. Then a shape spun away from the Ravenfather's outstretched palm, a rag-doll collapsing to the snow.

It groaned, as time came back. It twitched. It staggered to its feet.

And Odin laughed. Because it had worked. Titania, once queen of Spring, the mistress of ice and glamours, was now two feet tall, clad in candy-striped tights and a green tunic, and wearing a jaunty little acorn cap.

*"No!"* she squeaked, in a voice that was more comical than frightening. *"You can't! I Won't! I am eternal! I am..."*

But whatever she had been, she was that no more. Odin walked over, reached out, picked her up in one hand, and stuffed her in a sack which he had belted at his waist.

"Ho. Ho. Ho." said Odin, with definite malice aforethought. Behind him, the Four Horsemen of the Apocalypse began to applaud.

"So," asked the figure who Eddie could only, disbelievingly, now see as Santa. "Are you going to come and help me catch the rest?" He gestured to the remaining traitorous Fae, who had all been transformed into toy-making slaves along with their Queen. They were legging it across the hillsides, screaming.

Connor the Beige answered for all of them.

"Fun as it looks, ye ken, we have tae get back to the Major. Lots o' cleaning up tae do, I reckon. And the war isnae over just because old Schprinkler is in a wooden onesie!"

Odin Julnyr nodded, running his fingers through his beard.

"All right. And I know it's not the right day for it, but I think you've earned one Christmas wish each. What'll it be?"

Percy grinned.

"New eyebrows, please! Mine have gone all floppy!"

"A nice bottle of afterlife-compatible whiskey for the husband," said Mrs H.

"Some trousers that aren't shorts!" put in Lucky.

"A new sporran!" shouted Connor.

"A ten-gallon bottle of wig spray," said Saint Germain. "It also doubles as harpsichord polish, you know."

Fyodor shrugged. "What do you get for the vampire who already has good looks, charm, amazing fashion sense and staggering humility?" He smiled, showing a lot of fang. "A new sniper rifle, please. I hear there's a great big bugger made by Harkonnen Industries that can take down a zeppelin with one shot!"

Patience leaned over on her motorcycle and found Eddie's hand. She gave him that certain look – the one which made him think she was reading cue-cards stapled to the inside of his skull. This time, though, it didn't make him feel small. This time, she followed it up with a tiny smile.

"Tell my friend Eddie where his brother is. He came all this way, and we seem to have distracted him somewhat, haven't we?"

Odin fished around in his sack – where Titania still struggled, adorably[50] – and brought out a yellowed envelope. He passed it to Eddie, who received it with numb fingers.

"Your choice if you open it or not, big man," said the Allfather. "Just remember, he made his choices too. You others – you'll find a little something next to your bedrolls when you get back to base. Wherever that is. Believe me, it works every time!"

He turned back to Eddie as he saddled up his big Vincent. Under the jolly-old-gift-giver, there was still plenty of Viking to go round.

"What about you, lad? Want to be normal again? Forget about the curse of the dragon blood? How about wealth? Fame? Fortune? A cuddly toy? I haven't got all night!"

Eddie thought about it for a second.

"I'd like twenty-two pounds fifty, a new suit, and reservations at the best restaurant still standing in London," he said. "Can you do that?"

Odin nodded.

"When you get back to base, as I say..." He fired up his bike, and blasted a sooty cloud of exhaust across the snow.

Eddie had faced slobbering horrors, cannibals, Nazis, tanks, golems, the British Army's catering service and a horde of wicked elves in the past few days. Still, it took all his courage to swallow the lump in his throat, and raise his head to look Patience straight in the eyes.

"Miss Goodhallow, if you'll allow me the impertinence of asking, would you at all be interested in going on a... that is, eating in the same... while I was in the vicinity... together... sort of thing?"

Patience laughed, as the Wild Hunt sped away all around them,

---

50 The worst part is, eventually the wicked queen's mind *did* adapt to the cute-as-a-button little form she'd been twisted into. She changed her name to Holly, and today holds the record for largest number of teddy bears assembled in a single shift. Deep inside her, the remnant of her power and savagery rages, sometimes giving her a distinct but tiny nervous twitch. But that's all. And, of course, with Titania gone, William Shakespeare's 'A Midsummer Night's Dream' was returned to the world of literature. Though a single, moth-eaten copy of 'Three Nincompoops of Sutton Coldfield' was once presented to a book collector in Oxford, who wrote it off as a terribly poor hoax.

filling the air with the detonation of unburned petrol and a spray of powdery snow. It wasn't an unkind laugh, though. In fact, it may have been the most happy and sincere laughter to be heard in the Spring Lands of Fae for a thousand years.

"Eddie Weatherfield, that has to be the worst, lamest, most pathetic attempt to ask me out on a date I've heard in 275 years." She gave his hand a little squeeze. "So of course, I'd be delighted."

It was many, many miles back to England. Flying by motorcycle should have seemed like a risky proposition.

But Eddie didn't look down the whole way home.

# Epilogue – Brokenwaters Station, New Zealand, 1999

Connor Weatherfield was almost knocked from the steps of the Woolshed (now with a capital W, of course, as it was in fact a very up-market bed and breakfast) as his youngest, Charlie, came barreling past, out into the sunlight. There was no way that Connor could follow right now; he was tethered to the end of a long telephone cable, through which a far-off studio executive in Auckland was offering him inconvenience and money in equally large amounts.

Well. *More* inconvenience. A lot of it was already here, because apparently the rocky tussock-land of Brokenwaters was just the perfect place to shoot a movie about… well, about something expensive. That local feller was attached to direct, so Connor expected it was more horror nonsense. Certainly, the truck-fulls of extras looked weird enough. Like something from his old grand-dad's bedtime stories.

"Elves over here! Dwarves, to make-up! Orcs, that salad bar is for *everyone!*"

A menial with a megaphone was standing in the middle of the homestead yard, sweating and laden down with clipboards. Young Charlie almost knocked him down too as he ducked and weaved between the throng of outlandishly costumed actors, looking for his great-grand-dad. He knew just where to find him.

Grampa Eddie was sitting in his old recliner, out the front of the aircraft hangar, the sun reflecting off of his special glasses; one half thick and clear, the other half jet black. The Le Rhone Avro was pushed to the back now, and a new Piper and a Bell helicopter took up the space. Charlie launched himself into his grampa's lap with the force of a small torpedo, squeezing the old man almost in half.

"Grampa! There's funny looking things everywhere! And guys with cameras, and a lady with lots of drinks and ice creams, and all! Is this the circus?"

Eddie recovered a little, bundling Charlie, who was all of five years old, up onto his lap. He folded away the book he'd been reading and smiled.

"Not really, lad, but it's a good enough description. No, this is worse. This is *movies.* They're making a film from a very old story. I met the writer once, you know."

"They've got a wolf that's as big as dad's car, but it's not a wolf, it's a robot," reported Charlie, with all the seriousness only a five year old can muster. Eddie grinned even wider. All of his family – and it was a big one, now – remarked on how good his teeth were for a man of 76.

"I beat up a robot, once. Huge thing. Black as a coal-bucket and taller than a house. I chopped it up with a sword."

Charlie looked at him with a mixture of awe and disbelief. He felt the need to one-up his grampa.

"They've got elves and dwarves and orcses and a troll and everything," he said. "I want the big catapult troll toy for Christmas, and a bike, and some chocolate covered peanuts, but Chad Glenton at school says Santa is just your dad in a beard."

Eddie's mind was still sharp, after all these years, but memories tended to unmoor it a little.

"Chad Glenton's an idiot, then," he said. "I met Santa once. Big guy. Motorbike. Helmet with horns on. If it wasn't for him, I would never have married your great-granny." A truck bumped by, carrying a pack of extras dressed as orcs and elves. "Then again, that was back during the war."

Charlie tried a final riposte. Sometimes, if his grampa got really, really into a story, he'd reach into his cardigan and pull out a paper bag full of boiled sweets.

"Grampa Eddie, what *did* you do during the war, anyhow?"

The patriarch of the Weatherfields sighed, well aware of the scam. He rummaged deep in his pocket, trusting in the sorcery of old age to provide him with suitable antique candy in his time of need.

"Kid," he said, watching a wizard, a dwarf and an orc trying to light their cigarettes, around the corner of the barn out of the wind. "You wouldn't believe me if I told you."

# THE END

*If you liked this book then please consider leaving a review on Amazon or wherever you bought it from.*

*It would mean a lot to us.*

# Other books by Drew Bryenton from
## sci-fi-cafe.com

Fullchrome Afterburn

Elysium Burning
Chains of Tartarus
Soul Crusher

Halo of Thorns
On Black Wings of Vengeance

**Available from AMAZON and other good bookstores**